TRIAL AND ERROR

ALSO BY ROBERT WHITLOW

A Time to Stand

The Witnesses

A House Divided

The Confession

The Living Room

The Choice

Water's Edge

Mountain Top

Jimmy

The Sacrifice

The Trial

The List

THE CHOSEN PEOPLE NOVELS

Chosen People

Promised Land

THE TIDES OF TRUTH NOVELS

Deeper Water

Higher Hope

Greater Love

THE ALEXIA LINDALE NOVELS

Life Support

Life Everlasting

TRIAL AND ERROR

ROBERT WHITLOW

THOMAS NELSON
Since 1798

Trial and Error

Published in Nashville, Tennessee, by Thomas Nelson. Thomas Nelson is a registered trademark of HarperCollins Christian Publishing, Inc.

Interior design by Mallory Collins

Thomas Nelson titles may be purchased in bulk for educational, business, fundraising, or sales promotional use. For information, please email SpecialMarkets@ThomasNelson.com.

Library of Congress Cataloging-in-Publication Data

Names: Whitlow, Robert, 1954- author.
Title: Trial and error / Robert Whitlow.
Description: Nashville, Tennessee : Thomas Nelson, [2021] | Summary: "A small-town lawyer has been searching for his daughter for eighteen years. Now another young woman is missing, and he's determined to find them both-no matter the cost"-- Provided by publisher.
Identifiers: LCCN 2020037093 (print) | LCCN 2020037094 (ebook) | ISBN 9780785234654 (paperback) | ISBN 9780785234661 (library binding) | ISBN 9780785234678 (epub) | ISBN 9780785234685
Subjects: GSAFD: Christian fiction. | Legal stories. | Suspense fiction.
Classification: LCC PS3573.H49837 T76 2021 (print) | LCC PS3573.H49837 (ebook) | DDC 813/.54--dc23
LC record available at https://lccn.loc.gov/2020037093
LC ebook record available at https://lccn.loc.gov/2020037094

Printed in the United States of America

HB 07.10.2023

To those who pray for the restoration of families.

May the circle be unbroken.

God sets the lonely in families,
he leads out the prisoners with singing.

—Psalm 68:6

PROLOGUE

BUDDY SMITH SAT ON A GREEN VINYL CHAIR IN THE expectant fathers' waiting room at the Milton County Memorial Hospital. He stretched out his lanky 5'11" frame and ran his fingers through his light brown hair. The minute hand on a large round clock on the wall clicked forward. It was 3:00 a.m. Buddy yawned. Amber Melrose, his girlfriend, was in the labor and delivery suite.

To Buddy's right sat a man wearing faded jeans and work boots with red Georgia clay caked on the sides. The man leaned back, rested his head against the wall, and pulled a red ball cap down over his eyes. A minute later he snorted, and his head jerked up. He rubbed his eyes and glanced at Buddy.

"Did I snore?" he asked. "My wife claims I start making a racket even before I'm asleep."

"I wouldn't call it snoring."

"What did it sound like?"

Buddy thought for a moment. "More like the noise you'd make when telling a little kid what a pig sounds like."

The man laughed and slapped his thigh with the palm of his hand. "That's exactly what Crystal claims. And she's usually right."

Buddy cracked a smile.

"I'm Sammy Landry," the man said, extending his hand to Buddy. "Crystal is about to pop out our fifth pup. She likes having me around when she checks into the maternity ward and they stick in the epidural, but after that she doesn't want me bothering her while she works. The nurse knows to bring me back when it's time for the big push."

Leaning forward, Buddy listened closely to what the man was saying.

"Babies look gross when they first come out," Sammy continued. "But every woman in the room thinks they're beautiful. I'm cool with holding a newborn after they clean it up, but I give it back to Crystal as quick as I can."

Buddy hadn't thought about anything Sammy mentioned. Though he was lagging behind in the dynamic of becoming a father, he was determined to catch up. He and Amber didn't attend any prenatal classes together, and they'd broken up twice during her pregnancy, first initiated by Buddy, more recently by Amber. Anxious and private about the imminent arrival of a baby girl, Amber had angrily ordered him not to come to the hospital. But when her mother called and told him Amber was in full-blown labor, there was no way Buddy was going to lie in bed, staring at the ceiling and wondering what was going on. He'd hopped in his souped-up car and sped through the quiet streets to the hospital.

Patty Melrose, who was with her only daughter right now, had vacillated between resentment toward Buddy and insistence that he and Amber get married. Now that the big day had arrived, she seemed positive and excited. Three times she'd come to the waiting room and given Buddy an update as the contractions became stronger and closer together.

Amber's father hadn't come to the hospital. Buddy hoped the deranged former security guard wouldn't barge into the waiting area. John Melrose's profane, vocal negativity about Buddy and Amber's relationship was scary, and the young couple never hung out at her house. Whenever possible, Amber grabbed the opportunity to spend the night with friends, and it wasn't unusual for Buddy to pick her up for school across town. Hoping to follow in the footsteps of her older brother, Amber couldn't wait to leave her parents' household. The big question was whether she would be with Buddy after she left.

"Do you have a name picked out?" Sammy asked.

That was one item Buddy could check off the new-father to-do list. "Elise," he replied.

"Nice," Sammy said with a nod. "We're having a girl too. Crystal wasn't too keen about the name I picked out, but she named the first four, so it was finally my turn. We're naming our daughter after the greatest president this country has ever had."

Sammy didn't continue. Buddy waited and thought about his AP American History class.

"Washington or Lincoln?" he asked tentatively.

"Reagan," Sammy replied with a big smile. "You wait and see. When our girls are in high school, they'll be putting Ronnie up there with the ones you mentioned." Sammy adjusted his cap. "Is this your first kid?"

"Yes."

"I figured that. I mean, how old are you? Twenty?"

"Eighteen."

Sammy gave a low whistle. "Man, I thought we started early. I was twenty-one and Crystal was nineteen when our son was born. He's almost twelve. Are you still in school or did you drop out and go to work?"

"I'm a senior at the high school and will graduate in a couple of weeks. My girlfriend finished early because she got pregnant."

"It's good they let her do that." Sammy eyed Buddy closely. "You look kind of familiar. Do you play any sports?"

"I ran cross-country, and I'm on the baseball team."

"That could be it," Sammy said. "Crystal's nephew plays baseball. His name is Jeff Minshew."

"Jeff plays shortstop, and I'm in right field."

"Are you that fast kid who steals all the bases?"

"Yeah. My problem is getting on base in the first place."

"Tell me about it." Sammy shook his head. "Once the pitchers started throwing curveballs that dropped out of the sky for strikes, my baseball days were over."

Buddy had more trouble with fastballs. His hand-eye coordination didn't match his foot speed. He'd recently started wearing contacts. They helped, but it was too late to salvage his batting average.

"Have you lived in Clarksburg your whole life?" Sammy asked.

"Yeah, I was born in this hospital."

"Me too. Crystal grew up outside Atlanta. She wasn't a city girl, but she likes to tell people that's where she's from. Who are your folks?"

"My father is Marvin Smith—"

"Rascal is your old man?" Sammy interrupted, using the universal nickname for Buddy's father. "My folks rented a house from him for years. It was a mile outside of town on Newberry Road."

Buddy knew the rural two-story dwelling. He'd spent two

weeks the previous summer scraping and repainting the white frame exterior.

"Does he still own it?" Sammy asked.

"Yeah. Once he buys a place, he usually holds on to it."

"My brothers and I had a blast at that house. We practically lived in that creek out back. We thought it was huge at the time, but when I drove by there the other day, it wasn't much more than a wet spot with a trickle of water in the bottom."

"It depends on the time of the year. It spills over onto the yard when there's a big rain."

"Oh, that was the best. We'd play football until we were so covered with mud that our granny couldn't recognize us."

The door opened and a nurse stuck her head into the room. Buddy held his breath.

"Mr. Smith?" she said.

"That's me," Buddy answered, hoping his voice wouldn't crack.

"Congratulations. You're the father of a healthy baby girl."

ONE

THE YOUNG MOTHER GRABBED A TISSUE FROM A BOX ON the corner of Buddy's desk and pressed it against her eyes. When the new client intake screen appeared on his computer monitor, Buddy typed in "Sue Ellen Ford—Domestic Matter." He waited patiently for the distraught woman to regain her composure. Sue Ellen blew her nose and stuck the crumpled tissue into the front pocket of her jeans.

"Who referred you to me?" Buddy asked.

"Gracie Blaylock at the courthouse said you were the best lawyer in town for this sort of emergency. One of my nieces played on her summer league softball team last year. I called Gracie because I figured she'd know who I should talk to. She told me you don't usually handle divorce cases but have a heart for people who are trying to"—Sue Ellen stifled a choking sob—"find their children who have been kidnapped."

Buddy leaned forward. The young woman's words changed everything. He'd not seen his only child since his daughter was a newborn. Years of fruitless searching had caused him to lose hope of ever finding her.

"Go ahead," he said.

"I don't really want a divorce. I just want my son back. I mean, I've thought about leaving Jackie a bunch of times over the years, but when I walked down the aisle and said 'I do,' I meant it. Now I wish I'd listened to my mother, who told me to kick Jackie out and hire a lawyer over a year ago."

"What is your son's name and date of birth?"

As he entered the responses, Buddy stayed calm and professional on the outside, but anger rose up within him. To wrongfully deprive a deserving parent the right to be with his or her child was inexcusable.

Three days earlier, Jackson Ford Sr. had left Milton County, Georgia, with the couple's three-year-old son, Jackson Ford Jr. Claiming he was going to visit his grandmother in Knoxville, Tennessee, Jackie's actual goal was to kidnap his son and abandon Sue Ellen and their six-year-old daughter, Emily.

"Has he ever taken Jack for an overnight trip before?" Buddy asked.

"No, this was the first time. I didn't want him to do it, but we'd been fighting a lot, and it was easier to say yes and try to keep the peace. If I had known this would happen, I would have done anything to keep him from—" The young woman stopped, and her tears returned.

"You didn't know," Buddy said softly. "You couldn't have known."

"I'd been receiving text messages from Jackie all along saying they were doing fine, which made me feel good because things between us have been so awful. But when he didn't come home like he was supposed to, I called his grandma. She told me she'd not seen or heard from him in weeks. I immediately called and texted Jackie. Nothing. I rushed down to the sheriff's department, but the detective told me I had to prove little Jack was in danger or that his daddy had violated a court order giving me custody before they could do anything. Is that right?"

"Unless there's a court order limiting a parent's rights, either the father or mother can exercise custody over a child."

"That's horrible! A mother ought to have the right to be with her child!"

"You do, but you'll need to get an order from a judge before law enforcement personnel can step in and act."

"How long will it take?"

"Given the circumstances, I think we can convince a judge to act quickly. What have you done on your own to try to track them down?"

"After calling everybody I could think of, I went to the cell phone company to find out where Jackie was when he texted me. They said he'd terminated his contract, and even though they had the cell tower information, they couldn't give it to me because I wasn't on his account."

Buddy was impressed with Sue Ellen's creativity. And disturbed by her husband's advance planning.

"According to a recent Supreme Court case, that kind of information can't be disclosed to a third party without a search warrant," he said. "Were you and your husband ever on the same cell phone plan?"

"Yes, but he changed it a few weeks ago to save money. By the time a court does something, who knows where Jackie and little Jack will be?"

"There are other things we can do. I know you talked to your husband's grandmother. What about other relatives and friends? Have you spoken with them?"

Sue Ellen laid several sheets of paper on the edge of the desk beside the box of tissues. "Gracie said you would want that information. I've made so many phone calls and sent so many emails that I haven't slept more than a few hours over the past two days. Nobody has heard anything."

"They'll take it more seriously once the police contact them." Buddy flipped through the sheets of paper. "Do you have copies of all this information?"

"Yes. Those are for you."

"What about your bank accounts?"

"We only have one, and I've checked it several times a day. He hasn't taken out a penny."

"If your husband is relying on cash, that will eventually run out, and he will have to go to a bank or use a credit card."

Sue Ellen shook her head. "We don't have any credit cards. Jackie does most of his work for cash. He's an auto mechanic."

"Does he have a business name?"

Buddy entered the information Sue Ellen provided.

"Another thing you should know," she continued, "Jackie was always looking at those survivalist websites and talking about living off the grid. I'm afraid he's going to change his name and go underground."

"What kind of vehicle was he driving? Do you know the license plate number?"

"He left in an old pickup that he took in as a trade. I don't even think he'd transferred the title into his name. That will make it harder to track him down, won't it?"

"What's the name of the man who owned the truck?"

Buddy entered that information as well.

"Jackie was trading vehicles all the time," Sue Ellen said.

"Sometimes the titles weren't clean because the cars had been wrecked, totaled, or water damaged in a flood or hurricane. I tried to tell him it was a bad idea to mess with that stuff, but he said the government didn't have any business sticking its nose into car trading so long as people had the chance to check out vehicles on their own."

"Any chance he dealt in stolen cars?"

"Maybe," Sue Ellen answered slowly. "Like a lot of things that went on, I stopped asking questions because it just caused a fight."

"What is your husband's relationship like with your son and daughter?"

"Jackie worships little Jack." Sue Ellen grabbed another handful of tissues. "And ignores Emily. Sometimes I think the only reason Jackie married me was so he could have a son. He wanted another baby right after Emily was born. I got pregnant real quick but had a miscarriage. It was another year and a half before I became pregnant with little Jack. When the ultrasound came back showing a boy, it was the best time of our marriage. I really thought we'd turned the corner, and Jackie might start being a father to Emily and the baby. But it didn't last."

"Why would Jackie want to kidnap little Jack?"

Buddy knew it was an emotionally packed question and hated to ask it. But he needed to know. More tears preceded an answer.

"He doesn't want anyone to raise little Jack but him," Sue Ellen managed after a few moments passed. "He wants our son to be just like him, and if I'm around, that can't happen. My mother saw it early on, but I didn't think anyone could be that messed up."

There were always two sides to every domestic dispute, but Buddy couldn't imagine a scenario in which Jackson Ford Sr.

came off looking like anything except a rogue. He'd heard nothing that justified running off with his son.

"What about your husband's computers, social media, and email accounts?"

"Jackie has an email account but took his laptop with him when he left. I don't know his password and doubt he'll send any emails. He's paranoid about a lot of stuff and believes the government spies on people through the cameras in cell phones and computers."

Buddy held up the papers Sue Ellen brought in. "This is a good start for contacts," he said. "Is there anyone on here that Jackie would be more likely to communicate with?"

"I highlighted a few names. One would be Boyd Lipscomb. He and Jackie both like to buy and sell cars, and they agree about a lot of political stuff. I've called Boyd several times since Jackie left, but he's never answered. I even drove out to where he lives to see if maybe Jackie had gone there, but I was afraid to knock on the door. I'm desperate enough to do anything."

"Leave him to me. I'll try to talk to him or hire an investigator who works with me to do it."

"Be careful. Boyd is a gun fanatic. At least Jackie never got into that."

"Have you had any conversations with Jackie's immediate family?"

"His grandmother in Tennessee is the only one he cares about. His father abandoned Jackie and his mom when Jackie was three or four years old—" Sue Ellen suddenly stopped and put her hand to her mouth. "I hadn't thought about that. Jackie is doing the same thing, only taking little Jack with him."

"What about his mother, brothers, or sisters?"

"Jackie was an only child. His mother remarried and had other kids. They live in Kentucky and stick to themselves. None of them came to our wedding, and they never invite us to family gatherings."

Buddy leaned back in his chair. "Write down everything else you can think of about Jackie's personal and business relationships and email it to me. Don't worry about trying to figure out whether or not it's important. I'll sort through it. I'll prepare an affidavit for you to sign, which will be the foundation for an emergency hearing in front of Judge Claremont. He's familiar with my involvement in these types of situations."

"Gracie said you and the judge are kinfolks."

Buddy never emphasized the fact that he and Judge Nathan Claremont were first cousins once removed.

"The judge and my mother are first cousins, but that doesn't mean he gives my clients preferential treatment. He'll rule in our favor based on the facts and the law." Buddy scrolled to a final screen. "Was there anyone else in the picture for either one of you?"

"What do you mean?"

"Did either one of you have an affair during the marriage or are you in a relationship with another person at this time?"

"I don't know for sure about Jackie, but I've been faithful. Like I said, I took my marriage vows seriously. When I first met Jackie, he was quiet and kind of shy. He hadn't dated much. He was a hard worker and really wanted kids, or I guess at least a son. I thought that meant he would be a family man."

"How is Emily doing?"

Sue Ellen sighed. "She misses little Jack more than she does her daddy. My father has always been the male figure in her life, not Jackie. He ignores her."

"Anything else?"

"There's so much," she said, shaking her head sadly. "I'm a private person, and I've kept my problems to myself and our marriage difficulties behind closed doors. I hate that this is going to come out in the open so people can gossip."

"Even negative publicity can be good, because it gets the word out about little Jack. You're the victim here. No one has the right to judge you."

"I don't see it that way," Sue Ellen answered sadly. "Little Jack is the victim."

"Which is why I'm going to help you," Buddy replied.

"What about paying you? I don't have much money, but my parents say they'll help."

"I'll email a contract for you to sign and return. Don't worry about the money. We'll work it out. What are your parents' names and their address? I'll put them on the contract too."

Sue Ellen gave him the information. "My mama is praying like crazy for us," she said.

"In situations like this, I tell people to call on whatever help they believe is out there."

"I can't imagine never seeing little Jack again or holding him." Sue Ellen sniffled.

Buddy handed Sue Ellen a packet of information. He didn't tell her that if not quickly resolved, cases like hers could gather dust for a long time. Just like his search for Elise.

After Sue Ellen left, Buddy pushed aside two other projects and spent over an hour engaged in preliminary research. Jackson Ford Sr. had no criminal record. He'd not even received a traffic ticket during the past ten years. He'd been sued twice in small-claims court by people dissatisfied with the repair work he performed on their cars. Both cases settled. Buddy studied the Ford family photos. There was no denying the resemblance between father and son. Little Jack shared his father's dark brown eyes, square chin, and short curly brown hair. In a recent picture, both of them were dressed in blue jeans, work boots, and identical T-shirts with a hot rod car printed on the front. The photo would have been cute if not for the fact that Jackie was trying to clone his son. Emily looked more like her mother, with sandy hair and scattered freckles. In a family portrait taken nine months earlier, the intense expression on Jackie's face as he glared at the photographer caused an involuntary shiver to run down Buddy's spine.

TWO

GRACIE BLAYLOCK HOISTED A LARGE CANVAS BAG OF softballs over her shoulder and carried it to the pitcher's mound. Compact and physically fit, she placed the bag on the ground and finished her stretching exercises. It would be twenty minutes before the group of fifteen- to seventeen-year-old girls on the Milton County summer softball league team began to arrive. After quickly rotating her left arm several times in windmill fashion, she adjusted the yellow cap that covered her short blond hair. Taking out a ball, she rocked back and forth a couple of times before whipping her arm over her head and releasing the ball with a snap so that it shot forty-three feet from the mound to home plate with fierce velocity.

When she was an all-star pitcher in high school, Gracie's hair was much longer and a golden ponytail hung down her back. Her hair would snap to the side like a blond whip when she released a two-seam fastball at close to seventy miles an hour. During her senior year, she'd accepted a friendly dare from the boys' baseball coach and successfully struck out five male batters in a row before a few of the better players made weak contact. Without practice, the boys had trouble adjusting to her riseball.

The canvas bag contained a mix of white and yellow balls. Gracie practiced pitching, not so she could compete, but as a way to stay loose and blow off stress inherent in her job as clerk of court for Milton County. Each time she hurled a ball that caromed off the wire backstop, she relaxed a tiny bit more.

"Hey, Coach," a young female voice called out from behind third base. "Do you want me to put on a catcher's mitt?"

Heidi Casey was a tall, redheaded girl with long arms and a face full of freckles. During her first year on the summer team, Heidi was a gangly fifteen-year-old with little hope of playing in high school. Gracie saw her potential, and now the rising senior had the second-highest batting average on the team and the ability to throw out runners at home plate from deep left field. Gracie threw one more pitch.

"No," Gracie answered. "But you can help me pick them up."

Gracie held the bag open while Heidi tossed in the balls. Several more girls arrived. The players came in all shapes and sizes. There were muscular country girls who could hit a softball over the fence and smaller girls who relied on speed and quick reflexes. Gracie always began and ended practice with a brief prayer. The team wasn't sponsored by the local school system, and no one had ever complained.

"Has anybody heard from Reagan Landry?" Gracie asked when they'd gathered in a circle. "She hasn't been here for over two weeks and hasn't returned my calls or texts."

"I talked to her mom the other day at the grocery store," said Laura Anselm, a scrappy second baseman. "All she said was for me to pray for her."

"Then let's do it," Gracie replied.

"I'll pray," Heidi volunteered.

One of the highlights of Gracie's day was listening to one of the girls pray. Ninety minutes later practice wound down as the sun crept toward the tops of the tall pine trees beyond the left field fence. Heat was a perpetual part of life in Georgia, and drops of sweat carved paths down the reddish dust on the girls' faces. Gracie was just as hot as they were, and her voice was raspy from yelling instructions by the time they formed a final circle.

One of the younger girls, who rarely spoke, lifted her right hand. "Coach, did you hear about the man who kidnapped his little boy? My mom was talking about it with one of her friends."

"A kidnapping?" a girl asked.

"How can a parent kidnap their own kid?" another girl responded.

"I know a little bit about the situation," Gracie said. "And it would be right for us to pray for the boy. His name is Jack."

The girls joined hands again and bowed their heads. When no volunteers stepped forward, Gracie prayed, "God, we know that you are the best and greatest Father in the world. You love and take care of each and every one of us. Wherever Jack is tonight, we ask you to watch over him and bring him safely home to his mom and sister."

The circle broke up. Laura helped Gracie load their equipment into the trunk of Gracie's car, placing the bag of softballs beside a set of golf clubs.

"How often do you play golf?" Laura asked.

"Not as much as I used to."

The only reason Gracie had taken up the sport was to spend time with Barry, her former boyfriend. Within six months, she was regularly beating him, even when playing from the men's tees.

Gracie grabbed a couple of waters from a cooler and handed

one to Laura. Emblazoned on the side of the cooler was the Milton County Generals logo. The previous year, the girls' high school softball team, known as the Lady Generals, unveiled a modified mascot, switching out the white-haired old general for a vibrant older woman with white pigtails. The new figure lasted three weeks before the school principal nixed it. The controversy made it into the local newspaper. Gracie bought a T-shirt with the female general galloping across the front at a fund-raiser held by the softball team but didn't wear the shirt in public. She needed the votes of men as well as women to remain in office. Neutrality was an inherent part of her job description.

Laura dangled her legs off the bleachers. "Would you let me pitch an inning if we get ahead in one of the early games in the tournament?" she asked. "I've been working on my changeup and four-seam fastball."

The team already had three solid pitchers, but Gracie knew Laura was itching to be involved in every play. Physics worked against the second baseman. Laura's diminutive size made it harder to generate the ball speed needed to be an effective pitcher.

"The fastball sets up the changeup, my strikeout pitch," Laura continued. "It comes out looking the same, then dies and drops when it reaches the plate. Maybe I can come early before our next practice and show you how much I've improved."

"Okay, but the fastball has to have enough zip on it to get the job done too."

Laura swung her legs a few more times. "Maybe I need to add a riser," she said. "I've tried, but it always ends up too high because I'm releasing it lower than the other girls. How tall were you when you were my age?"

"About the same as you. Be here thirty minutes early on Thursday, and we'll work on it."

Laura's mother pulled into the gravel parking lot, sending up a cloud of grayish dust.

"Thanks!" Laura said brightly as she hopped down onto the ground.

Gracie waved bye but stayed seated on the low bleachers. She loved everything about the softball field. The green grass, the brown infield, and the blue sky, the smell of a top-quality leather glove, the orderliness of the white lines that framed the field of play. It was a controlled world where the rules were clear and results easy to quantify. She stayed until the sun dipped below the tops of the pine trees.

/ / /

The sign in front of the large older home located two blocks from the courthouse read "Blair C. Smith, Attorney at Law." Buddy's father spent most of his adult life buying, selling, and renting real estate in and around Milton County. Rascal purchased the house from a local physician whose mother lived there until her death and turned it into a commercial property.

Buddy's law office took up the main floor of the house. He rented out spaces on the second floor to a nonprofit organization dedicated to building affordable housing for low-income families and to a semiretired financial planner who came in a few hours a day to check his mail and deposit the checks he received for managing his clients' money.

Rascal earned his nickname as a mischievous boy and proudly carried it with him through his entire life. He even left instructions that Marvin "Rascal" Smith be chiseled on his tombstone. Beatrice Smith honored the request when her husband dropped dead from a heart attack at age sixty-four.

Buddy stopped beside the desk of Millie Graham, the office manager and bookkeeper who'd worked for his father and now helped him. Millie wore her gray hair pulled back in a tight bun that dared a hair to escape. The office manager still showed up for work every day wearing a dress, stockings, and nice shoes. Her memory and attention to detail were legendary and made her excel at her job. Even though it was 5:45 p.m., Millie was still at her desk. She usually worked until 6:00 p.m. because the supper hour was the prime time to contact residential tenants who might be behind on their rent.

"Don't forget the secretarial candidate coming in tomorrow morning for an interview," Millie said. "She's been working as a waitress at the Dinner Bell but wants to be in an office."

Buddy did most of his own typing, and Millie kept his calendar. He'd had several secretaries over the years, but it was hard to find a good one. Millie wanted an assistant to spell her as much as to help Buddy, and he'd reluctantly agreed to consider a new hire. They'd already interviewed one candidate.

"Does this girl know it might not be a permanent job?"

"Yes. She just wants some experience."

"We'll see," Buddy replied noncommittally.

The initial documents in the Sue Ellen Ford case were on Millie's desk.

"Cut the filing fee checks in the Ford case so I can take this to the courthouse in the morning," Buddy continued. "I'm going to try to schedule an emergency hearing in front of Judge Claremont as soon as possible."

"I read the file. The husband sounds like the kind of jerk who could actually disappear with the son."

"Yeah," Buddy replied. "This won't be like the father who took off with his children for Idaho. By the time he made it to Mississippi, the kids were acting out so badly he drove back and handed them over to their mom."

"One other thing," Millie said as she raised her right index finger. "What do you want to do about the Grants? As of tomorrow, they will be three months behind on their rent."

"They caught up the payments when they received their federal tax refund."

"It's June. Are you going to wait until next April before filing a dispossessory warrant? Their rent is month to month, not year to year."

"I know, I know."

"Your father would—"

"Sometimes let it slide, sometimes not."

"Mostly not."

"Let me talk to my mother about it," Buddy said. "Mr. Grant's father used to work for her at the house on Lexington Avenue. She liked him a lot."

Millie sniffed. "I'm just doing my job."

"And you do it well. The Grants are a special case because of their history with our family."

Leaving the office, Buddy took a detour and slowly drove past the house where the Grant family lived. It was a single-story brick dwelling, built in the 1950s, with three bedrooms and two baths. Rascal had owned it long enough to replace the roof shingles twice and extensively renovate the interior after a drunken tenant trashed it on his way out of town in the middle of the night.

The yard was well maintained, and the house looked to be in good shape. The problem with the current tenants was their dependence on seasonal work. Kenneth Grant repaired the large equipment that harvested soybeans, field corn, and cotton. The work paid well during the harvest period, but he had a lot of downtime, and his efforts the previous year to start a lawn maintenance business to bridge the gaps resulted in capital outlay for equipment with not much profit. Buddy could see two commercial mowers sitting idly on a trailer parked next to the house.

Seeing the equipment, Buddy suddenly had an idea that would help Ken Grant satisfy his rent obligation.

THREE

AFTER EARNING AN ASSOCIATE DEGREE IN BUSINESS management from the local community college, Gracie went to work at the clerk of court's office. Eight years later she was promoted to chief assistant clerk. When her boss decided not to seek reelection, a lot of people encouraged Gracie to run. She wasn't sure she had the stomach for the rough-and-tumble world of Milton County politics, but her competitive juices kicked in. Also, she knew that if she lost the election, she would be out of a job because her opponent would bring in his own chief assistant. In the end, she won by a narrow margin, and Milton County had its first female clerk of court. Now, unless she made a big mistake, her job was secure. Incumbents rarely lost in small southern towns where people valued familiarity over the unknown.

Having arrived home after practice, Gracie placed the large bag of softballs in a small, cramped closet filled with bats, balls, gloves, hats, cleats, and other softball-related paraphernalia, enough to outfit an entire team. There were also leftover yard signs from her political campaign with "Grace Blaylock for Clerk of Court" printed on them in red, white, and blue letters. Opening the door to the small fenced-in yard, she greeted her dog. Opie was a four-year-old soft-coated wheaten terrier. The thirty-five-pound animal jumped up and placed his paws on her waist while Gracie rubbed the dog's curly-haired head. She'd rescued the dog from a backyard breeder who was about to be shut down by the county animal rescue department. The spirited terrier had deep, dark, soulful eyes.

In some ways, Opie rescued her. Gracie had fallen into a nagging depression after the three-year relationship with Barry fell apart. The golf addict moved to Birmingham and four months later married another woman. It turned out the newlyweds had been secretly communicating before Barry broke up with Gracie.

Abandoning the dating game for a while, Gracie had focused on work, softball, family, and faith for the past year. Taking a break from dating was easy because the number of suitable bachelors within a twenty-mile radius of the courthouse was small. Recently, Gracie's sister, Lauren, had started pressuring her to sign up on a Christian dating site. That was how Lauren met her husband, and she was convinced Gracie could also find true love and a godly soul mate through the right profile and photos.

"Did you keep all the squirrels and chipmunks off the property?" Gracie asked Opie.

The dog fixed his gaze on Gracie. Now that she was home, he would follow her around the house closer than if on a leash. Gracie was the epicenter of his world.

The single-story house that Gracie rented from the Smith family had heartwood-pine floors throughout. Opie's paws pattered on the wood as he followed her into the small kitchen and lapped water from a metal bowl. Gracie sorted through her mail. People occasionally sent business mail to her home address, and she set aside three letters to take to the courthouse in the morning.

Opie lay on the floor outside the bathroom while Gracie took a shower and changed into gym shorts and a cotton shirt. The house was air-conditioned, but the early summer heat pressed against the walls and roof from all directions. Gracie fixed a salad that included a generous helping of local peaches and watermelon. Lunch at one of the restaurants clustered around the courthouse square was usually her big meal of the day, and unless she had a community or church event to attend, she ate a light supper.

Gracie's mother and father lived on a 150-acre farm near the eastern edge of Milton County. The nearest neighbor was half a mile away. Maxine Blaylock was an avid vegetable gardener and every spring planted a full acre of tomatoes, green beans, okra, cantaloupe, watermelon, and peanuts. Gracie's father owned a herd of fifty Black Angus cattle, mostly cows with calves, a few steers, and an ornery bull confined in a smaller enclosure. A meal at her parents' house usually included something grown on the property.

As a young girl and teenager, Gracie enjoyed walking in the woods, playing with one of the family dogs, or holing up in her room with a book. She still read but now preferred to unwind by watching movies. She liked everything from romantic comedies to comic-book action flicks. She also kept a few nature shows saved in her TV queue. Opie's ears always perked up when the sounds of wildlife came through the speakers in the small den Gracie had converted into an entertainment area. He especially liked shows about African wild dogs and would stand directly in front of the screen with his stubby tail straight up in the air when the dogs yapped in communication. The roars from a lion pride made him nervous.

Gracie kept a chore list on her refrigerator. This evening she was scheduled to clean and dust the living room and den, using a special liquid product on the old wooden floors. While she was dusting the den furniture, her cell phone rang. She glanced at the caller ID. It was her mother.

"Hey, baby girl," her mother said when Gracie answered.

Gracie was the third of four children, but her mother still liked to call her "baby girl," mainly because Gracie was the first female child.

"How's the team shaping up?" Maxine asked.

Gracie gave a quick coach's summary and then asked a gardening question: "Are you irrigating yet?"

"Oh yeah. It's been dripping for over a week Will you be able to come out for dinner on Sunday? Noah and Bethany will be here with their kids."

"Probably."

"Just let me know."

Gracie could sense something else was on her mother's mind but knew it wouldn't come out until the older woman wanted it to. For her mother, no conversation should be rushed.

"How's Daddy feeling?" Gracie asked.

"Hating the hot afternoons, but he feeds and waters the cattle early in the morning and gets in a nap in the hammock after lunch."

"If he wants to come in one day and have lunch with me, just let me know."

"He mentioned that this morning, but he thinks you're so busy that he'd be bothering you. I told him that was nonsense."

"You're right. His vote counts too."

Maxine chuckled, then was quiet for a moment. "I don't want to bother you either," she said, "but I heard about a sad situation from Frances Mulhaven this afternoon and wanted to talk to you about it. It has to do with her granddaughter Reagan. Is she on your team this summer?"

"She came to the first couple of practices, but I haven't seen her since."

Gracie told Maxine what she'd heard from one of the girls during the prayer time at softball practice.

"That makes sense," Maxine said. "Frances called me about an hour ago to tell me Reagan ran away from home, and they don't know where she is."

"Did she leave by herself?"

"It seems that way, but it's hard to know. She turned seventeen a few weeks ago. I asked if she'd gotten into drugs or was running with a bad crowd. Frances didn't have a clue, and my questions made her cry so I shut up. You know Sammy and Crystal Landry, don't you? They're Reagan's parents. She's the youngest of their five children."

"Sammy works for Linton Construction?"

"That's right. He's a supervisor. Crystal taught preschool for years. The family has been calling everybody they can think of without success. The sheriff's department knows about it and set Reagan up as a missing child because she's not yet eighteen, but they haven't located her either."

"It sounds like the family is doing all they can."

"Yes, but after I talked to Frances, I thought about Buddy Smith. Is he still tracking down children kidnapped by one of their parents?"

"He is. I referred a woman to him yesterday."

"Do you think he might be interested in helping with this?"

"I don't know," Gracie said slowly. "Buddy is a lawyer, not a private investigator. And he gets involved when a parent wrongfully takes off with a child."

"Think about it. I'm worried Reagan will end up on a poster like the missing children you see at Sam's Club. I know most of those kids have been gone since they were little. It hurts my heart to see them, and to think about Reagan being someplace bad and in danger . . ." Maxine paused.

"I'll talk to Buddy," Gracie said.

"Thanks," Maxine said with relief. "It makes me feel better to know that at least I tried to help."

"But don't say anything to Frances. Not yet."

"Right, right. I almost brought it up but had sense enough not to. One other thing. Have you talked to Lauren recently?"

"Not this week."

"She really wants to come over to your place one evening after the boys are in bed so you can work together on the internet dating thing."

Gracie bristled. "And she asked you to say something to me about it?"

"Yes, she did," her mother replied slowly. "And before you say no, it won't hurt anything to give it a try. I had my doubts until Lauren met Jeff, but I couldn't ask for a better son-in-law. He came out last Saturday and got our small tractor running. I'd told your father we were going to have to buy a new one, but now it's running great."

"I don't think Lauren included 'must be tractor mechanic' as a requirement for the type of man she was looking for."

"I know. But anyway, it wouldn't hurt to give one of those websites a try. You could just do the one that worked for Lauren and Jeff."

Gracie was the only one of her siblings who wasn't married, and whether her mother intended to put pressure on her or not, she occasionally did.

"I'll set something up with Lauren."

"Good."

"And tell her not to put you up to calling me about it," Gracie added. "She's thirty-three and I'm thirty-five. We should be able to communicate as adults."

"You're right. Hope to see you on Sunday for dinner after church."

"Love you," Gracie said. "Talk to you soon."

"Love you, baby girl. Remember, I'm always proud of you."

After the call ended, Gracie started to text Lauren but decided not to. She'd waited half a biblical lifetime to meet the right man. Another day's delay to begin the process wouldn't hurt.

Once she finished cleaning the two rooms, Gracie plopped down in her TV room to watch a movie. She selected a chick flick, but the plot involved a teenage girl who ran away from home in an effort to make her estranged parents begin to communicate. Gracie felt uneasy. The girl in the movie hid out in safety at a friend's house, but the story was too close to the darker dangers possibly facing Reagan Landry. Gracie turned off the movie half-way through.

/ / /

Buddy bought a smoothie before stopping by to see his mother. Beatrice Smith lived in a historic home on Franklin Street, a tree-lined boulevard with Victorian- and colonial-style houses built in the 1880s and 1890s. General William Tecumseh Sherman and his Union troops burned Clarksburg to the ground in November 1864. As a result, no antebellum structures remained in Milton County. Post–Civil War upheavals delayed significant rebuilding for more than a decade. As things slowly improved, the few prosperous families who wanted to live in town settled along Franklin Street.

Rascal Smith sold the house on Lexington Avenue where Buddy and his two sisters grew up and bought the Franklin Street residence as a way to validate his financial success and social status to anyone who looked down their nose at a man who got his start selling weekly-premium life insurance policies to millworkers. But in a town like Clarksburg, new money never impressed old money unless there was a lot more than Rascal ever had in the bank. As a trader, he encumbered existing property to fund future expansion, which occasionally made cash flow tight and bankruptcy two or three bad deals away. But he was a survivor. Now that Rascal wasn't on the scene, Buddy was paying off debt while keeping his mother comfortable.

He parked his Audi behind his mother's Mercedes. The German luxury vehicle was another effort by Rascal to establish his bona fides. Beatrice, who cared little about the make of the car she drove, liked the lines of the cream-colored Mercedes vehicle and deemed the tan seats more comfortable than the leather couch in her living room. She only drove about twelve thousand miles a year, and Buddy hadn't yet suggested she trade in the aging vehicle for a new model. He texted his mother to let her know he was in the driveway. She didn't like him to barge in unannounced.

Beatrice met him at the door wearing a blue-and-yellow housedress and white sandals. Unlike her husband, she came from a respectable family with deep Milton County roots. Everyone who knew the Smiths shared the same opinion—Beatrice was the best thing that ever happened to Rascal. He didn't deny the truth, and his desire to provide for his wife and family was Rascal's most admirable quality. Recently turned sixty-seven, Beatrice looked several years younger and could have attracted suitors if she wanted one. Buddy leaned over and kissed her on the cheek.

"Good afternoon, Mama," he said formally. "I got too hot and sweaty walking to the courthouse to give you a hug."

"Come in where it's cool," she replied. "I'll get you a glass of tea."

"I just finished a smoothie."

"If you squeeze a couple of lemon slices into your tea, it can be a fruit drink too."

Buddy followed his mother into the kitchen. The spacious room had the most natural light of any part of the house. Black-and-white tile squares covered the floor. The wooden cabinets were white, and there was a round antique farm table in one corner. Neatly stacked on the table were newspapers, books, and different types of magazines. Beatrice always kept a pitcher of freshly brewed iced tea in the refrigerator. She filled a cut crystal glass and positioned three lemon wedges on the rim.

"What have you been reading?" he asked, thumbing through the collection on the table.

"A little bit of everything."

Buddy picked up a thin book about bonsai trees. Beatrice liked to grow flowers, and the beds around the house featured various colors at different times of the year. The most spectacular display was the early spring explosion of purple and white azalea bushes along Franklin Street. The large mature bushes formed a wall of blossoms that caused people to slow down and admire the vivid colors.

"Are you thinking about taking up bonsai?"

"Heavens, no. Reading about them is close enough for me."

Beatrice sat down at the table with a smaller glass of tea. "I should have asked—are you hungry?"

"No, I might have a snack later."

"A bowl of ice cream around nine o'clock?"

"Maybe." Buddy smiled and shifted in his chair. "I need to talk business with you for a minute. It's about the Grant family. They're behind on their rent."

"If I was going to grow bonsai, I'd try to train an azalea," Beatrice said, picking up the book and showing Buddy a photograph of a miniature bush with pink flowers. "It would be quite a conversation piece."

"Is that your way of telling me not to bother you about the Grant family?"

"Yes. Your daddy took care of that sort of thing. I know you want to keep me informed, but I don't want the responsibility."

"Okay, but at least let me tell you what I'm thinking. Ken Grant bought a bunch of lawn maintenance equipment that's sitting idle at his house. I thought he could satisfy part of the rent by cutting grass for us. I would surprise the tenants by offering his services free of charge for a month. Then, if Ken did a good job, some of them might hire him. I wouldn't ask him to come here. I know you like the crew you already have."

Beatrice nodded. "That's a clever way to handle it. I bet Doris Fletchall would welcome it. Her husband had a stroke and can't go outside in the heat. Another one is Gracie Blaylock. I saw her cutting her grass the other day when it must have been ninety-five degrees outside."

"I hadn't thought about Gracie. She refers cases to me from time to time, so I owe her a favor."

Beatrice took a sip of tea. "Gracie stops by to see me sometimes when she goes out for a walk. I love talking to her, and she has the friendliest dog."

"Are you interested in another dog?" Buddy asked, raising his eyebrows.

Beatrice shook her head. "Once Starr had to be put down, that was it for me and pets."

Starr was a cuddly bichon frise who lived to be eighteen. Rascal liked the furry white animal so much that he let him ride around in the car with him.

"What else have you been reading?" Buddy asked.

Beatrice handed him a book of poetry. It was a book of cinquains, five-line variations on Japanese haiku. Each poem featured a watercolor painting. The paintings caught Buddy's attention. He liked to draw and sketch, mostly with pen and ink.

"I like these illustrations," he said. "They're precise. I never could control watercolors."

"I like everything you've ever drawn."

"Spoken like a true mother," Buddy said, draining the last drops of tea from his glass. "Is there anything you need me to do around here before I leave?"

"The lightbulb in the stairway to the basement burned out, and I'm not tall enough to reach it."

"I'll be glad to change it."

Taking a new bulb from a closet near the kitchen, Buddy went halfway down the stairs and replaced the light. His mother had no business trying to descend into the dark and musty basement without a bright light. When the bulb came on, Buddy noticed a large cardboard box on the bottom step. It was a trip hazard, so he went down the steps to move it out of the way. The box was surprisingly heavy. He lifted the lid. It was filled with papers bearing his father's spindly handwriting. Glancing up the stairs, Buddy picked up a few sheets. They were kind, romantic notes written by his father to his mother. Buddy was tempted to read them but didn't. His mother didn't talk about her grief and filled her life with many friends, but Buddy knew she often felt sad and alone. She must have come down to spend time reading what Rascal wrote to her.

About to return the lid to its place, Buddy saw a long, narrow envelope with the corner of a check sticking out. He opened it. Instead of notes or letters, the envelope contained canceled checks. The first one he took out was dated ten years earlier and made payable to "Bearer." Buddy's eyes widened when he saw the amount. Drawn on his father's money market account with the First National Bank of Milton County, the check was in the amount of $10,000.

Buddy quickly removed all the checks from the envelope. Each of them was for $10,000 and made payable to "Bearer," which meant anyone in possession of the check could walk into a bank, endorse it, and deposit the money, or, in the case of the issuing bank, request $10,000 in cash. There was no rational, legitimate reason to conduct business in such a way. There were fourteen checks, one per year, totaling $140,000. Buddy's heart sank as he considered the possibility that his father might have been involved in something fraudulent or illegal. He turned the checks over to see had who received and deposited them.

There was an illegible scrawl in the space for endorsements until Buddy reached the earliest check.

Written clearly in a woman's handwriting on the back of the check was the name Amber Melrose. Amber always shaped the "o" in Melrose so that it looked like a heart. In faded blue ink on the endorsement line was the familiar tiny heart. Issued seventeen years earlier, the check was dated around the time Amber and Elise left Milton County and dropped out of sight.

Shocked, Buddy stared unseeing across the basement toward the fiberboard wall where his father hung his tools. Within seconds several things were clear. Rascal had financed Amber's escape from Clarksburg. But he didn't stop there. His father not only aided Amber's initial flight but enabled her to permanently disappear, an act that stymied Buddy's later efforts to track down his former girlfriend and daughter. And Rascal maintained contact with Amber until several months before his death. The final payment was less than sixty days prior to his fatal heart attack three years ago. Buddy felt sick. Rascal was aware of how desperately Buddy wanted to find Amber and Elise, yet he never told his son that he knew where they were.

Buddy quickly rummaged through the box. Somewhere in the jumble of papers might be hidden the information he'd been desperately seeking since he began his search: Amber's address. There were receipts for repairs to rental houses, property surveys, real estate closing documents, even a list of Christmas gifts for Beatrice. Buddy reached the bottom of the box. Nothing. He began again, this time going much slower. Partway through the second search, his mother opened the door at the top of the stairs.

"Buddy, are you all right?" she asked. "I started worrying you might have fallen."

"I changed the lightbulb," he replied, shielding the cardboard box from his mother's line of sight with his body. "I'll be up in a minute or two."

"Okay. I'm going to water the flower beds."

"Good idea. Take your time."

The door closed. Buddy again reached the bottom of the box. Still nothing. There were fifteen or sixteen similar-looking boxes stacked to the left of the staircase. Buddy had always assumed they contained miscellaneous information related to Rascal's business dealings. His father was a disorganized pack rat who never threw anything away. That's why he hired Millie Graham. Going through all the boxes would take hours and couldn't be done tonight. And Buddy faced a more immediate issue—whether to talk to his mother about his discovery.

Sticking the envelope in the back pocket of his pants, Buddy replaced the lid and returned the box to the stack. He was about to climb the stairs when he had another thought. Sitting down on a higher step, he inspected the back of the checks a second time. Amber took the first check to the First National Bank of Milton County, the same bank on which it was drawn. Most likely Rascal notified a bank officer that a teenage girl would be coming in with the check. There were several bank employees who'd worked at the bank for many years and might remember the transaction. It wasn't common for a seventeen-year-old to have such a large check, especially one made payable to "Bearer." And Amber likely requested cash if she was going to leave town for good.

Subsequent checks were presented at banks in Atlanta, Savannah, Chattanooga, and St. Louis. Of the final four, three were negotiated in Atlanta at a well-known bank with branches across the country. The scrawl Amber adopted as her legal signature after the first year no longer contained an "o" shaped like a heart, but the way she formed her "A" bore a strong resemblance to her original handwriting. After that, the signature circled around a few times and died in a small loop that could be interpreted as an "e." To him, the illegible name spoke of the ongoing desire for anonymity. Returning upstairs to the kitchen, he glanced at the clock and realized he'd spent almost an hour doing a job that took less than a minute.

Grabbing a bottle of water from the refrigerator, he made his way through the living room and stepped onto the wide front porch that stretched across the entire front of the house. There was a large swing to the right and a pair of wicker chairs with a small table between them to the left. His mother was standing with her back to him and watering a spectacular cluster of tall orange gladiolus. Beatrice turned around, smiled, and waved. Seeing her contented face, Buddy suspected she hadn't looked at the checks or, if she did, she had no idea what they were for. It wasn't the right time to drop a bomb on his mother's world.

"I'll talk to you tomorrow!" he called out.

His mother turned off the water. "What were you doing in the basement?" she asked. "I know it's messy, but I don't want you wasting your time straightening up down there when you have more important things to do."

"It wasn't a waste of time."

FOUR

OPIE SLEPT IN A COMFY DOG BED IN THE CORNER OF Gracie's bedroom. It was hard for an animal bred to protect Irish farmhouses from varmints to turn off his genetic wiring, and if he heard a strange noise in the night, he issued a series of sharp barks that caused Gracie to jerk awake. The dog went to bed shortly after the sun set and liked to greet the day as soon as the sun appeared. That schedule suited Gracie. Early mornings were a prime time of the day for her. She enjoyed drinking a cup of freshly ground coffee sweetened with cream and sugar at the kitchen table or while sitting on a small deck built onto the rear of the house. This morning the outside air was cool and pleasant, so she chose the deck.

Gracie read a chapter each in the Old and New Testaments, then opened a prayer list she kept on a tablet. She liked routine and had organized the extensive list so that items appeared daily, weekly, monthly, and annually. When she received an answer, she recorded the result. Sometimes a sick person recovered. Other times the person died. Regardless of the outcome, Gracie faithfully made an appropriate entry and moved the request to a separate file.

Sue Ellen Ford and little Jack had been added within the past forty-eight hours. This morning Reagan Landry made her first appearance on the daily list. To make room for them, Gracie moved two other prayer concerns to weekly reminders. Another went from weekly to monthly. It wasn't just a record of requests; it was also a celebration of answers. One of Gracie's cousins who'd been laid off from his job had found a new position for better pay, and she entered the answer followed by an exclamation mark of thanks. Moving down the list, she was prompted to pray for a woman who worked for her at the clerk's office who was having marital problems. Recently, the couple had agreed to counseling. Gracie changed her prayer reminder to focus on that aspect of the situation. After forty-five minutes she reached the annual items that she hadn't seen for a year.

The first one that popped up was a prayer that Buddy Smith would find his daughter, Elise. The situation had been on Gracie's prayer list for a long time, but after years without progress it had been relegated to annual status. As clerk of court, Gracie had seen the original birth certificate. For some reason the document issued to Amber listed the female baby's father as "Unknown." There was the possibility that Buddy wasn't the father, but he believed he was and Gracie had no reason to doubt him.

Buddy and Gracie had known each other since sharing the same third-grade classroom in elementary school. Gracie was a chubby little blonde, and Buddy was the smartest boy in the class. That winter he drew an amazingly detailed picture of a dog romping in the snow and gave it to Gracie, who still had the drawing in a box that contained memorabilia from her school years.

In the tenth grade, she and Buddy shared a table in biology

and partnered in dissecting a frog, growing green bean seeds in pots with different brands of fertilizer, and doing an experiment to illustrate Mendel's laws of genetics using colored M&M candies. As part of the genetic project, the teacher required a fifteen-minute verbal presentation of Mendel's principles to the entire class. To Gracie, who'd not completely grown out of her chubby stage, fifteen minutes standing in front of the class sounded like fifteen hours, but Buddy boldly stepped in. He wrote most of their paper and allowed Gracie to demonstrate the concepts while he spoke about them. The teacher gave them both an A, but Gracie knew who'd earned the grade. During that time, she'd developed a secret crush on Buddy and whenever possible positioned herself near him during lunch or study hall. He was nice to her but was mostly oblivious to her presence. That summer Gracie played summer league softball and showed up for their junior year fit, attractive, and with more confidence than ever before. She walked into chemistry class hoping to share a table with Buddy, but he was sitting next to a new girl, Amber Melrose. Gracie had to find another lab partner.

Amber had sailed into the high school after living all over the country and immediately threw herself into cultivating relationships with the boys—not the girls—in their class. A decent athlete, she briefly played on the softball team but soon quit. Once she and Buddy paired up, they were inseparable.

In a conservative area like Milton County, a high school pregnancy, especially involving someone as well-known as Buddy Smith, was a big deal that generated a massive amount of talk and gossip. Amber didn't seem to care. During their senior year, she flaunted her increasing baby bump and accepted the special accommodations she received from teachers. Buddy was so fixated on Amber that he appeared immune to negative opinions. The scuttlebutt around the school was that Buddy and Amber were going to marry upon graduation. It didn't happen, and Amber abruptly left town shortly after the baby's birth. Gracie heard several versions of why they broke up and Amber disappeared, but she never learned the truth from Buddy.

Tapping the tablet with her finger, Gracie prayed that Buddy would find his daughter and be able to establish a good relationship with her. She didn't add anything about Buddy reconnecting with Amber. She didn't have to pray about that. Gracie never believed they were a good match for each other when they were in high school, and nothing since then had changed her opinion.

Closing the tablet, Gracie sat quietly in her chair for a few minutes with Opie lying contentedly at her feet. Beginning her day with the Lord was the foundation for everything else that followed. Gracie relished the final moments of quiet and peace before entering the high-stress world of the courthouse.

Before leaving for work, she made sure the dog had plenty of water in his outside bowl. He could find shade under the deck or beneath several large trees in the small backyard.

Gracie parked in a space reserved for "Clerk of Court." She was fourth in line in the local governmental hierarchy, ranked behind only the two superior court judges and the county sheriff. Sometimes the status she held still seemed unreal to her.

"Morning, Brenda," Gracie said to her chief assistant.

"Hey," Brenda replied. "I sorted your mail."

Gracie's position hadn't earned her a private office. Instead, her desk rested against the back wall so she could oversee everything that took place: filing lawsuits and other pleadings, recording deeds, notifying jurors when it was time to serve, maintaining court records, assisting the judges with the court calendar, helping attorneys, and performing anything else the county commissioners wanted done. The clerk's office employed six people, five women and one man. Jeremy Prater, the lone male, was a young man who wanted to become an appraiser in the county tax department. Gracie knew about his goals and had assigned him to the real estate department.

Managing people was a lot like coaching a sports team, and Gracie brought the same approach to the office that she'd perfected on the softball diamond. That meant cross-training among different positions and fostering a willingness among her employees to help wherever and whenever needed. She'd fired two people since becoming clerk, both for pushing back against that expectation.

The morning passed quickly. Automation in Milton County wasn't as sophisticated as in metropolitan areas. There was a lot of hands-on work with paper records and documents. Around 10:30 a.m., Judge Claremont, the senior judge, threw Gracie a major curve when his administrative assistant called to tell her the judge had decided to take a few extra days off the following month. This had a domino effect on the court calendar. By the time Gracie finished, it was lunchtime. She walked across the street to the Crossroads Café.

Buddy leaned back in his chair and read Jennifer Stockton's résumé. The secretarial candidate was a tall girl with a thick country accent. She'd completed several business courses at the local community college. Jennifer's references confirmed the young woman was a hard worker with above-average organizational skills.

"I brought a typing sample," the dark-haired nineteen-year-old said, laying a few sheets of paper on the edge of Buddy's desk. "And I'm prepared to take a typing test."

The samples included court pleadings in both a civil case and a criminal case. Jennifer had correctly laid out the headings and format and selected the proper font size. Buddy didn't see any errors and liked what he saw. But training people wasn't his favorite activity.

"That won't be necessary based on your coursework."

"And I'm a self-starter who isn't afraid of taking initiative."

"Is that something your career counselor at the community college told you to say?"

The young woman was perched on the edge of her seat. Her face flushed. "Yes, sir. But it's true."

"That's okay," Buddy said with a wave of his hand. "How soon could you start?"

"As soon as you like. My boss at the restaurant knows I'm looking for an office job and told me not to worry about working out a notice."

Buddy wasn't afraid of making a quick decision. "You have the job," he said. "Come in tomorrow."

"I do?" Jennifer asked, her eyes wide.

"Yes." Buddy nodded with a smile. "But be sure that you make Millie happy."

"I will. I know she can teach me a lot."

"Millie will set you up with everything you need."

The young woman beamed. "Thank you, Mr. Smith. I really appreciate the chance to work for you."

Nobody in the office called him Mr. Smith, but Buddy didn't correct her. It might be a good idea to keep things formal for at least a couple of weeks. He escorted Jennifer to the office manager's desk. Millie had already prepared a new employment packet for the young woman. Jennifer left with the information in her hands.

"How did you know I would hire her?" Buddy asked.

"We both know some fresh blood will be good around here."

Buddy walked across the street and filed the complaint for divorce and the motion for an expedited custody hearing in *Ford v. Ford*. There weren't any clouds in the sky, but the air was humid, which would make the heat later in the day even more oppressive. Instead of returning to the office, he made his way to the First National Bank of Milton County.

Inside the front pocket of Buddy's jacket were the two checks that Amber negotiated at the local bank. Unlike his father, Buddy didn't have any accounts there. He entered, and a young woman approached him.

"How may I help you?" she asked.

"I'm Blair Smith. Is there a vice president available?" Buddy handed her one of his business cards.

"Let me check with Ms. Brockington."

A middle-aged woman emerged from a side office and introduced herself.

"I knew your father," she said with a smile. "I had several opportunities to work with him. He was quite a character, very entertaining to talk to."

It was a common description of Rascal.

"Could we speak in private?" Buddy asked.

They went into a small enclosed office in a corner of the main floor. Ms. Brockington closed the door and sat behind a shiny wooden desk.

"How long have you been with the bank?" Buddy asked.

"Twenty years. I started as a teller."

Buddy removed the two checks from his jacket but kept them in his hand. "I have a question about a couple of transactions that took place a number of years ago. Both of them involved my father's money market account. One was seventeen years ago, the other shortly before his death. If you need to see any formal paperwork before you talk to me, I'm the executor of his estate, but my questions don't involve confidential information. They have to do with these checks."

He handed her the checks. The bank officer examined the front of each document, then the back.

"Obviously, writing a check to 'Bearer' for $10,000 is unusual," Buddy continued.

"Yes, it is."

"And I'm interested in finding out if you, or someone else who worked here at the time, assisted my father or the holder of the checks when they were presented to the bank."

Ms. Brockington held up one of the checks. "I remember the most recent one. Your father came in with a young woman and obtained my approval for delivery of cash."

"You're sure?"

"Yes," the bank vice president responded slowly. "It was a situation that made me personally uncomfortable, but there was no reason not to honor your father's instructions. The money was in the account. The woman was quite a bit younger than he was."

Buddy suddenly realized Ms. Brockington suspected Amber was his father's mistress.

"No, no," he said quickly. "There was nothing wrong between my father and the woman. She was the mother of his first grandchild."

"Oh," Ms. Brockington said as she visibly relaxed. "That makes sense now."

"In a way it might, but not totally. Tell me everything you can remember."

"Details are fuzzy. I was puzzled why your father would write a check payable to 'Bearer.' He could have simply withdrawn the money himself. It seemed like an unnecessary step. And a transaction for that much in cash isn't a common occurrence. We don't report cash withdrawals to the feds unless they exceed $10,000."

Buddy wasn't interested in discussing bank regulations. "What do you remember about the woman? Was she alone? Did she have a child with her? What did she look like?"

Ms. Brockington thought for a moment. "All I remember thinking is that she was attractive. Maybe her hair was dark, but I'm not one hundred percent sure. She was alone except for your father. There wasn't a child with her."

Amber was a natural brunette in high school.

"Where did you meet with them? Try to remember any snippets of conversation. That could help bring back more information."

"Uh, I think we went directly to one of the tellers who took over from there. I believe I simply initialed the authorization for disbursement of the cash."

"Do you remember the teller?"

"No."

"Does the name Amber Melrose mean anything to you? I suspect she's the woman who negotiated the check."

"No," Ms. Brockington replied and shook her head. "I realize you're the executor, but I may have told you more than I should."

"I'm not going to take your deposition or anything like that," Buddy said reassuringly. "I'm just trying to unravel a mystery from the past."

"Sorry I can't be of more help."

Even though he'd confirmed what happened, Buddy left the bank feeling unsettled. Information didn't necessarily lead to progress. All he'd done was verify what the checks already told him.

Shortly before noon, Buddy received a call from Christopher Henley, a fellow lawyer who was one of Buddy's best friends. Chris was a junior partner in Clarksburg's largest firm, a group of five attorneys. Vince Nelson, the senior partner in the group, was a white-haired lawyer who'd served several terms in the state senate and held more political power than anyone else in Milton County. Buddy hated facing off against the unflappable southern gentleman who treated his opponents with respect as he skillfully gutted their claims.

"Did you forget what day it is?" Chris asked in an accent that revealed his Tidewater roots outside Richmond.

Buddy looked at the calendar on his computer. There were no special notations.

"Are you supposed to buy my lunch today?" he asked.

"No, you should be buying mine. It's my anniversary. I'm leaving the office early to take Marissa to Atlanta for a fancy dinner and spend the night. The kids are already at her parents' house."

"Congrats. Why didn't you ask me to keep the kids?"

"They'd love eating pizza and playing your video game system, but Marissa couldn't relax knowing they weren't being supervised by a responsible adult. But listen, I called to ask if you'd heard the news about Jason."

Jason Long, a local pediatrician, was a mutual friend.

"What's going on? Are he and Katie having problems?"

"No, but someone filed a malpractice claim against him on Monday."

There were very few lawsuits against doctors or hospitals in Milton County. Local juries were reluctant to award damages against health-care providers because their purpose was to help people and they deserved community support. Any malpractice litigation immediately became a top item of local legal gossip.

"What are the allegations?"

"It has to do with a little boy who contracted bacterial meningitis and ended up in a coma. He began suffering seizures once he woke up and still has neurological problems. The plaintiffs claim Jason didn't diagnose the condition soon enough."

"Will your firm serve as local counsel?"

"Probably. The malpractice insurance company will bring in lawyers from Atlanta, but they'll want Mr. Nelson sitting in on the depositions and at trial."

"Who's representing the plaintiff?"

"Nobody we know. They hired a lawyer from New York. I checked him out. He's a big deal with a lot of multimillion-dollar verdicts."

"Most of those kinds of attorneys have lost big too. That doesn't show up on their websites."

"True. Anyway, be aware of what's going on with Jason. I'm sure he's torn up about it."

"Thanks for the heads-up."

After the call ended, Buddy leaned back in his chair and

thought about Jason. The pediatrician was a dedicated doctor who cared deeply about his young patients. Chris was right. A malpractice suit would devastate Jason.

It was noon, and Buddy was hungry. Going down the street to the Crossroads Café, he sat at a table for two.

/ / /

Gracie glanced around the restaurant and saw Buddy Smith sitting alone. Usually, Buddy would be surrounded by a posse of friends at lunch, so this was her chance to ask him in person about helping Reagan's parents track down their daughter. She headed directly for his table.

"Are you eating alone today?" she asked brightly. "Or is someone joining you?"

"I'm solo," Buddy replied.

Gracie didn't move.

"Would you like to join me?" Buddy asked after an awkward silence of several seconds.

"Thanks," Gracie said, sitting down.

Their waitress appeared. The Crossroads Café was a comfort food diner known for southern cooking, but it also offered a decent chef's salad, which Gracie ordered.

"I'll have the stuffed green pepper special with sautéed squash and baby peas," Buddy said without looking at the menu. "And extra butter for the corn bread, please."

"I'd like a piece of corn bread too," Gracie added.

They sat in silence for a moment. Gracie wasn't sure how best to bring up Reagan's disappearance.

"Thanks for meeting with Sue Ellen Ford," she said.

"Glad to help. There's an expedited hearing for custody in front of Judge Claremont set for two o'clock this afternoon. After the judge grants Sue Ellen sole custody of the kids, I'll ask the sheriff's department to help track down Jackie."

"Okay, and if there's anything I can do, let me know," she said.

"What do you have in mind?"

"I'm not sure," Gracie stammered. "I mean, you know what you're doing. That's why I recommended you."

The waitress arrived with their food. Gracie offered up a silent blessing. Buddy went directly for the piping-hot corn bread that came in the shape of a miniature loaf. He cut it in two and spread butter that instantly melted. He took a big bite and closed his eyes.

"This is a good batch," he said. "It's always better when James is working in the kitchen. I saw him there when I came in. Eat it while it's hot."

Gracie sampled the corn bread, which had the perfect combination of coarse golden meal and a touch of sweetness. They ate in silence for a few moments. Buddy seemed preoccupied. Over the years, Gracie would occasionally ask about his search for Elise.

"I was praying this morning for you and Elise," she said.

"You did what?" Buddy burst out so loudly that Gracie saw people in the restaurant turn and stare in their direction.

"Uh, it comes up as a reminder once a year on my prayer list," she managed. "And today was the day. I thought I'd mentioned it to you before, but if you don't want me to—"

"No, no." Buddy returned his fork to his plate and shook his head. "I appreciate it. But I can't believe you did that."

Buddy stared at her. Not sure what to say, Gracie ate a bite of salad.

"I may have missed what you said at first," he said. "Why did you pray about Elise today?"

"It came up, just like a reminder on a calendar."

"That is so weird," he said.

"Why? Has there been some progress?"

Buddy looked around before answering. "Yes," he said, lowering his voice. "I uncovered some information last night at my mother's house that might help me locate Amber and Elise. I believe my father was in touch with Amber after she left Clarksburg."

Gracie's eyes widened. "And you didn't know about it?"

"No. And I doubt my mother did either."

Gracie silently absorbed the news. "That's . . . uh—" she started but then stopped.

"Terrible," Buddy said flatly.

An even longer period of silence followed as they both ate. It was clear Buddy was preoccupied with whatever he'd uncovered. If Gracie was going to talk to him about Reagan, she needed to act quickly. Buddy stood up.

"I'd better get going so I can prepare for Sue Ellen's hearing," he said before she could bring up the subject.

"Hope it goes well. I'd like to talk again soon."

"Okay," Buddy replied. "Lunch is on me today. And you'll be getting a letter from Millie. I'm going to pay Ken Grant to provide a free month of lawn care for all the residential tenants. I know your yard is small and you keep it up, but it's a way to help Ken. If you like his work, maybe there's something he can do for you in the future."

"Thanks."

Gracie watched as Buddy left the restaurant. She inwardly kicked herself for missing her best chance to talk to him about Reagan.

FIVE

AFTER LISTENING TO SUE ELLEN FORD FOR FIVE MINutes, Judge Claremont told Buddy that he'd heard enough and signed an order granting Sue Ellen immediate and total custody of little Jack and Emily. Buddy included the girl in case Jackie tried at some point to grab her too.

"Thank you, Judge," Buddy said as he closed his file. "Once the sheriff's office confirms that the boy hasn't been turned over to the mother, I'll be asking that the father be held in criminal contempt of court."

After making sure Sue Ellen understood how the process would work, Buddy slung his jacket over his shoulder for the short walk to the sheriff's office. He handed the custody order to the officer in charge of serving court documents.

"Anyplace else I should check?" asked an overweight, middle-aged officer named Reynolds.

Buddy flipped through his file until he found Boyd Lipscomb's name and address. He copied the information onto a slip of paper.

"Try here. Even if Ford's not there, Lipscomb may know how to get in touch with him and notify him that law enforcement is involved. Maybe that will get his attention and convince him to turn himself in."

"Or run farther."

"Yeah, that's also a possibility."

The officer slipped the address into a file folder along with the order.

"Who works missing children cases now that Detective Watkins is gone?" Buddy asked.

"Detective Harkness."

"Is he available?"

"Detective Harkness is a woman. Started a few weeks ago."

"Sorry," Buddy said.

"Hey, better to make the mistake with me than her," the officer said and shrugged. "Do you want me to see if she can talk to you now?"

"Yes, please."

Buddy followed Reynolds down a narrow hall into a large room with dividers. There were at least six cubicles. They stopped in front of one where a young woman in her thirties was sitting. Detective Harkness was wearing blue jeans and a yellow cotton shirt. A cowboy hat rested on the corner of her desk, and when she stood up Buddy saw Western-style boots on her feet. The new detective had long, straight black hair with dark eyes.

"Mayleah Harkness," she said in an accent that sounded southern but without a Georgia drawl.

They shook hands, and Buddy glanced at her desk. Next to the hat was a cluster of photos of adults and children who looked similar to the detective.

"Welcome to Milton County," he said. "Where are you from?"

"Oklahoma," she responded. "How may I help you?"

Buddy explained why he was there, including his interest in finding children kidnapped by their parents.

"I just left the courthouse with a custody order in a new case," he said. "It may come across your desk soon, and I wanted to give you a heads-up."

"Okay. Most of my caseload is going to involve claims of child abuse, neglect, and molestation, but missing children are also my responsibility."

"Is that what you did in Oklahoma?"

"Only for the past year. Before that I worked homicide in Tulsa."

The phone on the detective's desk buzzed. She answered and listened. Placing one hand over the receiver, she picked up a business card with the other and handed it to Buddy.

"I need to take this call," she said.

Buddy put the card in his pocket. Having a woman detective working on the case was a plus. Detective Harkness might be even more zealous than a man in trying to track down little Jack.

Back at his office, Millie was working on the monthly financial statement for the law firm.

"Take a break," Buddy said. "I'd like to talk to you in my office."

"Why not here?" Millie asked. "We're alone."

"My office, please. There's something in there I want to ask you about."

With a huff, Millie followed him. Buddy opened the top drawer of his desk and took out the envelope he'd discovered in his mother's basement.

"Are you familiar with my father's money market account at First National Bank?" he asked.

"Yes. We closed that account after he died, and you moved all the funds to the Commerce Bank and Trust."

"But when the First National account was open you'd reconcile it for him, correct?"

"Yes," Millie replied slowly. "Why? I feel like you're cross-examining me. Did I do something wrong? We reconciled all those accounts when we closed out his estate."

"Do you know anything about these checks?" Buddy slid the envelope across the desk. Millie picked it up and quickly thumbed through the canceled checks. Buddy watched her face, which revealed nothing.

"Where did you find these?" she asked without looking up.

"In a box in my mother's basement. Did you see who endorsed the first check?"

Millie blinked her eyes a couple of times. "Your father made me promise never to tell you about these payments."

"He's gone now. And whatever he pressured you into agreeing to no longer applies."

Millie didn't respond.

"I went by First National Bank and spoke to one of the vice presidents," Buddy continued. "Ms. Brockington remembers my father coming into the bank with a young woman to cash the final check a few months before he died. It had to be Amber."

"Well, you've found them," Millie said. "And you're certainly smart enough to figure out what he was doing."

"No, no," Buddy said, holding up one hand. "I need you to talk to me about this."

"You have the checks." Millie returned the envelope to Buddy's desk. "I knew about them because I balanced the account. There's nothing to tell. Your father made me promise never to talk to you or your mother about the payments, and I agreed to keep it secret, even if he died before I did."

"So all these years you knew about the existence of these checks?"

"Yes."

"And never said anything to me about it, even when you knew I was trying to track down Amber and Elise?"

The older woman glanced at the floor for several moments before looking up with a sad expression on her face.

"Maybe it's time you found someone else to manage the finances around here," she said. "I've thought about retiring and spending more time in my garden. I'd be willing to work out a notice, or you could hire Kipper Bookkeeping Service. Jane in their office would be glad to jump right in—"

"Millie, I don't want you to quit or retire," Buddy interrupted. "And I don't want to hire someone else. My mother didn't know about these payments?"

Millie pressed her lips tightly together. "You'd have to ask her. But we never discussed it. That was part of the agreement I had with your father."

"Where did he send the checks? They were negotiated at banks from here to Atlanta, Savannah, Chattanooga, St. Louis, and back again."

"I didn't mail any of them for him."

"And you don't know where he might have kept a record of Amber's address?"

"No."

Buddy thought for a moment. "Did you ever hand-deliver a payment to Amber or see her when she came to town to pick one up?"

The change in expression on Millie's face revealed the answer.

Buddy leaned forward. "When and where?" he continued.

"No," Millie said in reply and shook her head. "That was part of the promise."

Buddy was about to explode but knew it wouldn't help. Millie might clam up.

"Don't you think there's a time to put aside my father's wishes and respect my desires?" he asked, trying to sound calmer than he felt.

"You have the checks," Millie repeated.

"Why did he make the payments? Did Amber blackmail him and demand financial support for her and the baby? I have a right to know."

And for the first time in his life, Buddy saw tears appear in Millie Graham's eyes. She quickly wiped them away.

"Your father loved you," she managed. "And in his own way he always wanted the best for you. You may not agree with what he did, but the only things he really cared about were taking care of your mother and making sure you and your sisters had a good future. When you graduated from law school, passed the bar exam, and decided to return here to practice, he was so proud."

"What does that have to do with anything?"

"It has everything to do with it!" Millie responded emphatically. "Don't you see?"

"You mean—" Buddy started and then stopped in dismay. "My father paid Amber so that she and the baby wouldn't be part of my life?"

"From the time you were a little boy, everyone knew you were smart and would succeed in life. Your father never asked my opinion or talked openly to me about his reasons for giving

Amber money. But if he had, I'm not sure I would have disagreed with him. It's hard to know the right thing to do when a child is suddenly caught up in adult challenges."

Buddy stared past Millie as he talked. "As a teenage father, I would have been saddled with a wife and child who would hold me back from becoming the kind of son who would make my father proud."

Millie didn't respond. Resentment boiled up inside Buddy—not against the bookkeeper for hiding information from him, but against his father for his manipulation of such incredibly personal and important parts of his son's life.

"He had no right to do that," Buddy said. "And he should have talked to me. If not when I was eighteen, then later when he knew how much I wanted to find Elise."

Millie threw her hands up in the air. "I've thought about this a lot over the years, and it's been a burden to my soul. I don't blame you for being mad at me."

"I'm a lot madder at him than I am at you."

Millie rubbed her forehead with the bony fingers of her right hand. "Okay," she said with a determination in her voice that was familiar to Buddy. "I'm going to break my promise because I can't think of a good reason not to. When the baby was around seven years old, I gave Amber a check in the parking lot of the Southside Grill."

The Southside Grill was a local hangout for high school students, especially on Friday nights after football games. Many a late-night rendezvous between Buddy and Amber started at the grill.

"You saw Elise?"

Millie nodded.

"What did she look like?"

Millie closed her eyes for a moment before opening them. "There's no question that she looks like you. If you take a photo of you at six or seven and turn it into a girl, you'll have a close picture of her. I saw her sitting in the rear seat of the car with the window down. She didn't get out of the car, but I saw her face. She has your eyes, hair color, even the shape of your mouth. I'm not sure, but I think she was skinny."

Buddy's stomach flipped. The fact that he had a daughter who resembled him made everything much more real. The few photos taken when Elise was an infant at the hospital revealed a vague similarity to his own baby photos. With this new information, he couldn't wait to go to his mother's house and drag out an album of photos from when he was in the second grade. At that age, he'd been a skinny kid with light brown hair and dark brown eyes who was just beginning to realize that his only real sports skill was blazing speed.

"And Amber?" he asked.

"She was wearing dark sunglasses. Her hair was blond and cut short. She was wearing jeans and a T-shirt. We didn't talk at all. I handed her an envelope with the check, and she left."

"Blond hair? It was brunette when she came to the bank with my father a few years ago."

"Women change their hair color."

"I know, I know. Did she have on a wedding band?"

"No. And I checked. She was wearing rings on several fingers, but nothing on the left ring finger."

"What kind of car was she driving?"

Millie hesitated. "I'm not good at types and makes. I think it was small and white, but I'm not sure."

"Any other children in the car?"

"I didn't see any."

"What state was the license plate from?"

"I don't remember that either. Buddy, it was all over in a few seconds. The only thing I really focused on was the little girl. She was looking at a book and glanced up at me for just a second or two. I don't remember her clothes. It was her face I wanted to see. The resemblance to you was so strong."

"Why did you personally deliver that particular check to Amber?"

"Because Rascal told me to do it."

"Was it the only time?"

"Yes."

"Did you and my father talk later about Elise? Was he curious about her?"

Millie shook her head. "No. Neither one of us ever said a word about it."

/ / /

After she returned to the courthouse, Gracie mulled over her conversation with Buddy. Her prayer for him and Elise was going to move in the opposite direction—from once a year to every day.

"The Office of the Courts in Atlanta called," Brenda said. "They're sending another judge to fill in while Judge Barnwell is gone."

Judge Dixon Barnwell was on active military duty as a JAG officer for three months. That meant retired superior court judges with emeritus status had been coming to town for short periods to help with the caseload. Gracie called Atlanta and learned that a former judge named Bryant Williams would be traveling to Clarksburg the following week.

"He's from Statesboro and has your contact information," the coordinator said. "He'll arrive Sunday afternoon and will need accommodations for four weeks. He's agreed to stay until Judge Barnwell returns."

There were two motels in Milton County, neither suitable for a judge. Gracie had housed the other visiting judges with a local couple who ran a bed-and-breakfast in a large, older home on Franklin Street not far from Buddy's mother. Gracie explained what she had in mind.

"Sounds okay, but make sure the judge can bring his parrot. That created a hassle the last assignment he took."

"A parrot?"

"Yes. And it's nonnegotiable."

Gracie wasn't sure if pet birds were allowed at the bed-and-breakfast. "I'll find out and get back to you."

Gracie called Vivian Hunt at the bed-and-breakfast and told her about the unusual request.

"Thanks for letting us know," said Vivian. "We can make it work. I've had people who snored so loudly it rattled the pipes. In case the bird makes a racket, I'll put the judge in a room that's separate from the other bedrooms. It's downstairs near the kitchen, which is convenient for meals and has a nice view of the vegetable garden."

"Sounds perfect. I may bring him over in person."

Later, on her way to softball practice, Gracie stopped by Buddy's office to pay her rent and schedule a specific time to talk to him about Reagan. She handed the rent check to Millie Graham.

"I have good news," Millie said when she handed Gracie a receipt. "We're going to provide free lawn service by Ken Grant for a month to all our residential tenants."

"Buddy told me about it at lunch today," Gracie said, glancing past Millie's desk toward the lawyer's office. "I'd like to set up an appointment with him to talk about a new case I want to refer to him."

"Let me check for an opening on his calendar. Is there a day that's best for you?"

"I can make most times work. It won't take long. Maybe fifteen minutes."

While Millie looked at her computer screen, Buddy emerged from his office wearing his running gear and with a gym bag in one hand.

"Twice in one day," he said to Gracie.

"I was paying my rent and wanted to set up an appointment to talk about a new case," she replied. "It'll only take a few minutes to provide the background information so you can decide if you can help."

"You've got a fairly full day scheduled tomorrow," Millie said.

"Do you have time now?" Buddy asked Gracie.

"I have to be at the ballfield in a few minutes for practice."

"I'm going to start running again. Why don't I swing by and we can talk after practice?"

Gracie knew she would be hot and sweaty. "Uh, okay," she said.

Buddy turned to Millie. "Did you know Gracie struck me out when I was playing ball in high school? I had no chance."

"He wasn't used to hitting a rising fast-pitch softball," Gracie explained. "It moves differently than a baseball."

"It looked like magic to me," Buddy replied as he continued toward the door. "But that was before I got contacts. See you later."

"I remember the girls' softball team was really good when you were in school," Millie said after Buddy left. "Much better than the boys' baseball team that he played on."

"We won two regional championships and made it to the state semifinals my junior year."

"Was Amber Melrose on that team?" Millie asked.

"Yes, but she was a bench player," Gracie said, then paused. "Buddy mentioned Amber and his daughter today during lunch at the Crossroads Café. He discovered some new information at his mother's house that may help him find them."

"We had the same conversation," Millie sighed. "I felt bad for not telling him about the payments his father made to Amber, but Rascal swore me to secrecy. It was a relief having it all come out in the open. It's been a burden on my shoulders for a long time."

Gracie froze. Millie had mistakenly assumed that Buddy had shared a lot more with her than he had.

"I'm praying for all of them," Gracie managed.

"That's good. I'm sure Buddy is going to ramp up his efforts to locate them."

Gracie left the office with the bookkeeper's startling revelation swirling around in her head.

SIX

BUDDY PARKED IN A GRAVEL LOT LARGE ENOUGH FOR only five or six cars. A winding path led away from the lot and intersected the high school cross-country course near its midpoint. It had been over two years since he'd gone for a run. He stretched for a few minutes before jogging toward the course. Completing half of the five-kilometer route would be a good goal. He took it easy. He'd run the course so many times in training and competition that at one time he knew every tree and rock. Pine trees that were seedlings when he was in high school now shaded the path with thick, long needles on closely connected branches. Neighboring hardwoods grew more slowly, but they, too, were much bigger than when Buddy first ran the course at age thirteen. The only tree that remained eternally the same was a massive, ancient pin oak that marked the halfway point of the course. A foot-wide horizontal streak of bark on the tree had been worn smooth by the hands of countless runners who touched it on their way past in a tradition that began many years before. Buddy brushed his hand across the smooth bark as he jogged past the tree. Sprinting the last hundred yards, he knew his legs would be sore in the morning, but it felt good to be back in the race, even at a much slower pace.

Leaning against his car, Buddy gulped down a sports energy drink. He turned the air-conditioning in his car on full blast, but it didn't have a chance to cool down much during the short drive to the softball field. He sat on a low bleacher to watch. The girls were taking batting practice. One of the shorter girls was pitching. Her fastball was rising too much and going out of the strike zone. Gracie jogged over, spoke to her for a moment, then wound up and threw a pitch with her left hand that shot out straight but magically rose shortly before reaching the plate. The girl in the batter's box swung and completely whiffed. Buddy shook his head. Unlike his running ability, Gracie's pitches seemed as sharp and deceptive as ever.

Three more batters hit before Gracie called everyone together near home plate. The girls stood in a circle for several moments before joining hands and bowing their heads. Prayer was never part of the routine for the boys' baseball team. Buddy's coach used profanity for emphasis and motivation. The girls separated.

The petite pitcher helped Gracie gather up the practice balls, then hoisted the large bag over her shoulder and carried it from the field. Gracie came over to him. Her hair was tucked beneath a ball cap, and her cheeks were tinged with the reddish dust from the infield.

"You've still got it," Buddy said.

"What do you mean?"

"You'd still strike me out."

"Maybe the contacts would make a difference."

"I doubt it."

Gracie took a sip of water from a bottle.

"What did you want to talk to me about?" Buddy asked.

"It's about a girl named Reagan Landry," Gracie said, placing the water on the bleacher seat beside Buddy. "She was on the team at the beginning of the season but stopped showing up a couple of weeks ago. Her family is worried because—"

"I know Reagan," Buddy cut in. "She was born at almost the same time as Elise. Her parents are Sammy and Crystal Landry."

"That's right. Reagan ran away from home. The family filed a missing person report with the sheriff's department, but so far they haven't been able to track her down. I know you just took on the Sue Ellen Ford case, but they were wondering if you could help find her."

It had been several years since Buddy talked to Sammy, but he hadn't forgotten the time he'd shared with the jovial expectant father in the waiting room at the hospital.

"I'd like to help, but they need a real investigator, not a lawyer. Do you know if they've talked to the new detective who is overseeing crimes against juveniles?"

"I'm not sure. Who is it?"

"Mayleah Harkness. I met her today when I took over the custody order signed by Judge Claremont in Sue Ellen Ford's case. She seemed sharp. As clerk, you may be able to get the sheriff's department going when an average person can't. If Detective Harkness knows you're personally interested in a matter, I'm sure it will receive top priority."

"I don't know," Gracie said.

"Don't hesitate to use your political influence for a good cause. It's not like you're seeking a political favor for yourself."

"Okay," Gracie said and nodded slowly. "But are you sure you can't get directly involved?"

"I'll talk to Sammy and Crystal. If Reagan is caught up in illegal activity, the police will track her down because of that."

The look on Gracie's face revealed that she hadn't considered the possibility that Reagan was a criminal.

"I assumed she's an innocent runaway," she said.

"Let's hope so." Buddy stood up. "I'll call Sammy, but you should contact Detective Harkness. It will be better coming from you than me."

After Buddy left, Gracie jogged a couple of times around the ballfield. On her way home she received a call from her sister, Lauren.

"Where are you?" Lauren asked.

"Leaving softball practice."

"Perfect. Jeff is going to bathe the boys and put them down for the night so I can come over and help you set up your dating profile."

Gracie was looking forward to a shower and the absence of anything resembling work. "Let's do it another time. I had a tough day at work."

"So did I, and I wasn't paid for it," Lauren responded. "When I was rocking Mark this afternoon, I felt a surge of inspiration for you and don't want to let it pass."

Mark was eighteen months old. The sturdy little boy played hard and slept harder. Lauren's willingness to sacrifice time when she could rest herself touched Gracie.

"Okay, you win," Gracie said. "Give me time to clean up."

"Awesome, see you in a bit. If you're in the shower, I'll play with Opie. I've missed him."

Gracie fed the dog after arriving home and took a shower. When she emerged wearing pajamas, Lauren was sitting on the floor holding one end of a thick rope. Opie had the other end in his mouth and was shaking it back and forth. Lauren shared Gracie's blond hair but was taller. The only regular exercise she had was chasing her boys around the house. After obtaining a college degree in psychology, Lauren worked for several years as a counselor at the local mental health clinic. Now she was a stay-at-home mom but planned on returning to work when both boys were in school.

"Let's go into the kitchen," Gracie said. "We can use my laptop."

The sisters sat beside each other at the small kitchen table. Lauren accessed the profile creation screen for the dating website that she and Jeff had used.

"Do you have any chocolate?" she asked. "I didn't eat dessert before rushing over here."

"No, but I can give you a peach."

"That's okay. I need to focus on you and nothing else." Lauren pointed to the box reserved for entering data. "Keep this in mind. You can't be too generic. Don't say, 'I like to hike.' You have to write that you 'love to climb mountains and see the horizon painted on a blue-and-green canvas.'"

"I don't like to hike," Gracie answered.

"I know. It's just an example. Unless you want to attract a dud, you need to prove that you have an imagination and write something that stands out from the crowd. Maybe something about golf. A lot of women play golf, but you're really good."

"I haven't played more than three rounds since Barry broke up with me. And I only took it up because he liked it."

"Then ended up being a better golfer than he was."

"I enjoy going for walks with Opie," Gracie said.

"'Likes to walk dog,'" Lauren said as she typed the words on the screen. "That will stand out."

"No need to be sarcastic."

"Only until you give me something decent to work with."

Gracie slid the laptop over in front of her and began typing: "I enjoy spending time with my dog. I love watching him discover the world through his nose, which is ten thousand times more sensitive than a human nose."

Lauren nodded. "That will get tons of hits from veterinarians."

"I wouldn't mind marrying a veterinarian. He could work with large animals or household pets; either is fine with me."

Lauren ignored Gracie's response. "Let's cut the technical comment about comparison of noses and add something different," she said.

"Okay, I'll get serious," Gracie said. "I don't want to waste your time."

Gracie thought for a moment, then edited the sentence: "I enjoy spending time with my dog, Opie, and watching him discover the world through his nose. Opie loves me unconditionally, and that's the way I want it to be with the man I love."

Lauren was looking over Gracie's shoulder as she typed. "That's better," she said approvingly. "It not only speaks about your desire for a relationship but lets any guy know that loving you unconditionally must be his goal as well. I'm going to show that to Jeff. Now you have to make it clear that you're not always serious but like to have fun too."

"I am a serious person. That's not going to change."

"Not only are you serious, you're a rock that everyone who knows you can stand on. But you don't want to attract a needy guy looking for a mama substitute to baby him. How do you define fun?"

Gracie pointed at Opie, who was curled up at her feet. "Walking Opie is fun."

"We're creating this profile so you can find a mate, not a second dog."

"I love softball," Gracie suggested. "Lots of men watch fast-pitch when it's on TV. It's as exciting as any other sporting event."

Lauren furrowed her forehead for a moment, then clapped her hands together. "That's it!" she exclaimed.

As her sister resumed control of the keyboard, Gracie watched the words appear on the screen: "I'm a fierce competitor who loves sports and knows how to play, not just watch. Teach me something new, and I'll be all in."

"Fierce?" Gracie asked.

"Trust me. The kind of strong guy you want will love it. And when you challenge a man, it makes him want to test you and see if you can back up your words."

"It sounds exhausting."

"You set the rules. Doing sports together can be a small part of the relationship, but it will mean a lot to the guy. Wasn't Barry proud of you when you beat him at golf?"

"Not always. He had to win at least half the time to maintain his fragile ego."

"Did you let him win?"

Gracie shrugged. "There were a few times I missed a putt I probably could have made."

"Bad girl for letting him win." Lauren leaned in closer to the screen. "We need to work in that you're a confident, professional woman without saying you're the Milton County clerk of court. That's intimidating. A guy might think you're going to make him pay his traffic tickets."

"I don't have anything to do with traffic tickets."

Lauren tapped the bottom of the keyboard without hitting

any letters, then began to type: "At work I'm a boss who cares about the people working under me. I motivate with loyalty, not fear."

"That's true," Gracie agreed.

"I know," Lauren replied. "Everything we're including is the truth. And this takes some of the edge off the other sentence."

"I like it except that I wouldn't say 'under me.' That's demeaning."

Lauren moved the cursor across the screen, then typed, "At work I'm a boss who cares about the people working with me. I motivate through loyalty, not fear."

"Better," Gracie said.

"Some sites recommend putting in what you don't like. I think it's better to do that in person so you can explain things. Nobody likes a negative person. But it's not bad to include a weakness so long as it doesn't disqualify you in the eyes of the man you want to meet."

"You're my sister. What are some of my weaknesses?"

"Where do I begin?" Lauren rolled her eyes and looked upward toward the ceiling. "It's hard to pick just one."

Gracie chuckled. "I can be too trusting," she suggested. "That's what happened with Barry. I should have seen the signs that he'd lost interest in me."

Lauren shook her head. "Barry didn't lose interest in you; he lost his mind. That was his weakness, not yours."

The two women sat in silence.

"Even though you're an elected official who works at the courthouse, you would enjoy being a hermit six months out of the year," Lauren said.

"That's not true."

"Yes, it is, and you know it."

"I can be shy. And I need alone time to recharge my batteries. Extroverts help keep me involved with people."

"All true. You're way more self-aware than most of the people who were in my caseload when I worked at the mental health department."

Gracie began to type: "I can be shy and withdrawn. When I don't like to be around other people, I need a man willing to coax me out of my shell."

"I love it," Lauren said. "Along with everything else, you're sending a clear message that you want a champion to ride in on a white horse, rescue you, and love you unconditionally."

"This isn't realistic," Gracie said.

"Yes, it is," Lauren replied emphatically. "Your champion is waiting in cyberspace, and we're going to call him forth. Be optimistic. I selected the best shots from the photos you sent me."

Gracie was curious to see the pictures that made the cut. There was a head shot right after she'd had her hair trimmed and styled.

"I never wear my hair like that. The girl at the shop is the only one who can give it that much body."

"It's okay. She'll do your hair on your wedding day."

The next picture was a candid shot of Gracie standing in front of the muscadine vines at her parents' home. She was laughing.

"I like that one," Gracie said.

"Me too. It's what pops up on my phone when you call. Let's delete the third one I picked out and include a photo with Opie since you mention him by name in the profile. Check your phone for a good one."

Gracie scrolled through the saved pictures. Opie turned up more than she'd expected. She found one with the terrier sticking his nose into a rose blossom.

Gracie showed it to Lauren. "This fits with him exploring the world through his nose."

"It's too feminine."

Gracie kept looking and opened one of Opie leaping into the air to catch a Frisbee. Gracie was standing in the background in a green-and-white dress. She showed it to Lauren.

"That works," her sister said. "When was that taken?"

"One afternoon with Barry at the park on Montgomery Avenue. I was throwing the Frisbee and Barry was taking the pictures because—" Gracie stopped.

"You were better at throwing the disk than he was," Lauren provided, finishing the thought. "Hey, this photo is something good that came out of your relationship. Maybe it can help launch you into true happiness."

Gracie reviewed everything they'd decided to include on the website. "I don't say anything about being a Christian," she said.

"Because it's a Christian dating site. That's assumed."

Gracie looked at the photos one last time. Except for her hair, the pictures weren't an over-the-top portrayal of how she looked.

"I hate that so much emphasis is based on physical appearance," she said.

"You have nothing to hide, and there's nothing wrong with physical attraction as part of the process."

"That sounds like your degree talking."

"Experience. Post it and let the fireworks begin. You are going to get a lot of interest."

Gracie poised her index finger over the enter key, then withdrew it. She glanced at her sister. "I need to sleep on it."

She was surprised by her sister's response.

"No problem," Lauren replied. "Falling in love is a big decision."

SEVEN

BUDDY LIVED IN A HOUSE ON MONTFORD STREET THAT he bought from his father a couple of years before Rascal's death. The single-story white frame dwelling rambled across a flat lot with a large backyard. Custom-built for a school principal and his librarian wife, the house had built-in bookcases in several rooms and was one of the nicer residential rental properties Rascal owned. When Buddy first asked about purchasing it, his father quoted a sales price significantly above market value but quickly backed down when Beatrice protested. The house was only a couple of minutes away from Franklin Street, a factor that became more relevant sooner than anyone expected when Rascal suddenly died.

The bookcases were filled with a mix of military history, novels by lawyers, and poetry books. When Buddy entertained guests, they didn't spend much time inside the house but spilled out onto a large screened-in porch that ran along the rear of the house and a patio with large stone pavers. He liked to grill, and his steaks were famous among his friends and acquaintances. Most of the year, the porch was Buddy's favorite room. That's where he set up a comfortable chair and read or drew.

After taking a shower, he ate a smoked turkey sandwich on the porch beneath a slowly turning fan. The rear of the house faced east, and as the sun set, the silhouette of the house became more and more elongated on the green grass. Eventually, the shadowy roofline reached the base of an ancient pin oak tree. Eating the final bite of his sandwich, Buddy phoned his mother.

"How was your day?" she asked when she answered the phone.

"Busy," Buddy replied, giving his stock answer. "Would it be okay if I came over for a few minutes?"

"Of course. What did you eat for supper?"

"A turkey sandwich."

"I have a leftover piece of pot roast that I was about to put in the refrigerator, but I'll keep it out if you want to eat it."

Buddy loved pot roast cooked all day in a slow cooker. Even though he'd eaten a sandwich, he could make room for more food.

"I'm on my way," he said.

Beatrice was in the kitchen when he arrived. The envelope of checks was in the rear pocket of Buddy's pants. In addition to the pot roast, there was a serving of mashed potatoes and creamed corn on the plate.

"Why the big dinner?" he asked.

"I didn't cook any of it. Our supper club ate over at the Llewellyns' house. They insisted I bring home a plate to eat tomorrow, but I'd rather give it to you."

Buddy took a bite. As expected, the pot roast was fork-tender but had a surprising kick to it. "This is spicy."

"Patsy cooked it with yellow peppers. It's called Mississippi pot roast."

Beatrice filled two glasses with tea and sat at the table with him. "What do you want to talk about?" she asked.

"I just came over to see you."

"That's not the way you sounded on the phone. You have something on your mind."

Buddy's heart started beating faster. He ate a bite of creamed corn.

"I saw Gracie Blaylock today," he said as a delaying tactic.

"How's she doing?"

"Great." Buddy ate another bite of pot roast. "She sent me a new case the other day involving a woman whose husband ran off with their three-year-old boy. I'm going to see what I can do to help."

"Do you think you can find him?"

"I hope so. It will be tough."

Buddy continued to eat. Beatrice didn't seem interested in holding up her end of the conversation.

"Gracie told me about another situation," he said.

Beatrice listened with concern as he told her about Reagan Landry's disappearance.

"I remember the family," Beatrice said. "I've seen Frances Mulhaven from time to time over the years, and I'd always ask how Reagan was doing. Frances knew Amber left town when her baby was a few days old."

Beatrice never referred to Elise by name. She always called her "Amber's baby."

Buddy lowered his fork to his plate. "When Amber left, what conversations did you and Daddy have about it?" he asked.

"Nothing you don't know. If your father was upset about something, he dealt with it by crawling into a shell. I learned it was better to leave him there until he was ready to come out on his own terms."

"But when he eventually did come out, you must have talked. Now that he's gone, what can you tell me now that you couldn't then?"

"You're making him sound harsher than he was," Beatrice replied with a pained expression on her face. "He loved you and cared a lot about what was going on, even if he didn't know what to say or do about it."

Rascal may have hidden the truth. Buddy wouldn't.

"Oh, he did something," Buddy replied, pushing his chair away from the table.

He took the envelope from his pocket, found the first check, and placed it on the table in front of his mother.

"What's that?" she asked.

"Look at the date and who endorsed it."

Beatrice picked up the copy of the check, stared at it for a second, and turned it over. Her eyes widened.

"Why in the world would he write a check for $10,000 to Amber Melrose?"

"I was hoping you might be able to tell me. There were thirteen other checks after that. One per year until shortly before he died."

Beatrice suddenly dropped the check as if it were on fire. A look of shock and bewilderment crossed her face.

"You didn't know anything about this, did you?" Buddy continued in a softer tone of voice.

Beatrice stared down at the check. "No," she managed. "Where did you find it?"

"In a box at the bottom of the basement stairs. All of the other checks are also payable to 'Bearer,' which means anyone could deposit it in a bank. The endorsement on the other checks is illegible, but I'm sure he gave them to Amber."

"I can't believe what—" Beatrice started, then stopped.

"There's more," Buddy said.

He told her about his visit to the bank and the conversation with Millie Graham.

"Millie delivered one of the checks to Amber at the Southside Grill when Elise was around seven years old."

"She saw Elise?" Beatrice asked as tears flooded her eyes.

It was the first time Buddy could remember his mother saying his daughter's name.

"Yes, and Millie says she looked a lot like me at that age."

Beatrice reached for a napkin from a holder on the table and wiped her eyes. "I don't know what to say," she said and slowly shook her head. "I was feeling blue the other day and went downstairs to read some of the sweet notes your father sent me over the years."

More tears coursed down Beatrice's face. She caught her breath as the tears gave way to a sob. Getting up, she hurriedly left the kitchen. Buddy had never seen his mother break down like this, not even when his father died. He wondered if he'd made a mistake.

Taking his plate to the sink, Buddy scraped the food into the disposal. When his mother returned, she'd stopped crying, but her eyes were still red. She had a photo album in her right hand.

"I found some pictures you probably want to see," she said, sitting down at the table with a tissue in her hand.

It had been years since Buddy looked at family photos. His mother carefully organized events year by year. One of his sisters was older and one younger, with Buddy in the middle. When he was seven, his older sister was nine years old and his younger sister five. In a photo on the first page, Buddy was standing between the girls. They were all dressed in their Sunday-best clothes. It was Buddy's skinny stage. He was wearing khaki shorts and a pale blue polo shirt. The girls were in frilly dresses.

"Maddie looks a lot like you in that Easter Sunday picture," Beatrice said, pointing to the younger sister. "Maybe that gives us an idea about Elise at that age."

Buddy peered closely at his little sister. They continued through the album. Every time he saw his face, Buddy tried to superimpose a female version onto his shoulders. They reached the end.

"I hope it's okay that I threw out the rest of my supper," he said, leaning back in the chair. "I lost my appetite."

"That's fine," Beatrice replied with a dismissive gesture of her hand. "The pot roast was too spicy for me."

They sat in silence for a moment.

"Would you like to look at the album when you were eighteen?" Beatrice asked.

"Are there baby pictures of Elise in it?"

"No, those are in a special little album. I always kept them separate in a book no one else knew about."

Buddy glanced at his mother in surprise. "Would you ever look at it?"

"Every year on Elise's birthday and sometimes at Christmas."

Displays of emotion were rare for Buddy. But the realization that his mother had traveled her own road of private pain touched him deeply. Tears appeared in his eyes. His mother reached out and laid her right hand on his.

"Everybody tries to work through the difficult things in life in their own way," she said. "Once I realized Elise was gone for good, I kept my thoughts and feelings to myself. Your father never wanted to talk about it. I guess I know one of the reasons why. He felt guilty for keeping what he knew about them a secret."

"You and I are in this together now," Buddy said. "Let's look at both albums."

/ / /

Gracie was in the twilight realm between sleep and wakefulness when her mother called early the following morning.

"Is everything okay?" Gracie asked.

"Yes," her mother replied, then immediately followed with, "No. I didn't want to bother you again so soon, but I saw Frances last night, and she looked so sad. I didn't mention anything about Buddy Smith, but I couldn't get him out of my mind. Did you get a chance to talk to him about Reagan?"

"Yes, he's going to talk to Sammy and suggested I get in touch with a detective at the sheriff's department. He thinks they're more likely to do something if they know I'm interested in the case. I'm going to do it today."

"That all makes sense," Maxine said. "More and more churches are praying for Reagan's return."

"Good. Maybe you could also say a personal prayer about Buddy's efforts to locate his daughter. There's nothing to mention publicly, but I'm praying about it."

"The girl back in high school? What was her name?"

"Amber Melrose. She left town shortly after Elise was born. Buddy recently uncovered some new information that might help him track her down."

"If he finds her, I hope it has a happy ending."

"Me too." Gracie pushed the start button on the coffeemaker.

"Tell Frances I'm going to reach out to the detective at the sheriff's department."

"Thanks, baby girl. Love you."

After the call ended, Gracie took a cup of coffee onto the back deck for her prayer time. When she finished, she decided to take Opie for a morning walk.

A powerful thunderstorm had moved through the area during the night, and the air was cool and fresh. Green leaves blown from the trees by the high winds dotted the sidewalk. Opie loved walks, and every sense was on high alert. His four-inch bobbed tail remained straight up in the air, and his nose constantly twitched from side to side. Gracie kept a tight grip on his leash in case a squirrel made an appearance. If one did, a sharp bark from Opie sent it scurrying up a tree or dashing across the yard. They passed the bed-and-breakfast where Judge Williams was going to stay and approached Beatrice Smith's house. Buddy's mother was outside watering her flowers. Gracie waved.

"Gracie!" Beatrice called out after her. "Could you come over if you have a minute?"

There was a three-foot-high retaining wall along the sidewalk. Opie easily bounded up the four steps onto the brick walkway that led to the long front porch. Beatrice was misting a cluster of large purple flowers in a shady part of the yard. She turned off the hose. Opie pulled on the leash.

"Good morning," Beatrice said, stepping closer so she could pat the dog's head. She was wearing colorful gardening gloves. "How are you and Opie doing?"

"Fine."

Beatrice continued to scratch Opie's neck.

"What are you watering?" Gracie asked.

"Purple iris."

The petals on the large flowers curled down like lavender waterfalls.

"I'll cut some for you," Beatrice said.

"That's sweet, but—"

"Don't be silly. Wait here."

Beatrice went inside the house. Opie sniffed around the base of a large tree. There was a squirrel's nest in the upper branches. The yard had a peaceful, welcoming feeling. Beatrice returned with kitchen shears and several damp paper towels.

"We'll wrap them in these," she said. "As soon as you get home, put the flowers in water, and they should be fine for several days. It makes me happy to know they'll have a good home."

Beatrice clipped six long stalks and secured them with a small rubber band. She talked as she worked. "Buddy came over last night for a late supper and told me Reagan Landry ran away from home."

"It looks that way. I'm going to see if I can help the family find her, and Buddy is going to talk to Reagan's father about the situation."

"Reagan was born on the same day as Amber's baby."

"That's what Buddy said."

"We talked about Amber and Elise last night," Beatrice continued. "Then, when I saw you walking down the street, I thought about what a good friend you were to Buddy in high school."

"I don't know about that. He helped me get a good grade in tenth-grade biology."

Beatrice handed the bouquet to Gracie. "Maybe the flowers can remind you to pray for Buddy. He has a lot on his mind," she said.

"I will."

At home, Gracie put the flowers in a clear glass vase and placed it in the center of the kitchen table. She'd always liked Beatrice Smith, but the gracious widow seemed more like a kindred spirit than ever. Praying for Buddy created a bond between them.

/ / /

Buddy stopped off at a client's place of business for an early meeting before driving to the office. Jennifer was receiving instructions from Millie. The new secretary greeted him, then stepped across the hall to her workstation.

Buddy paused at Millie's desk. "How's it going?" he asked.

"I like her," Millie replied. "I talked to her about our different bank accounts and how they work. She learned about attorney trust accounts at the community college and did basic bookkeeping at the restaurant. I'll show her how we keep track of the rental business."

"So long as you supervise her."

"Of course." Millie raised her eyebrows and added, "I have to supervise you too."

Buddy smiled. "And I appreciate it. I'm glad you're not thinking about quitting this morning."

"No," Millie said with a shake of her head. "I slept soundly last night."

"And I talked to my mother," Buddy said. "She never knew about the payments to Amber."

"That's not surprising. I hope she's not upset with me."

"No. She was more interested in looking at photos of me when I was seven."

Buddy took the picture of him and his two sisters wearing their Sunday best from his shirt pocket and laid it on Millie's desk.

The bookkeeper adjusted her glasses and leaned forward. "At that age Maddie is a female version of you," Millie said.

"That's what I thought. Is that how Elise looked when you saw her at the Southside Grill?"

Millie picked up the photo for closer inspection.

Jennifer's voice interrupted them. "Mr. Smith, do you want me to go over federal court practice information or the corporate forms first?"

"Uh, corporate documents. I do a lot more of that than federal court litigation."

Jennifer left. Millie handed the photo back to Buddy.

"Elise definitely favors Maddie," she said. "The shape of their faces, the eyes, the mouth."

Buddy took the picture into his office and positioned it in the corner of the frame that contained his certification to practice before the Georgia Supreme Court. He had a busy morning scheduled. Phone calls and unexpected interruptions were part of a lawyer's normal routine. But today was especially disruptive. Jennifer buzzed him.

"Sammy Landry is calling. Do you want me to take a message?"

"No, I'll talk to him. He's returning my call."

The call came through.

"Hey, Sammy," Buddy said. "It's been awhile."

"Yeah, too long. Thanks for contacting me. I hate that it's about something like this."

"I want to help," Buddy answered. "Would you like to get together over lunch and discuss it?"

"You'd do that?"

"Sure. Can you take a break from work?"

"Yeah, I have a good crew. My oldest boy is one of the foremen."

"How about Smoke?" Buddy suggested. "I haven't gone there recently."

"That's my language. You set the time?"

Buddy quickly calculated what he needed to accomplish before taking a break. "Twelve thirty?"

"Perfect."

The barbecue restaurant served traditionally smoked pork shoulders, country-style ribs, and chicken, all doused in a tangy red sauce that mixed sweet notes of local honey with the smoldering fire of red pepper flakes. But Buddy's favorite item on the menu was Brunswick stew, accompanied by a thick slab of crusty corn bread. Named after its place of origin on the Georgia coast, the Brunswick stew at Smoke floated in a tomato roux with flavors as complex as a French bordelaise sauce or Mexican mole. It contained smoked chicken and pork along with fresh tomatoes, corn, diced potatoes, lima beans, bits of sweet Vidalia onion, and secret spices.

Arriving before Sammy, he sat at a table covered with a plastic red-and-white-checked tablecloth. The waitress knew Buddy's drink preference and automatically brought him a glass of sweet tea with three lemon wedges positioned on the rim. A few minutes later the construction supervisor hurried through the front door and saw him. Sammy had put on weight over the past seventeen years and lost most of the hair from the top of his head.

"Thanks for taking the time," he said, removing an Auburn hat and placing it on the table.

"No problem, but please put that hat on the floor so I don't have to look at it," Buddy answered.

Buddy had received his undergraduate and law degrees from the University of Georgia, one of Auburn's rivals.

Sammy grinned. "A supplier gave it to me. If something is free, it's for me."

The waitress returned with a pad in her hand, and they placed their orders. Buddy could see dark circles underneath Sammy's eyes.

"Before we talk about Reagan, how is the rest of your family doing?" Buddy asked.

The question seemed to relax Sammy. Except for typical life challenges, the rest of the Landry clan was okay.

"We have six grandkids," Sammy said. "I look old enough to be a grandpa, but Crystal doesn't. She's an amazing woman."

"Are you still playing golf?"

"Every chance I get. It stresses some folks out, but it relaxes me. Would you like to join us sometime? We're always looking for a fourth."

"So long as no one makes fun of me. My driver has a mind of its own."

Their food arrived. Sammy had ordered ribs with collard greens and pickled onions.

"How are you going to corral your breath?" Buddy asked after they'd eaten a few bites. "I can smell the onions on your plate from here."

"I'll stay off the roof. I don't want anyone to get a whiff and fall."

Buddy focused on the stew. He waited a few minutes before bringing up the reason for their meeting.

"Tell me about Reagan," he said. "What happened?"

"I don't really know." Sammy shook his head. "She's the baby of the family, so I guess we spoiled her. Things have been rocky for the past year, but I left it mostly up to Crystal to deal with her. She's always been better with the kids when they have problems. I'm the one who takes the boys fishing and hunting and the girls to sporting events. Anyway, there were a bunch of big blowups with Reagan over the past three months, and about the time the school year ended, she started spending a lot more time with friends instead of at our house. Crystal didn't like it, but I thought it was better to keep the peace than start a war."

Buddy remembered a similar pattern with Amber but couldn't imagine that Reagan was fleeing an abusive home life.

Sammy continued, "A couple of weeks ago she didn't come home from an overnight, and we haven't seen or heard from her since. We called everyone we could think of, and nobody could help."

"Could help or would help?"

"Yeah, I thought a couple of her friends might be covering for her, but we sat them down with their parents and they swore they didn't know anything."

"Did Reagan have a car?"

"That was another mistake. All the others had to work and pay on a vehicle, but we just dumped one in Reagan's lap. The sheriff's department entered the license plate number into some database in case she gets pulled over, and her name is in another database for missing children."

"What about social media contacts?"

"I don't know anything about that stuff. Crystal gathered up the information along with the passwords, and we took it to the sheriff's department when we filed the missing person report. The guy we talked to said it would take awhile for them to sort through it. I got huffy at the way he treated us. It made me feel like they had more important things to take care of."

"That's where Gracie Blaylock may be able to do some good. She's going to contact the detective in charge."

"Yeah, government people scratch each other's backs. I'll take the help any way we can get it."

Buddy took another bite of food. "I'm a lawyer, not an investigator, but I'll be glad to see if there's anything I can add to the search. Give me your email, and I'll send over a contract and release forms since Reagan is a minor."

"We'll pay whatever it takes. I try to be upbeat, but we're worried sick."

As they were finishing their meal, Sammy took a long drink of tea. "Tell me, what's going on in your world?" he asked. "And don't give me the standard 'Everything is fine' answer. Did you ever get married?"

"Not yet. I've dated a lot but never got close. My most recent girlfriend was a travel agent in Savannah. Things were going great until she went on a free cruise and met another guy. I've been out of commission for the last three months."

"Better to stay off the aisle than walk down it with the wrong woman," he said. "And marriage ain't easy for anyone."

"To be fair, I'm not sure I was the right man for any of them."

Sammy ate a bite of collards. "And your daughter who was born the same day as Reagan? When I told Crystal we were meeting for lunch, she said to ask how she's doing."

"I don't know. Elise has been out of the picture since she was a few days old and her mother left town. I've tried to find them for years but haven't had any luck."

Buddy could tell his answer shook Sammy because of what he was now facing with Reagan.

"I'm sorry," Sammy said, his face showing the empathy he felt. "That's a long time to be looking."

EIGHT

TURNING ON HER LAPTOP, GRACIE READ HER PROFILE for the dating site. She then took a deep breath and said a quick prayer to supplement what she'd already written and pressed the send button. Not waiting even a minute to see if she received any responses, Gracie closed the top of her computer and texted Lauren:

It's done!

Her sister replied with a succession of happy faces, red hearts, and a tiny couple in formal wedding attire holding hands.

As soon as she arrived at the courthouse, Gracie tried to set up an appointment with Mayleah Harkness, but the detective wasn't available, and she had to leave a voice-mail message. Criminal jury trials were scheduled for the following week, and Gracie received a steady stream of phone calls from people wanting to avoid jury duty. Some of the excuses were more creative than others.

"My cat is going to be neutered on Monday, and I'll need to be with her during surgery and take care of her the rest of the week," one woman said breathlessly. "There's no way I can serve on a jury. I have written proof from the veterinarian's office."

Medical excuses from a potential juror's treating physician and single-parent situations with a minor child or children at home were the most common types of justification authorizing a person not to report to the courthouse. The pet-care plea was rare.

"If you or a close family member was undergoing surgery, you could be excused," Gracie replied evenly. "But not for a pet."

"Lucy is like a member of the family," the woman responded. "I found her abandoned near the trash bins at the supermarket on Baxter Street and brought her home. She's had two litters of kittens. I gave some of them away, but now I'm taking care of eight cats. I live in a tiny two-bedroom apartment, and this has got to stop."

Gracie could imagine the feline chaos in the confined space. "Have the other cats been spayed or neutered?"

"No, I was going to start with Lucy. And I'm worried one of her daughters may be pregnant. I thought about taking her to see the vet on the same day as Lucy's surgery. Do you think that's a good idea?"

"It's usually best to spay and neuter all pets."

"Then I'm going to take Ninny in on Monday too. She is the craziest little thing. You've never seen a cat act like she does. When someone rings the doorbell, she will—"

"Wait, wait," Gracie cut in. "I didn't say that taking your cats to the vet is a legal reason to avoid jury duty."

"But I thought you understood what I'm facing."

Gracie paused. All Judge Claremont cared about was having a large enough pool of jurors to move forward with trials. The judge didn't monitor the excuses issued by the clerk's office.

"If I put your name on the list for the next term of court, will you be able to make arrangements to be here regardless of your pet situation?"

"I'll do my best."

Gracie checked the calendar and gave her the date.

"I was going to visit my aunt in Tallahassee around that time—" the woman began.

"No," Gracie interrupted. "That's not a legal excuse."

"Okay, I'll be there," the woman surrendered.

"I'll make a note in my records. I hope Lucy's surgery goes well."

One of Gracie's assistants overheard the last part of the conversation as the call ended.

"Is that someone related to Lucy Brogden?" the assistant asked. "She's having gallbladder surgery next week."

"No," Gracie replied. "We were talking about Lucy the cat."

"A cat?"

Gracie held up her hand. "Don't ask."

Shortly before 2:00 p.m., Detective Harkness called.

"Thanks for getting back to me," Gracie said. "I'd like to meet with you and discuss the Reagan Landry case. Let me know when you're available, and I can swing by the sheriff's department."

"No," the detective said, then paused.

Gracie swallowed. Apparently her status as an elected official wasn't as potent as Buddy Smith thought.

"Let me see," Detective Harkness continued. "I have an appointment with one of the assistant DAs later this afternoon and could stop by the clerk's office when I'm finished. Would that be convenient?"

Tonight was the first softball game of the season, and Gracie wanted to leave work promptly at five so she could prepare for the game. The district attorney's office was on the second floor of the courthouse.

"Could you be here by four thirty?" she asked.

"Yes, that should work."

"Great."

The clerk of court and the tax appraiser's office shared use of a small conference room on the first floor. Shortly after 4:00 p.m., Detective Harkness arrived. The detective was a woman about the same age as Gracie, with dark hair and an olive complexion. She stood at the counter with a folder in her hand.

Gracie introduced herself: "Call me Gracie. This is a small office, and we're not formal except when it comes to the judges."

"I'm Mayleah," the detective replied with a friendly smile.

Gracie led the way to the conference room and held the door open for the detective, whose cowboy boots made a tapping sound on the tile floor. They sat down at the table, and Mayleah opened her file.

"It looks like Reagan Landry is set up as a runaway," the detective said. "We haven't done anything except flag the license plate number on her vehicle and enter her name and personal information into a national database for missing children. What's your interest in her disappearance?"

Gracie explained the personal connection between her mother and Frances Mulhaven. "I also talked to Buddy Smith, a lawyer who represents people in cases of parental kidnapping. He suggested we check Reagan's social media accounts," she added.

Mayleah opened the folder. "The mother provided access to that information. I'll run the names through our database and see how many have a criminal record. When I was in Oklahoma, I worked several cases like this. Sadly, some of the young women ended up being trafficked."

Gracie's mouth went dry. She'd considered that possibility, but to hear it spoken so bluntly was a blow.

"It's only been a couple of weeks," Mayleah continued. "Which is good, but you're right to want to move quickly."

"What else can I do?" Gracie asked.

"Let the family know I'm working on it." Mayleah paused. "And if you're willing to look at Reagan's Instagram account and other online contacts, it often helps to have a second set of eyes involved."

"Okay."

Mayleah handed the information to Gracie, who left the room and copied it. The detective seemed like an efficient, organized woman.

"How are you adjusting to life in Clarksburg?" Gracie asked when she returned.

"It's a change from Tulsa," the detective replied. "But one of my sisters and her family live in Atlanta. After I went through a divorce, I decided to relocate, and she convinced me to apply for jobs in Georgia."

"Did you try to find a position in Atlanta?"

Mayleah shook her head. "No, it's too big. But Clarksburg and Milton County are pretty small, which is going to take getting used to."

Gracie had a busy life, full of interaction with family and people in the community and at church. But she instantly liked Mayleah.

"Let's get together sometime," she suggested.

"I'd like that," Mayleah replied.

The detective took out her business card, wrote on the back, and handed it to Gracie. "Here's my cell phone number."

Gracie held the card lightly in her fingers for a moment, then had an idea. "I know it's short notice, but I coach a girls' softball team," she said. "We have a game tonight at seven o'clock, and if you don't have any other plans, you're welcome to come. We play at the Milton County High School field."

"Fast-pitch softball?"

"Yes."

"That brings back memories," the detective said. "I played on my high school team for a couple of years, but we weren't very good."

"You should come."

"I'm busy tonight, but text me the schedule, and I'll check it out another time."

They left the conference room. As they did, Gracie got a better view of the detective's boots that looked like they were made from some kind of lizard skin.

"We'll talk soon," Mayleah said. "Reagan's case will stay on my desk until I have something to report."

Buddy was in the middle of drafting a contract for a business client when his phone buzzed.

"Deputy Reynolds is calling," Jennifer said. "He says it has to do with the Ford case. Do you want to talk to him?"

Buddy hesitated. He was under a strict deadline for completion of the contract. "Okay," he said.

"I'm at Boyd Lipscomb's residence," the officer said. "He says he's willing to talk to you about Jackie Ford."

Buddy sat up straighter in his chair. "Put him on the phone."

"I tried that, but he wants to do it in person. If you can drive out here, I'll wait for you. It should take about fifteen minutes from your office. Otherwise, I can try to set something up another day when we can both be here."

Buddy didn't want to miss the opportunity. The contract would have to wait.

"I'm on my way."

"You'll see my patrol car in the driveway. We'll be sitting on the back porch. Come around the house. Don't worry about the dogs. They bark but don't bite."

Buddy told Jennifer where he was going. "I have a client scheduled for an appointment in forty-five minutes," he said. "Call and see if he can reschedule for tomorrow morning."

Buddy drove west from Clarksburg on the road toward Atlanta. He knew the area where Lipscomb lived. Four miles from town he turned right onto a narrow two-lane road and traveled a little over a mile. He slowed when the road crossed a narrow stream on a one-lane bridge. Three hundred yards farther he turned onto a dirt road for another half mile. A mailbox sitting at a crooked angle announced the number for the residence. As Buddy drove up a short hill, he could hear dogs barking as they ran toward him. He parked behind the deputy sheriff's vehicle.

Three large brown dogs and an even bigger black dog circled Buddy's car like wolves around a wounded caribou. Buddy was a fast runner but doubted he could outrun the pack. With no option except to trust Officer Reynolds's word about the dogs, he opened the door. One of the brown dogs leapt into his lap. Before

Buddy could knock him away, the animal licked him on the chin. All three brown dogs seemed friendly. Buddy got out of the car. The black dog eyed him suspiciously from a distance.

Boyd Lipscomb lived in an unpainted wooden house perched on top of the hill. A low-roofed shed as big as a barn stood to the right of the house. Inside the shed Buddy could see a collection of cars and pickup trucks. Two dump trucks were parked beneath the trees next to the shed. With the brown dogs bouncing alongside him, he made his way to the rear of the house. A screened-in porch rested on exposed wooden posts. He could see Officer Reynolds and another man sitting in rocking chairs. Reynolds stood as Buddy approached and held open the porch door.

"The dogs aren't welcome inside," Reynolds said.

Buddy climbed three steps and let the door slam shut behind him. The dogs whimpered on the ground below. Boyd Lipscomb was a large man in his mid- to late forties. He was wearing a dirty white T-shirt, jeans, and an orange ball cap. A bulge in his right cheek and a Styrofoam cup beside his rocking chair announced his use of chewing tobacco. He didn't get up when Buddy entered. Instead, he picked up the cup and spat in it. There was no place for Buddy to sit. Given the environment, he didn't mind standing.

"I don't want no trouble," Lipscomb said.

"I told Boyd that he could get charged with aiding someone in the commission of a felony if he chooses not to cooperate," Reynolds said. "He has a prior conviction on his record for selling stolen property and doesn't want anything else tacked on."

"A car I had no way of knowing was stolen," Lipscomb objected. "I lost the $6,000 I paid for the car and served three years on probation."

Buddy wasn't sure about the legitimacy of Officer Reynolds's threat of prosecution, but it was enough of a gray area that he didn't have a problem using it as leverage to dislodge information. He got straight to the point. "Where did Jackie Ford take his little boy?"

Lipscomb glanced at Reynolds. "What if I don't know exactly where he's at? That ain't a violation of the law, is it?"

"You admitted that you knew Ford was going to take off with the kid," Reynolds replied. "Then you sold him a car with fake plates on it."

Lipscomb extracted a massive wad of chewing tobacco and dropped it into the cup. Like most of his teammates on the high school baseball team, Buddy had sampled chewing tobacco but never got past the queasy stomach phase. The amount of chew Lipscomb had forced into his cheek was impressive. He spat into the cup, and any remaining bits of tobacco flew from his mouth.

"I know he was on his way to Oklahoma," Lipscomb said. "He was going to stay there or go on to Montana. It all depended where he could best hook up with folks living off the grid."

"Do you know who and where?" Buddy asked.

"I got ideas, but you can't let nobody know where you got this information. These are some heavy-duty dudes who don't want the government knowing anything about them. If Jackie drove on into Montana, I swear I'm not sure where he landed. I just heard him talk about going there a couple of times."

"What's the name of the place in Oklahoma?" Reynolds asked.

Lipscomb rubbed his jaw before answering. "It's near a little town called Red Oak or Red Pine, something like that. I heard Jackie say it was an Indian settlement where most people don't want anything to do with the feds."

"Do you know how to contact him?" he asked.

"Nope. I already showed Officer Reynolds the number I had for Jackie in my phone. We tried to call, and it ain't in service."

"What kind of car did you sell him?"

"A white 1998 Ford Taurus. It had a salvage title because it got flooded in a hurricane, but it ran good. Jackie worked on it off and on for a couple of months."

"Where did the license plate come from?"

"I didn't have nothing to do with that," Lipscomb said as he turned to Reynolds. "That was all Jackie. I keep my junks back in the woods. He went in there and took off a plate."

"When did you first find out that Jackie was going to leave town with his son?" Buddy asked.

"I don't recollect. He didn't talk much about anything. A month or so ago, he asked if I was interested in buying five cars all at once. He said his old lady was getting on his nerves, and he was thinking about moving away with that boy of his." Lipscomb looked at Reynolds again. "That shouldn't be no crime if it's his own young'un."

"How much money did you give Jackie for the five cars?" Buddy asked.

"Over $40,000 with the Taurus thrown in. One of them was his favorite piece, a 1968 Pontiac Firebird. That tipped me off that he was serious about a change in locale. He was getting rid of all his stock."

"Cash money?" Buddy asked.

"Always."

"Where are the cars now?"

"I only have one left. It's a Fiat ragtop. Not many people around here want to mess with one of those. If you want, I can show it to you."

Buddy looked at Officer Reynolds. "What do you think?" he asked.

"I owned a Fiat when I was younger and swore never again," the officer answered.

Boyd Lipscomb laughed out loud. "That's good," he said. "I didn't see that one a-comin'."

Reynolds spoke to Buddy: "Let's take a recess on this conversation and see if Boyd's been on the level with us."

"Hey, everything I've said is the gospel truth!" Lipscomb protested.

"Is there anyone else who could give us information about where Jackie might be?" Buddy asked.

"Not that I know of. Like I said, he mostly kept to hisself. I done told you everything I know. I got nothing to hide."

Buddy and Officer Reynolds walked together away from the porch and toward their vehicles. The brown dogs followed. The black dog stayed behind at the bottom of the steps.

"Thanks," Buddy said as soon as they were out of earshot. "You went way beyond serving the order."

"Hey, I'm in law enforcement," Reynolds replied with a smile. "And working over Boyd Lipscomb was my afternoon entertainment. I have two boys and a girl of my own. My kids are my life. I hate what this Ford guy did running off with his son. It's not right, even if it's his own kid."

They reached the officer's patrol car.

"Do you think Lipscomb told us everything he knows?" Buddy asked.

"Probably not. My biggest worry is that he has a backdoor way to get in touch with Jackie and tip him off. With that much money changing hands, there could have been a side deal for extra money down the road. I'll write up a report as soon as I'm back at the department."

"Give it to Detective Harkness. When Lipscomb mentioned Oklahoma, I immediately thought of her. She'll have contacts there."

"Yeah, but she may still consider this a domestic matter, not a criminal case."

"Talk to her. You convinced the tobacco-chewing guy on the porch that it could be a criminal case."

Reynolds grinned. "Boyd was easy to bluff."

NINE

BUDDY STAYED LATE AT THE OFFICE SO HE COULD FINish drafting the business contract. He then drove directly to his mother's house to continue his search for clues. Beatrice didn't respond to his text letting her know he'd arrived, so he unlocked the door. He immediately began calling out to let her know he was there. "Hello! It's Buddy!"

There was no answer. He stopped at the base of the staircase in the foyer. His mother's bedroom was on the second floor. He called out again: "Mom! I'm here!"

Still no answer. The Mercedes was parked next to the house. Buddy called his mother's cell phone. It went to voice mail. He went up the stairs two at a time. Inside his mother's bedroom he saw the wallet where she kept her driver's license. Going back to the main floor, Buddy looked in the backyard to see if she was watering any flowers or bushes. The garden hose was neatly wound up where she normally kept it. Stumped, he concluded his mother must have gone out for a late-afternoon walk.

Taking a glass from a kitchen cabinet, Buddy opened the refrigerator. A high-pitched shriek caused him to drop the glass, which shattered on the floor. He spun around and faced his mother, who was standing in the doorway that led to the basement.

"Why didn't you let me know you were here?" she demanded. "You had your back to me behind the refrigerator door, and I didn't know it was you!"

"I texted, dialed your cell phone, and have been calling out all through the house," Buddy answered calmly. "I thought you'd gone out for a walk or a friend picked you up to go someplace."

Beatrice patted the pocket of the faded gray slacks she was wearing. "Oh, I must have left my phone here in the kitchen."

Buddy looked at the round table in the corner. His mother's cell phone was lying next to a magazine.

"Let me clean up that broken glass," Beatrice said.

"No, I dropped it," Buddy answered. "What were you doing in the basement?"

"I've been down there most of the afternoon. I've gone through ten boxes looking for anything else that might help you find Elise."

"I was going to do that," Buddy said as he opened the utility closet and took out a broom and dustpan. "It's why I stopped by."

"I wasn't sure when you'd be able to do it, and I couldn't keep from wondering what was there."

"Any luck?" Buddy asked as he began to sweep up the broken glass.

Beatrice took a folded piece of paper from the other pocket of her slacks and handed it to him. "Less than five minutes ago I found this."

Buddy leaned the broom against the kitchen counter and unfolded the single sheet of notebook paper. Written in Amber's handwriting was a short letter:

Mr. Smith,

Thanks for the check. We had to move again, and it came exactly when I needed it. I'll call you next month with a new address.

Amber

Buddy read it three times. "Was there an envelope?" he asked.

"No, it was stuck in the middle of one of those charts your father used to make about how to manage the rental property."

"Was there a date on the chart? That might give us a clue."

"I didn't think about that."

"Show me."

Leaving the kitchen, they descended the steps into the basement. Beatrice took the lid from a box and rummaged around in the contents.

"There are a bunch of charts in here," she said. "Now I'm not sure which one it was. They all look alike to me."

"Let's take the box upstairs."

They returned to the kitchen, and Buddy placed the box on the round table.

"I'll finish cleaning up the glass while you look," Beatrice said.

Buddy took everything from the box and inspected it. Several papers and pieces of business correspondence were dated. His mother dumped the broken shards of glass into a trash can.

"Most of this stuff is from the years I was away at college," he said.

"Your father saved everything."

"Which is good now."

"Who knows?" Beatrice sighed. "But finding the letter made me more sad than happy."

Buddy stopped and looked up. "Why?"

"Because it's another example of him keeping a secret and me not knowing. I mean, I'm sure he believed he was doing something good. And Amber appreciated it. But he didn't tell either one of us about it. And now he's gone—" Beatrice stopped.

Buddy wasn't sure how to respond. His mother's words mirrored his thoughts. Instead of speaking, he stepped over and put his arms around her shoulders. He held her for several seconds.

"I'm going outside," Beatrice said. "The hydrangeas are drooping. When it gets as hot as it did today, they need an extra drink."

"Would it be okay if I continue looking?"

"Yes. But it's too much for me."

Downstairs in the basement, Buddy saw the boxes his mother had opened but went through them again. In addition to charts and graphs, they contained invoices, letters to tenants, copies of dispossessory petitions, and bundles and bundles of canceled checks from the era when banks mailed them each month to the account holder. None of the other checks were made payable to Bearer, Amber Melrose, or Amber with another last name.

Toward the bottom of one box he found a sheet of paper with three phone numbers scribbled on it. One of the numbers was marked with a star and the initials "AM." The area code was unfamiliar. There was nothing on the paper to indicate the date, but most of the documents in the box were about five or six years old. That was about the time Amber cashed a check in Tennessee. A quick search on his phone revealed that the geographic region for the 423 area code included Chattanooga, Tennessee.

His heart beating faster, Buddy debated whether to call the number. The possibility of hearing his daughter's voice caused an involuntary shiver to run down Buddy's spine. Taking a deep breath, he dialed the number. It rang twice before a recording announced it was no longer a valid number. Deflated, Buddy stared at his phone for a moment, then glanced at the sheet of paper and realized that in his haste he'd incorrectly transposed two of the numbers. He slowly entered the correct number. This time it rang several times.

"Hello?" a female voice answered.

Buddy instantly tried to discern from a single word whether Amber was on the line. After seventeen years, he wasn't sure.

"Amber?" he asked tentatively.

"No."

"Elise?" he quickly added.

"You must have the wrong number," the woman responded and hung up.

/ / /

Attendance at summer softball league games wasn't limited to the family members of the players. Fast-pitch softball in Milton County had a long history of success. Winning attracts fans, and residents of the community followed the program year-round. As the team trotted onto the field for the first inning, Gracie glanced into the stands and saw the faces of people who'd come to the games during her playing days. At the end of one of the bleachers she was surprised to see Mayleah Harkness. The detective was talking to someone, and they didn't make eye contact.

The score after six innings was a nail-biting 1–0. The visiting team loaded the bases with two outs in the top of the seventh inning, but the batter at the plate hit a line drive straight at Laura Anselm, who jumped into the air and snagged it. Postgame celebrations after a win lasted longer than postmortems following a loss. It was several minutes before Gracie could make her way to where Mayleah was sitting.

"Glad you were able to make it," Gracie said.

"Me too. My other plans fell through, and I remembered your invitation. That was an exciting game."

"The team played great. Would you like to grab a bite to eat? A lot of the girls go to a local drive-in after a game. Coaches and adults are welcome."

Mayleah hesitated for a moment. "I bought a bag of peanuts at the concession stand, but that's not a real meal," she said.

"The Southside Grill gives a bit more variety," Gracie said. "Do you know where it is?"

"It's the place that still offers drive-in service?"

"Right, but we'll eat inside. I'll see you there in fifteen minutes. It'll be neat for the girls on the team to meet you. You're the only female detective working with the sheriff's department, right?"

"Yes."

On the way to the diner, Gracie looked in her rearview mirror. The detective was following in a glistening white pickup truck that would make the majority of the men in Milton County green with jealousy. Gracie and Mayleah pulled into parking spaces next to each other. The jubilant members of the team had taken possession of a group of tables and pulled them close together. The carhops wore in-line skates, and a young man glided past Gracie and Mayleah as they entered the restaurant.

"This place should be in a movie," Mayleah said.

"It was," Gracie responded. "A film crew came here a year ago and spent a week."

Laura was standing nearby and overheard Gracie's comment. "I was an extra in the movie," she said. "It's about a girl who worked at a diner and fell in love with a rich guy who looked down on her. She taught him how to skate. It wasn't that great, but it was fun seeing a place I know."

"Were you in some scenes?" Mayleah asked.

"For like a nanosecond."

Gracie and Mayleah walked up to the counter to order. There weren't a lot of healthy options on the menu.

"What do you recommend?" Mayleah asked.

"If you don't want something fried, the grilled chicken sandwich is good."

They each ordered the chicken sandwich. Gracie added a side of thin and crispy onion rings that were her favorite. The detective included coleslaw.

Gracie led the way to the area where the girls were gathered. There were a few parents off to the side. Gracie introduced Mayleah to the group and told them where she worked. They sat at a table with Heidi, Laura, and a couple of other girls. The teammates were buzzing about the game.

"I don't think I could get a hit off their pitcher if I faced her ten times," one of the girls said.

"She had an awesome screwball," Heidi responded. "It cut away from me at the last second. I chased it a couple of times."

Gracie smiled and took a drink of water from a large paper cup.

Laura turned to Mayleah. "Coach Blaylock was the best pitcher who's ever played in Milton County," she said.

"There have been a lot of good pitchers," Gracie said. "Vanessa Morgan had a great fastball with a lot of movement on it."

A cashier called their number and Gracie left to get the food. When she returned, several more girls had moved their chairs so they could be closer to Mayleah.

"I also played lacrosse," Mayleah was saying. "It was popular among Native American tribes in the East. The Cherokee word for it means 'little war.' Hundreds of men would play at once."

"Hundreds?"

"Yes, it was fierce. Broken bones and other serious injuries happened all the time."

"Do you speak the Cherokee language?" Heidi asked.

Mayleah rattled off a string of words.

"What did that mean?" Heidi asked.

"I said how much I enjoyed watching your game and that you are brave and courageous girls because you stood at the plate and tried to hit a ball thrown so fast in your direction."

"I love the sound of your language," Heidi said. "Do you have a Cherokee name?"

"My father named me Ahyoka, which means 'she brought happiness.'"

"That's beautiful," several girls said at once.

Gracie and Mayleah moved over to a table for two to eat their food.

"Does anyone call you Ahyoka now?" Gracie asked.

"Only my grandmother. Mayleah is my legal name. My maiden name was Fairweather. We're part of the Long Hair Clan. I thought about going back to Fairweather when I left Oklahoma, but I've used Harkness for so long that I left it alone."

Gracie knew very little about the Cherokee people. When she heard the word "clan," she thought about Scotland. Gracie gave Mayleah a few onion rings.

"These are good," the detective said after she sampled one.

"I try to eat healthy, but I can't resist these every so often."

"Have you lived in Clarksburg your whole life?" Mayleah asked.

"Since day one."

"Tell me about your family."

While they ate, Gracie gave a summary. Mayleah was a good listener, a characteristic that probably served her well as a detective. Gracie found herself saying more than she normally would have.

"What about Mr. Smith, the lawyer?" Mayleah asked. "He came by the sheriff's department the other day to discuss a case. What's his background?"

The question startled Gracie. "Buddy Smith?"

"Yes."

"Uh, he grew up here too. We were classmates in school, and he came back to Milton County after law school. He has a couple of sisters who are married but don't live here."

"Is Buddy his real name?"

"No, it's Blair, but he's always gone by Buddy. His mother lives in a beautiful old home on Franklin Street. It's the one with the porch across the front and a yard full of flowers."

"I've driven down Franklin Street but don't remember specific places," Mayleah said.

"I rent a house owned by the Smith family," Gracie continued. "They own a lot of real estate."

"Is he married with children?"

"Buddy never married," Gracie replied slowly.

She was about to mention Amber and Elise but didn't. It didn't feel right to reveal such personal information about Buddy to someone she'd just met. Heidi and another girl returned and began asking questions about being a detective. When it was time to leave, Gracie gathered the team together in the back corner of the restaurant.

"Tonight was a huge first step," she said. "You beat a team of all-stars. Show up for practice tomorrow ready to get better. Our next opponent is from Newton County. Those of you who played varsity this past season remember what they did to us in the regional semifinals. A lot of the same girls will be on the summer league squad."

"How about that tall pitcher?" Heidi asked. "I hope she was a senior and graduated."

"I haven't seen their roster. But their program is like ours. They're always training younger players to step up and play."

The girls gathered in a circle, put their hands together, and yelled, "Team!"

Other customers in the grill clapped and cheered.

"Thanks again for inviting me," Mayleah said as the meeting broke up. "It was fun. I'll try to make it to another game soon."

"And you'd be welcome to come to practice if you want. The girls really like you."

TEN

THE FOLLOWING DAY KEPT BUDDY BUSY AT THE OFFICE, but in the back of his mind, he continued to think about the remaining boxes in his mother's basement. After a quick stop at home, he drove to Franklin Street and resumed his seat on the bottom step.

One of the boxes contained nothing but copies of correspondence his father considered important enough to save. There were threatening letters to Rascal from tenants and copies of the replies from either Rascal or Norman Kaufman, the lawyer Rascal used before Buddy passed the bar exam. Now deceased, Norman remained infamous in the bar for the length of his correspondence, pleadings, and any other type of legal document. If one paragraph would cover a topic, Norman used three. It was an effective way to justify his bill. If a tenant had to be evicted, Norman would prepare a long complaint that laid out the downward spiral of a relationship that began beautifully and descended into bitter betrayal by the tenant. Buddy went through five boxes without finding anything pertinent to his search.

Off to one side was a plastic container different from the other boxes. Curious, Buddy brought it over to the place where he was sitting and lifted the lid. It was filled with small notebooks. Opening one, he saw his mother's small, neat handwriting. At first he thought it was a diary but quickly realized it was a collection of her thoughts intermingled with short prayers. Flipping through the pages he saw familiar names, including his own. Interestingly, his mother often wrote "Blair," not "Buddy."

"Buddy!" his mother called out from the top of the stairs. "Find anything?"

"No, I'll be up in a minute."

He brought the box of notebooks with him. His mother took a plate of food from the microwave and placed it on the kitchen table beside a glass of tea. There was a large piece of baked chicken with rice and gravy and a bowl of okra and tomatoes. She seemed brighter and less sad.

"This should be better than a sandwich," she said. "Leftovers from the McMillians. I'll enjoy watching you eat it more than if I ate it myself."

Buddy's stomach growled. "Thanks," he said, then pointed to the box near his feet. "I didn't find anything else about Amber or Elise, but I came across this. It contains your notebooks."

Beatrice lifted the lid of the container. "Oh, I have bunches of those. It started years ago as an assignment for a Sunday school class, and I never stopped."

"I hope it was okay that I read a few pages from a couple of them."

"Sure. I don't have any secrets."

Buddy took a bite of food. The contrast between his mother and his father couldn't have been starker. Beatrice joined him at the table with a glass of tea.

"I noticed that you called me Blair. Usually only people who don't really know me call me that. It was different seeing it in your handwriting. It made me feel"—Buddy paused and met his mother's gaze—"special, if that makes sense."

Beatrice smiled. "It does. Because that's the name I gave you. I'm fine calling you Buddy since that's what your daddy liked, but in my heart you've always been Blair."

"What else did you write about me?"

"Lots of stuff. You'll probably be bored, but you're welcome to take the journals home with you. If nothing else, they'll bring back memories, some good, some bad."

"Bad?"

"A little bit. I've always tried to keep things positive since I don't think God spends much time worrying, so I pray solutions, not problems." Beatrice ran her fingers through her hair. "The past twenty-four hours have sure put that to the test."

"Yes. Do you still do this?"

"Every night."

/ / /

At home, Buddy took the box of notebooks onto the back porch. He had a favorite chair that was both a rocker and a recliner. Propping up his feet, he grabbed a random journal and began to thumb through it. The language was so typical of his mother that it made him smile. She included details from life, concerns about problems, and notes of thankfulness. The pages opened a window to parts of her soul that he didn't know existed. He'd always considered his mother to be a decent judge of people, but the insights she had about folks in Milton County whom he now knew were striking. Her prayers were concise and direct, her thanksgiving specific. Going to the bottom of the box, he found one of the earliest notebooks. The pages were yellowed with age. It was from his high school years when he was in the ninth or tenth grade. Turning to a page toward the middle, he found an entry asking the Lord to help Buddy and Gracie Blaylock do a good job with their presentation in class. He vaguely remembered the class but not a joint project. The next line caught his attention: "Gracie is a sweet girl with a pure heart. Bless her with a lifetime of joy and happiness."

Buddy took the book from the box and placed it on a table near the front door so he wouldn't forget it in the morning.

/ / /

It was 8:30 a.m., and Buddy was hungry. He'd stopped by the jail to see a client and left home before eating breakfast. When he passed the courthouse, he saw Gracie Blaylock getting out of her car. The journal was on the passenger seat beside him. He dialed her number and watched as she stopped and took her phone from her purse.

"Hello," she said.

"This is Buddy Smith. Have you had breakfast?"

"Not really. I drank some coffee and ate a cup of yogurt."

"Unless you're too busy, I wondered if we could meet for breakfast at the Crossroads before you start your day."

"I guess a few minutes won't make a difference."

"Great. See you there."

Gracie returned her cell phone to her purse. While eating her yogurt, she'd enjoyed looking at the purple irises Beatrice Smith had given her and, as requested, she'd prayed for Buddy. She was startled when he called. He'd never invited her to breakfast, or lunch or dinner.

Breakfast was a busy time at the restaurant. There was an initial rush of construction workers and laborers who wanted a hearty meal before beginning a long day in the hot sun. Most of them would be gone by now, replaced by the second shift of professionals. Buddy was sitting at the same table for two where they'd recently had lunch. He held up his coffee cup in greeting, and she walked over to him.

"I reserved our table," Buddy said with a smile when she sat down across from him. "Thanks for coming on such short notice."

Their waitress appeared. Gracie had already had her morning quota of coffee and ordered orange juice. The middle-aged woman topped off Buddy's cup and took their orders.

"Don't you drink coffee?" Buddy asked.

"One and a half cups at the house is my limit. Otherwise, it would be hard for me to sit still at my desk."

"It's two for me, but I'm making an exception today. I came across something last night at Mom's house and wanted to show it to you."

A faded notebook lay on the table beside Buddy. He opened it to a page marked with a slip of paper and pushed it across the table.

Gracie read the words Beatrice wrote about her. "That is so sweet," she said.

"Do you remember the biology project she mentions?"

"Yes, it had to do with Mendel's law of genetics. We used pieces of colored candy to show how it worked. You did most of the work on the paper and gave the presentation in class because I was so shy."

"You remember that?"

"Women have good memories," Gracie said with a smile. "Where did you find this?"

"Digging through records in my mother's basement while trying to find more information about Amber and Elise."

"It's precious that she's letting you read this."

Buddy sipped his coffee. "Can this be a confidential conversation?" he asked.

"Sure."

"I told you the other day that my father maintained contact with Amber after she left town. There was more to it than that. He paid her a lot of money from the time Elise was born until shortly before he died. My mother and I didn't know anything about it until recently."

Gracie started to interrupt but didn't want to get Millie Graham in trouble.

"What I didn't anticipate was the level of pain this was going to cause my mom," he said. "It hurt her deeply, worse than anything I've seen in my life."

Buddy stopped. Gracie waited for him to continue. Suddenly, she realized Buddy was struggling with his emotions. The waitress returned with their food and placed it in front of them. Neither of them moved. Tears welled up in Gracie's eyes. She grabbed a thin napkin from a dispenser in the middle of the table and wiped them away.

"I'm sorry," Buddy said. "I don't know what came over me."

"It's okay. Let's just sit here without saying anything for a minute."

Gracie turned sideways in her chair. She was afraid that if she looked directly at Buddy's face, she'd burst into tears. Beatrice

Smith must be struggling with a tremendous sense of betrayal and shattered trust. Several people Gracie knew were dining at the restaurant, and they caught her eye and waved. She waved back. When she looked again at Buddy, he, too, seemed more under control.

"Doing a little campaigning?" he asked with a slight smile on his face.

"Always," she managed. "And there's nothing wrong with caring about your mother. Beatrice is one of the most gracious ladies I've ever met. I stopped to talk with her for a few minutes the other day, and she sent me home with a beautiful cluster of purple flowers."

Buddy nodded. "That's her. But finding out about the money my father secretly gave Amber has been tough. And I didn't realize until recently that my mother has been grieving this whole time about not seeing Elise."

Gracie barely breathed as Buddy told about the photo album Beatrice put together and her longing for her first grandchild at Christmas and on birthdays. It was heart-wrenching. Gracie's food remained untouched.

"She kept all this completely bottled up inside," Buddy continued. "And now my father is gone so they can't try to work it out. Anyway, when I saw you getting out of your car at the courthouse, I wanted to show you the entry in her journal. I didn't know I was going to dump all this other stuff on you."

Their waitress returned. "Honey, is there something wrong with your food?" she asked Gracie. "I can send it back and get you something else if you want."

"No, I'm sure it's fine," Gracie answered. "I'm a slow eater."

The waitress gave her an odd look and left.

Buddy chuckled. "That was creative, but it's my fault that you haven't eaten."

"What you're talking about is so much more important than food."

"I appreciate you feeling that way."

"And I'll be praying for her."

An idea flashed through Gracie's mind. "And you could pray too. It would be extra special if you did it with her."

"That's not an area of expertise for me," Buddy said doubtfully. "It might give her a heart attack."

"No, it would affect her heart in a good way."

/ / /

Buddy and Millie arrived at the office at the same time. Jennifer's older-model car was already in the small parking area.

"Does Jennifer have a key to the office?" Buddy asked Millie.

"Yes, I gave her one yesterday. I assumed it would be okay with you."

"That's fine."

The phone rang and Millie answered. "Detective Harkness calling about the Ford case," she said.

"I'll take it in my office."

The detective spoke first. "I read the report from Officer Reynolds about your meeting with Mr. Lipscomb, and I'm willing to open an investigative file in the Ford case."

"That's great news," Buddy replied, slowly lowering himself into his chair.

"Do you think you can get a criminal contempt order from a judge?" Mayleah asked.

"Yes, because he hasn't delivered the boy to his mother pursuant to the custody order."

"Okay, if you can assure me that's in process, I'm going to contact law enforcement in the Red Hill area and see if they can locate Ford and his son. It will be better coming through me than you doing it privately. Do you have current photos of the boy and his father?"

"Yes. I'll scan and send them to you."

Encouraged by how proactive the detective was willing to be, Buddy quickly scanned and sent the photos.

/ / /

Gracie carried her sympathy for Beatrice and Buddy Smith with her to the clerk's office. Rascal's conduct sounded like something that would happen in Hollywood, not Clarksburg. She was working her way through her phone messages when Brenda came over and told her the Honorable Bryant Williams had arrived.

"He's not supposed to get here until the weekend," Gracie said in surprise.

"He's here now," the assistant said, pointing to the counter where a lanky, well-dressed man over six feet tall and sporting a black goatee streaked with gray stood looking down at his cell phone.

Gracie left her desk and walked over to the counter. "Judge Williams," she said, extending her hand. "I'm Gracie Blaylock, clerk of court."

"Madam Clerk," the judge said, bowing slightly and speaking with an aristocratic southern accent. "I know I've arrived in town unexpectedly, but if possible I'd like to check into my accommodations today. That way I'll be ready to assist Judge Claremont first thing Monday morning."

"I made arrangements at a local bed-and-breakfast," Gracie answered. "I'll call the owner and see if there's a room available."

Gracie returned to her desk and phoned Vivian Hunt.

"Does he have the bird with him?" the proprietor asked.

"He didn't bring it into the courthouse," Gracie replied in a hushed voice. "If that happens, it will be up to Judge Claremont to deal with it."

Vivian laughed. "His room is almost ready. Give me at least an hour, then send him on. I've already cleaned the kitchen, so if he wants something to eat, he'll need to grab it downtown."

"Thanks for being flexible."

Gracie delivered the news to the judge.

"Excellent," he said with a slight nod. "On that note, I might as well check in with Judge Claremont now and see if I can help with anything since I'm here and have some time. Also, where is Vince Nelson's office? I've known Vince since his days in the General Assembly and thought I might swing by and see him while I'm in town."

"It's only a couple of blocks," Gracie said. "Turn right when you leave the courthouse. You can't miss the office. His name is on a large sign."

After the judge left, Brenda came over to Gracie's desk. "Did he seem creepy to you?" she asked.

"No, he was very polite," Gracie answered. "He sounds like he stepped off a cotton plantation."

"That could be good or bad."

"True."

Brenda lowered her voice. "Maggie over at the county commissioner's office told me he lost the judicial election in his home county because of a financial scandal and problems with a young female DA. In spite of that, they gave him emeritus status because of his political connections in Atlanta."

"Let's not bring that talk into the courthouse," Gracie said.

"Okay, but I thought you should know."

ELEVEN

BUDDY STOPPED AT MILLIE'S DESK. "I'M ON MY WAY TO the sheriff's department. Contact Amanda Byrnes in Judge Claremont's office and find out if he can see me anytime today or tomorrow on an uncontested contempt matter in *Ford v. Ford*. It will take five minutes or less. Text me what you find out. Amanda is good about squeezing me in."

At the sheriff's department, Officer Reynolds wasn't available, but one of the clerical workers gave Buddy what he needed for his hearing in front of the judge.

"Is Detective Harkness in?" Buddy asked.

"I think so. Do you want to see her?"

"Yes, please."

Buddy's phone buzzed as a text message came in from Millie:

Go immediately to the judge's chambers. He has an opening.

Buddy spoke to the clerk: "Sorry, I have to be in court in a few minutes. Tell Detective Harkness I'll talk to her later."

Buddy entered the courthouse through a side entrance. Retrieving the file from the clerk's office, he took the stairs two at a time on his way to Judge Claremont's chambers.

"Thanks for working me in," he said to Amanda.

"Glad to do it. You're seeing Judge Williams in the small courtroom. He came into town early and just met with Judge Claremont. They made a decision on the spur of the moment and he's going to help with handling expedited matters today."

"Judge Williams?"

"Bryant Williams. He's going to be assisting for the next month until Judge Barnwell returns."

"What's he like?" Buddy asked quickly.

"No idea," Amanda said and rolled her eyes. "Except that he comes across like a character from *Gone with the Wind*."

Buddy wasn't sure how that would impact Williams's judicial philosophy.

The small courtroom was a compact, windowless room with a witness stand and two tables where lawyers could sit with their clients. There was no jury box and only two benches for spectators. Buddy stopped to straighten his tie before opening the door and entering the courtroom.

Judge Bryant Williams was sitting on the bench and chatting with the court reporter, a young woman who also worked for private attorneys when not needed at the courthouse. The judge glanced up when Buddy entered.

"What do you want?" the judge asked.

"I'm Blair Smith, Your Honor. Judge Claremont's assistant told me you were available to hear expedited matters. I'm here on a motion to hold a defendant husband in criminal contempt for failing to deliver a minor child to the mother."

The judge turned to the court reporter and smiled. "Ms. Norfield, do you have the calendar?"

"Yes, sir. I should have given it to you, but we started talking and—"

"That's fine."

The court reporter handed a sheet of paper up to the judge. Buddy eased forward to the table where plaintiff's counsel sat when presenting arguments in the small courtroom.

"It looks like I can give you a few minutes, but you'd better talk fast," the judge said. "I value efficiency in my courtroom."

Before Buddy could begin, the back door opened, and Chris Henley entered along with a man Buddy didn't recognize.

The judge glanced up at Chris and asked, "Who are you?"

"Christopher Henley, Your Honor. Vince Nelson and I represent Bridgewater Limited Partners. We've filed a motion seeking a preliminary injunction to freeze the company's assets until they can be equitably divided. Mr. Callaway, a managing partner, is with me to offer testimony in support of the motion. Our motion was added to the calendar a short time ago."

"You work with Vince Nelson?"

"Yes, sir."

"Come forward and be heard. Mr. Stuart, I'll get to your matter later."

"It's Smith," Buddy said, emphasizing his last name.

"Does that make a difference in how I choose to proceed?" the judge asked.

"No, sir." Buddy swallowed and stepped away from the table as Chris made his way forward. Chris caught Buddy's eye and gave him a look of unspoken apology.

"How is Vince doing?" Judge Williams asked.

"He's fine, sir," Chris replied. "He told me to send his regards and looks forward to seeing you during your time in Milton County."

"Tell him I'll call, and we'll get together for dinner."

"Yes, sir."

"Proceed with your proof," the judge said.

For the next hour, Chris presented testimonial and documentary evidence in support of the preliminary injunction. Disputes between business partners can be ugly, but a falling-out is especially rancorous when the partners at one time were close friends. Chris's client was angry and didn't try to hide it. He couldn't resist inserting personal digs directed at one of the other partners. Buddy knew there was another side to the story, but Mr. Callaway had won the race to the courthouse. Buddy checked his watch. He hadn't planned on sitting in the small courtroom doing nothing for this long. The rear door of the courtroom opened and another lawyer entered, accompanied by a man wearing a blue suit.

"No!" Mr. Callaway shouted from the witness stand and pointed at the two men.

"Your Honor, I represent Mr. Scarboro," said Bill Lynwood, a local lawyer who specialized in business law. "We just learned about the motion for preliminary injunction filed by Mr. Callaway and would like to be heard."

"I'm not going to make Mr. Henley start over," the judge replied. "But you can offer your proof when he finishes."

Buddy checked his watch and saw Chris do the same. Bill Lynwood was notoriously long-winded, which could be an effective strategy.

Buddy stood. "Your Honor, could you tell me when to return so I might be heard on my motion? It will be unopposed."

"You may certainly leave," the judge answered. "But I'm not

going to specially set your motion. On these types of calendars it is first come, first served in my courtroom."

Buddy wanted to point out that he'd arrived prior to Chris and his client but knew it was pointless. Chris was talking to Bill Lynwood. They continued to whisper back and forth. Finally, they faced the bench and Chris spoke.

"Mr. Lynwood and I would ask the court for a recess so we can discuss this matter with our clients."

"There's nothing to discuss," Mr. Callaway blurted from the witness stand.

"There is if your lawyer says so," the judge replied. "Step down."

"We'll report back in thirty minutes," Chris said.

"Take your time," the judge said with a wave of his hand. "I'm always in favor of the parties working out their differences."

After the group left the room, the judge turned to Buddy. "Mr. Swain, you may proceed."

Not wanting to correct the judge a second time, Buddy placed the file in front of the judge.

"This is a domestic matter. Before you is the clerk's file along with the sheriff's report of unsuccessful efforts to serve the defendant with Judge Claremont's order granting my client immediate custody of the party's minor son. Upon information and belief, the defendant father has taken the child and left the state. Because Mr. Ford has not complied with Judge Claremont's order to immediately turn over the child to the mother, I ask that you find Mr. Ford in criminal contempt. The sheriff's office is ready to initiate an out-of-state search for the child."

While Buddy talked, the judge flipped through the file. "You didn't personally serve the defendant with the order?"

"No, sir. He can't be located."

"Motion denied."

Startled, Buddy paused for a moment. "Your Honor, the sheriff's department confirms diligent efforts to locate Mr. Ford. He chose to make himself unavailable by leaving the state."

The judge tapped the file. "I don't see any proof that he left the state. Your client's affidavit contains conclusions based on speculation."

Sue Ellen's affidavit and testimony had satisfied Judge Claremont. Buddy wasn't prepared to relitigate that issue; however, he wasn't prepared to back down.

"There is attempted service by Officer Reynolds of the Milton County Sheriff's Department. He tried to locate the defendant at his last known address and other places where he might be found."

The judge shoved the file across the bench toward Buddy. "That's repetitive. I'm not going to hold a man in criminal contempt so close in time to the alleged kidnapping of his own child. You've not proven the occurrence of criminal contempt beyond a reasonable doubt. If you want to come back and request civil contempt, I will consider it."

Civil contempt could eventually lead to criminal contempt but wouldn't provide the quick remedy Buddy needed to justify Detective Harkness's help in finding little Jack. Without her assistance, Buddy would have to rely on his own effort to track down father and son or hire a private investigator like Jim Brim. He inwardly kicked himself for taking a chance with a judge he didn't know. He should have waited for Judge Claremont.

"Prepare an order with my findings so it can be placed in the file," Judge Williams continued. "I want Judge Claremont to know that I've already ruled on this motion."

"Yes, sir."

/ / /

Gracie called Vivian Hunt to let her know that Judge Williams wouldn't be arriving at the bed-and-breakfast until late in the afternoon.

"Why does that not surprise me?" Vivian responded. "But at least the room is ready. Where is the bird staying while the judge is at the courthouse?"

"I don't know. I've been so busy getting ready for court next week that I didn't think about it. I hope it's not in his car. The high temperature this afternoon is going to be in the nineties."

"Parrots live in the jungle. Maybe the heat doesn't bother them."

"That would be parrot abuse."

"It will be air-conditioned at my place. Are you going to give Judge Williams directions to the house or bring him yourself?"

"I was going to let him follow me just to make sure everything is okay. These retired judges can be temperamental."

"The last one you sent over was like a second grandfather to my grandkids. He and Mikey got along great."

"Judge Clarke was a nice man. I wish he could have come back, but he didn't want to spend any more time away from his family. I'll send you a text when Judge Williams and I leave the courthouse."

After the call ended, Gracie saw Buddy standing at the counter to return a file. She assisted him herself and saw the label: "Ford v. Ford."

"Bad news," Buddy said, shaking his head.

"What happened?"

"The visiting judge denied my motion to hold Jackie in criminal contempt. It was an ambush."

Gracie knew the definition of criminal contempt, but she didn't understand exactly how that impacted Sue Ellen's efforts to recover her son. "Does that mean Jackie can keep little Jack?"

"No, no. Judge Claremont's original order gave Sue Ellen sole custody pending a supplemental hearing. That's still valid. But the sheriff's department can't help me track down Jackie unless he's held in criminal contempt of court and therefore potentially guilty of a crime."

"Oh. That is a big deal," Gracie acknowledged.

"Yes, and Detective Harkness was primed to go."

"Can you talk to Judge Claremont about it?"

"That thought crossed my mind, but Judge Williams is making me prepare an order that will discourage Judge Claremont from reaching a different conclusion. Judges don't like to step on each other's toes."

"But Judge Williams is a visiting judge."

Buddy shrugged. "That may not make a big difference. Sue Ellen is so fragile, I hate to give her the bad news."

Not wanting Mayleah Harkness to incorrectly assume that a criminal contempt order against Jackie Ford was imminent, Buddy returned to the sheriff's department after leaving the courthouse.

"Is Detective Harkness available?" he asked the same clerk who'd waited on him earlier.

"I'll check," the woman replied.

Cream-colored vinyl chairs lined two walls of the waiting area. Buddy sat down, avoiding a chair with a red stain that looked suspiciously like dried blood. A couple of minutes later several cars, their sirens blaring, left the parking lot. After fifteen minutes passed, Buddy prepared to leave. He could always call the detective or send her an email. He stood just as Mayleah Harkness entered the waiting area. The detective was wearing a white blouse, a dark skirt, and regular shoes instead of cowboy boots.

"Sorry you had to wait," she said. "But I was on the phone with someone in Oklahoma about the Ford matter."

"That's what I need to talk to you about. I've hit a snag in the legal process."

The detective led the way to her cubicle. After they were seated, Buddy explained what transpired in front of Judge Williams.

"It's too bad that he denied the request for criminal contempt," Mayleah said.

"Yeah, and I didn't want you to tell your contacts in Oklahoma that a criminal contempt order justifying Ford's arrest and extradition to Georgia was imminent."

The detective didn't immediately respond. Instead, she turned to her computer monitor.

"The lack of a contempt order doesn't mean I can't help," she said while typing on her keyboard.

"Really?" Buddy asked in surprise. "I assumed that would shut you down for now."

"Judge Williams may not agree with you, but I don't have to agree with him."

"Okay." Buddy sat up straighter.

"I've already opened an investigative file, which can serve as a reason to track down the defendant. If we find him quickly, then you'll have new evidence to present to the judge that confirms Ford fled the state with his son. That seems like the main sticking point." Mayleah pointed to her monitor. "I've already exchanged emails with the sheriff in Haskell County, Oklahoma. That's where Red Hill is located. He has the photos and is dispatching an officer later today to see if anyone matching the defendant's description is in the area. It's a sparsely populated community, and a newcomer with a little boy might attract attention. I'll let Sheriff Blackstone know that we don't currently have a criminal warrant so he needs to be discreet."

"That's perfect."

Mayleah checked her watch. "I'd better be on my way to the courthouse for a bond revocation hearing. I'll let the assistant DA know that Judge Williams can be a stickler for process in case that changes how she wants to proceed."

"I hope it goes better for you than it did for me."

/ / /

It was close to 5:15 p.m., and Judge Williams hadn't appeared. Gracie was about to ask Brenda to take the judge to the bed-and-breakfast.

"Madam Clerk, I'm ready to depart for my lodgings!" the visiting judge called out from across the office.

After Buddy's bad experience, Gracie wasn't amused by Williams's flowery rhetoric. She grabbed her purse.

"It's about five minutes from here," she said crisply. "Where is your car?"

"In Judge Barnwell's reserved spot. I assumed that would be acceptable."

"Yes, sir."

"I enjoyed the afternoon calendar," the judge said as they walked toward the side exit nearest the parking area. "I was particularly impressed with the Native American detective who testified in a bond revocation proceeding. What can you tell me about Detective Harkness?"

The judge's interest in Mayleah made Gracie even more uncomfortable. She kept her answer extra brief. "She's only been here a couple of months."

Gracie sped up as they walked down the sidewalk. The long-legged judge had no trouble keeping up with her.

"I need to swing by the pet store to retrieve my parrot before we go to the bed-and-breakfast," he said. "The proprietor was kind enough to board him for the day."

There was only one pet store in Clarksburg.

"It's in the opposite direction," Gracie said.

"You're not returning to the courthouse, are you?"

Gracie doubted the excuse of being late for softball practice would work with the judge. "No, sir."

Once in her car, Gracie turned on the air-conditioning full blast. Judge Williams followed in a large Buick. It was a five-minute drive to the pet store, which sold everything from turtles to tarantulas. Gracie intended on staying in the car, but the judge insisted she join him. Benny Hargrave, the owner, was a kind, eccentric man who'd retired to Clarksburg and opened the store more as a hobby than a business enterprise. A large gray parrot was perched on a stand beside the cash register.

"We've had a wonderful day," Mr. Hargrave said to the judge.

"Madam Clerk, let me introduce you to Bailiff. He's an African gray parrot, by most accounts the most intelligent species of talking bird in the world."

Bailiff was about twelve inches long with a black beak, gray body feathers, a circle of short white feathers around the eyes, and a cluster of red tail feathers.

"Who's the smartest of them all?" Judge Williams asked the bird.

"Judges, not lawyers," the bird replied. "Judges, not lawyers."

Gracie manufactured a slight smile.

"Pretty lady," the bird said, looking at her.

"Bailiff speaks the truth, even when he's not under oath," the judge said.

"He said that to every woman who came into the shop," Mr. Hargrave added.

The judge beamed. "Which proves he's smart."

Judge Williams held out his hand, and Bailiff stepped onto it. Williams stroked the back of the bird's head, and the parrot lowered his head in pleasure.

"No crackers for Polly," Bailiff said. "Steak and lobster."

"How big is his vocabulary?" Mr. Hargrave asked.

"Over one hundred words, and he can put them together with understanding," the judge replied.

Gracie doubted the last comment but didn't want to get into a debate. "Your Honor, I have another appointment," she said.

"Certainly," the judge replied.

"Don't be late," Bailiff said, as if to prove the judge's claim that the bird could comprehend language.

"Bring him back anytime," Mr. Hargrave said. "If you'll give me advance notice, I'd like to arrange for some of the schoolchildren to meet him."

"Better yet," the judge replied, "I'll come myself so they can really see what Bailiff can do. I enjoy showing him off to kids."

Bailiff hopped into a portable cage. "Go to jail," he said.

Gracie watched as the judge placed the cage in the rear seat of his car and tethered it with a harness similar to that used in a child's car seat. He certainly seemed to care for his parrot.

When they arrived at the bed-and-breakfast, Gracie introduced the judge to Vivian Hunt, then quickly excused herself.

Driving to the ballfield, Gracie couldn't get Brenda's comment about the judge having issues with a young female DA out of her mind. That made her suspicious of his interest in Mayleah. No doubt the detective could take care of herself, but that didn't lessen Gracie's negative thoughts.

A couple of girls were already at the ballfield when Gracie arrived. She went into the restroom and changed clothes. Normally, she looked forward to a shower after softball practice. Today she wanted one before practice. Judge Williams made her feel dirty.

Later that evening, when she arrived home from the ballfield, Gracie saw Lauren's car in the driveway.

"You didn't have a fight with Jeff, did you?" Gracie asked as Lauren got out of the car.

"No, we're doing great. But since I haven't heard from you, I concluded you posted your profile and then let it collect dust like a grandmother's wedding dress."

"I'm busted," Gracie answered with a grin.

They went inside. When he saw Lauren, Opie retrieved his tug-of-war rope and dropped it at her feet.

"I know what I'll be doing while you take a shower," Lauren said.

Gracie returned wearing exercise clothes and with a towel wrapped around her wet head. Lauren and Opie were still playing with the rope.

"I need a rope like this for Mark," Lauren said. "He's teething and might enjoy it."

Gracie sat on the floor beside her sister. "That would make a funny video."

Gracie asked Lauren some more questions about her nephews, then mentioned Mayleah Harkness.

"You know how people say they want to get together but never do?" Gracie said.

"Like you and the dating site."

"Not exactly."

Gracie told Lauren about Mayleah coming to the softball game, the meal at the Southside Grill, and the detective's interest in helping find little Jack Ford and Reagan Landry.

"Was the Landry girl into drugs?" Lauren asked.

"I don't know."

Gracie then mentioned Mayleah's interest in getting to know Buddy Smith.

"Does Buddy have a girlfriend?" Lauren asked.

"I'm not sure, but he usually has someone with him when he comes to social events sponsored by the local bar."

"You need to be more like this detective," Lauren declared.

"You think I should be interested in Buddy Smith?"

"No, no. Buddy Smith isn't right for you. I mean more assertive about getting to know who around here is an eligible bachelor. We're in a small town, and with your position at the courthouse, you should be in the know about who's coming and going."

"All kinds of people filter through the courthouse. But you're wrong about Buddy. He's one of the nicest men I know. He's still trying to track down his daughter, who was born a few weeks after we graduated from high school."

"And that's supposed to make me respect him?" Lauren

answered, getting up from the floor. "You're always trying to see the best in people. Let's take a look at your profile."

Aware of her recent thoughts about Judge Williams, Gracie wasn't so sure she always looked for the best in people. She and Lauren sat at the kitchen table and turned on Gracie's laptop. Gracie sighed and leaned on her elbows.

Lauren glanced sideways at her. "What's wrong?"

"I have no faith in this."

"Don't fret. I have enough faith for both of us. There's living proof every time I see Jeff at the breakfast table."

The welcome screen for the site appeared. Gracie was about to enter her log-in information when Lauren reached out her hand and stopped her. "Let's guess how many responses you've received from men wanting to know more about you. You go first."

"Okay," Gracie said slowly. "I'm sure there are a lot of desperate men out there who are looking for a woman, any woman, to marry. You said this site is one of the smallest and most selective, so I'll estimate between ten and fifteen."

"Not far off from what I think, but I'm going to prove my faith and go higher and say fifty."

Gracie logged in. The photo of her with the fancy hairdo came into view. The screen was crowded with pop-up ads for upgrades to the dating service. Lauren gasped.

"What?" Gracie asked.

Lauren pointed to the right side of the screen. Gracie saw the number 357 with the words "See how many awesome godly men want to meet you" written beneath it.

"How is that possible in such a short period of time?" Gracie asked.

"We nailed it with the profile," Lauren replied with satisfaction. "I knew it was good."

"But over 350 responses?"

"Three or four days is an eternity on these dating sites. That's why you have to check regularly to see if a suitable candidate pops up."

"I can't do that on my work computer at the courthouse."

"You didn't link it to your phone?"

"No," Gracie said sheepishly. "This is an old email address that I rarely use."

"You're sneaky, but I love you anyway. Let's not waste any more time. Some of the first guys who showed interest in you may be married with children by now."

Gracie pushed the laptop toward Lauren. "You'll be able to evaluate them much faster than I can."

Lauren took over. Gracie could see that her sister relished the process. She quickly dismissed ten men before pausing when a man named Devin appeared.

"This guy is an accountant so probably has a decent job," Lauren said.

Gracie leaned forward. Devin was a handsome, serious-looking man born the same month and year as she was.

Lauren spoke: "The age is right, and he's good-looking, but if that's his idea of a smile, I don't think he's the one."

"Devin likes his dog."

There was a second photo of Devin with a Jack Russell terrier in his lap.

"But he's not looking at the dog or holding it like he cares. It's totally staged."

Gracie wasn't picking up on any of the nuanced traits identified by her sister.

"Let's move on," Lauren said.

There was a surprising number of responses from preachers and ministers. Lauren cut three in a row before pointing to one. "David looks like an interesting candidate. He lived overseas for several years. And before going into the ministry, he was a professional baseball player."

David had a nicely groomed beard and lively brown eyes. He was currently working as the administrative pastor for a church less than a hundred miles away from Milton County.

"He's three years younger than I am," Gracie said.

"Age differences that are important in high school don't mean as much when you're as old as you are," Lauren replied.

Gracie cut her eyes at her sister. "You are such a good cheerleader," she said.

"Truth-speaker is how I define my role. Click there so we can keep David as a possibility. Putting two people with strong administrative gifts together can work well because they can accomplish more as a team than as individuals."

"I like that."

"I know."

They continued plowing through the list. One man who worked in the human resources department for a large company caught Gracie's eye, and she stopped her sister.

"I'd like to find out more about him," Gracie said.

"No," Lauren said and shook her head. "First, his name is Barry. Second, he's almost ten years older than you are."

"A few minutes ago you said age wasn't a factor."

"Don't misquote me. Age is still important." Lauren examined Barry's photo. "He's handsome, but it looks like he's had some work done on his face."

"There's no way you can tell that!" Gracie protested.

"Also, he has two children in their twenties. Are they going to accept a thirty-five-year-old as their stepmother?"

"They're out of the house."

"It doesn't say that. Also, what about your children? Is Barry going to want to start all over creating a new family?"

"Okay, okay. Cut him."

Gracie was yawning repeatedly by the time they finished. Twelve candidates remained.

"Let's call them the twelve apostles," Lauren said, leaning back in her chair with satisfaction. "I just hope there's not a Judas lurking there. Your next job is to choose the three you want to respond to. And you can't procrastinate."

"But not tonight," Gracie replied, then covered her mouth as she yawned once again. "I can't believe you're not exhausted."

"Coffee at five o'clock this afternoon helped. Report back to me by the end of the day tomorrow."

"Yes, ma'am." Gracie saluted and prepared to log off the website.

"One more thing," Lauren said. "Let's pray."

They bowed their heads, and Lauren briefly but sincerely poured out her heart on Gracie's behalf. Encountering the depth of her sister's compassion in the prayer moved Gracie. She didn't add anything to Lauren's words except an amen.

"Thanks for caring," Gracie said when they raised their heads.

Lauren smiled. "You're a great sister and deserve a worthy soul mate. It's easy to want the best for you."

TWELVE

BUDDY ARRIVED EARLIER THAN USUAL AT THE OFFICE. Millie and Jennifer were huddled at the office manager's desk.

"Good morning. No interruptions, please," Millie said when he appeared. "We're going over the financial information for the rental business."

"No problem," Buddy replied and went directly to his office and closed the door. The first activity on his agenda this morning was to provide saliva samples to three different genealogical services along with the paperwork authorizing the companies to release his results to any relatives interested in knowing about him. He paid an extra fee to expedite the results. Though Buddy had delayed trying to locate Elise through genealogy websites, he felt compelled to do so now. He had no desire to open a Pandora's box of crazy family connections, but the possibility that it might help him locate his daughter overcame his reservations. A couple of hours later his phone buzzed.

"Detective Harkness is on the phone for you," Jennifer said.

"I have good news this morning," the detective said brightly when Buddy answered. "I believe we've found Jackson Ford and his son."

"That's fantastic," Buddy said, grabbing a pen to take notes. "What can you tell me?"

"A deputy showed the photos you sent to the owner of a local convenience store. The man confirmed that Ford and his son may be with an enclave of people living on several hundred acres about ten miles from Red Hill. The group is determined to live off the grid. They don't obtain Social Security numbers for their children and believe the federal tax system is unconstitutional. The sheriff knew it was the first place to look for someone like Ford wanting to hide."

"Did the officer make a positive identification?"

"No. If a patrol car shows up at their compound, everyone in the group disappears except for the head guy, who acts as a spokesperson."

"Is this group violent?"

"The sheriff said they probably have a stockpile of guns but keep to themselves. They like to file crazy lawsuits. The leader is a lawyer."

Buddy ran through his options. "There's no use sending my private investigator out there," he said. "He isn't set up to handle that sort of scenario."

"And I don't want to tell you how to do your job, but would this new information justify asking the judge to issue a criminal contempt order? Wasn't his objection based on not knowing Ford had actually left the state with the child?"

"That was part of it, along with the fact that I was acting so quickly."

"Which makes sense now."

Buddy paused for a moment. The judicial mind was a shifting landscape. There could be a creative way to approach the visiting judge.

"How was your hearing in front of Judge Williams?" he asked.

"Easy. No problems. If you like, I can testify about my conversation with the sheriff."

"That would be hearsay. You'd be testifying about what the sheriff told you, which someone else told him. Judge Williams is likely to kick me out of the courtroom for the second day in a row. Let me see if I can come up with a way to do this."

"You're the lawyer. I'll wait to hear from you."

While drinking a second cup of coffee, Gracie narrowed the list of twelve to three: Devin, the accountant; David, the administrative pastor; and Daniel, the director of a facility that offered occupational training for special-needs adults. Daniel spent his free time outdoors with his two golden retrievers and said he was "looking for a woman willing to love, dream, and grow together in ways that will change the world around us." Gracie sent the profiles of the three finalists to Lauren.

At the courthouse, she reviewed the final list of prospective jurors summoned for the following week. Gracie barely had more than the minimum number Judge Claremont expected, and she wasn't sure if Judge Williams was going to launch into a full trial schedule or not. If he did, there might be a shortage of prospective jurors. But worrying wouldn't help, and Gracie closed the screen on her computer.

She spent the next hour with members of the county administrator's office. The meeting lagged, and Gracie held her phone under the table to check messages. There was one from Lauren:

Devin!! Are you serious!!! And does every man you choose have to have a name that begins with D?

Gracie smiled and quickly replied:

Yes to Devin! Will talk to you about all the Ds later.

She had no explanation why the names of the three men she selected all started with "D," but there was no harm in creating suspense in Lauren's mind.

It was lunchtime when the meeting adjourned. Gracie called the sheriff's department to see if Mayleah was interested in meeting for lunch to discuss the Reagan Landry case.

After waiting on hold for almost five minutes, the woman who answered the phone came back on the line. "Detective Harkness is unavailable," she said.

Leaving the courthouse, Gracie walked across the street to the Crossroads. It was packed with a usual lunchtime crowd. As she looked around for a place to sit, she saw Buddy at the table where they'd shared breakfast. He was with a woman. When the woman turned her head slightly, Gracie realized it was Mayleah. The detective laughed and leaned forward toward Buddy. Gracie's desire for an update about Reagan, along with her appetite for lunch, evaporated.

/ //

Buddy had only a few bites of broccoli casserole left on his dinner plate when his phone buzzed. It was a text message from Millie.

"There's an open time slot in front of Judge Williams at one thirty," he said to Mayleah.

"I think we should take it."

"Okay, but this is a big risk. If Judge Williams doesn't like what I have to offer and holds me in contempt of court, you can take me to jail."

"At least it's air-conditioned."

Buddy rolled his eyes. He texted Millie, asking her to confirm the slot in front of the visiting judge. He then ordered two pieces of coconut pie. While they ate, he asked Mayleah about herself. The detective was surprisingly open and honest about her past. She'd moved to Georgia after divorcing a man named Clay. Her ex-husband had recently initiated contact to explore getting back together. Mayleah wasn't sure that's what she wanted to do.

"You've made me do all the talking," she said. "Tell me something important about you."

Buddy knew she wanted personal information, but telling the detective about his last romantic relationship, Krista, or one of his other girlfriends didn't seem like a good idea.

"I have a daughter who just turned seventeen," he said. "But I haven't seen her since she was an infant. I've been looking for her and her mother ever since they left town in the middle of the night. That's the main reason I started representing people like Sue Ellen Ford. I know how they feel."

He gave a quick version of his relationship with Amber in high school but left out the recent developments.

Mayleah finished her pie and placed her fork beside the plate. "It sounds like the trail has grown cold," she said. "Would you like my help?"

Buddy was about to take a drink of tea but stopped. "Amber hasn't broken any laws," he said.

"Not from a criminal perspective, but that doesn't stop me from acting on my own. I'd have to be careful not to improperly use any law enforcement resources to track them down. What was Amber's last name when she was in high school?"

"Melrose."

"And the date of birth for your daughter?"

Buddy gave it to her. Mayleah entered the information into her phone.

"But you have doubts her name is Elise."

"That's the name Amber and I agreed on when we were still together, but the birth certificate lists her as 'Baby Girl Melrose.' Because we weren't married, Amber had the right to select the name. She listed the father as 'Unknown.'"

"Why?"

"I have no idea."

"Did Amber ever try to have your parental rights terminated?"

"No, and it wouldn't have worked because I stood ready to pay child support."

"Who paid the maternity costs?"

"Amber qualified for Medicaid because her father was unemployed at the time, and she was considered indigent."

"Couldn't your family have paid the bills?"

Buddy cringed. It was another example of his father's selective use of financial resources. "I worked during the summer for my father and didn't have much money," he said. "My parents could have taken care of the bills but didn't."

Mayleah nodded. Buddy checked his watch. He sensed the detective was going to keep probing and wasn't prepared to tell her everything.

"I'm going to walk back to the office and then head over to the courthouse," he said. "Do you want to meet me there in fifteen minutes?"

"Sure. I have a good feeling about this."

"I hope you're right."

/ / /

Gracie ate a pack of cheese crackers at her desk. Shortly after she finished, her phone buzzed. It was Amanda from Judge Claremont's chambers.

"Judge Williams wants to see you in the small courtroom," the judicial assistant said.

"Do you know what it's about?"

"No. He just stuck his head in here and told me to summon you upstairs. That's the word he used."

"On my way."

Gracie pushed her hair behind her ears and climbed the stairs. Court records in rural areas like Milton County weren't yet fully electronic. If the judge wanted to know about a specific case, she'd have to return downstairs and retrieve the file. She pushed open the door to the courtroom. Wearing his black robe, the judge was sitting on the bench.

"Good afternoon," Gracie said. "I hope you're finding the Hunt house satisfactory."

"More than satisfactory," the judge replied. "And I like the location. I went out for a walk this morning through a very nice area of town."

"I'm glad. What can I do for you?"

The judge picked up several sheets of paper and held them in his hand. "Is this the jury pool for next week?" he asked.

Gracie approached the bench, and the judge handed her the papers. She quickly looked through them. "Yes, sir," she said.

The judge leaned forward. "Madam Clerk, how do you expect me to try cases when I don't have enough jurors to impanel twelve citizens in the box?"

"I don't know," Gracie replied, her mouth suddenly dry.

"Judge Claremont asked me to clear out a batch of the older cases on his docket, and I'd like to focus on matters expected to take a day or less. I can't do that unless I have sufficient jurors."

"I wasn't aware of that plan when I sent out the summons."

"How many jurors were summoned and how many were excused?"

"Uh, I can check that for you," Gracie said.

"That's not necessary, but I want you to bring in at least another twenty-five jurors by the middle of next week."

The back door of the courtroom opened. Judge Williams looked past Gracie.

"Mr. Smith and Detective Harkness," the judge said. "Ms. Byrnes told me you had a matter you'd like me to consider. Come forward and be heard."

Buddy gave Gracie an apologetic look as he and Mayleah walked past her to stand in front of the judge. Gracie prepared to leave.

"Madam Clerk," the judge said to Gracie. "You're not excused. Stay until Mr. Smith is finished. I have another question for you."

Humiliated, Gracie sat down.

The judge addressed Buddy: "Mr. Smith, I had a very pleasant encounter this morning when I went out for a walk. My route took me down Franklin Street, and I saw a woman watering an impressive display of flowers and introduced myself. It turns out that she's your mother."

"Yes, sir. She's lived on Franklin Street for a number of years."

Gracie felt the blood rush from her face.

"She invited me in for a cup of excellent coffee," Judge Williams continued. "I learned quite a bit about you and your family. Please accept my condolences for your father's early death. I went through a bit of a heart scare a couple of years ago. I'm better than ever now."

"That's good to hear, Judge," Buddy answered. "I've brought Detective Harkness with me—"

"Nice to see you again," the judge interrupted.

Mayleah was standing beside Buddy with her back to Gracie. "And you, sir."

"This has to do with *Ford v. Ford*," Buddy said, handing a file up to the judge. "Per your instructions, I prepared an order denying my motion to hold the defendant in criminal contempt; however, additional relevant events have transpired within the past twenty-four hours, and I'd respectfully ask you to hear my proof and reconsider your ruling."

"Is that why Detective Harkness is here?"

"Yes, sir."

"Then I'll hear what you have to say. Detective, come forward and be sworn."

Mayleah sat in the witness chair, and the judge administered the oath.

Buddy cleared his throat. "Detective Harkness, please tell the Court about your efforts to locate Jackson Ford and his minor child, Jackson Ford Jr."

As she listened, Gracie was impressed. Mayleah was comfortable on the witness stand and didn't refer to any notes as she testified about the information obtained from Boyd Lipscomb that led to Red Hill and Haskell County, Oklahoma.

Judge Williams interrupted her. "Do you have an affidavit from the sheriff in Oklahoma?" he asked.

"No, Your Honor," Buddy interjected.

"I'm talking to the witness, Counselor," the judge replied curtly.

"No, sir," Mayleah answered. "And Sheriff Blackstone hasn't been able to confirm that Ford and his son are at the compound near Red Hill. We thought it wise not to alert anyone in the area about the search. Given what's transpired, Mr. Ford is a flight risk."

"Very well," the judge said. "Proceed."

"That's all," Mayleah said. "With your permission, I'd like to inform Sheriff Blackstone that if he locates Ford, he can arrest him. The boy would be placed in protective custody until his mother could claim him."

The judge turned to Buddy. "Mr. Smith, what if I issue the contempt order and it turns out that Ford and his son aren't there?"

"We would continue searching."

"That's what I would say if I were in your position," the judge replied. "I'm going to issue an order, but I want language included that it will expire immediately if Ford and his son are not in Haskell County. Also, I'm going to limit it to five days."

Buddy stepped closer to the bench. "Judge, I anticipated that might be the direction you'd go in the case, and I've already prepared an order if you're willing to handwrite a sentence limiting it to five days."

The judge glanced down at the sheet of paper, read it, then picked up a pen and scribbled something.

"Thank you, sir," Buddy said.

The judge turned to Mayleah. "You may step down, Detective. You're always welcome in my courtroom."

As Buddy and Mayleah left the room, Judge Williams turned his attention to Gracie. "Madam Clerk," he said, clearing his throat. "What is your plan to increase the number of jurors available next week? If necessary, I'll bring this up with Judge Claremont."

"I have a proposed solution," Gracie replied. "I'll pull the list of jurors scheduled for the next session of court and personally contact as many as necessary to obtain the number you'd like to have available. I know many of the individuals in the jury pool and should be able to satisfy your expectations."

Judge Williams eyed her for a few seconds. If he rejected her suggestion, Gracie knew she might be in for a scolding from Judge Claremont.

"Proceed and give me a report by tomorrow morning."

"Yes, sir."

Gracie fled the courtroom and walked rapidly down the stairs to the clerk's office. She called Brenda over to her desk and told her what they had to do.

The assistant's eyes widened. "Is that legal?" Brenda asked. "People can't volunteer for jury duty."

"We're not asking them to volunteer. They're being summoned and given the chance to fulfill their obligation during a different term of court. If the judge approves the process, then it's legal."

"But if a lawyer picking a jury finds out about this, they might object and cause a stink."

"If they want to do that in front of Judge Williams, I pity them," Gracie answered. "He'll chop off their head and make them carry it out of the courtroom."

"Is he that bad?"

Gracie thought about the anxiety she felt when the judge talked to Buddy about his mother. Judge Williams was a threat inside and outside the courtroom.

"I can't comment on that," she said. "Thank goodness we already have the list for the next term. I'll look it over and mark the names of people most likely to say yes."

"If we do that, how can we make sure we have a proper cross section of the jury pool? We can't just bring in retirees looking for something to do."

"Let's keep that in mind." Gracie paused. "And pray this works."

/ / /

With a certified copy of Judge Williams's order to send to Oklahoma in hand, Buddy drove Mayleah back to the sheriff's office.

"I'll contact Sheriff Blackstone," Mayleah said as Buddy pulled into the parking lot.

"Thanks, and I really appreciate what you did in court. It's uncommon for a judge to pivot so quickly."

"I told the truth, the whole truth, and nothing but the truth," the detective replied. "Why do you think Gracie Blaylock was in the courtroom?"

"I don't know. The county commissioners are too cheap to pay for a full-time court administrator, which means the clerk's office has to perform a lot of support duties for the judges. The local bar association would get behind Gracie if she made a push with the board of commissioners to create a new position. It needs to happen, but I guess she'd rather do the work than play politics."

/ / /

Sue Ellen Ford started crying when Buddy told her there was a chance they'd located her husband and little Jack.

"Where are they?" she asked between sniffles.

"Oklahoma, but don't mention it to anyone. I'm not sure who you can trust with the information."

"I understand. When will you know something for sure?"

"It should be soon. The detective working with me knows we have to act fast. If the police in Oklahoma find them, you'll need to fly out there immediately to pick up your son because Jackie will be in jail."

"Just let me know. My mother can take care of Emily."

Toward the end of the day, Buddy checked in with Jennifer to see how she was doing with her workload.

"I've finished scanning in the filing. It was exciting to read the order the judge signed in the Ford case. Do you think they'll catch the father?"

"That's the hope."

"I've learned so much already by working here," Jennifer said. "My family can't believe what I'm doing. Thank you again for hiring me."

"You're welcome." Buddy paused. "And make sure you don't talk about cases to anyone outside the office. The confidentiality rules regarding the attorney-client privilege cover you too."

"Yes, sir," Jennifer replied, but her face suddenly flushed.

"Have you talked about something you shouldn't?" Buddy asked sharply.

"Maybe," Jennifer said as she slowly shifted her feet. "My grandma knows Sue Ellen Ford's grandmother. They've been praying for the little boy to come home. My grandma and I are real close, and I wanted to encourage her."

"What did you tell her?"

Jennifer swallowed. "That her prayers might be answered soon."

"Anything else?"

"I guess I mentioned that the police thought the little boy was in Oklahoma."

Buddy's first thought was to terminate Jennifer on the spot. But he couldn't remember if he'd emphasized the attorney-client rule to her since she started working for him.

"They taught you about client confidentiality in your courses at the community college, didn't they?" he asked.

Tears filled Jennifer's eyes. "Yes, sir. I was so excited that I didn't think clearly. Am I in trouble?"

Jennifer's last question sounded so childlike that it reminded Buddy how young she was.

"I'm not going to fire you," he said. "But you'd better call your grandmother immediately and tell her not to say anything to anyone about the Ford case. If she's already done so, let me know."

"Yes, sir. I'll do it right now."

A few minutes later Jennifer reappeared in his doorway. Her face was extra pale. "Mr. Smith, my grandma sent an email to the prayer chain at her church repeating what I said."

"How big is the church?"

Jennifer told him. It was one of the three largest congregations in the area.

"What is a prayer chain?"

"A place to post requests that are sent to everyone who signs up to receive them."

Buddy clenched his jaw before responding. "Let's pray no one who receives this prayer chain mentions the situation to someone who tips off Jackie Ford."

THIRTEEN

FIVE MINUTES BEFORE GRACIE HAD TO LEAVE FOR SOFTball practice, she confirmed attendance of the twenty-fifth extra juror for the following week.

"We've done it," Gracie said to Brenda. "Marvin Quinn is going to report for duty on Monday."

"And I have another one," Brenda replied. "Rosa Estrada is coming."

"I don't know her."

"Her mother works with my mom. Rosa is in her early twenties and helps the male-female ratio along with providing ethnic diversity."

"Good," Gracie sighed. "We probably still have too many older white folks, but it's not nearly as big a deal for civil trials as criminal cases. If either one of the judges was handling criminal cases, I'm not sure this would work."

"It's a good thing so many people like you and were willing to say yes."

Her heart beating a little faster than normal, Gracie walked upstairs to the small courtroom. She peeked inside. Judge Williams wasn't there. Going down the hallway to Judge Claremont's chambers, she found Amanda at her desk.

"Is Judge Williams still here?" Gracie asked. "I need to talk to him about the jury pool for next week."

"No, but I have Judge Williams's cell phone number if you need to reach him."

"That's not necessary," Gracie replied. "But can you leave him a message that I was able to summon extra jurors for next week?"

"I can," Amanda said slowly. "But before he left, Judge Claremont told me Judge Williams was only going to handle bench trials in which the parties waive a jury."

"What?" Gracie sputtered. "One of my assistants and I just spent all afternoon contacting people to come in!"

"Sorry," Amanda apologized. "I didn't know."

The judges were the kings of the courthouse and could be arbitrary with impunity.

"Well, a lot of people are going to be sitting in the courtroom on Monday morning wondering why they're here," Gracie said.

She went downstairs and broke the news to Brenda, who didn't try to hide her shock. "Do you want me to come in tomorrow and try to call the new folks and tell them not to come?" the chief assistant asked.

"No, that makes it look like we made a mistake when we didn't."

After changing clothes, Gracie headed toward the ballfield. As she was pulling into the parking lot, her phone vibrated. It was Buddy Smith. Wanting a few minutes of peace and quiet, she thought about letting the call go to voice mail but answered.

"How are you?" the lawyer asked.

"Fine," Gracie said curtly.

"Wasn't that a great development in the Ford case? Mayleah Harkness worked her magic with Judge Williams."

"Yeah, I just hope they catch Jackie and lock him up."

"You're not going to mention what happened in court to anyone, are you?"

"No. I wouldn't want the word to get out and then someone warn Jackie."

"Right, I figured you'd make that connection. What was going on with you and Judge Williams this afternoon? It looked like we interrupted something."

"He had questions about the jury pool for next week. Look, I'm at the ballfield and don't have much time to talk."

"Okay, bye."

Laura Anselm was firing balls toward the backstop from the pitcher's mound. Gracie got out of her car and stretched. Taking the large bag of balls from the trunk of the car, she slung them over her shoulder and walked to the mound.

"Would you mind catching while I pitch?" Gracie asked Laura. "I need to burn off some steam. I won't be throwing anything except inside fastballs. You know, the kind of pitch that either hits the batter or makes them jump away from the plate."

Laura's eyes widened. "Yes, ma'am."

Buddy showered and prepared to go to Chris Henley's house for a cookout with a large group of friends, including Jason and Katie Long. Along the way, he picked up a container of potato salad from a local deli for his contribution to the food. As a bachelor,

Buddy could still get away with bringing a food offering that wasn't homemade. Chris's wife, Marissa, met him at the door and took the potato salad from him.

"This is perfect," said the auburn-haired woman with a pixie nose and freckles. "I didn't have time to make any, and this is way better than anything at the grocery store."

"Great."

"I wish Krista could join us sometime soon," Marissa said as she led the way to the kitchen at the rear of the house. "I enjoyed talking to her the one time we met. She has so many amazing stories of places she's been that I have to dream about until the kids are older."

"Uh, we broke up three months ago."

"What?" Marissa spun around and her mouth dropped open. "Did Chris know about it?"

Buddy couldn't lie to protect his friend. He'd called Chris seeking sympathy the day it happened. "Yeah, but he probably forgot to mention it."

"Hmm." Marissa sniffed.

"Krista and I were like ships that passed in the night but didn't end up docking at the same port," Buddy continued.

Marissa gave him a wry look. "If you can joke about it, the breakup must not have hurt too much," she said.

"You didn't see me right after it happened."

Even with two small children, Marissa could lay out a spread suitable for a *Southern Living* cover. A recent heat wave had abated, and there was already a small group of people standing in the shady backyard. Marissa gave Buddy a gentle push toward the double doors that opened onto the area.

"Hang out with your friends. And when it's time to cook the

steaks, make sure Chris doesn't turn them into beef jerky. He gets distracted and forgets to watch the meat."

It was a cloudy evening, and a nice breeze was blowing from the northeast. Jason and Katie Long were talking to another couple. The doctor saw Buddy and immediately came over to him.

"I was hoping you'd be here," Jason said. "And I promise not to talk business for more than a few minutes. I get annoyed when people corner me at social events and ask me to diagnose what's wrong with their kid who's at home sick with a babysitter. But can I ask you a few questions about what the insurance company lawyers are telling me in the malpractice case? You prepared our wills, so we have an attorney-client relationship, correct?"

"Yes."

For the next twenty minutes Jason talked to Buddy about the case filed against him. Jason was more friend than client. Buddy listened patiently and offered a few insights into the legal process.

"That helps," Jason said. "I don't want to ask the lawyers in Atlanta a stupid question."

Chris came over to them. "You've been standing over here by yourselves long enough for Jason to take your temperature and blood pressure."

"I'm leaving before that happens," the pediatrician said and moved on to another group of guests.

"I'm glad I wasn't wearing a blood pressure cuff when I was in front of Judge Williams the other day," Buddy said to Chris.

"He's been great to me," Chris replied. "I've won three straight cases."

Buddy shrugged. "You're a good lawyer. But the Vince Nelson factor may be in operation."

"Possibly." Chris grinned and then grew serious. "How is

Jason doing? I assume he was talking to you about the malpractice claim. We haven't met with him yet because the insurance company hasn't officially hired us as local counsel. The primary lawyers are with a firm in Atlanta and are super territorial."

"This is tough on him. He really cares about his patients and doesn't believe he made a mistake."

"Speaking of tough, Marissa raked me over the coals a few minutes ago for not telling her you broke up with Krista. She says you didn't seem too upset."

"I'm okay now," Buddy replied.

"I saw you having breakfast the other day at the Crossroads with Gracie Blaylock. Have you ever thought about asking her out? She's as local as they get, and there wouldn't be a need to bring her up to speed on your life story."

"My life story?"

"You know what I mean. It takes time to unpack the real person in any relationship. And she knows what it's like to be around a lawyer. Gracie is attractive and strikes me as a straightforward person."

"She certainly knows how to throw strikes," Buddy replied. He told Chris what he'd observed at the softball field.

"I'm just trying to steer you in a direction that might work out for you," Chris said. "And if I didn't mention Gracie, Marissa would be all over me later tonight. She was intrigued by Krista, but after she met Gracie at a political event a couple of years ago, she came home telling me the two of you would make a good couple. Women can pick up on these things."

"So I've heard."

The back door opened and Marissa called out to Chris: "Are you ready for the steaks?"

Chris gave her a thumbs-up.

"Your wife also believes I'm supposed to supervise the cooking of the steaks," Buddy said.

"She's right about that too."

/ / /

When the girls gathered in a circle to pray at the end of practice, Laura prayed, "Lord, please be with Coach Blaylock and take away the stress and tension she felt when she got here this afternoon. We don't know what's causing it, but you do. And help us do well in the tournament tomorrow."

The prayer made Gracie smile with appreciation. After the last girl left, she picked up the bag of softballs and carried it to her car. At home, she played in the backyard with Opie before bringing him into the house and feeding him supper. The unconditional love of the dog, expressed through dark eyes that were pools of devotion, was an added balm to her soul. Gracie fixed a salad and ate on the small deck at the rear of the house. Even though she was alone, a sweet presence enveloped her as the shadows lengthened.

The following morning the softball team assembled at the high school to depart in a caravan to the tournament. There were two ballfields at their destination, and the round-robin format required all four teams to play one another. Gracie's team and another team came into the third game with two wins and no losses. As the only undefeated teams, they would play for the championship.

The title game was set to start at 2:00 p.m. Milton County's opponent was the host team for the tournament, and there was a big crowd of local supporters in the stands. Gracie didn't consider herself a great speaker, but she had a couple of motivational talks patterned after what she'd heard as a teenager. Gracie's high school coach knew how to fire up a team. Gracie enjoyed telling the girls that nothing was impossible if they believed in one another and played with fire and passion. With loud whoops they ran out onto the field for the first inning.

Gracie had used her two best pitchers in the early games, which meant several backups, including Laura, would have to pitch. The game was tied 5–5 when Gracie moved Laura from shortstop to the pitcher's mound. Both teams were hitting well. Laura struck out the first batter she faced and pumped her fist in excitement. She walked the next batter. The next batter was one of the most skilled players on the other team. The girl completely missed one of the best rising fastballs Laura had ever thrown. Gracie, who was on the steps of the dugout, inched closer to the field to watch. Laura threw another rising softball that sailed over the catcher's head and allowed the runner on first to scamper down to second base. Her next pitch was a changeup. The batter swung and made solid contact. The ball rose higher and higher in the air and sailed over the fence in dead center field. It was the longest home run of the day. Gracie gasped at the mammoth hit. Laura hung her head as the girl rounded the bases and was mobbed by her teammates at home plate. The next batter ripped a triple down the third base line. By the time Laura recorded the final out, the score was 9–5.

"We'll get 'em back," Heidi said when the Milton County team filed slowly into the dugout.

Laura did her part by hitting a single and stealing both second and third. She made it home on a weak grounder to second base. But the game ended with Milton County on the short end of a 10–7 score.

"I lost the game for us in that one inning," Laura said morosely to Gracie after the presentation of the championship trophy to the winning team. "I was too pumped up after striking that girl out and lost control."

"That can be a challenge for anyone. Do you remember when I showed up for practice yesterday? It took thirty pitches for me to calm down. If I'd tried to pitch when I was so amped up, it wouldn't have gone well."

"Yeah, you were throwing so hard that it hurt my hand even wearing the catcher's mitt. Is everything okay for you now?"

"Nothing has changed except in here," Gracie answered, pointing to her heart. "Your prayer helped more than you know."

Laura perked up. "Thanks."

"Yes. And because you've got such a great heart, you're always going to be a winner. Gather the team together."

Laura stepped into the open space in front of their dugout. "Circle up!" she called out.

/ / /

Buddy spent most of Saturday morning doing something he rarely did: playing a round of golf. Sammy Landry called and offered to pay the greens fees as a way to reimburse Buddy for agreeing to help them find Reagan. They were joined by two of Sammy's friends. The conversation was light until Buddy and Sammy were walking up the twelfth fairway by themselves.

"The detective from the sheriff's department told Crystal that she was working with Gracie Blaylock and you," Sammy said. "I appreciate Gracie putting her weight behind the investigation to get things moving."

"I agree. And based on my experience with Detective Harkness in another case, she won't push the search for Reagan off to the side."

Sammy was silent for a moment before continuing. "I've been racking my brain trying to come up with anything that might explain why Reagan took off so suddenly. It's hard not to let your mind run wild. Like I told you the other day, we've had more spats with her than the other kids, but nothing crazy. She's headstrong, which I was proud of until this happened." Sammy took a few more steps. "I'm afraid that she's someplace where she can't call or communicate with anyone," the father said, voicing his greatest fear.

Buddy could feel the torment of Sammy's soul. "Sammy, I'll make this a priority as high as if Reagan were my own daughter."

"Thanks, that helps."

Buddy ended up shooting a low score. One of Sammy's friends claimed the long layoff probably enabled Buddy's body to forget any bad habits that usually plagued his game.

"It's a physiological fact," the friend said when Buddy crushed a drive past two fairway bunkers. "The signals from your brain to your muscles aren't getting scrambled."

"And you didn't cheat," Sammy said as they walked off the eighteenth green. "Or break one of my clubs."

Inside the clubhouse, Buddy took his cell phone from a locker where he'd left it so he wouldn't be interrupted. He had a text message from Mayleah Harkness asking him to call as soon as possible about the Ford case. Leaning his golf bag against the wall of the clubhouse, he placed a call to the detective, but it went to voice mail. As he drove away from the country club, Mayleah's name appeared on his phone.

"Sheriff Blackstone from Haskell County called me a couple of hours ago. They have the Ford boy."

"Yes!" Buddy pulled off onto a service road for the golf course and stopped. "What about Jackie?"

"Not sure of his condition. He's in the hospital."

"Did they have to shoot him?" Buddy asked in shock.

"No. The sheriff gave me a brief rundown. They went to the compound at the crack of dawn. A man came out and denied knowing anything about Jackson Ford or his son. Then the head guy showed up and threatened some kind of lawsuit, alleging violations of their civil rights. While the sheriff talked to the leader, a deputy walked around to the back of the property and found a tent pitched behind one of the buildings. A little boy stuck his head out the entrance. The deputy recognized him from the photo we sent. It was the Ford boy."

"That changed everything."

"Yes. The deputy didn't try to speak to the kid, but returned to the sheriff and told him what he'd seen. A few seconds later Jackie Ford came speeding around the building and sideswiped a patrol car. The officers pursued him with sirens blaring. About a mile from the compound, Ford ran off the road and flipped the car. When the officers came on the scene, they saw the boy. He hadn't been wearing a seat belt and bounced around inside the car when it wrecked. He seems to be okay except for some cuts and scrapes. Jackie was knocked unconscious and is in the hospital. The sheriff didn't know the extent of his injuries."

"I'll let Sue Ellen Ford know immediately so she can go out there. That boy needs his mother."

"I'm going too."

"You are?"

"Yes. I'll make sure everything goes smoothly and then swing by Tulsa."

FOURTEEN

THE FOLLOWING DAY GRACIE WAS EATING SUNDAY DINner with her family. The main meal was over, and they were having warm peach cobbler with ice cream for dessert when the house phone rang.

"Don't answer it," Gracie's father said. "Whatever it is can wait."

Ignoring her husband, Maxine placed her napkin beside her plate and went into the kitchen. An ancient phone hung on the wall near the refrigerator.

"Hello," she said.

There was a large open pass-through in the wall between the kitchen and the dining room, and Gracie could see her mother standing by the fridge with the phone in her hand.

"Hallelujah!" Maxine exclaimed. "Praise God forevermore!"

Everyone at the table turned and stared. The thought shot through Gracie's mind that there was good news about Reagan Landry. Tingles ran down her spine.

Maxine hung up the phone and returned to the dining room. "That was Valerie Cook. She's in charge of the prayer network at

Antioch Church. The police in Oklahoma have rescued the little Ford boy who was kidnapped by his daddy. His mother is on her way to pick him up."

"I hadn't heard anything about that," Gracie's father said.

"Gracie was right in the middle of it," Maxine said, pointing across the table.

"Not really," Gracie replied. "I told the mother to contact Buddy Smith and see if he would get involved. The real hero is a detective who recently joined the sheriff's department. She moved here from Oklahoma and helped tracked them through her contacts."

"Is that the same detective you mentioned the other day?" Lauren asked.

"Yes. I also passed on information to her about Reagan."

"All this gives me hope for Reagan too," Maxine said.

Gracie and Lauren helped their mother clean up while everyone else played with the grandchildren in the backyard.

Lauren was scraping food off plates into the kitchen trash can. "Tell Mama about your search for a husband," she said.

"We're at the beginning," Gracie replied succinctly.

"We posted a profile and a few photos of Gracie," Lauren explained. "Gracie got more responses than a rich heiress who works part-time as a fashion model. It took us hours to narrow over 350 candidates down to a dozen, and she cut the list to three." She turned to Gracie and asked, "Have you heard anything from them?"

"Not yet," Gracie said in a subdued voice.

"You responded, didn't you?" Lauren asked.

Gracie shrugged her shoulders. "A visiting judge threw me a major curveball about the jury pool for next week, and then I spent all day yesterday at a softball tournament. When I got home last night, all I wanted to do was take a bath and relax."

Lauren sniffed. "You're hopeless."

"That's not true," Maxine retorted. "When Gracie commits to something, she always follows through."

/ / /

First thing Monday morning Buddy told Jennifer the good news about little Jack. "Sue Ellen Ford traveled out there yesterday to pick up her son. Detective Harkness went ahead of her."

"That's a huge relief," the young secretary said with a sigh. "I did what you suggested and prayed that nothing bad would happen because of my big mouth."

"It's always good to learn a lesson without negative consequences."

"Oh, I've learned my lesson," Jennifer said, nodding vigorously. "I'm not going to talk about anything that happens here."

"Good," Buddy said.

Thirty minutes later Buddy received a call from Mayleah. "How's everything going?" he asked.

"The little boy is fine. He told his mother that he and his father were on a camping trip."

"And Jackie?"

"Fractured neck, but it didn't damage the spinal cord so there's no paralysis. He's conscious and in a halo."

"Did Sue Ellen try to see Jackie?"

"Yes, but the sheriff said no. I'll leave it to you to sort out their ongoing domestic status."

Buddy wasn't surprised. After the intense pressure of a

conflict lifted, the natural impulse in some people was to take steps toward a return to the illusion of normalcy.

"I'll suggest Sue Ellen follow up with a counselor and request a restraining order for when Jackie gets out."

/ / /

Wearing one of her nicer dresses, a light blue outfit with a cream-colored necklace, Gracie arrived early at the courthouse on Monday morning. As people streamed into the courtroom, Gracie greeted them. There were a lot of familiar faces. Women complimented Gracie on her outfit, and she asked how children or grandchildren were doing. Those who didn't want to be there demanded to know when they would be excused.

"That depends on the lawyers and judges," Gracie answered pleasantly. "If you have a reason that prevents you from serving, you should mention it when you have the opportunity to speak."

Judge Claremont strode into the courtroom.

"All rise!" the bailiff announced in a loud voice.

Gracie took her place at the front of the courtroom to the judge's right.

"Court will come to order!" the bailiff continued. "The Superior Court of Milton County is now in session, the Honorable Nathan Claremont presiding."

"Be seated," Judge Claremont said into the microphone on the bench in front of him. "Judge Bryant Williams will be hearing nonjury matters and bench trials in the small courtroom down the hall. If that applies to you, please proceed there for a separate calendar call."

As people streamed out of the courtroom, Judge Claremont

continued, "When the clerk calls your name, please come forward and take a seat in the jury box. We're going to pick the jury in two cases. The second jury will return at ten o'clock in the morning."

The first time she'd summoned jurors, Gracie was concerned her voice might crack. Now she spoke as clearly and confidently as she did when shouting instructions to a softball player in right field. When she finished, Gracie gathered her notes to leave. On her way out, she spoke with several jurors who had additional questions. She saw Mayleah Harkness sitting in the back row. The detective stood when Gracie approached. She was wearing dark slacks and a light-colored top. A service weapon was holstered on her right hip.

"What brings you here?" Gracie asked. "This is a week of civil trials."

"I had to escort a couple of boys to juvenile court and thought I'd stop by and see if you could talk for a few minutes."

Gracie fielded two more juror questions as they made their way down the stairs to the conference room they'd used a few days earlier.

"I assume you've heard the good news about the Ford boy," Mayleah said when she sat down. "His mother is flying back with him from Oklahoma today. I flew in late last night from Tulsa."

"You went out there?"

"Yes, to help her and take care of some personal business."

"I was with my family yesterday when my mother received a call about little Jack. That wouldn't have happened without your help."

"It's great when something works out quickly. Anyway, I wanted to talk to you about Reagan Landry," Mayleah continued.

"Before I flew to Oklahoma, I was able to check out a few of the contacts her mother provided from Reagan's social media connections."

"Anything important?" Gracie asked.

"Do you remember the woman in her twenties who frequently responded to Reagan's posts, the one holding the little white dog in her photo?"

Gracie had spent several hours poring over the information without identifying anything she thought might be important.

"Yes, she always went overboard with the use of emojis and exclamation marks. What is her name? Katrina or Katarina."

"Katrina Caldwell," Mayleah said. "She describes herself as a twenty-five-year-old unmarried female who lives in Atlanta, works for an internet marketing firm, and loves her little dog. But I'm not sure that's her real name. When I ran a search through a criminal database, the name turned up as an alias used by a woman who'd been arrested in the metro Atlanta area a couple of times on drug charges, including the sale and distribution of methamphetamines."

"What's the woman's real name?"

"She used multiple aliases, but her real name is Patricia Nichols. When I checked the aliases on social media, every one of them had the same photo of a young woman with the little white dog." Mayleah paused. "And there was also a common thread in her comments on the Instagram pages for women Reagan's age and younger. After being active and friendly with them, Nichols mentions wanting to meet. She even offers to come to where the contact lives and do something the girl has indicated is a favorite activity. It could be anything from shopping to a music concert."

"Reagan likes country music," Gracie said. "I read how excited she was when she went to an outdoor event in Macon a few months ago."

"That's right. And in a response to Reagan, Nichols mentioned a friend who could get tickets to a much bigger show in Atlanta."

"When was that concert?"

"Two days after Reagan disappeared."

Gracie felt like a large stone had landed on her chest. She took a deep breath and exhaled, but the heaviness didn't budge. "What do you think?" she asked.

"I spoke to the sheriff about it first thing this morning, and he's on board for a full-blown investigation."

"Okay," Gracie managed.

"And try not to let your imagination run wild," Mayleah continued. "I know that's hard, but I've learned that if I focus on the things I do know, it helps me think clearly and not become distracted."

"I'll try. Is there anything you want me to do?"

"The same thing you did to help the Ford boy. That turned out well."

"I didn't do anything except put Sue Ellen in touch with Buddy Smith."

"You prayed, didn't you?"

Buddy cut short a phone call with an existing client so he could take a call from Mayleah, who gave him an update on Reagan Landry.

"I already filled Gracie Blaylock in on the details," Mayleah said when she finished. "I saw her this morning at the courthouse."

"What are the next steps regarding Reagan?"

"See what else I can find out about Patricia Nichols. I don't have contacts in Atlanta. Do you know anyone in law enforcement with the Atlanta Police Department or the Fulton County Sheriff's Department?"

"No," Buddy replied. "But I know a couple of lawyers who might suggest someone. I'll reach out to them. One is a former prosecutor; the other is a defense lawyer."

"Prosecutors have a lot more friends among police than defense lawyers."

"Maybe, but this defense lawyer puts on a huge barbecue every year and raises a ton of money for police causes."

"Okay, let me know what you find out."

"How was your side trip to Tulsa?"

"Good and bad."

Buddy waited, but Mayleah didn't elaborate. Instead, she changed the subject: "Do you ever go to the softball games for Gracie's team?"

"No, although fast-pitch softball is a big deal in Milton County. The high school team has been good for a long time, and everyone loves a winner," he answered.

Buddy got the hint. "Would you like to go?" he asked. "But it can be hot at those games. They start before the sun goes down."

"That's fine. I went to one recently and enjoyed it."

Buddy chuckled at the contrast between Mayleah and Krista, who considered sweating outside the walls of a sauna or on a sandy beach to be a sin.

"Sounds good," he said. "And Gracie will appreciate the support for the team."

Later in the day Buddy stopped by Millie's desk to obtain

a financial total. When she had given him the information he needed, he asked, "What did you think of Mayleah Harkness, the detective who stopped by the office last week?"

"Already?" Millie's eyes widened. "That was fast. Krista has been out of the picture for how long? Two months?"

"Three months," Buddy replied. "But don't go there yet with Mayleah. All we've done so far is spend time together working on the Ford case and the new file I opened for the Landry family."

"Okay."

"Oh, and she offered to help me find Elise."

"Did you tell her about the money your father paid?"

"No."

"No dinners together?"

"Not yet. We're going to a girls' softball game on Friday night. That hardly qualifies as a date."

"If she wants to share popcorn at the ballfield, it's a date."

A thunderstorm cut short softball practice. When the first large drops began to fall, the girls hustled off the field. Gracie barely avoided getting soaked as she ran to her car. By the time she arrived at home, the storm had passed, and the sun peeked back through the clouds. The temperature had dropped by fifteen degrees, and Gracie decided to take Opie out for a walk. The dog leapt up and down in excitement when he saw her take the leash from its hook on the wall near the back door.

"Yes, we're going on a walk," Gracie said as she attached the leash to the dog's collar. "But you're not going to jump into any mud puddles."

Still wearing her ball cap, Gracie left her neighborhood and turned down Franklin Street. Plenty of moisture remained on the leaves of the large trees, and an occasional drop fell on her or Opie, whose nose was in full operation as he sniffed every scent he could extract from the late-afternoon air. As she came closer to town, she passed the bed-and-breakfast where Judge Williams was staying. The judge's car was parked beside the house. Two blocks later she saw Beatrice Smith in the front yard picking up small limbs blown from the trees by the storm. She was wearing pink-and-white gloves along with a nice pair of slacks and a blouse not suitable for yard work. Gracie called out a greeting and Opie bounded up the steps from the sidewalk onto the yard.

"I'm leaving for dinner in a little while," Beatrice said. "And I didn't want this trash in the yard."

"If you can dog-sit Opie for a few minutes, I'll do it for you," Gracie offered. "I came straight from the softball field, so I haven't had a shower yet."

"Oh, it can wait—"

"I insist." Gracie took the limbs from Beatrice's hands and gave her the leash.

"Sit on the porch, pat Opie on the head, and make sure I don't miss anything. Where do you want me to toss the limbs?"

"There's a compost pile behind the house. If you can put them there, Buddy can grind them up in our old chipper."

It took four trips to clean up the front yard. One limb was so large, Gracie had to drag it. It had fallen to the ground within a foot of the left corner of the porch.

"This could have done some damage," she said when she picked up the end that had splintered from the trunk.

"Yes, I heard it snap."

Gracie returned from her fourth trip and climbed the porch steps. Opie was lying contentedly at Beatrice's feet.

"I think he likes your porch," Gracie said. "There are more limbs in the backyard. Could I help with that too?"

"No thanks. I'll do it tomorrow morning when I check on my plants. Did any limbs come down at your house?"

"I didn't check. As soon as I got home, I grabbed Opie's leash. It's been a hectic day at the courthouse."

"Did you see Buddy?"

"No, I don't think he had any cases on the calendar."

"He stays busy. Maybe too busy." Beatrice leaned over and scratched Opie's neck. "I know you and Buddy have been friends for a long time. I don't know anyone who prays for him and Elise except me and you. It's been hard on me, especially recently."

The ache in Gracie's heart for Beatrice that she felt at the Crossroads with Buddy returned. "Could I pray for you?" she asked.

"Yes."

"I mean right now."

Beatrice's eyes widened. Gracie knew praying on the front porch likely wasn't part of the kind woman's religious world.

"Okay," Beatrice said slowly. "I usually pray on my knees in my bedroom."

"Just relax in your rocker, and I'll stand beside this column. You don't even have to close your eyes."

Gracie bowed her head. Her first prayer was a short, silent one for herself—that she would say the right thing. She began by asking the Lord to direct Buddy's steps and quoted portions of verses she'd memorized. Then she moved into praying directly for Beatrice. Gracie chose her words carefully so as not to reveal that she knew much more than the older woman realized about Buddy, Rascal, Amber, and Elise. But she didn't shy away from addressing the pain in Beatrice's heart. At that point her prayer came forth with greater liberty and conviction. Gracie didn't stop until her spirit was clear.

"God, as you restore and heal Beatrice's heart, may the reality of your amazing love for her be a constant companion. In Jesus' name, amen."

Gracie opened her eyes and saw that Beatrice was staring at her.

"I closed my eyes for most of it," Beatrice quickly said, "but I had to take a peek at the end to make sure your face hadn't started glowing. That was so beautiful and personal. I wish I'd recorded it on my phone so I could share it with Buddy."

"Don't be surprised if he asks to pray for you sometime soon."

"That will be a day to mark on my calendar. Not to say anything negative about Buddy. He's been wonderful to me before and after his father passed."

A car slowed in front of the house, turned into the driveway, and stopped. Gracie stared at it for a moment. When the driver got out she felt her cheeks grow hot. It was Judge Bryant Williams.

"I'm sure you've met Judge Williams," Beatrice said, getting up from the rocker and handing the leash to Gracie. "He's staying down the street with the Hunts. Vivian fixes breakfast, but Bryant is on his own for supper. We talked the other day when he was out for a walk, and I agreed to go with him to Morgan's one evening, just so he'll know one of his options."

Morgan's Steakhouse was the most expensive restaurant in town. The interior was dark, the tablecloths white, the steaks aged. Gracie didn't say anything as the judge walked over to the porch steps. Williams was wearing an open-collared print shirt and white pants. Opie emitted a low growl.

"Madam Clerk," the judge said. "You have a way of turning up all over town."

"Gracie has been a friend since she and my son were in school together," Beatrice said.

The judge bowed his head toward Beatrice. "Good evening. Are you ready to be my tour host?" he asked.

"As soon as I get my purse."

Beatrice left Gracie and the judge alone on the porch. The spiritual high Gracie felt moments ago was gone, replaced by an intense desire to protect Buddy's mother.

"Beatrice Smith is one of the most gracious women in Clarksburg," Gracie said with a slight edge in her voice.

"And I'm looking forward to finding out more about her," the judge replied affably. "She was kind enough to agree to join me for dinner."

Gracie suspected her face revealed her disapproval.

"Judge Claremont's first case finished around five o'clock," Williams continued. "I was able to rocket through my calendar, so there's a chance I'll be available for jury trials on Wednesday. Your last-minute efforts to secure more jurors may not have been in vain."

"That's good," Gracie said curtly.

Beatrice returned. "Ready," she said to the judge, then turned to Gracie. "Thanks so much for stopping by. You did so much more than pick up a few limbs for me."

FIFTEEN

AFTER WATCHING THE TAILLIGHTS OF THE JUDGE'S CAR recede in the distance, Gracie wasn't in the mood to return home and think about dating a stranger. However, Lauren's loving yet insistent voice compelled her to log on to the dating site and respond to Devin, the accountant; David, the administrative pastor; and Daniel, the manager of the facility for special-needs adults. Daniel had the initial advantage. Any man who served others for a living and owned two beautiful golden retrievers had a big heart. And Opie would love having playmates. But Daniel's life was filled to the brim, and Gracie wondered how he could carve out time for a relationship with a woman who lived over two hours away. As she stared at the screen, she faced the fact that Daniel had signed up for the dating service because he wanted to find a mate. She pressed the send button.

The following morning Gracie added Beatrice Smith to her prayer list. She'd never prayed for a woman in her late sixties to date the right man and steer clear of the wrong ones. Arriving at the courthouse, she had an email from Amanda Byrnes confirming that Judge Williams would be holding jury trials the remainder of the week beginning Wednesday. Gracie called Brenda over and showed her the message.

"I could never do your job," Brenda said as she shook her head. "Dealing with all the changes would drive me crazy. People who think we gossip and drink coffee all day have no idea what we put up with."

Gracie was processing her mail when Mayleah came into the clerk's office. "Can we talk?" the detective asked.

"Yes."

They went into the nearby conference room.

"I have more info about Reagan," Mayleah said.

After the recent good news about Sue Ellen Ford, Gracie felt a surge of hopeful anticipation.

"Now that the sheriff has authorized an investigation, I've researched the rest of the people from Reagan's social media accounts. Most came up clean, but there were four more with criminal records in other states."

"What kind of crimes?" Gracie asked.

"Domestic violence for a husband and wife who live in Louisiana. They got in a fight and both were found guilty and received probation."

"What was their connection to Reagan?"

"A mutual friend. The only direct communication with Reagan came via comments when she posted a photo of herself at Jekyll Island with her family over spring break. The couple had vacationed there in the past and mentioned they'd stayed at the same hotel."

"That sounds innocent."

"I agree, but I made a note of it." Mayleah checked her phone before continuing, "Then there was a man named Earvin Parish who lives in Chattanooga and has multiple arrests for disorderly conduct, assault on a police officer, and petty theft. He's twenty-two years old and also has a record of criminal charges that occurred when he was a juvenile. He uses the nickname 'Easy' on his Instagram account. He's a nice-looking young man who shared Reagan's interest in music. He commented on three of her photos and told her she was cute."

Gracie remembered the young man. "Yes," she said. "Is he the one who owned the ski boat?"

"Correct. I followed up on that, and the photo he posted was from an advertisement in a magazine. There's no record of boat ownership for him in the Tennessee records. All that's titled in his name is a ten-year-old Honda Accord."

Gracie leaned back in her chair. "Lying is common online."

"True. Some innocent, some sinister."

"What's next with him?"

"I sent emails to the Chattanooga police regarding Earvin Parish. I don't have easy access to anyone with inside information. And I can't claim Reagan is in grave danger even though she might be."

"What does that mean for the investigation?"

"I have to keep grinding."

"Thanks so much for coming by to give me an update."

Mayleah nodded. "Sure. And I'll see you Friday night at the softball game."

"Since you're coming to another game, would you be able to come a little early to speak to the team? The girls would enjoy a pep talk from someone other than me, and then we can grab a bite to eat afterward. We don't have to go back to the Southside Grill—"

"I'll be with Buddy Smith," Mayleah said with a smile. "It was my idea to go to the game, and he accepted. He said the teams have won a lot of games going back to when you played in high school."

"Uh, yeah. Like you heard the other night at the grill, we've had a lot of good players over the years."

"One other question," Mayleah said. "Did Buddy's high school girlfriend, the mother of his daughter, play softball?"

"Just for a short time."

"Was she any good?"

"She was okay. But she didn't do anything special that I can remember."

Mayleah tapped the edge of the table a couple of times with her right index finger. "Do you think Buddy's daughter might be a softball player?"

Gracie didn't immediately answer. "It's possible," she said slowly. "But the percentage of high school girls who play competitive fast-pitch softball is very small."

"Amber grew up in a town where it's a popular sport, and it wouldn't be surprising if she encouraged her daughter to play. The big role softball has around here made me think about activities that Amber might take with her when she left town. But it sounds like she was more boy crazy than committed to sports."

"That's true," Gracie said more forcibly than she intended. "I mean, we were all interested in boys."

"Did you ever date Buddy in high school?"

Gracie felt herself blush. She knew the detective was trained in observing people's reactions and hoped Mayleah had turned off her investigative switch. "No, and I think Amber was his first serious girlfriend."

"Okay, I'll see you at the game," Mayleah said.

/ / /

Buddy had a late-afternoon appointment with Sue Ellen Ford for a debrief upon her return from Oklahoma. Sheriff Blackstone told her that Jackie was planning on leaving Red Hill, and they'd stopped him just in time. While she was in Buddy's office, he called a counselor who also worked for the battered women's shelter. The counselor scheduled an appointment for Sue Ellen and also recommended a child psychologist for little Jack and Emily.

"I guess I should be willing to talk to someone," Sue Ellen said when the call ended. "I mean, I have my mom, but if the woman is someone you trust, I'll do it."

"Yes. I think it will help more than you might think, for both you and the kids."

"Okay," Sue Ellen said with a nod. "I'm sure you're right. And thanks for all you've done. If you hadn't agreed to help, I don't know where my son would be today. Seeing him at home, safe in his own bed, makes me so thankful."

The young mother suddenly choked up.

"You're welcome," Buddy said with a smile.

Buddy stopped off at his mother's house on his way home. He hadn't seen her for several days. She answered the door wearing a nice dress.

"Are you going out with friends?" he asked. "I don't want to hold you up."

"My dinner plans fell through a few minutes ago, and I haven't had a chance to change. Come in."

They made their way to the kitchen.

"I thought your supper club with the Mitchells and the Barringtons was on Thursday nights," Buddy said.

"Yes, but my dinner this evening was with Bryant Williams."

Buddy was reaching for a clean glass in the cabinet near the refrigerator and stopped. "The visiting judge?"

"Yes, he's staying at the Hunts' bed-and-breakfast. Since they don't serve supper, I've been showing him places to eat."

Buddy placed an empty glass on the counter and faced her. "Are you going on dates with the judge?"

"I don't think so," his mother replied. "His family is in South Georgia, and he's up here alone for at least a month."

"He's not married, is he?"

"Of course not! Why are you questioning me like this?"

"I've appeared in front of him a couple of times and wasn't impressed with him. Maybe he's a nice guy away from the courthouse, but he suffers from a serious case of black-robe-itis."

"What's that?"

"A form of arrogance that hits a lawyer when he or she puts on a judicial robe and suddenly has a lot of power. It affects both men and women."

Beatrice sat down at the kitchen table. "Well, if you have to know, he's a widower whose wife died from cancer about a year before your daddy's heart attack. And I'm just being nice to him while he's here. He had to cancel tonight because of a jury trial that ran longer than he expected. You may think Bryant has a judicial disease, but he's been a perfect gentleman with me."

Buddy shrugged. "It's really none of my business if he takes you out to dinner."

"I'm glad you feel protective, but spending time with Bryant has helped get my mind off the situation with your father."

"And I shouldn't put you under a microscope. I have a date with someone new Friday night. I'm taking a detective who works for the sheriff's department to a summer league softball game. It was her idea to go see the team Gracie Blaylock coaches."

"What's her name?"

"Mayleah Harkness. She works cases having to do with kids."

Beatrice nodded. "I heard good things about her from someone at my bridge club who volunteers at the juvenile court."

"She's even offered to help me find Elise, even though there's no crime involved."

"Really?" Beatrice raised her eyebrows. "You've always said the police wouldn't get involved."

"That could be changing."

Beatrice ran her fingers through her hair. "I'm glad you're supporting Gracie's team. She stopped by the other evening when she was walking her dog and prayed the most beautiful prayer. It was like the Lord told her exactly what to say."

"Maybe she had a little help," Buddy replied, thinking about his breakfast conversation with the clerk.

"That's what I mean. I wish I'd recorded it on my phone or written it down, but it happened right before Bryant and I went to Morgan's Steakhouse."

"Who paid for dinner at Morgan's?"

"He did. No more questions!"

"Okay." Buddy held up his hands in surrender.

Friday afternoon Gracie checked to see if she'd received anything from Daniel before driving to the softball field. Over the past few days, the two of them had exchanged longer and longer emails. Gracie was surprised by how much she enjoyed sharing with him.

It also was fun reporting back to Lauren. Today there was nothing new in her in-box.

It was a cloudy day with the threat of a thunderstorm. The visiting team had already arrived at the ballfield. Most of the girls were younger than the players on Gracie's team, and she began revising her roster so that some of the second-stringers would have an opportunity to start. If a team had a ten-run advantage after three innings, the league had a mercy rule that suspended the game and awarded the victory to the team in the lead. Gracie didn't want the visitors to drive all the way to Milton County for three innings of play. As soon as Laura arrived, Gracie called the second baseman over and patted her on the back.

"Warm up on the practice mound," Gracie said. "You're going to be our starting pitcher."

"You want me to start?" Laura asked in surprise.

"Yes, just keep the ball in the strike zone and don't try to overpower the hitters."

As game time drew near, Gracie glanced up in the bleachers. Buddy and Mayleah were sitting beside each other. Mayleah had left her Western gear in her closet and was wearing shorts, a yellow top, and sandals. She and Buddy each had a bag of popcorn. Buddy motioned for Gracie to come over, and they climbed down from the bleachers.

"Coach, what should we expect tonight?" he asked.

"The other team has some younger girls, so I'm giving our backups a chance to start."

"They have a decent pitcher," Buddy replied. "I watched her warming up. The ball really popped when it hit the catcher's mitt."

"Thanks for the scouting report," Gracie said as she adjusted the ball cap on her head. "And I appreciate you coming out to support the team."

"Is Laura going to be the starting pitcher?" Mayleah asked.

Gracie was impressed with the detective's memory for names. "Yes, she's worked hard and earned it."

Buddy's assessment of the opposing pitcher proved accurate. The lanky girl retired all three batters she faced in the bottom of the first inning, but the Milton County team broke through in the fourth inning and scored three runs, making the score 3–2.

"Gracie will bring out one of her better pitchers in the top of the fifth and shut down the other team," Buddy said.

"The girl who's been pitching is solid."

"And it's time to make a switch before she makes a mistake."

Buddy's prediction that Gracie would change pitchers proved correct.

"How did you know that?" Mayleah asked when a new pitcher jogged out to the mound.

"Besides my superb legal skill, I'm a girls' softball genius," Buddy answered. "Also, during the last inning I noticed that a new pitcher was warming up along the right field line behind the home team dugout."

Mayleah laughed. The game ended in a 4–2 victory for Milton County.

"I'm hungry," Buddy said. "A small bag of popcorn wasn't a meal for me. Have you been to Smoke, the barbecue place on South Hamilton Street?"

"No, but whatever you suggest is fine with me."

This time of the evening on a Friday night, the dinner crowd at Smoke had thinned out, and there were more people drinking beer than eating pork. Buddy requested a table in a small overflow room that connected to the main dining area. It was much quieter than the rest of the restaurant.

"This is nice," Mayleah said.

"They don't open it during lunch, but the whole place was packed a couple of hours ago. A barbecue dinner on Friday night is the preferred way to end the week for a lot of people."

They ordered their food. Both Buddy and Mayleah selected the salad with burnt ends, but Buddy added a bowl of Brunswick stew and insisted Mayleah order a cup to sample.

"You'll thank me later," he said when the waitress left.

Buddy took a sip of water. They sat in silence. Mayleah didn't seem in a hurry to initiate a conversation.

Buddy cleared his throat. "This is the first time we haven't had a business reason to meet," he said. "What would you like to talk about?"

Mayleah smiled. "You can volunteer information, or I can interrogate you. Which do you prefer?"

"Interrogation," Buddy replied. "But only after you read me my Miranda rights."

At that moment the waitress arrived with the Brunswick stew. Buddy waited for Mayleah to sample it.

"This is good," she said. "There's a nice mix of heat and sweet."

"Another reason to like Milton County," Buddy replied.

Mayleah ate another bite before laying her spoon on the paper place mat. "I'm still not clear about how your parents felt about you and your daughter. How did they react? Did they offer to step in and help you and Amber as a young couple, or were they relieved that she left town?"

Buddy knew any chance of developing a relationship with

Mayleah Harkness would require honesty about Amber and Elise.

"That's been coming to light over the past few weeks in ways I'd never suspected." Buddy paused to take a sip of water. "Only a few people know what I'm about to tell you, so please keep it between us. But if you're going to help me find Elise, you need the full story."

Mayleah's normally inscrutable demeanor cracked when Buddy told her about discovering the envelope of checks in his mother's basement.

"That's incredible," she said. "And your mother never found out about this while your father was alive?"

"No, which has been very hard on her. And me."

As he related his mother's unfulfilled desire to know her first grandchild, Buddy saw Mayleah's compassion come to the surface.

"I'm totally in to help you for as long as I'm around to do so," she said.

"Are you thinking about moving?"

Mayleah picked up a napkin and held it to her lips for a moment before saying, "Since you poured out your heart to me, it's only fair to let you know there's a chance I might leave Milton County."

"You met with your ex-husband when you flew to Oklahoma, didn't you?"

"Yes, and we're talking to each other."

"We're talking to each other too."

"Yes," Mayleah replied with a slight smile. "But it's not the same. After my recent conversations with Clay, you and I should keep things on the friends level."

Buddy understood the words but was confused because Mayleah had been the one to initiate the date. If she wasn't interested in him, why would she ask to go out with him? Then he remembered Millie Graham's words.

"We didn't share popcorn at the game," he said.

"What?"

"If this was really a date, we would have shared a popcorn. You wanted your own bag."

"Yeah, and that's exactly what I was thinking," Mayleah replied with a grin. "If I didn't believe I was supposed to consider reconciling with Clay, I would share a bag of popcorn with you any day of the week."

Buddy knew Mayleah meant her statement as a compliment, but it stung.

"What would you like for dessert?" he asked. "I always save a corner of my stomach for something sweet. Either the peach cobbler or banana pudding is good."

"I'd like peach cobbler."

Buddy ordered the banana pudding. They shared.

SIXTEEN

DURING SUNDAY DINNER AT HER PARENTS' HOUSE, Gracie was able to provide Lauren enough additional tidbits of information about Daniel to satisfy her sister's curiosity.

"Svoboda," Lauren said, repeating Daniel's last name. "Where does that come from?"

"*Svoboda* means 'freedom' in Czech," Gracie answered. "His family immigrated to the US in the late 1930s before World War II. His grandfather was smart enough to see the problems coming with the Nazis and got out. Daniel has visited the Czech Republic and speaks some of the language."

"Gracie Svoboda," Lauren slowly intoned. "It would take some getting used to. At least I know what to buy you for Christmas this year."

"What?"

"Czech language lessons. You can start out listening to an app on your phone and then graduate to a personal tutor." Lauren paused. "No, the tutor won't be necessary because Daniel will want to handle that himself."

"He'll have to get used to my Georgia accent first. He's lived in Atlanta for six years, but before that he spent most of his life in Connecticut."

"When are you going to talk to him on the phone or meet him in person?"

"Soon," Gracie replied vaguely.

"What about Devin and David? Have you let them know they didn't win the Gracie Blaylock lottery?"

"Not exactly. I've traded a couple of emails with each of them. They both seem nice. Should I stop communicating with them?"

"No, no, and no," Lauren answered. "You only go exclusive when you're sure you want to burn your other bridges."

"What about Czech lessons?"

"It's six months till Christmas. Keep your options open."

Before Gracie left, her mother pulled her aside in the kitchen. "You're the clerk of court," Maxine said, "but Lauren still wants to boss you around like she did when she first learned to talk and tried to make you play her way. You were always the accommodating big sister."

"Some things don't change." Gracie lifted one shoulder in a small shrug. "How did you manage Lauren, Noah, and me at that age?"

Her mother smiled. "One day at a time. Anyway, I'm praying for you."

"It's been hectic on all fronts. At work, the softball team, and this online matchmaking thing." Gracie lowered her voice so that none of her family who remained in the dining room could hear. "And I've met several times with Mayleah Harkness, the detective who's looking for Reagan. There's nothing specific to report yet, but especially pray about that."

"I will."

Later that afternoon Gracie received a phone call from the detective. "I hope I'm not interrupting anything," Mayleah said.

"No, I'm driving home after dinner with my family."

"I'm on the road too. I spent the day with my sister and her family in Atlanta. After leaving her house, I decided to do some reconnaissance on Patricia Nichols."

"You found out where she lives?"

"Maybe. Through the database available at the sheriff's office, I found an apartment address she's used at some point in the past. The complex wasn't far out of the way. When I knocked on the door, a guy in his forties opened it. I asked if Patricia was there, and he told me he didn't know anyone with that name. Something about the way he answered made me suspicious, so I didn't leave. I moved my truck but kept the entrance to the apartment in sight. Five minutes later a woman came out. Even from a distance I could tell it was Nichols. She had shoulder-length black hair and was carrying the little white dog whose picture turns up in her Instagram and social media accounts."

Gracie had arrived home but stayed in the car.

"And she wasn't alone," Mayleah continued. "There were two other women with her. Nichols looked a little bit older than the other two, who were in their late teens or early twenties."

"Was one of them Reagan?" Gracie asked.

"No, but I took photos of Nichols and both of the women with her."

"Did anything look out of place or odd about how they interacted?"

"They seemed relaxed and happy. After a few minutes they took the dog for a walk to a common area at the apartment complex. They sat on a bench while the dog sniffed around in the grass. I stayed until they returned to the apartment. Next step is to try to identify the women with Nichols. Also, there's a chance Nichols is using a different name, so when the man who answered the door claimed he didn't know her, he may have been telling the truth."

"I'm not following you."

"She could be using an alias, as she does on social media, without telling everyone in her life."

Such a high level of deception was completely foreign to Gracie's world. "Have you told Buddy about this?"

"No. I called, but he didn't answer. I have a busy Monday morning, but I'll try to work on this tomorrow afternoon."

"Okay, thanks."

"And I enjoyed the softball game. Next time I'll probably come alone and try to spend some time with the girls."

"Buddy didn't like it?"

"No, he gave me expert commentary."

No more explanation came, leaving Gracie wondering about Mayleah and Buddy as a potential couple.

"Talk soon," Mayleah said and ended the call.

Gracie went inside the house and fed Opie an early supper. While the dog wolfed down his food, she offered up another prayer for Reagan. To keep from thinking about Buddy and Mayleah as a couple, she turned on her laptop and did a quick search of Czech language apps.

Buddy often spent Sunday evening working at the office. Taking a break, he opened the desk drawer where he kept the canceled checks his father gave Amber. Even though he'd memorized the details, it had been awhile since he'd looked at them. He pulled out the check endorsed in Chattanooga.

Before moving to Milton County, Amber's family lived in a small town near Chattanooga. Buddy knew the place had an odd name but couldn't remember what it was. Turning on his computer, he searched for towns near Chattanooga. As soon as the name Soddy-Daisy popped up, he remembered that was where the Melrose family lived. The specific check was negotiated five years earlier at a branch of the Citizens Tri-County Bank. Buddy confirmed that the Chattanooga bank had a branch in Soddy-Daisy.

Switching screens to the program he used to locate people, Buddy entered the name Melrose and Soddy-Daisy. His heart skipped a beat when a John David Melrose appeared. Amber's dad's name was John, but this John Melrose had been dead for twelve years. Based on the date of birth, the man could have been Amber's grandfather or great-uncle. Buddy continued checking. If he included Chattanooga, the number of people with Melrose as a surname exceeded one hundred. None of them were a match. Returning to the check, he stared at the endorsement. As was the case with the check presented at the First National Bank of Milton County, a negotiable instrument payable to "Bearer" in the amount of $10,000 should have been a memorable event at the bank. It might be worth contacting someone at Citizens Tri-County Bank to see if they remembered anything about it. His cell phone vibrated. It was Mayleah.

"You're working late," the detective said when Buddy answered.

"It's not that late," he replied, then paused. "How do you know I'm working?"

"I'm outside in your parking lot."

Buddy went to the front door and unlocked it. Mayleah was sitting in an unmarked car.

"I'm the one working late," the detective said when he approached the car. "I won't get off until midnight."

"I saw you called earlier and was going to get back to you tomorrow. Would you like a cup of coffee?"

"Sure."

Buddy led the way to the former kitchen that served as his break room. He glanced at the clock on the microwave. It was 9:15 p.m.

"Your choice." Buddy motioned to a rack that held individual cup options.

"I took a detour on my way back from Atlanta earlier today and checked out a potential lead in the Reagan Landry case," Mayleah said, removing the cup of fresh brew from the machine.

Buddy listened as Mayleah told him about Patricia Nichols. "Can I see the photos you took?" he asked.

Mayleah opened an album on her phone and handed the phone to him. "The first batch are from Nichols's Instagram and various social media pages. The next group includes the women at the apartment complex."

There was nothing overtly sinister about Nichols's social media picture. She was wearing a dark top and holding a small white curly-haired dog with a red collar. The dog's mouth was open, which made it look like it was smiling. The most distinctive aspect of the Nichols picture was a thick gold chain around her neck.

The first photo Mayleah took outside the apartment was from such a long distance that it was impossible to distinguish much except that there were three females accompanied by a white dog. Buddy couldn't tell which figure was Nichols. The photos became progressively better. By the time the women were sitting on the bench in the grassy area, Nichols's face could be clearly seen. She was wearing the same gold chain as in her social media photo. In the next picture, the young woman sitting in the middle had turned her head so that her face was visible. Buddy sharply sucked in a breath.

"She looks like Amber," he said. "That might be Elise."

"Which one?" Mayleah asked.

Buddy didn't immediately respond. Instead, he increased the size of the picture so that the young woman's face filled the entire screen. He studied her nose, the shape of her mouth, the color of her wavy brown hair. But the feature that grabbed his attention the most was her eyes and the slightly detached, amused expression that was Amber's trademark look. He stared for several seconds, then handed the phone to Mayleah.

"The one in the middle," he said.

Mayleah looked at her phone for a couple of seconds. "She could be the right age, but there's no way for anyone to give an opinion without a comparable photo of Amber from that time in her life."

Buddy turned around in his chair toward his credenza. Opening the bottom drawer, he took out the school yearbook from his senior year. He turned to the senior pictures and found Amber. Four other pages in the book were tabbed with faded Post-it slips.

He passed the yearbook to Mayleah. "That's a picture from about the time she found out she was pregnant. Other photos of her are marked with tabs."

Mayleah flipped the pages of the yearbook with one hand and held her phone with the other. Buddy waited.

Finally, the detective looked up. "I'm not seeing a family resemblance," she said.

"What?" Buddy exclaimed. "The expression on the girl's face and the way Amber looked at the camera in the senior picture are identical. They could be twins!"

Mayleah returned the yearbook to Buddy. "I'm sorry. It doesn't click with me. If these two women were side by side in a lineup, I wouldn't guess they were related. The hair color is similar, but that can be true for thirty percent of the women in America. And wavy hair can be natural or artificial. The eyes aren't the same shape. Neither is the mouth. The noses are close."

"I'm sure that's Elise," Buddy replied emphatically. "I'd like someone else to give an opinion."

"Gracie Blaylock?"

"Yeah. She and Amber weren't close friends, but she'll pick up on what I'm seeing."

Mayleah began touching the screen on her phone.

"What are you doing?" Buddy asked.

The detective didn't look up. "Calling Gracie."

Wearing her favorite pair of blue-and-gold pajamas, the school colors of Milton County High, Gracie curled up on the couch with a bowl of buttered popcorn beside her. She was watching a suspenseful movie, and when the villain suddenly appeared on the screen, she jumped and knocked the remaining popcorn onto the floor. Opie gobbled up the spoils.

"That's not good for you," she scolded. "Even if you like butter as much as I do."

While she was cleaning up the mess her phone vibrated. It was Mayleah Harkness. Gracie wiped her hands on a napkin and picked up the phone.

"Buddy and I need your opinion about something," Mayleah said. "I know it's late, but we're at his office. Could we swing by for a few minutes? It has to do with the photographs I took earlier today in Atlanta. I filled him in on what I found."

"You're at Buddy's office?"

"Yes. We can be there in less than ten minutes. It won't take long to show you the photos."

"Okay," Gracie said, scanning the floor to see if it was clean. "Come to the side door. Opie will bark to let me know you're here."

Gracie quickly threw on some exercise clothes, brushed her hair, and checked her teeth for bits of popcorn. She didn't see any white fragments but brushed her teeth to make sure. Opie barked sharply. Gracie tied the laces for her athletic shoes and went to the door. Buddy entered, followed by Mayleah.

"Were you working out?" Buddy asked. "If I exercise this late in the evening, it's hard for me to fall asleep."

"Not unless you call putting popcorn in my mouth exercise," Gracie answered. "Let's sit in the entertainment room."

Opie followed them. As soon as they sat down the dog came over to Buddy, who started scratching Opie's neck. The dog leaned against the lawyer's leg.

"It's been a long time since I was inside this house," Buddy said. "It looks great. Did you do something to the floors?"

"I forgot that Buddy was your landlord," Mayleah said.

"I try to be a benevolent landlord."

"And you are," Gracie said. "I hired Victory Flooring a couple of years ago to redo the floors in here and the dining room. I think they did a good job."

"I should have paid for that," Buddy said.

"You haven't increased the rent since I moved in. This place is a bargain."

Opie left Buddy's side to pick up two stray morsels of popcorn that Gracie had missed.

Mayleah took out her phone. "I'm going to show you the photos I took in Atlanta," she said. "Scroll to the right."

There were ten or twelve photos of the three women and the little white dog. Gracie easily spotted Patricia Nichols. The women were wearing nice shorts, short-sleeved tops, and sandals.

"There's no question that's Patricia Nichols," Gracie said.

"Does either of the young women remind you of someone you've known in the past?" Buddy asked.

"It's not Reagan," Gracie answered.

"How about the young woman sitting in the middle on the bench?" Buddy asked. "Anything familiar about her?"

Gracie scrolled through the photos again. There were four taken of the women on the bench. She focused on the young woman in the middle. She was wearing white shorts and a bright orange top. She had a nice smile.

"Her smile is similar to that of the girl beside her."

Mayleah looked at Buddy and raised her eyebrows.

"I'm going to ask her directly," Buddy said.

"Go ahead," the detective said.

Gracie was sitting on the sofa. Buddy left a side chair and joined her. Taking the phone, he expanded the image of the young woman in the middle.

"Doesn't this girl remind you of Amber?" he asked.

Her heart skipping a beat, Gracie leaned in closer. "I don't know," she said hesitantly. "It's been a long time."

"Do you have the high school yearbook for our senior year? I should have brought mine from the office."

"I have one."

"Please get it."

Gracie went into her bedroom. There was a bookcase in the corner of the room with several oversize books laid flat on the shelf.

"Here are the yearbooks from all four years of high school," she said when she returned to the living room and handed them to Buddy.

"Amber would only be in the ones from our junior and senior years," Buddy said. He quickly found Amber's senior photo and held it close to the phone.

"There are several similarities," he said. "You've already talked about her smile. But it was the eyes that triggered the connection in my mind."

Gracie studied the photo again and compared it to Amber. She also looked at Buddy, who had his head down looking at the yearbook.

"And this one too," Buddy said, flipping over a few pages to a candid shot of Amber at a pep rally. "You're in this one."

The picture was taken in the school gym during a pep rally. It was a close-up. There were five students in the frame. Gracie's blond hair was longer. She remembered the blue top she was wearing and the expensive dark jeans that made her feel stylishly confident. Her mouth was wide open in a full-throated scream. She was standing directly in front of Amber, who was smiling but not yelling.

"Maybe there is some similarity in the eyes," Gracie said cautiously as she held the phone close to the picture.

"It jumped out at me immediately."

"But overall I'm not seeing a family connection," Gracie continued. "It's not like a group photo with my siblings. The family resemblance for us is unmistakable. And this girl doesn't really look like you either. Elise would share Amber's and your features."

Buddy sat back against the sofa cushion. "I can't believe it's not clear to you," he said with frustration. "The girl in the picture also reminds me of my sister Maddie."

"You've been thinking a lot about Elise recently," Gracie said. "She's on your mind, and—"

"I've never stopped thinking about her since she was born!"

Gracie shut her mouth. There was no use stating the obvious or arguing about photographs on a phone when no one in the room knew the truth.

Mayleah broke the silence. "I'll continue trying to find out what I can about Patricia Nichols. I'd like to take a follow-up trip to Atlanta so I can talk to more people living at the apartment complex. And I also want to check out Earvin Parish, the guy who lives in Chattanooga and wanted to meet Reagan. His information on social media was bogus, which isn't uncommon, but he also had a petty criminal record and came across as potentially predatory."

"Chattanooga is where Amber cashed one of the checks my father gave her," Buddy said.

Gracie listened as Buddy told them about the connections between the Melrose family and Soddy-Daisy, Tennessee. She wasn't surprised that Buddy had brought Mayleah completely into the inner circle of his search for Elise.

"I'll do some preliminary research about Earvin Parish," Mayleah replied, "but it may make sense to drive up to Chattanooga."

"I'd like to go with you," Buddy said. "And even though Gracie dissed the possibility that Elise lives in the Atlanta area, that's where Amber cashed most of the checks."

"I didn't say it's impossible," Gracie protested. "But over five million people live there."

"And I'm not giving up."

"Don't give her a hard time because she agrees with me," Mayleah said to Buddy.

"Buddy, I hope you're right," Gracie said. "And I pray that Elise isn't in any trouble because she's hanging out with this Nichols woman. Nobody looked stressed in the photos, which is a good sign."

Buddy turned to Mayleah. "If you go to Atlanta, I want to be a part of that too."

"You can," the detective replied slowly. "But in my mind Patricia Nichols is connected to Reagan, not Elise."

Buddy threw up his hands. "I'm not going to argue with both of you," he said.

"Let's organize the logistics later," Mayleah said. "We've done all we can for now."

"Thanks for letting us come over," Buddy said to Gracie as they made their way to the door. "And I shouldn't have snapped at you. It's tough not to grasp at anything that might give me hope."

"It's okay," she said. "I understand."

SEVENTEEN

THE FOLLOWING DAY GRACIE WAS SITTING IN THE courtroom when Judge Williams issued a threat of a harsh prison term to one of Buddy's clients but then sentenced the young man to a boot camp program instead. Buddy was clearly pleased with the outcome. Gracie suspected the judge's leniency had more to do with his interest in Beatrice Smith than the ends of justice. Several minutes later Buddy nodded to Gracie on his way out of the courtroom. She joined him in the hallway.

"Were you in the courtroom when Judge Williams sentenced my client?" he asked.

"Yes."

"He had me on edge for a few seconds. I thought he was going to send that kid to prison for five years."

"He can be a challenge to work with," Gracie responded cryptically.

"Are you talking about the other day when you, Mayleah, and I were in the small courtroom?"

"Yes."

They descended the stairs to the main floor.

"He's been hanging around my mother and going to supper

with her," Buddy said. "I hope it's harmless, but I've been feeling protective."

"Have you talked to her about it?" Gracie asked, lowering her voice.

"A little bit, but she brushed it off. She put up with my father for all those years. He loved her, but everyone knows he could be a handful."

They reached the bottom of the stairs. Buddy stopped. "Maybe I should hang out with them one evening and see for myself how they're interacting. But that would be awkward."

"Very awkward."

Buddy paused for a moment. "But not as awkward if you were there too. Would you be willing to join me for a dinner with my mother and Judge Williams? As a woman, maybe you'd pick up on stuff I wouldn't."

"I don't think so," Gracie said doubtfully.

Buddy spoke more rapidly. "My mother thinks the world of you, so she'd welcome you being there. She was deeply touched when you prayed for her the other day. I'm sure she'd love having you around."

They reached the entrance to the clerk's office. Gracie's resistance was weakening. "Maybe," she said.

"Think about it and let me know. My mother isn't going to take Judge Williams to someplace like the Southside Grill, so you'll get a nice meal. They've already gone to Morgan's Steakhouse. I can request a repeat if that suits you."

"I'm not picky about the food."

"I'll take that as a yes."

"Okay," Gracie said, giving in with a grin. "You win."

"I'll find out what's on my mom's calendar and let you know."

"I have softball every afternoon except Wednesday," Gracie said quickly. "It usually lasts until six thirty."

"That won't be a problem, but I'll confirm with you."

Gracie watched Buddy as he walked down the hallway. She'd thought about going to dinner with him, but never with his mother and someone like Judge Bryant Williams tagging along.

/ / /

The next day a former client named Nan Mitchell came by Buddy's office to show off Trevor, her newborn baby boy. Buddy had helped Nan and her husband adopt a girl when they couldn't have a child of their own. Then, two years later, Nan became pregnant.

For Buddy, discussion of the differences among newborn infants was an art form limited to women. Both Millie and Jennifer took turns holding the baby. Jennifer, who had several younger siblings, handled little Trevor like a pro.

"Do you want a turn?" Nan asked Buddy when Jennifer returned the baby to her.

"I guess for just a second."

Nan placed the infant in Buddy's arms. Immediately, the baby screwed up his face as if preparing to scream.

"He doesn't like me," Buddy said, holding him out toward Nan. "He's about to cry."

"Or pass gas," Nan answered calmly.

As if on cue a tiny noise escaped the baby's diaper, and his countenance relaxed. Buddy brought him back in close to his chest.

"He's had a terrible time with gas," Nan continued. "Much worse than Catelyn."

That prompted a conversation between Nan and Jennifer about the causes of intestinal distress in infants. While they talked, Buddy looked down at Trevor. It had been awhile since he'd held an infant.

Buddy had cradled Elise probably only a half dozen times when Amber was in the hospital. Unlike Trevor, who was solid and firm, Elise had been soft and cuddly. She had perfectly formed lips and just enough wispy brown hair to refute any claims of baldness. Her eyes were dark dots of curiosity. Buddy was shocked by how much he cared for such a tiny creature. After Amber was discharged home, Buddy saw Elise only one more time. That took place one evening at Amber's house. They were all together in the messy kitchen. Buddy was holding Elise, who started to fuss. He leaned over and blew gently into her face. The infant settled down. Buddy could feel her melding into his arms as he held her close to his chest.

The visit had ended abruptly when Amber's parents got in a huge fight that spilled over into the kitchen. John Melrose wasn't as tall or as strong as Buddy, but he packed an internal rage that threatened imminent danger.

"You!" he yelled at Buddy. "Who invited you over here?"

"I did," Amber said. "He's been asking to see me and the baby ever since we came home from the hospital."

"You've seen 'em, now get!" John Melrose bellowed.

Amber's father roughly pulled Elise from Buddy's arms, then turned and shoved the infant into Amber's chest. The young mother reflexively brought her arms up to support the baby and prevent her from falling to the floor. Buddy felt himself tremble on the inside in a combination of fear and rage. Elise started to cry.

"Go!" Amber yelled at Buddy as she attempted to soothe Elise.

Buddy glanced quickly at Elise then back at Amber's father, who took a step toward him. Buddy left the house. But he didn't immediately leave. He stood for quite a while in the front yard debating what to do. Many, many times over the years he'd wondered what would have happened if he'd insisted on staying to be with Amber and Elise.

The following day one of Amber's closest friends, a girl named Blakeney Lockett, came to the rental house where Buddy was putting new brackets on a gutter. He came down from a ladder.

"I've been trying to find you all morning," Blakeney said anxiously. "Amber and the baby left her parents' house last night."

"Is she staying with you?"

"No, and I don't know where she's gone. She just called to say good-bye, then hung up."

"Good-bye?"

"Yeah, and I'm worried sick. I checked with everyone she would crash with and no one knows anything. I'm the only one she called."

Buddy left the job, drove directly to the Melrose house, and banged on the door. He didn't care if John Melrose answered or not. Instead, Amber's mother opened the door. She looked like she hadn't slept.

"I want to see Amber," Buddy demanded.

"She's gone. Left last night with the baby."

Amber's mother closed the door. Buddy heard the lock click shut.

Buddy banged on the door for over a minute more, but no one returned. He left. When he called later, Amber's mother gave him the same message and told him to stop calling or coming by.

For several days Buddy tried to track down Amber and Elise by reaching out to anyone in their circle of friends. But Blakeney was the only person who'd had contact with her. And she claimed she hadn't heard anything else. Beatrice didn't have any suggestions, and Rascal grunted when Buddy asked his advice. It was the beginning of a long, fruitless search.

Holding Trevor Mitchell, Buddy thought about Elise, and he blew gently into the baby's face. The infant twitched his nose and teased Buddy with a tiny smile. Buddy blew again.

/ / /

Jennifer buzzed Buddy in his office. He was deep in the middle of a research project and didn't answer. An hour later he checked his voice-mail messages. Included in the batch was one from Mayleah.

"I'm calling to talk about our road trip," the detective said when Buddy called.

"To Atlanta?"

"No, this one is to Chattanooga, and I thought we could include metropolitan Soddy-Daisy."

Buddy leaned back in his chair. "Great. I'm in."

"I've been digging for information about Earvin Parish. I spoke to a detective with the Chattanooga Police Department and told her about the search for Reagan Landry. She did some checking and called back an hour ago. Parish was recently arrested for domestic violence, but the case was dropped when the woman refused to go forward with the prosecution. The victim gave her name as Kimberly Landers."

"Landry, Landers." Buddy perked up.

"It got my attention too."

"Were any photographs taken of the victim?"

"Not by the police. Maybe at the hospital. According to the police report, the doctor at the hospital reported that Landers had bruises to her right arm and leg and showed up at the ER because she was afraid her right arm was broken. She told the triage nurse that her boyfriend hit her, and an ER doctor called the police. Parish was arrested at the hospital and quickly made bond. A few days later his lawyer sent the police an affidavit in which Landers swore no abuse occurred. I have a copy of the affidavit and can send it over."

"Did she give another explanation for the bruises in her affidavit?"

"That she was intoxicated and fell."

"Do you have the hospital records?"

"No. The detective was cooperative enough to send me the affidavit but wouldn't include the medical records without patient consent or stronger proof that Kimberly is Reagan."

"We should compare the signature on the affidavit with a recent writing sample from Reagan."

"I had the same thought and asked Gracie to get multiple writing samples from Reagan's family. If they look similar, then I definitely think a trip is in order."

Buddy was silent for a moment. "Do you think the detective in Chattanooga could check out the Melrose family in Soddy-Daisy?"

"Not unless there was an open criminal investigation, but that doesn't mean we can't ask some questions. Check out the affidavit, and I'll let you know what I receive from Gracie."

Shortly after the call ended, Buddy received an email from

Mayleah with Kimberly Landers's affidavit attached. It was three paragraphs long and clearly prepared by Parish's attorney. Nothing about the language sounded like a seventeen-year-old woman. In the affidavit, Landers claimed she was nineteen years old, a detail that would eliminate her from consideration as Reagan, but there was no confirmation of age, such as a copy of a birth certificate or driver's license. Landers didn't address why she told the triage nurse that Parish struck her. The young woman merely stated that she fell down some stairs while intoxicated and Parish transported her to the hospital. Buddy suspected that with the right input from an attorney at the local DA's office, Landers might revert to the truth. The signature was clear and legible.

After going for a run, Buddy stopped by his mother's house. A large pot was simmering on the stove.

"What's that?" Buddy asked. "It's too hot outside for soup."

"It's chili. When I told Bryant about my venison chili recipe, he asked if I'd cook some for him."

It had been years since Beatrice made chili. It was one of Rascal's favorite meals. Rascal wasn't a hunter, but he would occasionally get ground venison from one of his tenants and bring it home.

"Where did you get the venison?"

"Ken Grant. He was one of your father's main suppliers. Rascal said he knew how to handle the meat properly."

Buddy leaned over to smell the food in the pot. "What time is the judge coming over? I don't want to be in the way."

"Not till tomorrow evening. Chili always tastes better the second day after the flavors meld. Virginia Clausen is going to bake some corn bread for her family and give me a pan too. My corn bread always turns out too crumbly to serve for company."

Buddy sat at the kitchen table and told his mother what had gone through his mind earlier in the day while holding newborn Trevor Mitchell.

"The details you remember amaze me," Beatrice said, shaking her head. "Most of it is a blur for me."

"I realize now just how young and immature Amber and I were. And I wish that things would have turned out differently."

"You were in love," Beatrice sighed. "As strict as your daddy was with your sisters, he was just as lenient with you. He believed you were too smart to make a mistake."

"He was wrong."

"After you found out Amber was pregnant you wanted to act like an adult, and we tried to let you do that. You stayed at the hospital the night Elise was born." Beatrice was silent for a moment. "I even talked to your father about letting Amber and the baby live here because the situation at her house seemed so bad. He wouldn't hear of it."

This was new information to Buddy. He started to respond but didn't want to run the risk of making his mother sad.

"Hey, what do you think about Gracie Blaylock and me coming over tomorrow night to eat chili with you and Judge Williams? I'm not trying to barge in, but it would be fun."

Beatrice managed a tiny smile. "Is this your latest strategy for how to protect your mother?" she said.

"Yes. And I know how much you like Gracie."

"True." Beatrice paused. "I think it's a great suggestion."

"Should you check with the judge?"

"We're eating at my house, not the courthouse. And based on what you said the other day, I'd like to see how he interacts with you outside the law field."

It was an angle Buddy hadn't considered. His mother would be performing her own evaluation.

"I won't feel comfortable calling him Bryant."

"What do you call Judge Claremont when you see him at our family reunions?" Beatrice asked. "I don't remember you calling him Natty."

"'Judge' is always the safer path."

"I told Bryant six o'clock for dinner."

"I need to check with Gracie, but could you make it seven? That way she'll be finished with softball practice."

/ / /

Gracie was driving home from the Landry house when her phone vibrated and Buddy Smith's name appeared.

"Do you like homemade venison chili?" the lawyer asked.

"It's been a long time since I had any."

"That's on the menu tomorrow night at my mother's house for our dinner with her and Judge Williams. She makes an excellent venison chili and is getting corn bread from Virginia Clausen. I suggested we meet at seven so you'll have time to change after softball practice. Mother was excited when I mentioned that you'd come."

Gracie turned off a rural road onto the main highway into town. "That will be pushing it on the time," she said.

"Should I call her back and change it?"

"I'm the coach. The girls won't have a problem quitting a few minutes early. I worked them hard the other day after the rain shower that passed through."

"Great. I'll be glad to pick you up, or we can meet at my mother's house."

Buddy's comment reminded Gracie that the dinner wasn't really a date with him. "I'll meet you there," she said. "It's close by, and there's no need for you to drive out of the way."

"Okay. I really appreciate you doing this. My mother also wants to see how Judge Williams interacts with me in a social setting."

"Sounds like everybody will need to be on their best behavior."

The fact that Buddy's mother wanted to see how Judge Williams treated her son meant that her relationship with the judge might be serious. Once home, Gracie called Mayleah.

"Sammy and Crystal Landry gave me several writing samples," Gracie said to the detective. "When I mentioned the affidavit, they wanted to jump in the car and drive to Chattanooga. But after we talked, they understood it was better for you to check out the situation. They're just sick with worry."

"I'm sure they are. I'm about to start a meeting at the sheriff's department, but I'll email the affidavit to you, so see what you think."

Gracie took care of Opie before turning on her laptop. She had two lengthy emails from Daniel and one each from Devin and David. Gracie skimmed all of them but didn't answer. She then opened the email from Mayleah and read the affidavit. Even though she wanted to find Reagan, Gracie couldn't keep from hoping it was a dead end. She increased the size of the signature on her screen and took out the writing samples.

The first letter to compare was the shape of the "L" for Landry and Landers. Even to Gracie's untrained eye, there were clearly more differences than similarities. When she moved to other shared letters the distinctions remained, until she checked out the lowercase "n." The "n" in Reagan and the "n" in Landers looked identical, all the way down to the way she finished the letter. Gracie's heart started beating a little faster as she held the samples close together. Encouraged, she ran through the remaining shared letters. Nothing else seemed to match. The common formation of the lowercase "n" could be a coincidence or a signpost. She scanned in the writing samples obtained from the Landry family and sent them to Mayleah and Buddy.

EIGHTEEN

AS SHE STOOD TO THE SIDE WATCHING THE GIRLS FINish batting practice, Gracie repeatedly checked her watch. She'd set a peach cobbler to start cooking on timed bake, and it would need to come out of the oven in twenty-five minutes. One of the younger girls hit her second home run of the afternoon.

"Round the bases," Gracie said to the young power hitter. "I want you to get used to it."

"That's what happens when a fastball meets a fast bat!" Heidi called out. The pitcher took off her glove and clapped her hands for her teammate.

"Nice job!" Laura said. "Glad you're on our team!"

The young player, her face flushed with excitement, trotted over to Gracie.

"If you can hit like that in a real game, I'm going to move you up in the batting order," Gracie said.

Two batters later, Gracie raised her fingers to her lips and gave a sharp whistle. The girls gathered around her.

"We're going to knock off a few minutes early," she said.

"Do you have a date?" Heidi asked.

"No," Gracie answered. "But I'm going to a friend's house to eat venison chili and don't want to be late."

The mention of venison sparked several remarks. Eating wild game was common for Milton County families. After a minute Gracie called for quiet.

"Okay, let's pray," she said.

Team building required many stones, and as she listened to the girls pray, Gracie was thankful for the strength of the spiritual connections forming in the circle. When everyone grew silent for a few moments, Heidi ended the prayer: "Lord, let us become better ballplayers and people. Thank you for all my teammates and especially Coach Blaylock. May she not get sick eating deer meat and enjoy her date. Amen."

Laura turned to Heidi. "Why did you pray for Coach's date? Nobody eats venison chili on a date."

"You'd eat venison chili if Dayton Lancaster asked you to," Heidi retorted.

"Hey, that's not—" Laura started.

"Don't break the unity of the prayer circle," Gracie cut in.

"Is Heidi right?" Laura demanded. "Are you going on a date?"

Gracie hesitated. "A man my age is going to be there," she said. "We're eating at his mother's house."

Laura and Heidi glanced at each other. "It's a date," they said simultaneously.

Beatrice opened the door to let Buddy in. "Sorry," she said, wiping a stray strand of silvery gray hair from her eyes. "I picked up the corn bread from Virginia Clausen an hour ago. It was still hot from the oven. I brought it home and cut off a tiny corner because I couldn't wait to sample a bite. It's inedible."

"Why?" Buddy asked in surprise.

"She must have left out the salt."

"Couldn't you sprinkle some on top?"

Beatrice gave Buddy the same look he'd receive if he asked an expert witness a stupid question in a deposition.

"I believe you," he quickly said. "Do you want me to run down to Crossroads and see if I can buy a pan from them?"

"I wish I'd thought of that," Beatrice said. "It would have been way easier. I ended up scrambling around to throw together a batch myself. I found a recipe that my mother used, but it called for stone-ground cornmeal. Except for the Prater's Mill Fair in October, where could I find that these days? So I had to use the cornmeal I had on hand."

Buddy followed his mother toward the kitchen as she talked. "We don't have to eat corn bread," he suggested. "Rolls would be fine."

"You haven't even tried it!" Beatrice responded with exasperation in her voice.

They reached the kitchen. There were two pans of corn bread on the counter. Both had pieces missing from a corner of the pan.

"This is Virginia's," Beatrice said. "I've kept it warm in the bottom oven. I'll cut you a piece."

She handed Buddy a small sliver of the bread.

"I feel like a food judge," he said.

"Be serious and taste it."

Buddy put the entire piece in his mouth. "Yeah," he said before he swallowed it. "Salt makes more of a difference than I would have thought. You can't serve this to guests, but it would work great in your backyard bird feeder."

"Here's mine," Beatrice said. "It's still hot."

"I want butter."

"No, plain first."

Buddy took a nibble then put more in his mouth. He watched his mother's anxious face as he chewed and swallowed.

"Well?" she asked.

"May I have some more? I don't want Gracie and Judge Williams to eat all of it before I get seconds."

"Don't tease me," his mother said. "Is it really okay?"

Buddy nodded. "Yes. It's more coarse than what they serve at the Crossroads, but I like the flavor, and it will go great with chili."

"That's a relief. Help me finish setting up so I can go upstairs and get ready for—"

The front doorbell sounded and stopped Beatrice in mid-sentence. "See who it is," she said, shooing Buddy toward the foyer. "I'll run upstairs."

Buddy opened the door and found Gracie standing on the porch. She was wearing a peach-colored top, tan slacks, and white sandals. She held a glass dish in her hands.

"Welcome," he said.

"Is the judge here yet?" she asked.

"No."

Buddy led the way to the kitchen. "You didn't have to bring anything."

"Of course I offered to bring something. Your mother says you like peach cobbler."

"I love peach cobbler," Buddy said. "And it matches your shirt."

Gracie glanced down. "I didn't think about that."

"Mom is upstairs getting ready."

"Are we eating in the dining room or kitchen?"

"I don't know. What do you think?"

"Dining room."

Buddy put the cobbler in the lower oven that his mother used to keep food warm. While they set the dining room table, he told Gracie about the corn bread saga.

"That must have been nerve-racking," she said. "I never experiment with a new dish if I'm entertaining company. Would your mother mind if I cut some fresh flowers and brought them inside?"

"I'm sure she'd like that."

Buddy was impressed with the arrangement Gracie put together in a large, clear glass vase.

Beatrice came downstairs and into the dining room. "That looks lovely," she exclaimed.

"Thanks to Gracie," Buddy said. "She's the decorator."

Beatrice continued to admire the flowers. "I wish I could call you before the bridge club comes over here next Tuesday morning," she said. "How did you learn to do that?"

"My mother grew a lot of flowers, and my sisters and I would have competitions."

"This is a blue ribbon in my book," Beatrice said. "Did Buddy tell you about the corn bread?"

"Yes. It sounded like a close call."

Beatrice and Gracie continued into the kitchen. Buddy stepped into the living room and looked out one of the front windows that offered a view of Franklin Street. Several people Buddy recognized passed by. Growing up in a small town created the opportunity for community unknown to suburbanites and big-city dwellers. Out of the corner of his right eye, he saw a male figure approaching on the sidewalk. It was Judge Williams. The judge turned and climbed the three steps to the yard level, then continued toward the front porch. In his right hand was a birdcage. He was bringing his parrot to supper.

"Thanks again for setting the table," Beatrice said to Gracie when the women were alone.

"I'm glad I got here early enough to help."

"Taste a spoonful of chili," Beatrice said. "I'm not sure it's spicy enough."

Beatrice lifted the lid and handed Gracie a silver spoon. Gracie stirred the chili and made sure she had both meat and beans in the spoon.

"It's perfect for me," she said after sampling it. "But you can offer extra hot sauce."

"Buddy will add it, but I don't know about Bryant."

Gracie handed the spoon to Beatrice. The sound of male voices could be heard from the front of the house.

"He's here," Beatrice said. "How do I look?"

"Lovely."

Gracie followed Beatrice through the dining room and into the living room, where Buddy and Judge Williams were standing in front of the fireplace. Bailiff the parrot was perched on the judge's right shoulder.

"Two surprises!" Judge Williams exclaimed when he saw Gracie. "Madam Clerk. It's nice to see you."

The judge stepped over to Beatrice as if he were about to plant a kiss on her cheek. Instead, he stopped short and the bird lightly touched Beatrice's right cheek with his bill. Gracie watched

Buddy's reaction. His face revealed nothing. Beatrice stroked the top of the bird's head.

"What do you say?" the judge asked the bird.

"That's the right spot," the parrot said.

"I didn't know you were bringing Bailiff," Beatrice said.

"Is it okay?" the judge asked. "I can put him back in his cage."

The bird squawked as if he understood the judge.

"No," Beatrice said. "I'll put a towel on the back of a chair in the dining room. He can perch there."

"This doesn't sound like Bailiff's first visit for dinner," Buddy said.

"It isn't," Beatrice replied. "He came for tea one afternoon last week."

"And ate a cracker?" Buddy asked.

"Cracker?" Bailiff responded, then repeated, "No crackers for Polly. Steak and lobster."

The judge spoke to Buddy: "He actually likes crackers. He thinks they're steak."

Gracie watched as Beatrice created a place for the parrot to perch and positioned the chair close to the judge. Bailiff climbed from the judge's shoulder onto the chair and received a cracker as a reward.

"He'll be fine there," the judge said. "But I can't promise he won't interrupt our conversation and offer an opinion if we say a word or phrase that triggers a response."

They spent the next few minutes in the kitchen filling china bowls with chili. Beatrice cut individual pieces of corn bread brushed with melted butter. Judge Williams was gentlemanly in his interaction with Beatrice, but it was going to take more than a few moments of good manners to dispel Gracie's concerns. They assembled in the dining room. The judge gave Bailiff a large nut from a plastic bag in his pocket before they sat down. Gracie placed a cloth napkin in her lap. A loud crack signaled Bailiff's success in quickly opening the nut.

"Gracie, will you say grace?" Beatrice asked. "You prayed such a beautiful prayer the other day when we were together on the front porch."

The request caught Gracie off guard. She'd been focused on Bailiff and what he might say or do next. Her first thought was to trot out a rote prayer of thanks for the food followed by a quick amen. But deep inside she knew that would be wrong. She'd been invited to the meal for a reason. Closing her eyes, she waited for a couple of seconds. There was no sound in the room except the snaps of the parrot's beak as he continued to break apart the nut.

Gracie began by thanking God for Beatrice, the woman she was, the woman she'd been for Buddy, her daughters, her grandchildren, and others in the community; and the woman she would be for the remainder of the days allotted to her on earth. She transitioned to a prayer for Buddy, that God would touch him in the deepest places of his soul and give him the desires of his heart. Gracie thought about Elise and couldn't keep from asking that Buddy would someday be reunited with his daughter in the perfect way and at the perfect time. And then she prayed for Judge Williams, that his time in Milton County would be one of blessing and refreshing. Finally, she thanked God for the meal and said amen. Bailiff was quiet during the prayer and didn't interrupt. When Gracie looked up, Bailiff had his head tucked beneath one of his wings as if he, too, were praying.

Gracie's boldness from moments before was swept away by embarrassment. "I'm sorry that was so long," she said sheepishly.

"I'm not," Buddy said. "I've never heard anyone pray before a meal like that."

"That's not how I usually do it," Gracie started.

"Now you understand what I was talking about the other day," Beatrice said triumphantly to Buddy. "I had chill bumps running up and down my arms."

While Beatrice and Buddy were talking, Gracie was eyeing Judge Williams, whose expression didn't reveal what he was thinking.

"I don't want the chili and corn bread to get cold," the judge said.

"Yes, let's eat," Beatrice replied.

They focused on the food, but Gracie could feel Buddy's eyes on her. "Is that how you've been praying all these years for me and Elise?" he asked.

"Pretty much."

"Bryant doesn't know much about Elise," Beatrice said.

Gracie suspected Beatrice was trying not to be rude by allowing a conversation that made no sense to one person at the table. But Buddy might not want to air his past errors in front of a judge, even one who wouldn't be in town for very long.

"I can give you the short version," Buddy said.

Even a brief summary of the story touched Gracie and caused her heart to ache in a fresh way over Buddy's quest to find his daughter. And she realized something new—how much she wanted to meet Elise too.

Judge Williams turned to Beatrice. "I'm sure this has been hard on you as well," he said.

"Yes." Beatrice nodded but didn't elaborate.

As they ate, the parrot occasionally looked up, but his head mostly remained beneath his wing.

"Is Bailiff napping?" Gracie asked.

"Even though he's a talking bird and likes to express his opinion, he needs his alone time so he can decompress," the judge replied with a straight face. "I probably should have named him Judge."

Buddy laughed.

"Would anyone like to add hot sauce to their chili?" Beatrice asked brightly. "Buddy, I bet you do."

"Not right now, but I think this is the best batch you've ever made. And the corn bread is fabulous."

Buddy asked the judge a question about his previous judicial service, and the conversation shifted to Bryant telling courthouse tales. There was nothing wrong with the stories. It was the kind of conversation common at the courthouse, and Buddy slipped easily into the law talk. But Gracie longed for something deeper. As the judge rambled on, he revealed little of substance about himself. Partway through the conversation, he asked Beatrice if she had any bananas. When she returned with one, the judge handed it to Bailiff, who began to systematically remove the peel and eat the fruit. Buddy excused himself from the table to refill his bowl with chili. Gracie joined him in the kitchen.

"What do you think about the judge?" Buddy asked as soon as they were alone. "He has a much better sense of humor than I thought. And it was amazing when the parrot skinned that banana. I can see how Bailiff is therapeutic for him."

"Therapeutic? I have no idea what you mean."

"A psychologist might say that the bird is Judge Williams's alter ego and serves as a foil for his psyche."

"Buddy, that's nonsense."

"Probably," Buddy said with a grin. "But it does make for an interesting evening. I'm not sure the other lawyers in town will believe me when I tell them about it. You're going to have to be my credibility witness."

"To me, he's rattling on like a man who's used to dominating every conversation he joins."

Buddy raised his eyebrows. "Don't be so harsh, even if it's true. How can you pray for him and then throw him into the street?"

Gracie sighed. "I don't want to be overly critical, but superficial conversations about his exploits on the bench aren't going to reveal if he's the type of man you can trust to spend time alone with your mother. That's why you asked me to come tonight."

Buddy added a few drops of hot sauce from a small bottle to his chili. "What do you suggest?" he asked.

"Ask about his faith."

"I can't do that. It's too personal a topic."

"I'll do it then."

Buddy stayed in the kitchen for a few moments after Gracie left the room. The clerk of court had been a dominant force on the pitcher's mound, but she'd never come across as aggressive in person or on her job. And Bryant Williams seemed less arrogant than Buddy feared and more pleasant than he'd hoped. In a couple of the stories from the past, Williams was the object of the humor, which revealed a refreshing level of self-deprecation. Taking his bowl of now extra-spicy chili, Buddy returned to the dining room.

Gracie was speaking to the judge: "I'm always curious how a judge's faith affects his work."

The judge eyed Gracie curiously. "Have you ever asked Judge Claremont that question?" he asked.

"No, but I've never eaten venison chili and corn bread with him either."

Judge Williams didn't immediately respond, and Buddy shifted uneasily in his chair. Williams placed his spoon on the plate beside his bowl of chili. Buddy wasn't sure if the judge was going to explode or deliver a mild rebuke.

"It's interesting that you ask about that. Although I wouldn't have put it in those terms, I've been thinking about my perspective on being a judge quite a bit during my stay in Milton County. As a young, ambitious prosecutor, I primarily focused on advancing my career. That worked out well, and I was appointed to the bench by the governor when I was only thirty-four. Two years later I won my first campaign for reelection. At that point I thought I would be satisfied with what I'd accomplished. But I wasn't prepared as a person to best handle the responsibility a judge carries and the power he has over the lives of the people who appear before him. My reaction was to create a judicial persona, which ended up as a serious case of black-robe-itis. Have you ever heard of it?"

"I have," Beatrice answered perkily.

"I wonder where?" Williams said with a sideways glance at Buddy before continuing. "After many years, my attitude ended up alienating enough of the voters in my district that they ushered me out the courthouse door. I still fall back into my old patterns, but since coming here, I've been asking myself if change is possible and what that would look like. I assume you believe faith would be part of that process."

Buddy was listening with his mouth hanging partly open. Gracie looked only slightly less shocked than he did.

"Yes, sir," she said. "I believe faith should be at the center of life for everyone."

"That's why you pray like you do," Beatrice said, nodding her head.

"In your opinion, what would faith at the center of life look like for a judge?" Williams asked Gracie.

"I don't know about judges," Beatrice interjected. "But Buddy acts out the practical side of faith. He takes cases for people because they need help, not just to make a fee. And he treats everyone with respect, regardless of how much money they have or whether they might be able to do something for him in return."

"How do you know that?" Buddy asked.

Beatrice looked at Gracie. "Isn't that Buddy's reputation?"

"Yes, it is," she said.

"And to my thinking there would be opportunities for a judge to do the same sorts of things, only differently because he's a judge," Beatrice concluded.

"Your mother cuts to the heart of matters," Williams said to Buddy. "That's one of the reasons I've enjoyed getting to know her while I'm here. She's been part of the main reason for the self-analysis I mentioned earlier. She's made me think about myself without trying to pressure me to do so."

It was one of the most unique dinners of Buddy's life. The judge's receptivity to the combination of Gracie and Beatrice was a huge surprise. Gracie mentioned a couple of Bible verses, which the judge dutifully noted in his phone, and Beatrice shared about the priceless value of each person.

Partway through the dessert of peach cobbler topped with ice cream, Judge Williams held up his hand. "Enough," he said. "I'll consider your arguments."

"I'm not trying to be argumentative," Gracie replied.

"And you haven't been," Williams said. "But I need to take all this under advisement."

Before the judge left, Bailiff gave Beatrice another kiss on the cheek.

"Good night," the judge said.

"Good night, pretty lady," the parrot said.

The bird's final repartee convinced Buddy that the parrot was, in fact, acting as Judge Williams's surrogate.

"Would you like me to give you a ride home?" Buddy asked Williams.

"No, I enjoy walking after dark in a town where it's safe to do so. You take it for granted, but I've served in circuits in which the police parked a patrol car down the street from where I was staying."

After the judge left, Buddy and Gracie helped clean up in the kitchen.

"Would you like some chili to take home?" Beatrice asked them.

"Yes," Buddy answered. "So long as you include a big piece of corn bread."

"That would be wonderful," Gracie added. "And Buddy can have the rest of the cobbler."

"Done," he said immediately.

Beatrice yawned as they worked.

"Why don't you let us finish up?" Buddy asked.

"Are you sure?" Beatrice answered, unable to hold back another yawn.

"Gracie can supervise."

"Okay." Beatrice nodded. "It was wonderful having both of you here this evening. I enjoyed it a lot. I think Bryant did too."

"You'll find that out the next time the two of you are together without anyone else around," Gracie replied.

They divided the chili. While Buddy scrubbed the large cooking pot, Gracie straightened up the dining room.

"Find any cracker crumbs?" Buddy asked when she returned to the kitchen.

"Yes, along with bits of the other things Bailiff ate. Overall, he was fairly neat for someone without a napkin."

Buddy shook his head.

"What?" Gracie asked.

"For a dinner without alcohol, that was wild. All it took was a parrot at the table and you preaching to a retired judge."

"Did I come across as preachy?"

Buddy saw he'd hit a nerve that he didn't know existed. "No, I didn't mean it that way at all. Both you and my mother did a beautiful job of expressing yourselves. It was natural and credible because that's who you are on the inside."

"You found me a credible witness?" Gracie asked with a smile.

"Yeah, that's a fair statement."

"What did the judge think?"

Buddy dried the inside of the large pot with a dish towel. "It's hard to know. The fact that he took you seriously was a good sign. Did you get the impression he was putting on a show for my mother?"

Gracie shook her head. "No, and it made me see him in a different light. Not that I totally trust him, but he's willing to consider making some changes in his life. Maybe you'll get a chance to follow up with him when you see him at the courthouse."

"Or you will," Buddy replied. He returned the cooking pot to its place on the bottom shelf of one of the kitchen cabinets. "Would you like to sit on the front porch?" he asked. "I think there's a nice breeze blowing."

"Sure. I'm not in a rush to go home."

NINETEEN

GRACIE STOPPED OFF AT THE DOWNSTAIRS HALF BATH and checked her appearance in an oval mirror above the sink. Her hair looked fine, and she applied a light layer of fresh lipstick. Being in Beatrice Smith's house had been so natural to Gracie that she felt like a joint hostess, not a guest. But her emotions were still heightened by all that had taken place since she marched from the kitchen into the dining room to challenge Judge Williams about his faith. She took a few deep breaths to relax.

Outside on the porch, she found Buddy sitting in a white wicker rocking chair with a padded cushion. There was a matching chair beside it with a small side table between them. Two glasses of ice water rested on the table. A yellow light that wouldn't attract insects shone from the ceiling above the front door. Gracie sat down and took a sip of water.

"You know I don't believe like you do," Buddy said. "And I figure your question at the table to the judge was also directed at me as a way to force me to consider the differences between us."

"Not really—" Gracie started.

"Will the prosecutor please let me finish my answer?" Buddy cut in.

"Sorry."

"Anyway, regardless whether Judge Williams thinks about what was said around the table tonight, I was paying attention. And while I appreciate what you and my mother said about the way I practice law, that doesn't have much to do with what I believe about God. I'm just trying to be ethical and honorable."

Buddy stopped and stared across the porch toward Franklin Street. Outdoor post lamps projected a soft yellow glow into the approaching dusk. A dog barked in the distance. Gracie waited.

Buddy continued, "If I'm honest about it, my life has been a succession of trials and errors—a lot of false starts, wrong turns, and dead ends. I press on, but I've always felt stuck, and I want to get unstuck. Does that make any sense?"

"Yes."

"And the renewal of hope that I might find Elise, slim as it might be, has caused me to think about the man I want her to meet when she first sees her father."

Not wanting to make a sound that might disrupt Buddy's thoughts, Gracie sat perfectly still in the rocker.

He turned slightly and faced her. "I'd like you to pray for me. That I'll be the kind of man my daughter deserves."

Gracie immediately knew what she should say before she prayed: "I'll be glad to. But God wants you to be that man whether you ever meet Elise or not."

Buddy was silent for a few moments. "Maybe you're right, but I need something external to motivate me."

Gracie had another sentence on the tip of her tongue but left it lying there. Buddy's heart was open. That was the important reality of the moment.

"Okay, here we go," she said.

Gracie had never started a prayer by saying, "Here we go," but she quickly realized it was a perfect opening. She prayed for Buddy's journey, going all the way back to what she knew about his past into his present. She asked for the intervention of heaven for him and everyone close to him. And when she mentioned the name of Jesus, Gracie shivered slightly as the presence of divinity wrapped around them.

Gracie knew she had to voice what happened. "Did you feel that?" she asked.

"Yes," Buddy answered, raising his head and opening his eyes. "And thanks for making me say it before I could let myself doubt. If you're finished, I want to pray before I explode on the inside."

"Go ahead."

Buddy bowed his head and proceeded to pour out his heart in a torrent of words that would have swept Gracie from the porch if they'd had physical form and substance. Nothing in her religious experience matched what she heard. Buddy retraced the path she'd laid out in her prayer but made it his own, acknowledging where he'd erred and asking to be changed. He mentioned actions and attitudes. He spoke about opportunities lost and time wasted. He laid bare selfishness. He admitted responsibility. He wasn't emotional. He was thorough. Stunned, Gracie opened her eyes. Buddy was moving his right hand up and down as if emphasizing a point of law or evidence in the courtroom. Gracie knew she was witness to a miracle.

Finally, he stopped, opened his eyes, and looked at Gracie. "Something is happening to me right now," he said.

"Yes, it is."

Buddy closed his eyes, and a well of thankfulness overflowed in more heartfelt words. A trickle at first, it gained in force until Buddy's voice cracked, and he stopped. Gracie waited. When he didn't speak, she added a few simple words of thanksgiving and praise of her own. She opened her eyes as Buddy reached over and took a sip of water.

He stared at the glass for a moment. "That is the best drink of water I've ever had," he said.

Gracie smiled and pointed up. "There's more where that came from."

"What do you mean?" Buddy asked as he looked up in the direction of the porch ceiling.

"Jesus talked about living water flowing from those who believed. It's a way to describe the presence of the Holy Spirit."

Gracie's words weren't completely foreign, but they dripped with meaning unknown to Buddy moments before. He laid his hand on his chest. He'd never felt so full in a way that had nothing to do with eating a good meal.

"I want to write some of this down before I forget it," he said, glancing at his watch.

"I think that's a wonderful idea."

Buddy intended to get up from the chair to leave, but neither of them moved. He felt an invisible weight gently keeping him in place. He glanced at Gracie, who was sitting peacefully with her eyes closed. Buddy relaxed and didn't fight the blanketlike sensation. His senses were more acute: the sounds from the yard, the faint smells from the flowers, the shadows cast through the trees by the setting sun.

He took in a deep breath and spoke: "I've never felt more alive."

Gracie opened her eyes. "Me either. What's happening to you is rubbing off on me, and I like it."

They continued to sit beside each other in silence. When Buddy finally checked his watch, he was shocked to see that over fifteen minutes had passed since he mentioned leaving. He shifted in the chair and took another drink of water. Gracie glanced over at him and smiled.

"Thank you—" Buddy started, then stopped when Gracie raised her finger to her lips and shook her head.

"Go home," she said. "Write, draw, sit quietly, or do whatever you think you should. We'll talk soon."

Buddy couldn't stop smiling during the short drive home. He grabbed his sketch pad and sat on the back porch. Instead of drawing, he jotted down his thoughts and impressions, what he was sensing and seeing and feeling. It was an explosion like nothing he'd experienced before. It was unlike anything he'd ever written—the words were alive, the images real.

"This is different," he said to himself. And as soon as the words were out of his mouth, he knew the reason: "I am different."

Buddy wrote the simple statement on a fresh sheet of paper. He stared at the collection of three words. He suspected it would take a lifetime to plumb the depths of what it meant to be "different."

"Wow," he whispered. "This isn't what I expected."

Buddy had never considered himself a rebel, an agnostic, or an atheist, but after what transpired on his mother's porch, he knew he'd lived in practical agreement with all three of those labels. The joy and lightness and freedom he felt overwhelmed regret. He didn't try to rein in what was happening in his soul or force it to conform to any prior perception of religious stereotypes. He was different.

The box containing his mother's journals was still beside his chair. Taking one out, Buddy began to read the words with new eyes. His mother's expressions of simple, sincere faith no longer appeared as nice thoughts but dripped with power. Buddy was particularly drawn to prayers she'd prayed for him. That God would bless him, speak to him, touch him, direct him, protect him, and open his heart to receive divine love. Buddy found himself agreeing with everything she'd written and thanking God for answering.

He also had an irrepressible desire to talk to someone about what had happened. His mother deserved to know, but she was now sound asleep. He remembered Gracie's statement that they would talk soon. He suspected she didn't mean this soon, but that didn't stop Buddy from picking up his phone to call.

Tears began to stream down Gracie's face as soon as she was behind the wheel of her car. God had touched Buddy Smith. And Gracie was there to behold it. It wasn't the first time she'd been present when someone met the Lord. Each encounter was unique, but Buddy was special. She relived the prayer the Lord gave her, and the response that exploded from within Buddy's heart. Gracie began to express her thanks out loud and didn't stop until reaching her house. After giving Opie an exuberant greeting, she remained so excited that she couldn't sit still and walked through the house praising God until she began to shout. It was something Gracie had never done in public or private, but there was no suppressing what rose up within her.

When that passed, she turned on her tablet and found the place where she initially entered a request that Buddy Smith would come to know the Lord Jesus in a personal way. It had been an unanswered item for over a decade. She wrote the day's date and the answer. As she typed, Gracie returned to Beatrice's front porch and visited the miracle again in her mind.

Next to Buddy's name, she'd also written a prayer for Elise. Tonight anything seemed possible, but Gracie didn't pray that Buddy would find Elise. Instead, she fervently asked that even if Buddy never met his daughter on earth, Elise, too, would become a child of God. It was a transcendent request beyond earth and time. Gracie finished and closed the tablet. She was too worked up to go to bed, so she sat in the den with Opie on the sofa beside her. Gracie was stroking the dog's soft fur when her phone vibrated. Buddy's name appeared as she grabbed it.

"How are you?" she asked before he said anything.

"How do you think?" he asked.

"Better than at any other time in your life," she answered.

"Are you about to go to sleep?"

"No."

"If you're interested, I'd like to read some things I wrote when I came home. The words poured out of me."

"Yes, I'd love that."

Gracie curled her feet up beneath her and listened. She'd always considered Buddy naturally eloquent, but hearing what came from deep within his heart overwhelmed her a second time. When he mentioned being different and how that would take a lifetime to explore, she sniffled more loudly than she intended, and he stopped.

"Are you okay?" he asked.

"It's just so beautiful and personal. And I'm so honored that you'd share it with me."

"You deserve to know."

"Keep going," she said.

"That's it for now," Buddy said.

Gracie started to tell him what she'd prayed for Elise but felt an inner check and didn't. "Thanks so much for calling," she said.

"And to you for listening."

Later, Gracie lay in bed with her eyes open. Opie was already asleep, and she heard him snort. Sometimes the dog's legs would quiver while he unconsciously chased squirrels or chipmunks in his dreams. Gracie offered a final prayer of thanksgiving, rolled onto her side, and closed her eyes.

In the morning Gracie wanted to talk to someone besides God about Buddy Smith. She considered calling Beatrice, but Buddy had the exclusive rights to share what had happened with her. In the end, she settled on a call to her mother.

Before describing exactly what happened, she mentioned that Buddy Smith had met the Lord. Her mother cut in: "That's wonderful. Are you going to invite him to church with you?"

"Maybe," Gracie said thoughtfully. "Although I think I'd better leave that up to him and not be too pushy."

"Why were you eating dinner at the Smith house in the first place?"

Gracie didn't want to start a gossip fire about Beatrice and Judge Williams. "Beatrice cooked some venison chili and corn bread, and Buddy invited me to join them. I fixed your peach cobbler."

The mention of cobbler turned the conversation in another direction. After the call ended, Gracie realized it would be a challenge to talk to anyone about Buddy. Maybe she should leave it up to him to break the news that something "different" was in his life.

Arriving at the courthouse, she settled into her morning routine. Shortly before eleven o'clock, her phone buzzed. It was Amanda Byrnes.

"Are you alone?" the judicial assistant asked in a soft voice.

"You know where my desk sits, but I can listen."

"Listening. That's what I was doing earlier when Judge Williams came by to see Judge Claremont. They left the door cracked open, and I could hear what they were saying. I usually eavesdrop in case something comes up that I need to know about for my job. They went over some items on the calendar, and then Judge Williams started asking Judge Claremont a bunch of questions about you."

"What kind of questions?"

"About your background and family. How you got to be clerk of court. Whether you've ever been married."

"Married?" Gracie asked.

"Yes."

"Did Judge Williams bring up anything about church or faith?"

"Yeah, he asked where you went to church. That was one of the few things Judge Claremont didn't know. I kept waiting to see if they would say anything negative about the clerk's office, but they didn't, so I don't think you have anything to be worried about. But if I hear about a problem, I'll let you know."

"Thanks for calling and having my back."

"We have to do that for one another around here," Amanda responded.

"Absolutely."

/ / /

When Buddy woke up, the excitement and euphoria of the previous evening were gone. But as he stretched for a few moments in bed, he knew something else was present—a sense of peace. Normally, he stumbled around as he made the transition to wakefulness, but this morning he was alert and mentally sharp as he brewed a cup of coffee. After a few sips, he decided to do something he hadn't done in years: go for an early morning run. He left the house without a set route in mind. Making a turn down Franklin Street, he passed both his mother's house and the bed-and-breakfast where Judge Williams was staying. He then left the main road and made his way through neighborhoods with smaller homes. Reaching an intersection, he turned left and passed by the house where Gracie Blaylock lived. Buddy inwardly acknowledged the huge role Gracie had played in the good things that had taken place on his mother's porch, but he knew it was really about him and the Lord. He retraced his way down Franklin Street. It was still too early for his mother to be outside watering the flowers.

At the office, Buddy determined to greet Millie and Jennifer in a normal manner. But when he spoke to Millie, he smiled broadly and laughed.

The office manager gave him a strange look. "Is something wrong with my hair?" she asked, raising her hands to the sides of her tightly coiffed head.

"No, you look fine, uh, lovely." Buddy stopped and chuckled again.

He continued to his office, shut the door behind him, and leaned against it. The phone on his desk buzzed. He steadied himself for a follow-up question from Millie about what was wrong with him this morning.

He picked it up. "I'm sorry," he began.

"Excuse me," Jennifer said. "Mr. Varnego is on the phone. He needs to reschedule his appointment this morning, and I wasn't sure what to tell him."

"I'll handle it."

Buddy talked to the client, then moved into his morning routine. Several times he paused and checked to make sure the peace he'd felt upon waking remained. Around 11:00 a.m. he received a call from Mayleah.

"Good morning!" he said more enthusiastically than he intended.

"Good morning to you," Mayleah replied. "Detective Morrison, who's trained in handwriting analysis, believes there's at least a slim chance Reagan is using the name Kimberly Landers."

Buddy knew Detective Morrison to be a no-nonsense officer.

"But I wanted to tell you what the Chattanooga detective told me during our phone call. I'd mentioned your search for Amber the other day, and she jotted down some notes. She says there are several people with the last name Melrose living in the Soddy-Daisy area, with a lot more in Chattanooga."

"That's what I discovered in my research."

"That's not all. She talked with a man named Vick Melrose, who lives in Soddy-Daisy. When she asked if he knew a woman in her thirties named Amber Melrose, he told her that Amber is his great-niece."

"Does he know where she is?" Buddy asked, leaning forward in his chair.

"No. He claims that she's moved around a lot over the past few years, and he hasn't seen her in a while. He became suspicious when the detective asked if he would help track her down and refused to answer any more questions. I think it would be worth talking to him in person and laying out exactly why you want to contact Amber."

"Absolutely." Buddy opened the calendar screen on his computer.

"I was looking at next Tuesday."

Buddy moved to the calendar for the following week. "I only have one office appointment with a client who can come in another day. I'll block it off. Is there anything I should do to prepare?"

"No."

"Will you identify yourself as a police officer?"

"No, I'll be out of my jurisdiction."

Buddy paused for a moment. "Are you available for lunch today? There's something personal I'd like to tell you about."

"Yeah, if we can make it early."

"No problem. The Crossroads at eleven forty-five?"

"See you then."

Buddy hung up the phone and went out to Millie's desk. It was the fifth of the month, and the office manager was opening envelopes that contained rent checks from tenants.

"How is it looking this month?" Buddy asked.

"Pretty good," Millie said.

"I'm going to be out of town next Tuesday with Detective Harkness. We're going to talk to one of Amber's great-uncles who lives near Chattanooga."

"Is that why you bounced in here so chipper this morning?"

"No, that was something else. It had to do with time I spent last night at my mother's house with Gracie Blaylock. We went outside onto the porch after dinner—"

Millie held up her hand, palm out. "Whatever it is, I don't want to know," she said. "You, the detective, now the clerk of court. That's a roller coaster I'm not interested in riding."

When he arrived at the restaurant, Buddy saw Mayleah sitting in the back corner.

"I know you're on a tight schedule and hope you ordered," he said.

"No, I waited for you."

"I went for an early morning run, so I'm starving."

Buddy called over a waitress whom he knew well. "We're ready, Judy," he said. "And if you could bump her order to the front of the line, I'd appreciate it."

"Will do, Buddy," the middle-aged woman replied.

Mayleah selected a salad, and Buddy ordered a pork chop with candied yams, applesauce, lima beans, and corn bread.

"What's on your mind that we couldn't discuss over the phone?" Mayleah asked.

"I had an amazing experience last night at my mother's house and wanted to tell you about it."

Buddy had barely started when the waitress brought Mayleah's salad.

"You eat while I talk," he said. "No, I'll pray first."

Buddy bowed his head. He'd never openly prayed in public and didn't care who saw him do so.

"Thank you, God, for what you've done in my life and for this food. Amen."

"What has God done in your life?" Mayleah asked as soon as Buddy raised his head.

"That's what I want to tell you about."

Buddy was used to systematically organizing his thoughts and words. Today that ability deserted him. He stumbled, backtracked, and added extraneous information about Judge Williams's parrot. The waitress brought his meal.

"It sounds like a bizarre evening," Mayleah said.

Buddy continued talking while he cut his pork chop into bite-size pieces without placing one in his mouth.

Mayleah pointed to his plate. "It looks like you're preparing to feed a small child."

"I didn't want to stop talking."

"But you said you were hungry."

"I'm starving."

Mayleah laughed. "Okay, I'm assuming that you and Gracie ended up praying together on the porch after the meal, and it was very meaningful. Correct?"

"Uh, yeah. But that makes it sound a lot drier and more sterile than it was."

"Eat," Mayleah said and pointed to Buddy's plate.

Buddy dutifully ate a bite of pork chop.

Mayleah continued, "I know what you're talking about because I've heard similar stories from people close to me."

"Family members?" Buddy asked as he continued to chew.

"Yes. Including my ex-husband."

"What?" Buddy jumped in.

"Keep eating and don't interrupt."

Buddy ate a bite of candied yams.

"I'm not sure what to think," Mayleah said. "I didn't totally doubt what Clay told me, but I didn't completely believe him either. In the back of my mind, I couldn't shake the suspicion that he was using his story as a way to convince me to move back to Oklahoma and try to work things out between us. That's a total 180-degree turnaround, since he was the one who insisted on the divorce."

"Did he tell you exactly what happened to him?"

"A friend invited him to church and promised a wing dinner at one of the best sports bars in town if Clay showed up. My ex-husband loves wings and agreed to go. The minister preached a sermon, and Clay went forward for prayer at the end of the meeting. Now he claims that he's a different man."

"I totally get it. 'Different' has been a huge word for me over the past twenty-four hours."

Mayleah was silent for a few moments. "I'm happy for you," she said. "And I don't want to be selfish in the way I hear it. But I can't help wondering if what you're telling me also has something to do with how I need to relate to Clay."

"You mean, I'm saying what he might say?"

"Not exactly, but close enough that it gets my attention."

Talking and listening to Mayleah made one thing clear to Buddy: the detective was a friend and ally, nothing more. He felt a pang of regret coupled with relief at realizing the truth.

Mayleah continued, "Like I said the other night, I don't want to throw away what I'm building here to run back to Oklahoma, but I can't shake the possibility that I should consider it."

"I'm here as a sounding board if that's what you need," Buddy said.

"You're already doing it."

Mayleah got up from the table and reached into her purse for her wallet.

"No, I'm buying lunch," Buddy said. "I invited you."

"Not today," Mayleah said. "You can treat me when we go to Chattanooga."

/ / /

Shortly after noon, Gracie walked across the street to pick up lunch from the Crossroads. Deep in thought about how her attitude toward the visiting judge had shifted during the last twenty-four hours, she went directly to the to-go counter. Her order wasn't quite ready.

"Gracie." She heard her name and turned around to see Buddy at his usual table.

"Would you like to join me?" he asked when she made her way over to him. "I'm alone. Mayleah just left for a meeting."

"I'm getting takeout."

"You can still eat it at my table."

Gracie hesitated.

"Don't make me use this fork to threaten you," Buddy said, holding the raised utensil in front of him.

"I'm glad it's not a knife." Gracie smiled and switched her order to dine-in.

"How are you doing after last night?" she asked as soon as she sat down.

"Still different. And it's going to take awhile to get used to this. I woke up feeling so alive that I went for an early morning run. That may not sound like a big change, but it meant something to me."

"That's what matters."

"And I just told Mayleah about it. That's why I invited her to lunch."

The waitress brought Gracie's meal. Buddy's plate was almost clean. He ate a final piece of pork chop before continuing.

"I think she understood what I was talking about, but if she didn't, it was my fault because I'm not sure exactly how to explain it myself." Buddy paused. "Her main response was to let me know that her ex-husband recently heard a sermon that changed him and now wants her to consider moving back to Oklahoma."

"Is she considering that?"

"Yes, but she obviously doesn't want word to get back to anyone at the sheriff's office."

"Sure," Gracie said, then was silent for a moment. "God restores broken marriages, even after a divorce."

Buddy gave her a skeptical look. "Nobody that I've ever represented."

"Do you know Missy and David Whitaker?" Gracie asked.

"No."

"They remarried after getting a divorce and now have five kids."

"What about Sue Ellen and Jackie Ford? Do you think she should take him back when he gets out of jail?"

Gracie now regretted her comment. She didn't want to debate Buddy and wasn't sure what she believed about Sue Ellen and Jackie Ford's situation.

"All I can say is that it worked out for the best with Missy and David."

"Well, this is Mayleah's business, but I suspect I'll hear more about it when we drive to Chattanooga next week to talk to some people about both Reagan and Amber."

Buddy told her about Amber's great-uncle. Gracie was glad for the news and a change in subject.

"That could be huge," she said. "To finally find someone who might be willing to talk about what's been going on for the past seventeen years."

"Yes. Will you pray about it?"

"Absolutely."

TWENTY

LATE IN THE AFTERNOON, BUDDY CALLED SAMMY LANDRY to let him know about the upcoming trip to Chattanooga. Reagan's father seemed subdued. Buddy wanted to encourage him, but it would be tough to do so in good faith.

"Finding Reagan remains at the top of my list, and the cooperation we're getting from Detective Harkness couldn't be better," he said.

"And I appreciate all of that," Sammy replied. "But instead of the wait getting easier, it's been the opposite. I'm not sleeping. Crystal isn't sleeping. The constant questions we get from well-meaning people don't help either. They're like sticks of wood on a campfire. My mind is all over the place."

"What if we schedule a time to meet at the driving range and hit a bucket or two of balls?" Buddy suggested.

"I haven't done that since this all started. The only reason I played with you and the guys the other day was that it had been on the books for a long time."

"My hesitation is that it might ruin the new groove I discovered when we played. I'm scared my slice will rear its ugly head."

Sammy chuckled slightly, which was a golden sound to Buddy's ears.

"That's why it's both a great game and a terrible game," Sammy said. "I chase some of the fantastic shots I've made for years hoping they might come back."

They set a time for Saturday morning.

"And the first two buckets are on me," Buddy said.

"No way—"

"Yes, because you're going to be standing beside me giving me a lesson."

"Okay. Deal."

After the call ended, Jennifer came into Buddy's office with a FedEx packet and placed it on his desk. It was the results of his DNA test. Buddy read the summary sheet and chuckled. As suspected, he was a combination of many ethnic groups who washed ashore in America and created a new life. He was sixteen percent French, but there was almost as much English, German, Swedish, Spanish, and a lesser amount of Russian. Toward the bottom of the list was a small percentage of Native American—Cherokee.

He chuckled. "Mayleah and I are related."

Buddy propped up his feet on his chair and went through the rest of the DNA results. He'd read enough about the tests to know that the information looked more precise and scientific than it really was. However, it made for interesting reading. He shared a common ancestor with 312 people in the company's database. Buddy had checked a box that gave permission for his name and contact information to be released in case someone within the same subset wanted to connect with him. One of those could be Elise. In his heart he hoped; in his mind he doubted. There was a much greater probability that Amber's great-uncle in Tennessee would provide a viable lead.

Because he'd taken a run in the morning, Buddy stayed later than usual at the office. As he was getting ready to leave, he called his mother.

"Is there any venison chili in the fridge?" he asked. "I forgot to take home my leftovers."

"I saw that. But there's not as much as you'd think. I had some friends over this afternoon, and they wanted to taste it. They ended up eating seconds."

Buddy smiled at the thought of his mother's friends hunched over bowls of chili. "Would it be okay if I stopped by?"

"Yes, I'm not doing anything with Bryant this evening."

"Can I pick up something from the store and bring it with me?" he asked.

"Some strawberries if they look nice, and a pound of coffee. You know the blend I prefer."

"Dark Colombian roast?"

"Right."

Buddy stopped at the grocery store. He also grabbed a bunch of fresh asparagus, which was his mother's favorite vegetable. When he arrived at the house on Franklin Street, there was a much smaller pot of chili warming on the stovetop.

"Asparagus!" his mother exclaimed when she unpacked the grocery bag. "I almost asked you to get some. It may not be the best pairing for chili, but I've been craving some. I'm going to sauté it right now."

Buddy sat at the kitchen table while his mother washed the asparagus and put it in a pan with melted butter and two cloves of crushed garlic. Rascal didn't like garlic, so Beatrice had rarely cooked asparagus the way she preferred when he was alive. She put a lid on the skillet and sat at the table across from Buddy.

"I wanted to tell you what happened after you went upstairs last night," he began. "Gracie and I sat on the front porch and talked for quite a while. Actually, there was more praying than talking, kind of a carryover from the dinner table."

Beatrice's eyes opened wider. "What did you pray about?"

Buddy pointed at himself. "Gracie prayed first. You know what that's like, but then I was able to pray too. For much longer than ever before in my life." Buddy leaned forward. "And something happened to me. I can't exactly explain it, but I don't have any doubt it was real. I'd always thought praying was words directed toward God, but this was God touching me. Afterward, I went home and wrote for over an hour, scribbling as fast as I could what I was thinking and feeling and seeing. It poured out of me."

Buddy stopped. He could tell his mother was shocked.

"Would you let me read any of it?" she asked. "I was paying close attention to what you said, but that would help me understand better."

Buddy hesitated but then remembered the box of his mother's journals she'd willingly entrusted to him.

"Of course," he said.

Beatrice stepped over to the stove and checked the asparagus. "What did you think about Bryant?" she asked.

Buddy leaned back in his chair. "He wasn't the same as he is at the courthouse. And having a talking parrot as a dinner guest was a first. But I liked him."

"Bryant or Bailiff?"

"Both." Buddy chuckled. "But I meant the judge."

"I like him too," Beatrice said in a soft voice. "But I'm not sure I like him enough."

"Maybe you're filling a role in his life for something different. Were you surprised when he said getting to know you had made him evaluate his own life?"

Beatrice looked down at the table. "No," she answered with a slight smile before meeting Buddy's eyes again. "I haven't been as bold as Gracie, but I could tell pretty quickly that he'd gone astray over the years. The question was whether he wanted to find a way home."

Buddy was once again impressed by his mother. "What insights do you have about me that you're keeping to yourself?" he asked.

Instead of answering, Beatrice filled a bowl with chili, put some asparagus on a plate, and set the meal in front of him.

"Have you been reading my journals?" she asked.

"Yes."

"There might be some hints in there."

Beatrice fixed her own plate and joined him. She looked expectantly at Buddy. "Will you say the blessing?" she asked.

Not sure what to pray, he decided to keep it short. "God, thank you for this food and for my mother and what you did on the porch last night." Buddy started to say amen but hesitated. "And you know that I wanted to make things right for her the other day after we found out that my father gave Amber all that money without telling us. Maybe now I can help make that happen. Amen."

When he finished, Buddy expected to see tears in his mother's eyes. Instead, she was smiling.

"Sitting here and listening to you is a balm to my soul," she said.

"Would you like to hear the latest news about my search for Elise?" Buddy asked.

"Of course."

Buddy brought his mother up-to-date on the investigation.

"I'd like to see the photo of the young woman that the detective took in Atlanta to see if there's a family resemblance," Beatrice said.

Buddy pulled it up on his phone and showed it to her. "I think she's a combination of Amber and me, but Gracie and Mayleah Harkness claim the similarity is in my imagination."

Beatrice studied the picture closely before returning the phone to him. "Sorry, but I agree with Gracie and Mayleah."

"Okay. I know when I'm whipped." Buddy shrugged. "I'm not going to win an argument with three women."

He laid the phone on the table beside his chili. "But that's not all," he said. "There's a better lead."

Buddy told her about locating Amber's great-uncle Vick Melrose in Soddy-Daisy.

"Mayleah and I are going to Chattanooga next week to talk to the great-uncle. Hopefully, he'll tell me where Amber and Elise are living."

Beatrice ate the last piece of asparagus on her plate and touched her mouth with a napkin. "That makes me feel like you're closer than ever to finding Elise," she said.

"I wonder what it would be like to finally meet her. Where should that take place? What would I say? How will Elise react? What has Amber told her about me? Does Elise know anything about me at all? Has Amber made up a story about her past and—"

Beatrice reached out and placed her hand on Buddy's arm. "That's where you need to put into practice this new faith you found last night," she said. "You may even want to ask Gracie to pray about it, although I wouldn't be surprised if she was already doing so."

Buddy ate the last of his bowl of chili. "Is there any peach cobbler?" he asked. "Please tell me the ladies didn't finish that off too."

"No, there's plenty," Beatrice answered with a smile. "I'll warm it up. There's vanilla ice cream in the freezer."

While his mother heated the cobbler, Buddy went to his car and brought in the data from the DNA test. While they ate dessert, he shared the results.

"Your father always claimed to be part French," Beatrice said. "It was a few generations back on his mother's side."

"So that's not from your family?"

Beatrice pointed to the percentage for English. "That came from me. One of my aunts traced our family to someplace in the middle of England. Nothing fancy. They were farmers and working-class people."

"What about the Native American connection?" Buddy asked.

"Based on family rumors, I'll claim that too."

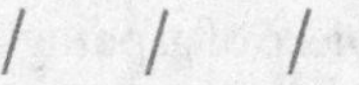

It was an unseasonably cool afternoon when Gracie arrived at the softball field. She spent time throwing softballs from the pitcher's mound into the backstop until the team began to arrive. The first girl on the scene was Heidi, who gathered up balls and brought them to Gracie. Gracie grabbed one and hurled a rising fastball across home plate.

"That would be hard to hit," Heidi said.

"Grab a bat, and I'll throw you a few," Gracie replied.

Gracie threw ten pitches. Heidi whiffed on five, fouled off three, and hit two weak grounders toward second base that would have been easy outs.

"What am I doing wrong?" Heidi called out from the batter's box.

"You're not picking up the ball with your eyes as soon as it leaves my hand. You're waiting until it's halfway to home plate, which is too late."

Gracie threw six more pitches. Heidi missed one, fouled one, hit a weak grounder, but also solidly connected with three balls and sent them into the outfield for potential singles or doubles. By this point several other members of the team were watching.

"Coach Blaylock, could you throw batting practice?" Laura called out.

"Not today," Gracie replied. "Our pitchers, including you, need the practice."

An hour and a half later the girls gathered in a circle to pray. Gracie glanced up as Mayleah pulled into the parking lot. After the prayer ended, two girls had questions about an upcoming game. As Gracie was answering, she saw Laura go over to the detective, who now sat on a low bleacher. It was ten minutes before Gracie walked over to join them.

"Come by the sheriff's department, and I'll give you a tour," Mayleah said to the second baseman as the girl walked away.

Mayleah turned to Gracie. "Buddy and I are going to Chattanooga next week—"

"I know," Gracie said. "I talked to him at the Crossroads after he met with you."

"Okay. And at some point I'm going to Atlanta to follow up my investigation into Patricia Nichols."

Gracie leaned against the end of the bleacher where Mayleah was sitting.

"I obtained a list of residents for the apartment building and called several of them," the detective said. "One woman was willing to talk to me and confirmed there was a lot of activity involving younger women coming and going from the apartment connected to Nichols. The neighbor believes a man lives there too. The way she described the man fit the description of the guy who opened the door the other day."

"Did you tell the neighbor that you're a detective?"

"Yes. That's why I believe she spoke with me. She's been concerned about the activity centered at the apartment but didn't know the name of anybody who lives there. She'd never heard of Patricia Nichols or Katrina Caldwell, the alias Nichols used for the Instagram account linked to Reagan."

Gracie felt a knot of anxiety in her stomach. "What's next?" she asked.

"Try to find out more." Mayleah paused. "Would you be willing to reach out to Nichols on social media?"

"How? I couldn't do something like that."

"You wouldn't do it in your own name. We'd create a fake presence and see if Nichols expressed an interest in meeting you. If she did, then we'd arrange something in a public place, and I'd record the conversation. It might give us a chance to find out what she's up to."

Gracie's head was spinning. "I'm the clerk of court, not in law enforcement," she managed. "And I'm thirty-five, not eighteen."

"You look younger," Mayleah said with a grin. "And we could

use a photograph taken a few years ago so long as nothing about your clothes or the setting of the picture dates you. All we need is a picture that will pass scrutiny when you show up in person. People post deceptively positive pictures on social media all the time. Yours would be an honest representation."

"I'd be scared to death."

"Nervousness would enhance your credibility."

Gracie shook her head. "If word got out in Milton County that I did something like this, I'm not sure how the voters, judges, or county commissioners might respond. It could ruin my career."

Mayleah placed her hands on her knees. "I mentioned it to the sheriff, and he thought it was a good idea so long as I supervise everything and make sure you're not put in a dangerous situation. I'd set up the social media account and create content based on what's attracted Nichols's attention to young women in the past."

"Why don't you do it with one of your photos from a few years ago?" Gracie asked.

"I'm going to whether you agree to do it or not," Mayleah replied. "But if you join with me, we can establish a social link that gives us a reason to meet with Nichols together at the same time. Everything would be totally false except for our own interaction. All the rest of our friend networks would be manufactured. That's not hard to do. We created bogus profiles for a case I worked on in Oklahoma, and I'd ask my former boss if I could borrow that data for this project. The success we had in the earlier investigation is what gave me the idea to use it here."

"What kind of investigation was it?"

"Sex trafficking."

Gracie sighed. "And you're sure the sheriff thinks this is a good idea?"

"Talk to him yourself. A lot of police work depends on the cooperation of the public. Instead of giving information, you'd be helping uncover it. It's all about finding Reagan and helping her and any other girls."

"Yes, and I do want to find her," Gracie said. "But I don't think I should do something like this. It's not who I am."

"This wouldn't be you. It would be someone we create."

Gracie didn't respond.

"It's just an idea," Mayleah continued. "And I'll understand if you say no."

Gracie relaxed. Mayleah's hard sell made her uncomfortable.

/ / /

After leaving his mother's house, Buddy returned to the back porch and reread what he'd written the previous night. There was a raw vitality to the words that poured out of him. They didn't need to be refined. He would make a copy at the office and give it to his mother.

Returning to the box of journals he'd found in the basement, he began to systematically read what his mother had written, some entries from more than twenty years earlier. Once again, he was impressed with her simple yet profound insights, expressed in succinct language. Family members figured prominently, but she also wrote about people throughout the community. The occasional mentions of Amber and Elise were like meteors shooting across the sky. He looked up from an entry about them that forced him to think about the situation in a new light.

In the past, Buddy had struggled more with anger at Amber for leaving than regret over what he could have done differently.

Although his mother didn't openly criticize Buddy, her honest words and prayers forced him to face the selfishness he brought to the high school relationship. Beatrice prayed for Buddy's heart to be tender toward the Lord and Amber. But during that time, he hadn't thought about God and related to Amber based on the happiness she could give him. Tonight, an aching sorrow stirred the depths of his being. Buddy looked up from the pages for a moment as a pair of tears slowly rolled down his cheeks and dropped onto the yellowed page of the journal in his lap. He blinked a couple of times and stared at the small circles whose margins were marked by sadness. A few more tears escaped from his eyes. Those he wiped away with the back of his hand. He'd never cried over his loss. Maybe it was time he did.

TWENTY-ONE

GRACIE CHECKED HER EMAILS THROUGH THE DATING site. There were two from Daniel, the second asking why she hadn't responded to the first one. Gracie went back to the earlier email and discovered Daniel was ready to meet in person and willing to do so at the time and place of Gracie's choosing. Other than an upcoming softball tournament, there were several open Saturdays within the next two months. Gracie stared at the calendar. The arrival of a new email from Mayleah gave her an excuse to delay a response.

> I've posted my Instagram profile and included links to fictitious people as well as to a couple of young women Patricia Nichols contacted in the past. I created a second-level link for me with those girls through other people in their network. Check it out. See you soon!

Gracie opened the link to Mayleah's fake social media account. The detective was using the name Ahyoka Lightfoot. The photo showed Mayleah on snow skis with a cup of coffee in her hand and a big smile on her face. A young Native American man, who looked to be in his late teens or early twenties, was standing beside her. Ahyoka longed for a life of adventure in Atlanta and listed herself as a recent high school graduate whose parents wanted her to go to college, but who didn't want to conform to family expectations. All the photos of Mayleah were taken from a distance and hid her true age. Gracie knew she had similar pictures stored on her own computer. Scrolling through the follower list, Gracie wondered which two women were the real people who'd connected with Nichols. Nothing gave her a clue. She picked up her cell phone and called Mayleah.

/ / /

Saturday evening Buddy was on his way to another dinner at Chris Henley's house, this time to celebrate the lawyer's birthday. Buddy pulled into the driveway at the same time as Jason and Katie Long.

"Go inside," Jason said to his wife. "I'm going to talk to Buddy for a minute."

"Don't be too long," Katie replied. "If Marissa says she's serving dinner at seven o'clock, she means it."

Jason waited until they were alone before he turned to Buddy. There was anxiety in the doctor's eyes.

"Has something new happened?" Buddy asked.

"Yes," Jason said in a low but intense voice. "The lawyers for the boy's family are talking to Cam Simpson about testifying against me."

"How did you find out?"

"One of my nurses is friends with a physician's assistant at his office. She said Cam is considering it."

Cam Simpson was a well-respected pediatrician at another clinic in Clarksburg. To convince a local doctor to testify that

Jason had been negligent would be ten times more damaging in front of a Milton County jury than bringing in a hired expert with a fancy diploma from a big city. Buddy could understand the panic in his friend's voice. Dr. Simpson was in his early sixties and considered by most the dean of pediatricians in the area. He'd been Elise's doctor when she was a newborn at the hospital. He'd also been an investor in a couple of real estate deals with Rascal, both of which turned out to be very profitable. Buddy remembered his father describing the doctor as a difficult business partner.

"What I want to know is, can I talk to Cam about it?" Jason asked. "The records from the hospital aren't the best, and there are statements in the triage nurse's notes that don't accurately describe what was going on. I have independent recollections of the situation because I was so concerned for the boy's status, and it would be important for Cam to know exactly what I did and why. I thought about calling the insurance company lawyers, but Katie reminded me that's why I asked you to help."

Buddy leaned against his car. It had been years since he'd seen Dr. Simpson. They didn't move in the same social circles.

"There's no legal prohibition against you talking to Cam, but there's a risk that if he gets involved, he might say you came to him and tried to convince him not to testify, which would make it look like you were manipulating the situation."

"I just want him to know all the facts."

"Who represents Cam locally?" Buddy asked.

"Chris's law firm." Jason motioned with his head toward the house. "That was my other thought. If Cam testifies, would that mean Vince Nelson has to get out of the case? Everyone tells me how important his presence in a courtroom will be to a jury."

"The Nelson firm wouldn't necessarily have to withdraw. Cam's testimony wouldn't have anything to do with their representation of him as an individual or doctor. One of the lawyers with the firm in Atlanta would cross-examine him."

Buddy could tell his analysis wasn't helping Jason. The doctor's face revealed his stress.

"I hate this," Jason said. "When I went to med school I always knew this was a possibility. But facing it in real life is so different from knowing it might happen."

"Let me think about it," Buddy answered.

Buddy followed Jason into the house. It was an Italian-themed dinner. Marissa had prepared an elaborate meal of lemon cream chicken with champagne risotto and prosciutto-wrapped asparagus. She paired the food with an expensive pinot noir wine. The table was set with fine china and a white tablecloth. Place cards directed the guests to their seats around the table. Buddy was to the right of Chris and next to Katie.

"When Chris said we were having Italian, I thought he meant a meat lover's pizza," Buddy said. "And my mother is going to be jealous when I tell her about the asparagus."

"If there are leftovers, you can take her a serving," Marissa said.

"There won't be," Katie piped up. "I'd rather have asparagus than dessert."

"We're having zabaglione for dessert," Marissa said.

"What's that?" Buddy asked. "I try not to eat anything I can't spell."

"Custard with fruit," Chris said. "I had a choice between that and chocolate cake."

The main courses were served from silver containers in the center of the table. Chris turned to Marissa. Buddy knew he was going to ask his wife to say a blessing for the food. It was a role she routinely fulfilled.

"I'll pray the blessing," Buddy said.

Everyone at the table stared at him. No one looked more surprised than Marissa. "Are you serious?" she asked.

"Yeah."

Marissa looked at Chris, who shrugged.

"Go for it," Chris said.

Buddy had volunteered on impulse. Now he felt the pressure to deliver. He bowed his head and thought about Gracie's prayer at his mother's house. He knew if he tried to copy that, it wouldn't work.

"God," he began, stretching out the name somewhat, "thank you for this food."

Buddy knew he could stop and be okay, but he didn't. He heard Chris stifle a laugh.

"We ask you to bless Chris and give him a good birthday and a fun time with his kids and his awesome wife who cooked this amazing meal for us that I'm sure is good even though we haven't eaten it yet."

Chris laughed out loud. "Sorry," the host said. "Are you finished?"

"No," Buddy answered. "And be with Jason and Katie while they're under a bunch of stress and help them in ways that only you can. I'm thankful for these friends who have included me in their lives even though I'm single. Amen."

Buddy looked up. Everyone was still staring at him.

"Didn't you close your eyes?" he asked. "You're supposed to do that during a prayer."

"What's going on with you?" Chris asked.

"Hey, I could ask you the same thing," Buddy replied. "At least I didn't laugh during the prayer."

"Maybe I was out of line." Chris grinned. "But you have to admit it was funny."

"I appreciated Buddy's prayer," Katie jumped in. "And you should be ashamed of yourself for being critical."

"Okay, I repent," Chris said and threw up his hands.

Buddy enjoyed the meal. The chicken was moist with a nice kick to the sauce due to cayenne pepper. Buddy had trouble cooking instant rice, so he could also appreciate the risotto. And the asparagus was crisp and flavorful. During the meal, he noticed that Katie, who was talking to Marissa, kept glancing sideways at him.

Finally, when Marissa stepped into the kitchen, Katie turned and spoke to him in a low voice: "Buddy, what's really going on?"

"What do you mean?"

"The blessing you prayed before the meal. That's not like you."

"Maybe it is, or at least it should be."

"Tell me more."

Buddy started giving her a quick, low-key version of recent events. Within a couple of sentences, the entire table was listening.

"And why was Judge Williams at your mother's house for dinner?" Chris cut in.

"He and my mother have been hanging out recently," Buddy replied.

Chris rolled his eyes. "If a witness in a deposition gave me that answer, I would not leave it alone."

"It's not like they're dating, at least not in the same way I date someone."

"That raises a lot of questions for me," Marissa jumped in.

"No," Chris said to his wife. "Buddy's dating life is off-limits to all female inquirers."

"I think everyone should be quiet and let Buddy tell us what he wants to about himself," Jason said.

Buddy began with what happened on his mother's front porch and the part Gracie played. He then summarized what he'd written in his journal about being different. Marissa Henley became teary-eyed. When Buddy finished, no one spoke for a couple of seconds.

"I shouldn't doubt you, but it sounds very subjective to me," Chris said slowly.

"That's because it's a matter of the heart," Marissa said with a sniffle. "I think it's beautiful. I've believed the same way ever since that special weekend at the church a couple of years ago. Remember, you only came the first night because Mr. Nelson made you work that weekend."

Chris didn't respond to his wife. Jason was looking at Buddy as if he were a patient with an unusual ailment.

"What are you thinking?" Buddy asked the doctor.

"I want to talk to you some more about this."

/ / /

"Hey, Ahyoka," Gracie said when the detective answered the phone. "What's the Instagram status?"

"It's only been active for six hours, and I'm already being followed by a bunch of guys."

"I'm not surprised. The photos are great. But are you sure it's okay to use your Cherokee name?"

"I thought it made me seem more exotic. How are you doing?"

"Fine," Gracie said, then paused for a moment. "Do you really think it might help if I did this too?"

"That would be the goal," Mayleah said calmly. "Like I said the other day, you and I would interact in a way that might increase the chance of Patricia Nichols contacting one or both of us. The only way to find out is to give it a try. Obviously, this isn't all I'm doing to locate Reagan. I've found another social media contact with a suspicious background. I'm investigating her too."

Gracie listened as Mayleah told her about a middle-aged woman in Atlanta with a criminal record who had personally communicated with Reagan.

"Beverly Linstrom is her name," Mayleah said. "The drug charges against her are for possession and distribution of methamphetamine, using younger boys and girls to sell."

"That is so bad," Gracie replied.

"And she went to prison for three years."

Gracie took a deep breath before continuing. "I'm in. What do you need from me?"

"Seriously?"

"Yes."

"Photos like the one with my cousin that suggests he's my boyfriend. I wouldn't include photos showing other people's faces unless I asked permission. Someone might randomly come across the post and identify them. My cousin wants to be a cop, so he thought it was a great idea. The only problem was making him realize he can't reveal who we are to anybody."

"Are there a lot of law enforcement officers in your family?"

"A bunch. My grandfather was a deputy sheriff. There are uncles, aunts, and cousins involved in one way or another. It's in my genes."

"I'll send pictures and you can pick the ones you think will work. Does this mean we should push back our trip to the apartment complex in Atlanta?"

"Maybe, but only by a few days. I don't want to put too much emphasis on any one aspect of the investigation."

"That makes sense." Gracie thought for a moment. "Oh, should I come up with a fictitious name?"

"I've done that for you and written the text and profile. All I need are the photos."

"How did you know I'd agree to do it?" Gracie asked in surprise. "I wasn't sure myself until a few minutes ago."

"A combination of woman's intuition and personal confidence that you would unselfishly take the risk."

"I don't feel overly brave. What's my fictitious name?"

Mayleah coughed slightly and mumbled something that Gracie couldn't understand.

"I couldn't make out what you said."

"Pixie Carpenter."

Gracie wrinkled her nose. "That sounds totally fake."

"Pixie isn't your real name. It's Patricia, same as for Nichols, but you like the whimsical sound of Pixie. You're looking to shed your conservative Deep South chains and explore your wild side, preferably in Atlanta, not Los Angeles or New York."

"I'm not sure I have pictures that will sync up with that theme."

"Something outdoors, in a flower garden, with a dog. Give me variety. The photos won't reveal how wild you are. That will come out in what you say about them."

"This feels so strange. Pixie?"

"Wait until you read the interchange between the two of us."

"What's that like?"

"I said wait," Mayleah said, a smile in her voice. "You have work to do. When can I expect to receive something from you?"

"I'll get started this evening."

Gracie was surprised by how much she enjoyed putting together an album for Mayleah. She had a nice photo with Ditto, a golden retriever she owned when she was in her early twenties. That prompted her to focus on that period of her life. As she did, Gracie was careful to avoid out-of-date fashion, which didn't prove very hard to do because she'd never been overly fashion conscious in the first place.

As part of her portfolio she included a more glamorous photo of herself and a man she briefly dated. They were at Tybee Island on the beach, walking away from the camera into a sunset. Gracie was wearing a loose-fitting white skirt and light blue top. The skirt was blowing in the sea breeze. After the photo session they went to dinner and had an argument and broke up soon thereafter. Since the picture didn't show either of their faces, Gracie decided to include it. Yawning, she forwarded the file to Mayleah and prepared for bed. Right before she turned off the light, her phone on the nightstand vibrated. It was Buddy. By the time she answered, he'd hung up without leaving a message.

/ / /

The next morning Buddy met Chris and Marissa in the lobby of their church. He was the only person in the parking lot wearing a tie. Marissa's face beamed in welcome, and she gave him a quick hug.

"Sorry, I should have told you the dress code is casual," Chris said. "It's a nice break because Mr. Nelson is so old-school about what we wear at work all week."

"Where are the kids?" Buddy asked.

"They have their own program," Marissa answered. "We'll pick them up later."

The church service was different from the traditional worship at the church his mother attended. The pastor was about the same age as Buddy and Chris. He read a lot of Bible verses and showed a couple of movie clips as part of his sermon.

"Isn't Todd a good speaker?" Marissa asked after the young pastor pronounced the benediction and the congregation stood up to leave.

"Yeah, he's fine," Buddy replied.

"But he would have a losing record in Milton County Superior Court," Chris said.

"Chris!" Marissa exclaimed.

"It's the church, so I have to speak the truth," her husband replied. "And you called me down for criticizing Buddy's prayer the other night. Frankly, I'd rather listen to Buddy anyway. There were things he said the other night that are still rolling around in my head."

"That's because there's so much empty space up there," Buddy said.

"No." Chris shook his head and spoke in a serious tone of voice: "It's because I know and trust you."

After they picked up the kids, Marissa invited Buddy to join them for lunch.

"Thanks, but I don't want anything to drive out the memory of the Italian chicken dish and asparagus you served last night. Besides, I'm going to swing by to see my mother and deliver the asparagus you sent home with me."

Chris stepped to the side and motioned to Buddy. "I know

Jason told you about Cam Simpson, but I'm not going to mention it to Mr. Nelson until you have a chance to talk to Cam."

"Are you okay with me giving it a try?"

"Yes. You could save everyone a headache."

"Okay, I just have to figure out the best way to approach him."

"Very carefully. From my experience, Cam always thinks he's the smartest person in the room. Usually, he's right."

Chris's comment didn't make Buddy feel optimistic.

Arriving at his mother's house with the asparagus, he found her eating a salad in the kitchen. She seemed subdued but perked up when he showed her the green stalks wrapped in prosciutto. While she warmed them up in the microwave, he told her about going to church with Chris and Marissa.

"Sara and Art Carbert go there. I think it's because that's where their children attend, and it's a chance to see the grandkids."

"It was okay, but I'm not sure where church is going to fit into my life."

"That's what Bryant thinks," his mother responded. "I took the plunge and invited him to go with me this morning, but he turned me down. He said he likes to relax on Sunday morning and read the Atlanta paper."

"Dad used to read the paper on Sunday afternoon."

"After he gave me the garden section." Beatrice took a metal bowl from the refrigerator. "Would you like a salad?"

"Sure."

Buddy sat at the kitchen table with his mother while he ate.

"Oh, it's not the garden section of the paper, but I have something for you to read," he said. "It's in my car."

Buddy left the house and returned with a few sheets of paper that he placed in front of his mother. She slipped on her glasses and began to read.

"Buddy, this is wonderful," she said when she reached the end. "Can I keep this? I want to go over it again."

"Absolutely. It's a start, but I have a long way to go before I catch up to you and Gracie."

"I've prayed for Gracie many times over the years," Beatrice said. "I'm not sure if those prayers are in the journals you have or not."

"There are more journals?" Buddy asked.

"Oh yes. The more recent ones are stored in the small closet in my bedroom."

"Can I read those?"

Beatrice ate a piece of asparagus. "I need to think about that."

Sunday afternoon Buddy obtained Cam Simpson's cell phone number from Jason. To be thorough, he also asked his friend to sign and fax back a simple attorney-client agreement that confirmed Buddy's representation beyond what he'd provided in the past.

"I almost never call Cam's cell because both our practices have grown so much that we don't cover for each other," Jason said.

"What would be the best time to contact him so I can set up a meeting?"

"He's an early morning guy who gets to the office at the crack of dawn. I'm not sure what he does then, probably reviews charts for patients coming in later in the day or catches up on paperwork."

"What if I showed up at his office at six o'clock in the morning and called him from the parking lot?"

"If a lawyer did that to me, I'd refuse to talk to him and put off the conversation for at least a month."

"Assuming he answers, what should I tell him about the case?" Buddy asked.

"I've been working on that and will send you something. It's a memo explaining the variables that went into my decision-making process for the patient. The insurance company lawyers wanted me to do it anyway."

"Excellent. Catching Cam early in the morning may be the best way."

"If that's what you think," Jason said slowly.

Later, Buddy read Jason's memo while eating a sandwich. He would distill it down to a few sentences, just as if arguing the case to a jury.

TWENTY-TWO

THE FOLLOWING MORNING BUDDY LEFT THE HOUSE while it was still dark. Dr. Simpson's practice was in a building close to the hospital. A pale yellow Porsche was parked in a space reserved for the physicians. Buddy read through Jason's memo one more time, then called Cam's cell phone. Just as the call was about to go to voice mail, the doctor answered.

"Dr. Simpson speaking. Who is this?"

"Buddy Smith. Thanks for taking my call. I'd like to meet with you if you have a few minutes."

"Are you the person sitting in a white Audi in my parking lot?"

"Yes, that's me."

"What do you want to talk about?"

"Jason Long. And I promise to be brief."

The phone was silent for a moment. Buddy checked to make sure the call was still active.

"Are you his lawyer?"

"One of them, but he's also my friend. That's what got me out of bed in the hope of catching you before your day begins."

There was another period of silence. "I'll open the back door."

Buddy walked toward the brick building. By the time he got there, Cam Simpson had opened the door. The pediatrician had aged since the last time Buddy saw him. The doctor's hair was totally white, and he stood slightly stooped over. He extended his right hand, and Buddy shook it.

"Are you still running marathons?" the doctor asked.

"No, I gave that up years ago."

"I remember reading an article in the newspaper about it."

"Yeah, the reporter tried to make it funny with the heading 'Lawyer on the Run.' I caught a lot of grief from folks about it."

"Would you like a cup of coffee?"

"Thanks."

Buddy followed Simpson down a hallway with examination rooms on each side into a compact office. There was a single-cup coffee machine in the corner.

"Pick what you like," the doctor said.

While the coffee brewed, Dr. Simpson sat behind his desk and focused his attention on his computer monitor. Buddy took a partially full cup of coffee from the machine.

The pediatrician spoke: "There's no need for you to trot out your legal skills and put them on display. I'm not going to testify against Dr. Long. Over the weekend I had a chance to review his office notes for prior treatment of the child. It was reasonable to suspect tonsillitis as the basis for the patient's symptoms upon presentation at the hospital. There weren't enough independent indicia of bacterial meningitis to justify a spinal tap until he ultimately ordered one."

Buddy remained standing. "That's good news," he said, raising his coffee cup. "I appreciate the coffee and will take it with me."

"No, sit down," the doctor said. "Now that you're here, there's something else I'd like to talk to you about."

Curious, Buddy took a seat in a plain chair across from the doctor's desk.

"I don't want to cross any lines," the pediatrician continued, "but I heard from the mother of another patient that you're representing the family in trying to locate Reagan Landry. Is that true?"

"Yes." Buddy sat up straighter in his chair. "In fact, I'm traveling with a detective from the sheriff's department to the Chattanooga area tomorrow as part of the investigation."

"Do you have a release from Reagan's parents granting you access to her medical records?"

"At my office."

"If you send it to me, I can speak with you."

Buddy checked the time on his phone. There was a chance Millie was at work. She occasionally arrived very early on Monday morning so she could get a head start on the week.

"Let me see if my office manager is there," he said. "She can scan one and send it over."

Buddy called Millie's cell phone. "Are you at the office yet?" he asked.

"Yes, and I'm glad you called. We have an emergency. There was a break-in over the weekend at Citywide Lighting. The front door was completely destroyed, and the tenant can't open for business until it's fixed. For some reason, the alarm malfunctioned. I think it's our responsibility under the lease to have an operational system and—"

"That can wait until I get there in a few minutes. Right now I'm at Dr. Cameron Simpson's office. Please scan and email the medical release form signed by Reagan Landry's parents over to him. The file is on the corner of my desk. I'll give you the email address."

"Okay."

While they waited, the doctor handed Buddy a business card. "Our office manager doesn't arrive for another hour and a half," the physician said.

"This is a woman who helped my father for years."

"How's he doing? Has he retired? I'm moving in that direction myself."

"He died from a heart attack three years ago."

"Sorry, I didn't know," the doctor grunted. "I must have missed the obituary."

Millie came back on the line, and Buddy gave her the email address. "Thanks," he said. "Have the police investigated the break-in?"

"They're on the scene now."

"Contact the security company and tell them what happened. As much business as we give them, I expect them to admit fault if there was a malfunction in the equipment that cost the tenant money."

The doctor printed the release from a compact printer on a table beside his desk and read it over. Buddy assumed it was sufficient, but based on Dr. Simpson's reputation he was prepared for an objection.

"This isn't what I prefer," the doctor said. "But you're here, so I'll talk with you."

Dr. Simpson hit several keys on his computer keyboard. "I've been Reagan's doctor since she was an infant. The last time I saw her was two months ago. As a patient gets older we discuss transition to a family practice physician who treats adults. I brought that up with Reagan and gave her information about options here in Clarksburg. She indicated it wasn't necessary since she would be leaving town. I assumed she meant going to college and didn't ask any follow-up questions."

"She just finished her junior year."

"I didn't pick up on that."

The doctor paused. Perhaps more than in any other profession, doctors second-guessed their actions.

"Now I wish I had," he continued. "Late yesterday one of our PAs received a call, supposedly from Reagan, asking us to fill a prescription for not only oxycodone but also Ambien, which I prescribed earlier this year when she was having trouble sleeping."

"Had you prescribed oxycodone in the past?"

"Last year after she dislocated her knee while playing soccer. The refill was out-of-date, but she'd altered the prescription."

"I suspected she might have a drug problem. What was the name of the pharmacy?" Buddy asked.

The doctor looked at the computer screen. "It was a CVS on Ponce de Leon Avenue in Atlanta. I checked and it's in the Midtown area."

The major thoroughfare connected the center of the city with several neighborhoods all the way out to suburban Stone Mountain.

"Did you call in the prescription?"

"Refills for an opiate and a sleep aid can't be justified without an appointment."

"If you called in the prescription and alerted the pharmacy, maybe they could help us find her. Can your office find out if the pharmacy has a way to contact Reagan?"

"I'll do it later this morning and let you know."

Buddy thought for a moment. "If she calls again, please instruct your day staff and the answering service to obtain any information they can, beginning with an address and phone number, and please notify me."

"Will do. And accept my condolences on the loss of your father."

On his way to the office, Buddy first called Sammy Landry and explained to him what he'd learned from Dr. Simpson. Sammy was heartbroken to hear about the probable drug use but encouraged that the pharmacy might be their link to finally finding Reagan. He pleaded with Buddy to let him know as soon as he received any more information, then hurriedly ended the call to go tell Crystal.

Buddy then phoned Jason to give him the much more positive news about Dr. Simpson's decision regarding the malpractice case. Buddy could hear background noise caused by his kids.

"That is great!" Jason replied with more enthusiasm in his voice than Buddy had heard in weeks. "Was my memo helpful?"

"It was totally irrelevant."

"Irrelevant?"

"Cam had conducted his own investigation beyond what the plaintiff's lawyers sent him and concluded your actions were reasonable based on the child's prior problems with tonsillitis. I barely had time to take a sip of the coffee he offered me."

"Do you think I should call him up and thank him?"

"Not for a while. When I know a judge is going to rule in my favor, I shut up."

"Okay." Jason paused. "I still can't believe you drove over there at the crack of dawn, and he invited you into the office for coffee. Should I let the insurance company lawyers know what you did?"

"Yes, they may want to depose Cam as a way to pressure the plaintiff. Do you think there's a chance he'll flip sides?"

"Once Cam reaches a conclusion, he doesn't budge."

/ / /

Gracie was drinking a cup of coffee when her cell phone vibrated. Usually the only person who called this early in the morning was her mother. Mayleah's name popped into view.

"Did I wake you up?" the detective asked.

"No."

"Have you been on Pixie's Instagram account yet?"

"I was going to wait until later to check it out. It's going to be weird reading about someone I'm not."

"There's more to be curious about than that. You've already received a message request from Patricia Nichols."

"What did she say?" Gracie asked in shock.

"That she had a favorite aunt named Pixie."

"Wow, it worked."

"Yes, but I had doubts too. Nichols also liked the photo of Ditto and claimed that she once owned a golden retriever who was like a member of the family. By the way, was Ditto the dog's real name?"

"Yes," Gracie answered, suddenly alarmed. "I should have changed it."

"I wouldn't be worried. It was years ago."

"We could change it or delete it."

"No, that would attract more attention than leaving it alone.

I haven't written a response to Nichols's comment, but I wanted to let you know about it."

"What are you going to say?"

"I'll send her a private message that Ditto recently died and ask her if she knows any breeders in the Atlanta area."

"That sounds so innocent and friendly."

"Which is what we want. My hope is that she'll offer to help. I'll post something too. The fact that you haven't mentioned Ditto's death publicly will reveal that I must be a close friend. Nichols will see your response to me, and that will pave the way for both of us to go to Atlanta. There's no way I'd send you to a rendezvous with her on your own."

The thought of a meeting with Nichols in Atlanta made Gracie's heart beat a little faster. This was the closest she'd ever been to an active police investigation. "Is there anything I need to do?" she asked.

"No."

"Are you going to talk to Buddy about this?"

"Not yet. He doesn't know about our fictitious social media accounts. I may mention it to him tomorrow. Oh, the photo of you and the guy walking toward the water at the beach was beautiful. Was he a longtime boyfriend?"

"He barely made the changing of the tide."

The call ended, and Gracie returned to her prayer list.

Several times during the morning at work, Gracie checked the social media account for Pixie Carpenter. She still had trouble getting past Mayleah's selection of a name but couldn't argue with success. Nichols quickly offered to help Pixie locate a dog breeder in Atlanta. Gracie's alias responded with a string of happy emojis. Ahyoka excitedly weighed in as well and asked if she could come. Nichols replied, "Yes."

/ / /

Late in the afternoon, Buddy stopped by the courthouse.

"Sorry I missed your call the other night," Gracie said.

"Yeah, I should have left a message. I'd been at a birthday party for Chris Henley and ended up telling the group around the table about what happened on my mother's porch."

Gracie raised her eyebrows. "How did that go over?"

"Better than I expected. It turns out I had allies in the room. Yesterday I went to church with Chris and his wife, but I'm not sure I'll go back."

Gracie wanted to ask why but didn't.

Buddy continued, "Anyway, I need to get back to the office for an appointment, but I'd like to talk to you before Mayleah and I go to Chattanooga tomorrow."

"Let's talk in the conference room. Would you like a bottle of water?"

"Sure."

"Did you hear about the break-in last night at Citywide Lighting?" Buddy asked as they walked down the hallway.

"Yes."

"My mother owns the building, and I've been interrupted all day. The sheriff's department is questioning one of the three men who own the company. He's a suspect."

"Why would he rob his own business?"

"He knew they had a lot of cash in the safe and believed he could steal the money and then collect from an insurance policy."

They reached the conference room. Gracie closed the door, and Buddy took a drink of water. She listened as Buddy told her what he'd learned from Dr. Simpson about Reagan and the prescription requests from the pharmacy in Atlanta. Her heart sank.

"Abuse of painkillers has been a problem at the high school for quite a while, especially with girls," Gracie said. "I talk to my team about it."

"That's good," Buddy answered. "But this news tells us that Reagan is likely in Atlanta, not Chattanooga, which means the trip tomorrow with Mayleah will mainly focus on Elise."

"Does Mayleah know about your conversation with Dr. Simpson?"

"Only via email. She wasn't available on the phone, so I sent her a written summary. That's what she'll need for her investigative file."

Gracie was silent for a moment. "We've been working a new angle on finding Reagan that's bearing fruit too," she said. "Mayleah may tell you about it tomorrow."

"Why don't you tell me?"

"Because I think she wants to do it." Gracie paused. "Or not."

Buddy shook his head. "No, Mayleah made it clear to me the other day that she doesn't want me showing up at the apartment complex so I can find out if Elise has been there. I want to be smart and not mess anything up."

"What we're doing doesn't have anything to do with Elise," Gracie said, kicking herself for bringing up the subject.

"Then there's no reason why you can't tell me."

"All right," Gracie surrendered. "But don't let Mayleah know. She set up fictitious Instagram accounts for herself and me. Within less than twenty-four hours, Nichols contacted me. Ahyoka is trying to set up a meeting for the three of us in Atlanta."

"Ahyoka?"

"Ahyoka is Mayleah's Cherokee name."

"How do you spell that? I assume that's the name she's using for the fake account."

"Buddy, please. Leave it alone. Mayleah says it's best that we keep this to ourselves. And that's what I want too. If word gets out that I did this, even though the sheriff knows about the plan, it would be hard to explain here at the courthouse, and I could be criticized or mocked."

"Okay, I can see that," Buddy replied. "And I'll let Mayleah bring it up with me if she wants to. I can play dumb."

"Thanks."

"By the way, what's your fake name?" Buddy grinned.

"Didn't you say you needed to get back to the office?"

Early the following morning Buddy met Mayleah at the sheriff's department. They'd agreed that he would drive to Chattanooga. The detective was wearing jeans, a soft white shirt, and her cowboy boots. She held a cup of coffee in her hand.

"No hat?" Buddy asked when she opened the door and got into his car.

"We're going to Chattanooga, not Laramie."

"Do you want to eat breakfast before we leave town?"

"Not for me."

"Then we'll swing by a drive-through window. I'm in the mood for a sausage biscuit."

There was a fast-food restaurant near the sheriff's department. Buddy pulled in behind an unmarked law enforcement vehicle.

"That's Detective Johnson," Mayleah said.

"I know. He's the one investigating the break-in at Citywide Lighting. My mother owns the building, so I spent a lot of time yesterday responding to the tenant. Any updates on suspects? I know Johnson was talking to one of the owners."

"Not that I'm aware of."

Buddy paid for his biscuit, unwrapped it, and took a bite. "Are you sure you don't want any?" he asked, holding it out to Mayleah.

"It smells yummy."

Buddy made another loop around the restaurant and ordered one for Mayleah.

"Thanks," she said. "I usually eat a yogurt at home, but the smell of the biscuit made my stomach growl."

"So that's what it was. I thought I had a flat tire."

Mayleah lightly punched Buddy in the arm. Reaching the city limits, they turned onto the road that would take them to the interstate.

Mayleah took a sip of coffee. "Sorry I wasn't available yesterday, but I read your memo about your conversation with Dr. Simpson. That's a hot lead."

"I talked with his office manager late yesterday afternoon and went over a protocol to use when contacting the pharmacist. They're going to let me know immediately if anything comes up."

"Reagan has been in Atlanta, but that doesn't mean she's living there."

"So you still want to check out Kimberly Landers?"

"Absolutely. I've learned to pursue all options until all but one are eliminated."

Fifteen minutes later they reached the on-ramp for the interstate.

"How are you going to entertain me during the drive?" Mayleah asked.

"That's your call," Buddy replied, glancing sideways.

Mayleah was silent for a few moments. "Tell me about growing up in Clarksburg. I'm interested in every detail."

"I'm not sure where to start."

"What's your first memory?"

"That's easy," he said. "I was three years old, and my father brought home one of those cheap plastic swimming pools you fill up with a garden hose. You know, the kind decorated with frogs and lily pads."

"Did it have a two-foot slide?"

"No, that probably would have cost extra. My parents put it in the backyard. My older sister and I couldn't wait to get in, so we put on our bathing suits and sat in the pool while my parents filled it up. It must have been in early April because the water from the hose was really cold. My sister jumped out when the water was about half an inch deep, but I refused to move. I can still see the goose bumps on my legs as the water got deeper. My father was sitting in a lounge chair with the hose in his hand laughing. I stayed in that pool until my lips turned blue and my teeth started chattering. And I didn't budge, even when the water spilled over the brim. I'm sure I remember that day because the water was so cold."

"Did your mother make you get out?"

"Probably. Your turn."

Mayleah's earliest recollection was of sitting on the back of a horse at an uncle's ranch when she was a toddler. "Later, I went through a serious horse phase as a young teenager and had dreams of competing as a barrel racer."

"Did you ever try it?"

"No. The quarter horse I rode was more interested in finding a shady spot to nibble grass than galloping across an arena. I set up three barrels in a field. Buddy would run to the first one, but once he made it around the barrel, he'd stop and take a break."

"Your horse's name was Buddy?"

"Yeah." Mayleah grinned. "After meeting you, it took awhile to scrub my horse's image from my mind when I heard your name. Did your father give you the nickname?"

"Yeah. He called me 'my little buddy' as a way to differentiate me from my sisters, and the name stuck."

"Does anyone call you Blair?"

"Lawyers who don't know me. My staff can always tell a new caller because they ask for Blair, not Buddy."

He decided not to mention his mother's journals.

"Would you like me to call you Blair?"

"No, I've made Buddy my own."

TWENTY-THREE

GRACIE CHECKED ON PIXIE CARPENTER'S INSTAGRAM account as soon as she woke up. Mayleah had continued to communicate with Patricia Nichols, who'd sent Pixie the names of several dog breeders in the metro Atlanta area. Gracie waited until she'd finished her prayer time before researching the breeders mentioned in the message. All of them had websites featuring golden retrievers. Seeing the puppies reminded Gracie how deeply she'd loved Ditto and grieved his passing. She glanced down at Opie, who was contentedly curled up on the floor at her feet.

"I love you too," she said to the beige terrier. "And to prove it I'll take you out for a morning walk."

At the mention of the word "walk," Opie's ears perked up and he jumped to his feet. After draining the last drops of coffee from her cup, Gracie grabbed the leash from its hook near the side door. It was a muggy morning. She was wearing shorts and a Milton County High School booster club T-shirt.

Following their usual route, she traveled through her neighborhood and then turned right on Franklin Street. When she passed the bed-and-breakfast, she saw Judge Williams's car parked in front of the rambling dwelling. Farther on, Beatrice was in the front yard watering her flowers. Reaching the edge of downtown, Gracie turned around to retrace her steps. A car pulled up beside her and stopped. An attractive young woman was driving a new minivan. She lowered the driver's-side window. Gracie didn't recognize her.

"Are you Gracie Blaylock?" the woman asked.

"Yes."

"I'm Marissa Henley," the woman said as Gracie stepped closer. "My husband, Chris, works at the Nelson firm. You and I met at an event sponsored by the local bar association a couple of years ago."

Gracie didn't remember Marissa. The social gatherings were a blur of faces. Opie woofed in greeting. Marissa reached out the window and patted the dog on the head. Gracie saw a large diamond on her finger.

"Anyway, I can't tell you how thrilled I am about what God is doing in Buddy Smith's life," Marissa said. "He was bursting to tell us the other night over a dinner at our house. He said it happened while he was talking to you on the porch of his mother's house down the street."

"It's been special." Gracie smiled and continued, "Or as Buddy described it, he feels different."

"Yes, he used that word with us. I don't want to hold you up, but would you like to join us for dinner one evening? I'd arrange for Buddy to be there too."

"That's very nice of you," Gracie said, then added, "But ask Buddy first. I'll feel more comfortable if he thinks it's a good idea."

"I understand. Have a great day."

Marissa drove off and Gracie continued back down the street. Buddy's mother was unwinding the garden hose from the reel next to the front porch. She had her back to Gracie, who didn't stop because she didn't want to be late to work. A few moments later her cell phone vibrated, and she took it from her pocket. It was her mother.

"Good morning," Gracie said.

"Hey, baby girl," Maxine responded. "Are you at work?"

"No, I took Opie for a walk."

"I talked to Frances Mulhaven last night. Is there anything I can tell her that might encourage her about the search for Reagan?"

"I believe that Buddy Smith recently gave some promising news about a lead to Crystal and Sammy. But Frances should hear it from them."

"Okay, honey. That sounds like the best thing."

Gracie entered her neighborhood. Maxine gave her an update about what was going on in her life and Gracie's father's.

"He claims the tomatoes this year are going to be the juiciest ever. The heirloom varieties are really producing."

"I want half a peck."

While her mother talked, Gracie took Opie off the leash. He trotted into the kitchen and began to lap from his water bowl.

"One last thing while I've got you on the phone," Maxine said. "Is there any news about you and a man? Lauren told me about the group of men who are interested in meeting you. She especially likes the one who works with special-needs adults."

"Yes, Daniel is my favorite too," Gracie said. "But I'm not sure about him. I received an email that repeated information from a previous one. It was like he cut and pasted it together."

"That's odd. Why would he do that?"

"Maybe he's communicating with multiple women."

"Heavens!" Maxine exclaimed. "That's not good."

"It's common on these sites, but the lack of personal attention turned me off."

Gracie sat down at a chair in the kitchen. She was already late for work but wanted to talk to her mother.

"Let me tell you what's been going on with Buddy Smith," she began. "But only if you promise not to say anything to Lauren. She doesn't like him because of what happened between him and Amber Melrose when we were in high school."

"That was years ago."

"Yes, and as I mentioned to you before, Buddy has been searching for them ever since. You know what happened the other evening on the porch at Beatrice's house, and I've already been spending a lot of time with him in person and over the phone."

"Tell me again about the porch."

This time Gracie described in detail what took place on the porch at Beatrice Smith's house. And this time Maxine really listened. "That gives me chills," she said when Gracie finished.

"It was amazing. And Buddy has been calling me ever since, sometimes late in the evening, to talk about what he's experiencing with the Lord. He's also brought me into his circle regarding the search for Amber and Elise."

Gracie ended by telling her mother about the invitation from Marissa Henley she'd just received.

"Buddy will say yes," Maxine said. "He's obviously interested in you."

"Maybe," Gracie said, then unleashed a torrent of words. "But today he's going to spend all day in the car with Mayleah Harkness, the detective. They're going to Chattanooga to check out another lead about Reagan, which I don't think will amount to anything, but they're also going to try to talk with one of Amber's relatives who might help them locate Elise. Throughout this whole time, Buddy has been treating me like a close friend, but I think he considers Mayleah a woman he wants to date, even though she's thinking about getting back together with her ex-husband in Oklahoma. I've kept this bottled up for weeks and really needed to talk to you about what I'm feeling and thinking. I'm confused—"

"You're not confused," Maxine cut in. "Your mind just needs to agree with what your heart feels."

The truth of her mother's simple statement stopped Gracie in her tracks.

"You're right. But what do I do?"

"Do? Nothing. It's up to Buddy to take a step toward you."

"Should I go to the dinner party at the lawyer's house if it comes up?"

"Yes, and be the woman of incredible character that makes me so proud of you I could burst."

Tears suddenly appeared in Gracie's eyes. "You're just hearing my side of things," she said.

"Which is plenty. And don't worry. I won't breathe a word of this to Lauren."

"Thanks. If things don't go anywhere with Buddy, I'd rather keep it between us."

"If that happens, it's because God has a better plan for you."

/ / /

The drive to Chattanooga passed quickly. Buddy shared a lot about his life, and he learned about Mayleah, her family, and her career. She revealed more details about the reason for her divorce.

"We'd drifted apart over a couple of years," Mayleah said. "Clay focused on his job in the oil fields, and I was building my career with the police department. We'd become more like roommates than husband and wife, but he was the one who finally forced us both to admit it. I argued at first but knew he was right. In Oklahoma you can get a divorce within ten days of filing the petition if there aren't any children and both sides agree."

"Ten days? That's even faster than Georgia."

"It was painless."

"Really? After five years of marriage?"

Mayleah was silent for a moment. "Only the process was painless," she admitted. "I'd finally worked through the embarrassment and grief stages caused by my failure, and then he popped up wanting to see if we could work things out. I've heard from him twice since you and I ate at the barbecue restaurant. He has a plan that involves going to counseling and attending church together."

They rode in silence. Buddy thought about his conversation with Gracie about divorce and remarriage. He wasn't sure what to say. A few moments later Mayleah received a text message from the detective she'd been communicating with about Kimberly Landers. She read it to Buddy.

"We should be able to make it to her precinct in less than an hour," he said.

Forty-five minutes later they caught a glimpse of the Tennessee River, which wound its way through the heart of the city. The precinct headquarters was in a modern brick building. Inside, Mayleah showed the receptionist her badge and asked for Detective Janice Richards. A minute later a woman about the same age as Buddy and Mayleah greeted them.

"This way," Richards said.

She led the way into the secure area of the precinct and opened the door of a small conference room. "Wait here while I get my laptop."

Buddy and Mayleah sat beside each other.

"Nervous?" Mayleah asked.

"Should I be?"

"Most people are uptight when they come into a room like this."

Buddy smiled. "So far today I haven't committed any crimes, and even if I did, they occurred in Georgia, not Tennessee."

Richards returned and opened her laptop. "I saw your email about the handwriting analysis on the affidavit," she said. "I asked one of our guys to look it over, and he couldn't reach a conclusion. After that I decided to get creative."

Richards positioned the laptop so all three of them could see it. "Because of the privacy laws, I can't share Landers's medical records with you, but I approached the security department at Erlanger Hospital and downloaded camera footage from the waiting room on the night she came in for treatment. I'm not sure what she looks like, but I spotted Earvin Parish based on mug shots taken at the time of his previous arrests. I've cued the video to the time when they're both standing at the check-in desk."

The images began with a hospital employee sitting at a desk. The camera was positioned on the wall behind him so that people came into the frame as they approached. An older man was standing at the counter. A few seconds later he moved out of the way, and a younger couple approached. The man was in his twenties with dark hair and a goatee. He was wearing a T-shirt with the name of a music group emblazoned across the front. The woman beside him was wearing a ball cap pulled down so low that it was impossible to see her face. She had short dark hair that looked to be the same color and length as the recent photos sent to Buddy by Reagan's family.

"That's Parish," Richards said. "There's no doubt about it."

"But you can't see the woman's face," Buddy said.

"Wait," the detective replied.

The conversation at the desk continued for a couple of minutes. Buddy opened a photo of Reagan stored on his phone. The young woman talked and gestured with her left hand while keeping her right hand close to her side. She continued to look down at an angle outside the camera's point of reference. Finally, she took off the cap and ran her fingers through her hair. As she did, she glanced up at the camera for a split second.

Mayleah spoke at once. "It's not her," she said.

Not yet convinced, Buddy didn't comment. The age and general appearance were close. He studied the photo of Reagan on his phone. The video continued. The young woman turned to the side so that her profile became clearly visible.

"You're right," Buddy said, holding up his phone. "It's not Reagan Landry."

Richards froze the frame and all three of them compared the images.

"I agree," Richards said. "They could be related, but the nose isn't right, and Landry has a longer, thinner face."

"Thanks for sharing the video," Mayleah said, sitting back in the chair. "We suspect Reagan is in Atlanta."

Buddy summarized his conversation with Dr. Simpson for Detective Richards.

"Tracking down a runaway who doesn't want to be found is a challenge," Richards said. "But that's an excellent lead."

Mayleah stood. "We're off to Soddy-Daisy. Any advice about the best way to approach Mr. Vick Melrose?"

"He was much more open when I asked a few general questions than when I inquired where his great-niece was living now. After the call, I ran a background check on him. He retired about twenty years ago from a textile company. He's widowed. No record of arrest or criminal charges. The address for his residence and phone number are the same as the ones you sent me. I wouldn't call in advance. I'd just show up. That way he can see that you're not a threat."

"That was our plan," Buddy said.

"This time of day, it should take you about half an hour to get there."

Buddy entered Melrose's address into his phone. During the drive, Mayleah told him about the connection between Soddy-Daisy and the forcible removal of the Cherokee people along the Trail of Tears in the 1830s.

"There's a chance my family came through here, but we don't know for sure," Mayleah said. "Everyone didn't travel together in a single group along the same route at the same time. It was chaotic, more of a death march than an orderly process. Often the soldiers made the people travel around white settlements because there was so much disease and sickness among the Cherokees."

Buddy glanced sideways at the detective, who spoke without emotion. "I'm sorry," he said. "Although words sound hollow."

"Thanks. I understand what you mean."

They reached Soddy-Daisy and Buddy slowed down. They turned onto the street where Mr. Melrose lived. It was a modest neighborhood with small ranch-style houses built forty to fifty years earlier. Rascal had bought, sold, and rented many similar dwellings in Milton County.

Buddy's heart started beating faster. "I'm more nervous than before I start a jury trial," he said.

"Which is why I think you should let me do most of the talking."

"You do?"

"I know it's asking a lot, but my instincts tell me it's for the best."

They reached the correct house. Constructed of red brick, it was a single-story structure with an open carport large enough for one vehicle. An older-model pickup truck was parked there. Most of the grass in the front yard had turned brown. Buddy saw window-unit air conditioners on each side of the house. He turned slowly into the short gravel driveway and parked behind the truck.

"It's a good sign that the truck is here," he said, then paused. "Are you carrying a gun?"

Mayleah cut her eyes toward him. "Yes, why?"

"I'm having flashbacks to Amber's father. He was a mean, aggressive drunk."

"Let's hope this member of the family is reasonable and sober."

/ / /

Gracie took a break to check the social media account for Pixie Carpenter. Each time she opened it, a boost of adrenaline shot through her. To be an investigator was an energizing occupation. She positioned her phone beneath the edge of her desk so that no one could see what she was doing. The photo with Ditto came into view. The announcement of the dog's death had attracted other sympathetic comments. Gracie felt bad that she was falsely eliciting grief from sensitive hearts. She thanked the people for their condolences. While she was on the account a private message came through from Patricia Nichols. Gracie quickly looked around to make sure no one was nearby. Except for her, everyone in the clerk's office seemed intent on doing his or her job.

Hey, I talked to a breeder this morning, and she has a litter of golden retriever pups that are weaned and ready for new homes. Would you like to see them this weekend? I'll arrange everything.

Gracie's heart was pounding. She and the detective had already set aside Saturday to go to Atlanta. The timing was perfect. But thus far, Mayleah had handled all communication. The question seemed straightforward. Before allowing herself to analyze the situation any further, Gracie entered a reply:

Just saw your message. Sounds great. How much $ are the pups?

A quick response appeared:

Not sure. It depends on male or female. But all are AKC registered and adorable! Where do you live and what time would you get here?

Gracie froze. Now she regretted entering into an online dialogue. Her profile described her as a "Georgia Girl" without revealing specifically where she lived. She didn't know what to do. Nichols knew she was online. If Gracie didn't respond, it might make her suspicious.

"Are you okay?" Brenda's voice and question caused Gracie to jerk.

"Uh, sure."

"You look worried. I have a question about a filing in a condemnation action."

Gracie quickly typed a reply to Nichols:

At work. Gotta go.

"Let me see what you have," she said to Brenda.

Five minutes later Brenda left. Holding her phone beneath the top of her desk, Gracie checked on Pixie Carpenter. There was no reply from Nichols. Gracie sent Mayleah a text telling her what happened. The message showed delivery, but the detective didn't respond.

"Madam Clerk!" a male voice called out from the counter. "May I have a word with you?"

Gracie left her desk and approached Judge Williams. The judge was wearing a blue suit, white shirt, and red tie.

"Yes, sir."

"In private."

"We could use the conference room."

"Lead the way."

/ / /

Walking side by side, Buddy and Mayleah climbed two concrete steps to the front door. The plastic doorbell button was cracked. Buddy pushed it and heard a faint chime inside. He glanced at Mayleah, who faced the door impassively. The knob turned and the door opened, revealing an older man wearing a white T-shirt, blue jeans, and white socks with no shoes on his feet. Vick Melrose looked a lot like Amber's father, only much older. Buddy guessed he was in his eighties. He eyed Mayleah.

"I'm Mayleah Harkness," the detective said. "And this is Blair Smith. Are you Mr. Melrose?"

"Yeah. What do you want? They don't allow no solicitation in this neighborhood."

"We'd like to talk to you for a few minutes about Amber, your great-niece. She and Blair went to high school together, and he wants to get in touch with her."

While Mayleah talked, the older man's attention shifted to Buddy, who tried to look calm and nonthreatening. Mr. Melrose sniffed, then pulled a well-used white handkerchief from the rear pocket of his jeans and blew his nose.

"Come on in," he said, moving to the side. "If this door stays open much longer, I'll lose the cool air I've stored up all morning."

Buddy held the door for Mayleah. They entered the living room of a small, cluttered house. There was a woodstove on one side of the room near the window. An aged air-conditioning unit was running at maximum capacity. A brown vinyl sofa covered with a faded yellow afghan was positioned next to a reddish-colored recliner. Three dirty coffee cups were on a low table. The wall opposite the recliner featured a mounted large flat-screen TV tuned to a news channel. Mr. Melrose picked up the controller and turned it off.

What immediately caught Buddy's attention was a black metal bookcase filled with photos in frames. There had to be at least thirty pictures. At first glance it was a blur of images. Buddy wanted to walk directly over to it but resisted. Mr. Melrose sat in the recliner and motioned to the sofa.

"Have a seat," he said. "Sorry about the mess. I haven't been keeping things neat since my wife passed."

"How long ago was that?" Mayleah asked.

"Six months ago tomorrow," the older man replied. "After fifty-six years of marriage."

"I'm so sorry," Mayleah replied.

"She'd been bad sick for a while so I'm glad her suffering is over, but it's tough being here all alone. I was sitting wondering when someone would come by to see me and the doorbell rang. It startled me."

As the older man talked, Buddy's concern that he might be a clone of John Melrose diminished.

"We didn't want to do that," Mayleah said.

"No, I'm glad for a bit of company. Why are you looking for Amber?"

Buddy spoke: "She was my girlfriend in high school, and we had a little girl together."

"What now?" Mr. Melrose asked with a confused expression on his face.

"Amber got pregnant our senior year," Buddy said plainly. "The baby was born about this time of the year. A week later they left town, and I haven't seen Amber or the child since. I was hoping you could help me make contact. The baby would be seventeen years old by now."

Mr. Melrose got up and went over to the bookcase. Buddy watched as the older man scanned the different levels.

"Here it is," he said, picking up a smaller frame from one of the lower shelves. "It's not the best picture."

He handed it to Buddy, whose heart was pounding. In the picture a young woman was standing beside a picnic table where two very young girls were sitting. The young woman didn't look like Amber.

"Is this Amber?" he asked.

"No, that's one of my other great-nieces who lives over in East Ridge. She's the one who gave me the picture. I'm not sure where it was taken, but the bigger girl is Amber's kid. I know that for a fact."

Buddy focused on the child, who looked a bit like his sister Maddie. She was around four or five years old and was wearing a one-piece swimsuit with a dolphin printed on the front. He continued to stare at the photo so he could absorb every detail.

"Does Amber have other children?" Mayleah asked.

"It's hard for me to keep up with my own grandkids," Mr. Melrose replied. "And now there are great-grandkids. Are you the woman who called me the other day asking about Amber?"

"No, that was someone with the Chattanooga Police Department," Mayleah answered. "And Amber isn't in trouble. It's like Blair said—we're just trying to find her and the child. He hasn't seen his little girl since she was an infant and would like to meet her."

Buddy looked up from the photo. "If you could help in any way, I would really appreciate it," he said.

The old man didn't respond. Instead, he blew his nose again, got up from his chair, and left the room. Buddy gave Mayleah a questioning look. She shrugged. As the wait dragged on, Buddy began to get nervous. He inspected the room more closely. There were old yellowed copies of the Chattanooga newspaper stacked beside the woodstove. On a small end table next to the recliner was a glass of water. A rack for keys hung on the wall near the front door. Mr. Melrose returned with a large black book in his hands. Written on the side of the volume in faded gold print were the words "Holy Bible."

"My wife is the one who kept this up," he said, opening the thick cover of the book. "I was too busy at work to pay it much mind."

Mr. Melrose squinted at one page before him, then turned to another one. "I can't find anything," he muttered. "I sure do miss Sally."

"May I help?" Mayleah asked.

The older man held the Bible out to her. "She was good about writing down whenever anyone in the family got married or had a child or died."

Mayleah held the volume so Buddy could see it too. Sally Melrose had recorded names, dates of births, marriages, divorces, and deaths in tiny handwriting on the preprinted family tree. The number of entries soon extended beyond the black-lined limbs into the margins and onto subsequent pages intended for other purposes. They turned the book so they could try to follow the connections.

"That's Amber's family," Buddy said as he pointed to her parents' names with the names and dates of birth for their children underneath.

"And that must be Elise," Mayleah said.

Written in small print beside Amber's name was Elise's date of birth.

"Mary Elise," Buddy said. "We never settled on her full name."

"That's right." Mr. Melrose nodded as he remembered.

"Did they call her Mary, Elise, or Mary Elise?" Buddy asked.

Mr. Melrose shook his head before saying, "That's out of my league. But she was a curly-headed thing when she was a young'un."

"What's this name beside Elise's?" Buddy asked.

"It looks like Charlie," Mayleah suggested, then looked up at Mr. Melrose.

"Did Amber have a son named Charlie?"

"Could be. But I recollect that's the man she married. He's a real smart guy who works for the government, so he and Amber moved all over the place with his work."

"Do you know Charlie's last name?" Buddy asked.

"No. I'm not good with names. It's been awhile since I saw that part of the family. John wasn't too sociable."

"That's Amber's father," Buddy said to Mayleah.

"Right," Mr. Melrose said. "He died some time back, not sure when."

There was no date of death for John Melrose recorded in the Bible. The name Patty Melrose was crossed out.

"Patty Melrose's name has a line through it," Mayleah said to Mr. Melrose. "What does that mean?"

"That means there was a divorce."

Buddy spoke: "I believe Amber was in the area about five years ago. Do you remember that?"

Mr. Melrose thought for a moment. "Do you know what time of year it was? We have a family reunion every five years in June."

Buddy took the canceled checks out of his pocket. There was one that Amber had presented to the bank for payment on June 5.

"Around June 5?" he asked.

"Yep," Mr. Melrose replied. "We always have the reunion the first week of June."

"Would you have any photos from the reunion?" Mayleah asked.

Mr. Melrose perked up. "That's a good question. Sally kept pictures in shoe boxes with the year written on the outside." He rose from his chair and left the room again.

"If we stay here long enough, we're going to get something good," Mayleah said.

"How do you know?"

"Because of Sally."

/ / /

Judge Williams held the door open for Gracie as she entered the conference room. He didn't say anything until they were both seated.

"Tell me the real reason why you and Beatrice's son came to dinner the other night."

Gracie froze.

"And don't try to come up with a story," the judge continued. "I can spot that a mile away."

"That's not the kind of person I am."

"I didn't think so."

Gracie rested her hands on the table in front of her. "Beatrice wanted Buddy to be around you in a social setting. After she brought it up, he asked me to come and offer an opinion if I had one."

"What did you say to Beatrice about me?"

"I haven't talked to her. The conversation at the dinner table led to a time of prayer for Buddy and me on the front porch. That's where my focus has been."

"On you and Buddy?"

"No." Gracie paused. "Well, yes, but mostly on what God is doing in his life. I'm usually not so bold about matters of faith, but for some reason that night I was."

"It irritated me," the judge said. "But later I appreciated it. Thanks for being 'bold,' as you describe it. People say all kinds of things behind a judge's back but not so much to his face. And as to the reason for you being there for dinner, I'm going to make it clear to Beatrice that I've enjoyed her company but don't want to give her the impression that I'm pursuing anything beyond companionship."

"Repeatedly taking a woman out to dinner sends a different message."

The judge held up his hands with his palms out. "I hear you. And I'll make it right."

TWENTY-FOUR

MR. MELROSE RETURNED WITH A SHOE BOX. THERE was a piece of masking tape on the side with a year written on it in black marker. He handed the box to Buddy without taking off the lid.

"I don't want to look at the pictures because it will make me sad."

The cardboard box was half full of photos thrown in without being organized. Buddy handed a bunch to Mayleah.

"No, let's do it together," the detective replied.

The first group included Christmastime. They sorted the pictures until they reached warm-weather scenes. Buddy stopped at a group photo taken with a lake in the background. The images of the people were very small, but he recognized Mr. Melrose standing in the middle.

Buddy showed the older man the picture. "Is this from the reunion?"

"Yeah, I can tell that even without my glasses. Sally is next to me."

A short, overweight woman with a broad smile on her face stood to the right of her husband. Buddy looked over the rest of the crowd. There were at least forty people of all ages. He couldn't identify Amber.

"Where's Amber or Elise?" he asked.

"I'm going to need my glasses for that," the older man said.

Mr. Melrose put on his glasses and held the photo in front of him. He touched the images with his right index finger.

"There's Bruce, J.F., Tim, Charlene, Vick Jr. He's my oldest boy and his family. There she is!" he exclaimed. "That's Amber."

Buddy leaned in closer. His former girlfriend had dyed her hair blond. Beside her was a man wearing a ball cap, T-shirt, and jeans. In his arms was a little boy who looked to be two or three years old. To the side of the man, with nothing visible except her neck and head, was a petite girl. Now that he could concentrate on one face, Buddy saw the similarity between the youngster in the photo on display in the living room and the preteen girl in the group shot.

"That's Elise?" he asked, showing the photo to Mr. Melrose.

"I reckon. And that's her mama, daddy, and little brother. Only you say you're the daddy."

Elise's hair was short, dark, and curly. She was smiling broadly.

"Now that we know they were here for the reunion, let's keep looking," Mayleah said.

Seconds later Mayleah discovered a photo of Elise standing at the plate with a softball bat in her hands.

"There she is playing softball," she said to Buddy.

"Yeah, we always do that," Mr. Melrose said. "It's all in fun. No strikeouts. The little ones run the bases."

"Buddy, she has your build," Mayleah continued. "See how long her legs are for her torso?"

Buddy was mesmerized. He turned the photo over. On the

back, Sally Melrose had written "Mary Elise Fleming—age twelve." He and Mayleah glanced at each other.

"Amber Fleming," Buddy said to Mr. Melrose. "Does that sound right?"

"Maybe," the older man replied with a shrug. "Like I said, I couldn't keep all that stuff straight in my head."

In total they found five images of Amber and Elise. Buddy's focus was on Elise. There was a photo of his daughter talking to a group of girls about the same age. The camera caught Elise in the middle of a laugh with her mouth open. In another shot, she was holding her little brother while they watched some older boys fly a kite. Her face seemed full of life.

"I can't tell you what this means to me," he said to Mr. Melrose.

"Is there anything else you can remember about Amber, Elise, or Amber's husband?" Mayleah asked. "Where they live? You mentioned her husband working for the government. What about Amber?"

"No," Mr. Melrose said and motioned with his hand in a semicircle. "There might be something here, but I don't know where it is or what it might be. Sally always sent out a bunch of Christmas cards."

"Do you have her address book?" Mayleah asked.

"No, I haven't seen it. She didn't send out any cards the last couple of years because she'd already gotten sick." Mr. Melrose paused. "But you know what? You can have those pictures. I can see they mean a lot to you, much more than to me."

"Thanks," Buddy said gratefully. "And if you come across something that might help me find Elise and Amber, would you let me know?"

"Yeah. Write down your name and phone number."

Buddy started to reach for one of his business cards, but decided it might be best not to reveal that he was a lawyer. "Do you have a sheet of paper?" he asked.

"Uh, you could use a scrap of newspaper."

Buddy tore off a piece of paper and carefully wrote down his name and cell phone number.

"Where would be a good place to put this?" he asked. "I don't want you to burn it in your stove."

"It's been so hot that it's hard to imagine I'll ever need to crank it up," Mr. Melrose said. "But it can get right chilly here in January and February."

The older man slid the piece of paper into the corner of the frame holding the picture of Elise taken at the lake. "I'm not likely to lose it if I put it in there," he said.

Buddy put the precious photos in the front pocket of his shirt. "Thanks again," he said, shaking Mr. Melrose's hand.

"It felt good talking to you," the older man said. "I reckon it's the right thing that you're doing. Every young'un ought to have the right to know their daddy."

"I'm glad you think so."

Midafternoon Gracie received a text message from Mayleah asking if she could talk privately. Gracie went to the conference room so she could be alone.

"You're on speakerphone with Buddy and me," Mayleah said. "First, we were able to rule out any link between Reagan and Kimberly Landers in Chattanooga. There was video footage from the hospital. Reagan is in the Atlanta area."

"Okay," she said.

"And Buddy wants to tell you about our conversation with Amber's great-uncle."

Gracie listened as Buddy related what they'd learned from Vick Melrose. Even the speakerphone couldn't mask the depth of emotion in his voice, which touched Gracie deeply.

"Mary Elise," she said when Buddy told her the full name Amber gave the baby girl. "Both names are beautiful."

"That's what I thought," Buddy replied. "Mary Elise Fleming."

"Now that you know her name, have you had any luck in tracking her down?"

"I did some preliminary research on social media after we left Soddy-Daisy," Mayleah said. "No matches turned up for Amber Fleming, Mary Elise Fleming, or Charles Fleming."

"Who is Charles Fleming?"

"Amber's husband," Buddy responded. He proceeded to tell Gracie about the family reunions.

"When is the next one?"

"Next summer, but there's no guarantee Amber or Elise will be there. Mr. Melrose said Amber's side of the family isn't close to the rest of them, most likely due to her father." Buddy told her about the photos Mr. Melrose gave him.

"Wow, he sounds like a very nice man. I can't wait to see them."

"And uncovering the names is a huge breakthrough," Mayleah said. "I believe it won't be long before we locate them."

Mayleah's words sparked an idea. "Buddy, have you thought about what you're going to say to Elise when you first meet her?" Gracie asked.

"I've written a bunch of speeches in my mind over the years. I'm not sure which one I'll use, maybe none of them."

"It'll come to you when the time is right," Gracie said.

Gracie started to daydream about what an encounter between father and daughter might look like. Mayleah spoke and jerked her back to reality.

"I saw that you've been active on Instagram," the detective said.

"Oh—"

"Pixie Carpenter," Buddy cut in. "I think it's perfect."

Even though she was alone, Gracie felt her face flush. "I was hoping you weren't going to tell Buddy," she said to Mayleah.

"Don't worry, I'm not going to blow your cover," Buddy replied. "But I can't promise that I won't call out 'Pixie!' the next time we have a bar association picnic."

"You better not!"

"As soon as we end this call, I'm going to respond to Nichols and move forward with a meeting on Saturday in Atlanta."

"I was worried I might have messed it up by not getting right back to her."

"No, you did great."

"There's even more good news," Buddy said. "I'm going with you to Atlanta."

"Buddy has pestered me into letting him tag along and promised not to get in the way," Mayleah said. "We'll take two cars. After we left Mr. Melrose's house, we compared the pictures of Elise at the reunion to the ones I took with my phone in Atlanta, and he admits it's not the same person."

"I really gave up on that idea when my mother agreed with you and Mayleah," Buddy said. "But you'll see. Elise's hair is curlier, and the color is a bit different. Oh, another thing. In one of the reunion pictures, she's playing softball. Mayleah says Elise has my legs, which sounds worse than it is."

Gracie chuckled. It was wonderful hearing the hope and excitement in Buddy's voice. "Your mother can be the judge of that too," she said. "Are you going to share all this with her?"

"Yes. If we get back in time, I'm going to her house tonight. If not, then tomorrow."

"And I need to get back to work," she said. "But thanks for calling. Mayleah, are you sure I didn't make a mistake in communicating with Patricia Nichols?"

"Don't worry," the detective replied. "But if there's a problem, I'll let you know."

/ / /

It was dark when Buddy and Mayleah reached the Clarksburg city limits. After leaving Mr. Melrose's house, they'd stopped by the Citizens Tri-County Bank. Buddy hoped to duplicate the success he had with Ms. Brockington at the First National Bank of Milton County, but the bank officer who met with them glanced at the canceled $10,000 check made payable to "Bearer," flipped it over, and returned it to Buddy, saying he couldn't help. Buddy wasn't disappointed. Even if someone at the bank had remembered the incident, he doubted they could have added anything to the treasure trove he'd received from Mr. Melrose.

Worn out physically and emotionally, Buddy yawned. If he ever had to stop practicing law, he wouldn't consider truck driving as a new profession. He turned into the apartment complex where Mayleah lived.

"This was a good trip," he said.

"Yes. I have a busy day tomorrow, but I'll try to find out more about the Fleming family."

Buddy waited for Mayleah to open the door, but she didn't. "Anything else?" he asked.

"May I tell you something serious?"

"Am I in trouble?"

"No."

"Okay," Buddy said tentatively.

Mayleah turned in the seat so that she faced him. "Spending time with you over the past few weeks has influenced me more than you realize."

"What have I done?"

"Shown me there's a love that won't ever give up."

Buddy had lived seventeen years in a world where the pursuit of his daughter was as constant as the sun rising in the east and setting in the west. To him, it was a natural part of life.

"That desire has been inside me since the first time I saw Elise at the hospital," he said after several moments passed.

"And you nurtured it even when you had little hope and it was painful to do so. You're a remarkable man."

With Mayleah's kind words lingering in his ears, Buddy slept soundly. When he awoke in the morning, he went for a morning run. He didn't mind the afternoon heat, but it was nice to exercise before the temperature climbed higher. He was already feeling much stronger and blew past another man out for a morning jog. Today Buddy's speed flowed from exhilaration.

Approaching his mother's house on Franklin Street, he checked his watch and knew she'd likely be drinking a cup of coffee in the kitchen. Walking up to the side door, he rang the bell. A few moments later his mother tentatively peeked around the sidelight. She was still in her pajamas and wearing a silk robe.

"I thought you might be the paperboy," she said when she opened the door. "He threw my paper on top of the porch last week."

"May I borrow a towel?" Buddy asked. "I don't want to sweat all over your kitchen."

Beatrice grabbed a towel from the half bath and handed it to him. "When did you start running again?" she asked.

"A few weeks ago. I didn't get to exercise yesterday because I spent all day in the Chattanooga area with Mayleah Harkness."

"Sit down and relax. You're still breathing hard. Do you want some orange juice?"

"Sounds good."

Buddy watched as his mother carefully filled the glass. It was a simple act of service in a long line of thousands and thousands gone before.

"Thank you," he said with extra emphasis that didn't do justice to his thoughts.

Beatrice topped off her coffee and added extra creamer.

"I have news," Buddy said.

"Good news, I hope."

"Yes."

His mother joined him at the table, and Buddy told her about the trip to Soddy-Daisy.

"Oh my goodness," she said when Buddy finished. "I wish you had those photos with you now."

"I'll bring them by on the way to work so you can keep them all day."

"It will be like inviting friends over," Beatrice said brightly. "I can't wait to see Elise, or should I start calling her Mary Elise?"

"I'm still using Elise. We'll find out when we meet her." Buddy stopped. “Did you hear what I just said? Not *if* but *when* we meet her.”

Beatrice smiled. “I heard,” she said before taking the last sip of coffee in her cup. “I’m going to get dressed now and water my flowers. Don’t forget to bring me those pictures.”

By the time Buddy returned with the photos, his mother had finished her morning watering routine and was in the backyard weeding a flower bed. She quickly removed her pink work gloves. He handed her the photos and pointed out Elise and Amber.

“I see a mix of you and Maddie in Elise,” Beatrice said. “And a huge dose of Amber, especially in her face. I can’t wait to take these inside and study them some more.”

“They’re yours for now.”

“May I show them to anyone?”

“Please don’t. Gracie knows about the trip, but I’m not going to say anything to any of my friends, at least not yet. Most people would only be interested in the gossip angle.”

“I have friends who don’t live to gossip.”

“I know, I know. If you have someone in mind, please check with me first.”

“What about Bryant? He heard about it the other night at dinner and seemed interested in helping you.”

“No, let’s not include him.”

“Okay. We’re having dinner tonight. He’s taking me to that new Greek restaurant on Selmer Street.”

“I’ve been a few times. Stick to the classic Greek dishes. They’re way better than the American food.”

Arriving at work, Buddy greeted Millie on his way into his office.

"Wait," the office manager said. "How was your trip to Chattanooga?"

Buddy stopped. "Fine. Any problems here?"

"No. When I came in this morning, I put something on your desk and saw the paperwork you received from the genealogy service."

"I doubt there's anything there that helps me."

"Anything come out of your trip to Chattanooga?"

Buddy chuckled. "Did you secretly go to law school without telling me? Mayleah Harkness and I met with Amber's great-uncle. He gave me some photos of Amber and Elise taken a few years ago at a family reunion. Amber got married and her last name is Fleming. I dropped the pictures off at my mother's house on the way in to work this morning. Satisfied?"

"No. More, please."

Buddy gave Millie a brief summary. He could tell she was soaking up every word.

"So finding those checks turned out for good," she said when he finished. "Are you going to let me see the pictures?"

"I hope so. My mother may stare at them so much the images disappear."

Millie let Buddy proceed to his office. Checking his voice-mail messages, he saw he had two calls from Dr. Cam Simpson.

TWENTY-FIVE

TURNING ONTO FRANKLIN STREET ON HER WAY TO THE courthouse, Gracie noticed Buddy driving away from his mother's house. On impulse, she turned in and parked beside Beatrice's aging Mercedes. Walking around to the front porch, she rang the doorbell. No one answered. Gracie returned to her car and was about to leave when she heard Beatrice call her name.

"Gracie!"

The older woman was coming around the corner at the rear of the house. Gracie greeted her.

"How about a cup of coffee?" Beatrice asked.

"That would be lovely. Cream and sugar, please."

"Inside or on the porch?" Beatrice asked.

Gracie smiled. "I'm partial to the porch."

"I understand."

Gracie sat in the same chair she'd occupied when praying with Buddy. It was a pleasant morning. As far as she knew, nothing urgent was waiting for her at work. And if something was, it could wait. She rocked back and forth while she waited for Beatrice to return.

"Here you go," Beatrice said, handing her a delicate cup that held steaming coffee.

Gracie took a sip. It was delicious. "I don't know why I stopped by, but this cup of coffee is a good enough reason."

"Oh, it's a special concoction I throw together. But I know why you're here."

"You do?" Gracie asked in surprise.

"To see the answer to your prayers."

Beatrice reached into the pocket of a yellow summer-weight jacket she was wearing and handed several photos to Gracie, who instantly knew what they must be.

"Buddy and Mayleah Harkness called me yesterday on their way back from Chattanooga and told me about these."

"He dropped them off a few minutes ago," Beatrice said. "I'm bursting to share the news with someone, and Buddy told me you already knew. The next thing I know, you show up at my door. I swear, sometimes I think you must be an angel."

"I'm not," Gracie replied. "Ask any member of my family."

As she looked at the pictures, Gracie felt an odd mixture of joy, curiosity, and anxiety.

"I was about to compare the photos with some of Maddie and Buddy at that age," Beatrice said. "Wait here while I get them."

After Beatrice left, Gracie tried to sort out her feelings. The source of her joy was obvious—a tangible hope that Buddy would finally get to meet his daughter. Curiosity, too, was understandable, because many unknowns swirled around that future event. But the anxiety was a surprise. It was actually closer to the surface than anything else. Gracie took a sip of coffee and decided it had to do with the possibility that Amber and Elise might reject Buddy and not want to have anything to do with him. It wasn't a far-fetched notion. If Amber had wanted Buddy to know his daughter, she could have initiated contact at any point over the past seventeen years. But she never did. Gracie couldn't imagine the pain that would result from a final rejection for both Buddy and his mother. Beatrice returned.

"Let's sit close to each other," she suggested.

They positioned the two rocking chairs so they could examine the pictures together. Beatrice picked out a lot of details. Gracie listened. The family resemblance with Elise was unmistakable.

"Now that he knows their last name, I'm sure it won't be long till he finds them," Beatrice said. "Elise would be four or five years older now. A woman can go through a lot of changes between ages twelve and seventeen."

Gracie could see much of Buddy in Elise, but Amber shared equally in their child. Seeing Elise brought back memories of Amber, which contributed to Gracie's anxiety.

"I'm so excited to have these," Beatrice continued. "Mayleah Harkness has really been a help to Buddy in his search for Elise."

"She's gone above and beyond any obligation she might have as a detective," Gracie replied.

"That's what he's needed. A champion to come alongside him."

Gracie licked her lips. "What do you think is going on with Buddy and Mayleah on a personal level?" she asked, hoping she sounded casual.

Beatrice looked directly at her. "Not as much as there is between the two of you. Buddy just needs to wake up and realize it."

"I don't want to be pushy about—"

"That's one topic on which I know to keep my mouth shut until he asks me," Beatrice continued. "But it's clear that you two have come into the same orbit. What happened on this porch last week proved it to me."

"That was about Buddy and the Lord."

"And you," Beatrice replied emphatically. "He told me how much he's enjoyed talking to you, calling you at all hours of the day and night."

Gracie didn't want to disagree with Beatrice because she hoped she was right.

"We've had a few good conversations," she admitted.

"And that's the best way for things to get started."

Gracie managed a weak smile.

"Bryant and I have had some good conversations too," Beatrice said. "But I don't think they're going to lead to anything else."

"Are you going to tell him that?"

"When it's the right time."

Gracie had a sudden urge to give Beatrice a hug. She leaned over, put her arm around the older woman's shoulders, and gave her a firm squeeze.

"Thank you," Beatrice said when Gracie released her. "I'm going to take that with me through this whole day."

/ / /

Buddy called Dr. Simpson. The pediatrician didn't answer, and Buddy left a voice mail. Before he could transition into another work project, his phone vibrated and the doctor's name came into view.

"Hello," Buddy said.

"I left you two messages yesterday," the doctor said. "Why didn't you return my call?"

"I was out of town."

"Reagan Landry returned to the pharmacy in Atlanta. The pharmacist on duty contacted our office, and I was able to speak to him while she was at the store. She still wanted refills for the oxycodone and Ambien, and based on my instructions, the pharmacist told her to come back this afternoon to pick them up."

Buddy glanced at the clock on his computer screen. He could be on Ponce de Leon Avenue in Atlanta by noon. Several appointments on his calendar for the day would have to be rescheduled.

"I can be there," he said.

"There's no guarantee that she'll show up. The pharmacist told her he had to have a faxed prescription from my office so he could fill the prescriptions, and it would take a day to receive it."

"What time did he tell Reagan to come back?"

"Two o'clock."

"Did she show him any identification?"

"She had a driver's license with a Clarksburg address and the correct date of birth based on my records. He was careful to verify her identity. One of the pharmacist's assistants said Reagan was with a group of three or four young women. The assistant asked for a phone number, and Reagan simply told her she'd be back to pick up the meds."

Buddy's mind was in overdrive. "Okay," he said. "I'll contact her family as soon as we hang up."

"And I've instructed my staff to notify me if any calls come in about her."

Buddy couldn't reach Sammy so he spoke to Crystal, who started crying when he told her the news.

"Thanks," she said.

"Keep trying to reach Sammy at work," Buddy said. "I want

the two of you to drive to Atlanta in a separate car in case we can convince Reagan to come home."

"Where should we meet you?" Crystal asked between sniffles.

"At the courthouse. How long do you think it will take you to get there?"

"Sammy is working in town today, so I'll pick him up at the job site. We can be there in thirty minutes."

"See you then."

Buddy was unable to reach Mayleah. He called her cell phone and then her extension at the sheriff's department number. As he prepared to leave the office, he briefly told Millie and Jennifer what was going on.

"What will you do if Reagan doesn't want to come home?" Jennifer asked.

"Maybe we can open a line of communication with her family that will lead to something positive in the future. Also, at least her parents can see that she's alive and hopefully safe."

"Is Detective Harkness going with you?" Millie asked.

"I haven't been able to reach her. I'm going to swing by the sheriff's department on my way to meet the Landry family at the courthouse. If Mayleah calls here, let her know what's going on and ask her to get in touch with me."

Buddy drove to the sheriff's department. "I need to get in touch with Detective Harkness," he said to the woman at the front desk when he went inside. "It's urgent."

The woman checked her computer. "She's out of the office interviewing witnesses and won't be back until around four o'clock."

Buddy gave the woman his contact information. "If she calls in, please ask her to contact me immediately."

When Buddy got to the courthouse, Sammy and Crystal hadn't arrived. He checked his phone. Still no response from Mayleah. It looked like the detective wasn't going to be able to help. Buddy didn't know Reagan and was reluctant to throw mother, father, and daughter into an emotional hurricane at a CVS pharmacy. Mayleah had the kind of professional skills needed for a high-pressure situation. On impulse, Buddy got out of the car and entered the courthouse.

It had taken Gracie two hours to work through her morning phone calls. She always tried to strike the right balance between letting people know their questions were important and processing the communication efficiently so she could move on to the next person. People contacted the clerk's office for help with a lot of matters outside the scope of Gracie's duties, which meant she became a traffic cop directing inquirers to the right county department or state resource. She recommended specific lawyers only to people she knew personally. Otherwise, she provided the number for the referral service offered by the local bar association. She didn't want to be accused of favoritism. She hung up from a sobering call with a woman who was seeking a divorce lawyer and mentioned domestic violence. In addition to the number for the bar association, Gracie suggested the woman contact the sheriff's department. Looking up, she saw Buddy. He motioned to her.

"I know this is short notice," he said, speaking rapidly, "but could you take the rest of the day off and go with me to Atlanta? There's a good chance Reagan is going to be at the pharmacy she visited the other day. Her parents are coming, but I'd rather have a third party with me to talk to her before bringing them into the situation."

"What about Mayleah?"

"She's working a case and is unavailable. And you know Reagan. I'm worried she won't talk to me."

Gracie took a deep breath. After processing the backlog of phone calls, her primary tasks for the day were complete with the exception of a quarterly report for the county commissioner's office, which wasn't due until the end of the week. Gracie could easily meet the deadline.

"And what exactly would I do?" she asked.

"Talk to Reagan, either with or without me. The first priority is to make sure she's safe and not in danger. Then find out if she's open to communicating with her family. In the best-case scenario, she'd be willing to come home with them."

"Are Crystal and Sammy okay with me being there?"

"I haven't told them. This all came up suddenly. They're going to meet me outside in a couple of minutes so we can go to Atlanta. I haven't talked over strategy with them. I'm still working that out in my own mind."

"I don't want to do anything without their permission."

"Of course."

"Also, I have softball practice," Gracie started, then stopped. "But if we're not back, I can contact the team captains and tell them what to do."

Gracie quietly informed Brenda that she'd be out the rest of the day. When she and Buddy left the courthouse, Sammy and Crystal were sitting in a car parked beside Buddy's vehicle. Buddy quickly explained why he'd asked Gracie to come. Crystal, who already had a wad of tissues in her hand, wiped her blue eyes.

"Thank you, Gracie," Crystal said. "Reagan has always thought a lot of you. It might be best if she saw you first. I'm desperate to talk to her but don't want to scare her off."

Sammy was wearing jeans and muddy boots. He cleared his throat and faced Buddy. "Like I've already said, I appreciate everything you're doing. But there are some things I want to say to Reagan."

"Honey, we can't start with that," Crystal said as she placed a hand on her husband's arm.

Sammy cut his eyes toward his wife. Seeing the interaction between Sammy and Crystal removed any doubt in Gracie's mind about the importance of her presence.

"I'll text you the address for the pharmacy in case we're separated on the way to Atlanta," Buddy said. "Dr. Simpson's office is supposed to let me know if they receive any additional communication from them about Reagan. I'm going to go over strategy with Gracie and then give you a call. We should arrive with plenty of time to spare so we can discuss the situation with the employees of the store."

Gracie slipped into the passenger seat of Buddy's vehicle. He pulled out of the parking space. Something rose up inside Gracie. "If it's okay, I'm going to pray right now," she said.

"Go for it," Buddy said with a sideways glance in her direction.

Gracie's prayer lasted all the way to the Clarksburg city limits. As she prayed, Buddy seemed to relax. He was able to take a few deep breaths and exhale. Gracie finished with an amen.

"Can you think of anything else?" she asked when she finished.

"No," he said. "That worked for me. I was tied up in knots."

Over the next fifty miles, they discussed different scenarios that might arise with Reagan. Gracie was impressed by the creative ways Buddy suggested to respond to multiple contingencies.

"Ready to call the Landrys?" he asked.

"Yes."

Buddy placed the call. Crystal was very interactive. Sammy didn't say anything for quite a while.

"Sammy, what do you think?" Buddy asked.

"I don't want to come across as harsh, but I think we should call the police and have them on the scene to arrest Reagan if she doesn't want to come home with us voluntarily," he replied. "They could take her to one of those places where they lock up minors for a night or two and teach her a lesson. A couple of nights should prove to her how much better life can be in Milton County."

Buddy looked at Gracie. He'd never seen this side of Sammy.

"Sammy can't take the unknown," Crystal said. "We both want this nightmare to end, but I think you and Gracie should have a chance to see if you can convince Reagan to come home voluntarily. If we force her, I'm concerned she'll run off again as soon as we turn our backs."

"Sammy mentioned the other day the possibility of Reagan spending part of the rest of the summer with her grandmother," Buddy said. "Are you still willing to do that?"

"She and Frances have a special relationship," Sammy said, his voice softening. "I hate to dump that responsibility on Crystal's mom, but she claims she's up to the challenge."

Gracie looked at Buddy and nodded her head.

"Okay, that will be something we'll keep in the back of our minds if she's willing to talk to us about it," Buddy said.

Crystal spoke: "Another thing you should know is that it

takes Reagan time to reach a decision. She doesn't make up her mind quickly."

"So you don't think she ran away on the spur of the moment?" Gracie asked.

"She had a plan," Crystal responded. "Also, I have an older sister who lives in Atlanta. Polly knows we're coming and can help if she's needed. If Reagan doesn't want to come home with us today, she might be willing to stay with Polly for a night or two before transitioning to my mother's house. They've always been close."

They continued to talk for several minutes before ending the call.

"What did you think?" Buddy asked Gracie.

"That Reagan's choices are ripping out her mother's heart and pushing her father toward the breaking point."

"And the exploding point," Buddy replied. "Sammy is an emotional guy, and he's ready to go off on her. I may end up having to speak for Reagan in a way that sounds like I'm her lawyer. Otherwise, she'll bolt because he'll come across as attacking her."

They reached the outskirts of Atlanta. The city had been creeping outward for decades with no end in sight. Even in the middle of the day, traffic was heavy. So far, Sammy had stayed right behind Buddy. They took the exit for Ponce de Leon Avenue.

"My heart is beating faster," Gracie said.

"Maybe you should pray again."

"No, I just need to believe what I prayed before we left Clarksburg."

When the pharmacy came into view, Gracie started looking for the best place for the Landrys to park so Reagan wouldn't easily see their car.

"Suggest the other side of the coffee shop," she said.

"Yeah, that should work. Any vehicle coming to the CVS would approach from this direction."

Buddy led the way to the spot. Sammy pulled in beside him and lowered his window.

"We can't see the entrance to the pharmacy," Sammy said.

"That's safer," Buddy replied. "Gracie is going to text you when Reagan arrives."

Gracie could see the anxiety on Crystal's face through the open window.

"Which won't be for another hour," Buddy continued. "Gracie and I are going inside to talk to some of the employees. I know it's hard, but it's best for you to wait here."

"Whatever you recommend," Crystal replied.

"You're the boss," Sammy added.

Relieved at Sammy's change in attitude, Buddy drove around the corner of the building and parked near the front of the store.

"Are you nervous?" Gracie asked.

"Yes, but let's get started. My butterflies usually leave when I start trying a case."

TWENTY-SIX

BUDDY GLANCED AROUND THE STORE. THE PHARMACY department was toward the rear.

"Let's talk to the head pharmacist," he said to Gracie.

They walked down an aisle filled with decongestants and flu medicine. The store was busy, and there were three pharmacists on duty. Buddy saw the name badge for Vladimir Pushkin, the pharmacist who'd communicated with Dr. Simpson's office. Buddy introduced himself.

"Ms. Landry is supposed to return around two o'clock," Buddy said. "When that happens, we'd like to talk to her. Do you have a place where we could do that?"

"Is this her mother?" Pushkin asked.

"No, a friend of the family who's helping me."

"We don't have a conference room," the pharmacist said. "But I can give you access to the break room."

Pushkin disappeared for a moment, then opened a door near the back corner of the store. Down a hallway to the left was a simply furnished room with a round table, plastic chairs, and a kitchenette.

"This is perfect," Buddy said. "How can we keep from being interrupted?"

"I'll announce that it's closed through the store intercom."

"Okay."

They were still standing in the break room when an announcement came over the intercom.

"Vladimir, you have a customer waiting for you."

"Gotta go," the pharmacist said.

"We'll hang out in the store and wait."

Buddy and Gracie stood before shelves of homeopathic and natural remedies. He picked up a bottle containing a substance intended to increase mental acuity and started reading the strange-sounding ingredients.

"Buddy!" Gracie said in an intense whisper. "It's Reagan!"

Buddy turned around and saw Reagan at the counter waiting to speak to a pharmacist. She was wearing jeans, a loose-fitting shirt, and flip-flops. She'd added several piercings to her face and ears in the short time since leaving Milton County. Her hair was hanging down on her shoulders. Pushkin came up to her and looked in the direction of Buddy and Gracie. He said something to Reagan and turned back toward the shelves where they kept the medicines.

"Let's go," Buddy said to Gracie. "You know what to do."

They started toward the young woman. Gracie was going to greet her in a quiet voice. They were six feet away when there was a loud cry from the middle of the store.

"Reagan!"

Buddy saw Sammy Landry standing in the greeting card aisle. Reagan turned and saw her father.

"Please, baby! We want to talk to you!" Sammy called out.

Reagan hesitated. Buddy and Gracie were now standing within a couple of feet of her.

"That crazy man is stalking me!" she yelled at the pharmacy tech. "Call the police!"

"No," Buddy interjected. "That's your father, and he just wants to know that you're safe. I'll ask him to leave if you agree to talk to me. You're in a public place. No one is going to hurt you."

Reagan stared at Buddy and Gracie for a moment. Buddy could see Sammy approaching out of the corner of his eye.

"Coach Blaylock?" Reagan asked with a puzzled expression on her face.

"Stop!" Buddy said, holding out his hand toward Sammy.

By this point everyone in the store was staring at them. Sammy stopped. Reagan looked at her father then Gracie. Buddy sensed the young woman was about to cry.

Gracie stepped forward and spoke in a calm voice: "Reagan, I'm only here to make sure you're okay. Nobody is going to force you to do anything you don't want to do."

At that moment a slender blond-haired young woman about Reagan's age appeared.

"Let's get out of here," the blonde said brusquely to Reagan. "You don't need the drama."

"Please," Gracie cut in. "There doesn't have to be any drama. All we want to do is talk to you for a few minutes."

Panic and confusion flashed across Reagan's face. The blonde grabbed Reagan's right hand, and in a split second the girls pushed their way past Buddy and Gracie and fled down the far aisle of the store. Buddy ran after them with Gracie behind him. The four of them went through the automatic doors in a row. The girls turned right and continued down the sidewalk. They couldn't outrun Buddy and Gracie, who were directly behind them.

"We're going to have you arrested!" the blonde cried out.

"Reagan, why are you running away?" Buddy asked. "Nobody is threatening you!"

Reagan didn't turn around. The girls reached a silver Cadillac SUV with heavily tinted windows. Buddy could see a young woman behind the wheel of the vehicle. Reagan jerked open one of the rear doors and hopped in. The blonde ran around to the front passenger seat, got in, and slammed the door behind her. The SUV shot out of the space and sped across the parking lot. At that point Sammy, who was breathing heavily, joined them.

"Did you get the license plate number?" he asked as the SUV turned a corner and disappeared.

"I did," Gracie answered and quickly entered the information into her phone.

Buddy was glad for Gracie's prompt action, but his focus was on Sammy. "What were you thinking?" he asked, facing his client. "We'd agreed that you and Crystal would stay in the background until we called you in."

"I couldn't sit in the car. I had to try. And then it seemed that Reagan had been standing at the counter for a long time, and I was worried that she'd leave before you and Gracie could talk to her."

"We were arranging a private place to talk to her," Buddy said.

"I didn't know that," Sammy answered, then pointed at the parking space where the Cadillac had been. "Whoever she's hooked up with is telling her what to do."

"That may be true," Gracie replied. "But Reagan was wavering. I could see it in her eyes."

Sammy didn't say anything.

"Where's Crystal?" Gracie asked.

"Over there," Buddy said, pointing in the direction of the pharmacy.

Crystal was walking rapidly toward them. "What happened?" she asked anxiously.

Buddy waited for Sammy to answer. To his credit, Sammy told Crystal exactly what took place. She started to cry.

"I'm afraid I messed it up," he said forlornly. "It all happened so fast."

Gracie stepped over and hugged Crystal, who leaned into her shoulder and sobbed. Sammy stopped talking. They stood in silence for several moments. Gracie rubbed Crystal's back until the grieving mother slowly pulled away.

"This is just a first step," Buddy said. "At least we know Reagan is in Atlanta."

"For now," Crystal said in a quivering voice. "She might run off to the other side of the country."

"It's possible," Buddy admitted. "But Gracie got the license plate number for the vehicle she's in. Detective Harkness just called. I'll pass it along to her so she can track down the owner."

"And then we can go to whoever that is?" Crystal asked hopefully.

Buddy glanced at Sammy before he spoke. "No, you may have been right. We need to have a law enforcement officer with us. It doesn't look like we'll be able to accomplish anything more here today."

"Tell me again what you said to her," Crystal said to her husband.

"I called her name and told her that we wanted to talk to her.

Buddy and Gracie were standing closer to her than I was. They said something and Reagan took off running with another girl."

"Did you talk to her?" Crystal asked Gracie.

Gracie explained the sequence of events. Her memory was very precise. There was nothing for Buddy to add.

"When the blond girl rushed up, things changed," Gracie said. "The people she's with are having a huge influence on Reagan. I wish there had been a way to get her off by herself, even for a few minutes."

"It didn't happen," Crystal sighed. "And it's going to be a long drive home to Clarksburg. Will you let us know what you find out about the license plate?"

"Yes," Buddy said.

Once the Landrys were gone, Gracie and Buddy returned to the pharmacy and spoke to Pushkin.

"I doubt the customer will return, but I'll post a notice on the company bulletin board," the pharmacist said. "That way her name will be flagged at any of our stores."

"Sorry for the disruption," Buddy said.

"We've seen a lot worse," Pushkin said with a shrug. "This store has been robbed several times since I've been working here."

The pharmacist's words triggered an idea for Gracie. "Were the surveillance cameras running?" she asked, glancing up at an opaque glass cover of the type that concealed a camera.

"Twenty-four/seven," Pushkin answered.

"Could we get a copy of the angle that best shows the face of the young blond girl and the girl we spoke to?"

"That would take a request from the police or an order from a judge."

"We can get that," Buddy replied. "Who should we contact?"

Pushkin left for a few moments and returned with a card. “Contact this person. She’s over security for the Atlanta region. I’ll file a report so she’ll know what happened.”

Buddy and Gracie left the store.

“Do you want me to drive?” Gracie asked. “I’d be glad to take a turn.”

“No, thanks. I do some of my best thinking while driving. The first thing we need to do is call Mayleah. She returned my call while we were in the store.”

The detective didn’t answer, and Buddy left a brief voice-mail message.

As they navigated their way through the streets toward the expressway, Gracie wanted to talk, but hesitated based on Buddy’s comment that he liked to think in the car. He remained silent until the city gave way to the suburbs. Gracie checked her watch. Barring a traffic accident, she’d make it to softball practice.

“I’m glad you came,” Buddy said.

“Why?”

“This isn’t the sort of situation to go through alone,” he said, then paused. “I wonder if things would have gone differently if Sammy hadn’t jumped in.”

“It’s impossible to know, and there’s no use guessing.”

Buddy glanced sideways at her. “Reagan was listening to you.”

“She’s with a bad crowd,” Gracie replied. “We just don’t know how bad it is. I’m afraid Crystal is right. Now that we’ve found Reagan, she may take off again.”

“Amber and Elise moved all over the place.”

They passed an exit with a lot of new commercial development springing up.

“I stopped by my mother’s house this morning,” Buddy said.

"I know. I pulled in right after you left."

Buddy looked over at her. "Did she tell you why I'd come over?"

"Yes, and she showed me the photos of Elise and Amber."

"What did you think?"

Gracie suddenly had a lump in her throat. "Amber and Elise may have crisscrossed the country, but your long search is almost over."

Buddy told Gracie more about the visit with Amber's great-uncle. It made her wish she could have been there too. Finally, Mayleah called, and Buddy filled her in on what happened at the pharmacy.

"The only way to find out what Reagan really wants to do is to get her off by herself," Buddy concluded. "Gracie had her on the fence until the other girl intervened."

"That's how it works in these situations," Mayleah replied.

"What situations?" Gracie asked.

"In which a young woman is being controlled by others. I doubt the oxycodone or the Ambien were for Reagan. Someone else in her new circle was behind the request and made her return to the pharmacy a second time. And they didn't send her alone. She was accompanied by a handler."

Mayleah's words sent shivers down Gracie's spine. She gave Mayleah the license plate number for the Cadillac.

"I'll have an answer within a few minutes after we hang up," Mayleah said.

"And we asked the pharmacist about obtaining the surveillance video so we have an image of the blond girl," Gracie said.

"We'll send you a photo of the security officer's card so you can send an official request," Buddy added.

"I'm at the sheriff's department and can follow up today. Sometimes those systems delete the data every twenty-four hours unless there's an override request to keep it."

"Anything else?" Buddy asked.

"The only question is how today's events impact what Gracie and I do on Saturday," Mayleah said. "I hope no one in Nichols's circle realizes that Pixie and Gracie are the same person."

Gracie hadn't thought about that possibility.

"To see if there's a problem," Mayleah continued, "I'll send a private message to Nichols and see if she responds. If she doesn't, it means your cover is blown. I may be outed as well."

Gracie glanced over at Buddy, who was staring straight ahead.

"Do you think we made a mistake in going to Atlanta?" Gracie asked the detective.

"Based on results, yes," Mayleah answered. "But it was worth a try. Don't be too hard on yourselves. There's no perfect formula for this sort of thing. You just have to be persistent and not give up."

"Do you think Reagan will run off someplace else?" Gracie asked. "Both Crystal and I had that thought."

"Maybe, but that possibility doesn't change anything we do over the next few days."

After the call ended, Gracie sent Mayleah an image of the security officer's business card. When they reached the courthouse, she opened the passenger door and prepared to get out. Buddy's phone buzzed. It was a text from Mayleah. He held it up so Gracie could read it:

License plate stolen. Don't know owner of Cadillac.

Several times during softball practice, Gracie checked the Instagram account for Pixie Carpenter. Mayleah had sent a private message to Nichols from Pixie with a follow-up question about the dog breeder. There was no reply. Gracie tried to hide her agitation from the girls on the team and stayed at the field after practice to throw balls into the backstop. A day that had started out promising ended with frustration for her and Buddy and crushing disappointment for Sammy and Crystal. Gracie released a rising fastball that ended up so high it would have sailed over the umpire's head. Glancing up, she saw Mayleah's truck pull into the gravel parking lot. Gracie took off her glove and walked over to the fence. Mayleah joined her.

"Where's the team?" the detective asked.

"Practice ended ten minutes ago. I stayed late to burn off stress. I saw that the license plate for the car was stolen."

"Yeah, lifted off another vehicle a couple of months ago. But now a description of the Cadillac and the number are flagged in the Atlanta Police Department system."

"And no response from Patricia Nichols to the last private message?"

"Not on social media, but I talked to her on the phone."

"What?" Gracie blurted out.

"The request came through the Ahyoka page. Nichols wanted to know how much I'd be willing to chip in for your new puppy since a purebred dog may cost close to $2,000. I suggested we talk it over and gave her the number for a burner phone. She called me a few minutes later. Now I have at least one of her cell phone numbers."

"What's she like on the phone?"

"She comes across as a really nice person who wants to help

you get a puppy. She's even willing to match whatever I put in. I suggested $500, and she said that was the figure she had in mind. I told her you'd do whatever it takes to replace Ditto and could come up with $1,000."

"What do you think she's up to?"

"To meet with us when we have $1,500 in cash in our pockets and either rob us or run some sort of con to give her the money. I think a con is more likely, but it could also be a hook to bring us into her circle of influence."

"As soon as she sees us, she's going to know we're not teenagers."

"Speak for yourself," Mayleah replied with a smile.

"How can you be so relaxed about this?"

"I'm not relaxed. I'm relieved. There's still an open door. And you're right. We're not going to look like teenagers. Do you think early twenties is a possibility?"

"Maybe," Gracie answered with a slow shake of her head.

"As you discovered earlier today, talking to someone in person can end very quickly unless you have a good plan."

"Buddy had a plan. Sammy jumped in and messed it up."

"And I want to minimize the chance of that happening again."

"Do we have a time and place to meet with Nichols on Saturday?"

"I wanted her to feel like she's in control of the situation, so I left that up to her." Mayleah paused. "She suggested the common area of the apartment complex where I took the photos. The oddest part is the time of day. She wanted to meet at eight o'clock."

"That's early."

"In the evening. She claims the breeder works a day job and meets with customers after hours. But we'll go down much earlier so we can watch what's going on at the apartment complex and learn as much as we can."

Gracie adjusted the ball cap on her head. "I saw Beatrice this morning, and she showed me the pictures of Elise. During the drive home from Atlanta, Buddy told me more about the meeting with Amber's great-uncle. I'm so glad that worked out so well."

"Yes, and I hope it's a breakthrough. I haven't had a chance to dig into the new information, though."

/ / /

Buddy stayed late catching up on work at his office. He took a break to search for current information about Amber, Charles, and Elise Fleming in the database available to attorneys through his legal research subscription. Often, the system quickly produced a treasure trove of residential addresses, debt history, marriages, birth of children, and arrest records.

In the past when he'd entered Amber's date of birth, the trail disappeared after she left town. Typing in "Amber Fleming" yielded results for women with that name in several places across the country. It took over an hour for Buddy to eliminate them from consideration. He didn't know Charles Fleming's date of birth, and his name yielded multiple results. He would have to save that search for another day. Buddy wasn't able to find any record of a marriage between Charles and Amber. The Flemings seemed as determined to live off the grid as a couple as Amber did when she was single.

When Buddy entered Mary Elise's name and date of birth, the first screen caught his attention. It showed that a girl named Elise Fleming, a minor, lived at an apartment in Chattanooga for two years and attended a private school. The lease period overlapped the check from Rascal that Amber cashed or deposited at the Citizens Tri-County Bank. Nothing else showed up for Elise all the way to the present. Buddy closed the program. He could contact the school and request information but doubted they would release it. Hopefully, Mayleah's research in the law enforcement database would prove more fruitful.

Emotionally and physically drained, Buddy went to bed early. He had a restless night and woke up from a disjointed dream in which he'd parked his car on a city street and couldn't find it. The peace that had been his companion since the evening on the porch had taken a vacation. Forcing himself out of bed, he went for a morning run. Sluggish at first, he found his legs at the start of the second mile and cruised through various neighborhoods for almost an hour. A final sprint brought him home, where he bent over and rested his hands on his knees as he caught his breath. The honk of a car horn caused him to stand up and turn around. It was Jason Long. The pediatrician pulled into the driveway and lowered the window. He handed Buddy a bottle of water.

"I saw you turning into your neighborhood," the pediatrician said. "You were ripping it. As a doctor, I recommend a drink of water."

"Thanks," Buddy replied as he unscrewed the top from the bottle and took a long drink. "I'm still holding out hope for Olympic gold."

"I wanted to give you some good news," Jason said. "I had a long phone conference with my lawyers in Atlanta yesterday afternoon. The plaintiff's attorney is going to take what's called a voluntary dismissal in the lawsuit. That doesn't end the possibility of a claim down the road, but it stops it for now."

"That's great news. If they dismiss, it's likely because they're concerned about their expert witnesses."

"Yes. My lawyers mentioned that the doctor the plaintiff's lawyer hired in New York ran into some disciplinary problems. Also, they found out that Cam Simpson, a well-respected local pediatrician, was going to express an opinion about liability favorable to me. That got their attention. My attorney suspects Cam sent them a report. They were surprised that we already knew about it."

"It's hard to keep a secret in Milton County."

"Yeah. Thanks again for showing up in Cam's parking lot at the break of day."

"Hey, I'll wake up early for my clients."

"This has been such a weight on my shoulders for the past two months that I'm not sure how to feel with it gone," Jason said earnestly. "And send me a bill. I want to pay you."

"Maybe, although I'd rather get a bowl of Brunswick stew at Smoke."

"A bowl? I'll buy you a quart."

"Sounds good."

Buddy prepared to turn away and go into the house. Jason's voice stopped him: "And I've thought some more about what you said the other night over at Chris's house. Katie and I have talked about it too. You don't make stuff up or exaggerate, so it got our attention. We'd like to get together to talk about it some more."

Buddy took another drink of water. "Would it be okay if I invited Gracie Blaylock to join us? She's far ahead of me about this sort of thing."

"Sure. Katie will like that."

Shortly after he arrived at the office, Buddy received a call from Mayleah. Surprisingly, she'd run into the same dead end as he had for Charles, Amber, and Elise. He told her about Elise's attendance at the school in Chattanooga.

"You're right. The school won't release any records to you," Mayleah said.

"What do you make of the whole situation?" Buddy asked.

"That the Flemings pay cash, avoid debt, and don't get arrested."

"Not many people in America can say that."

"And it's clear that as a family, they've wanted to stay hidden."

"Which makes me feel bad," Buddy said after a moment passed. "All I wanted to do was be in my daughter's life."

"People make choices for no reason or for wrong reasons. We all do."

/ / /

Shortly after Gracie arrived home from work there was a knock at her door. Peeking through the glass at the top, she saw that it was Lauren and both of her boys. Her sister had a large pizza box in her hand.

"Surprise!" Lauren said when Gracie opened the door. "Jeff is out of town for a business meeting until late tonight, and we decided to bring pizza for Aunt Gracie."

Opie was barking excitedly at the sight of the two little boys. Mark, the younger boy, seemed to grow an inch between visits and looked less like a toddler by the day. His older brother, T.J., thoughtful and less rambunctious, loved Opie. He immediately knelt down and began to rub the fur around the dog's face. Opie rewarded him with a quick lick to the nose.

"I thought that after we eat, the boys could play in the backyard with Opie," Lauren continued.

"Sounds like a plan," Gracie replied.

The pizza was from a local place willing to create three pies in one. The boys' third was strictly cheese. Lauren liked a Hawaiian theme with ham, pineapple, and onion. She knew Gracie was a pepperoni, mushroom, and black olive girl. They sat at the kitchen table. Opie settled down beneath the table at T.J.'s feet.

"How's it going with Daniel?" Lauren asked as she tried to capture an errant string of cheese.

Gracie told her about the strange email that repeated information from a previous one. "It made it seem like he was cutting and pasting," she said.

"He probably was," Lauren answered, securing the cheese between her teeth. "If you don't feel comfortable with him, it's time to move on to someone else. That's the beauty of these dating sites. You can minimize emotional damage. If it's been that long and you haven't agreed to meet, he's probably moved on too."

"This dating site thing is weird."

Lauren wiped her mouth with a napkin. "Look, this isn't like the days when our grandparents sat on the front porch, sipped lemonade, and chatted until the crickets began to chirp."

"I like sitting on porches," Gracie said.

"It's just a figure of speech."

"Not to me."

Lauren gave her a questioning look. Later, while they sat on the deck watching the boys run around in the yard with Opie, Gracie told her what happened with Buddy at his mother's house.

"You did a good deed. That's for sure," Lauren said. "But that doesn't mean you should date him. Didn't you tell me he's interested in a woman detective?"

"Yes. But she may get back together with her ex-husband in Oklahoma."

"Okay," Lauren said slowly. "I'm listening."

Gracie continued. "The way Buddy and I have been able to talk since the other night is what I want in a relationship. We have more in common than you might think."

"Like what?"

Gracie hesitated. She'd spoken too quickly. "Uh, we both grew up in Milton County and work with the law."

"That's true," Lauren said with a nod. "And I can imagine your conversation around the dinner table about the members of the jury pool for the next term of court. You can share stories about the people you each know."

Gracie bit her lower lip. They watched the boys in silence for a few moments.

"But seriously, your heart doesn't have to explain everything to your brain," Lauren said. "I hear what you're saying about communication with Buddy, especially about his new faith. You can ditch all men whose names start with 'D' so long as you realize you're setting yourself up for a huge hurt if Buddy doesn't share your feelings."

"Right now I have no solid reason to believe he does."

"But you have hope?"

"Yes."

"Hope isn't a bad thing," Lauren said, patting Gracie on the arm. "Buddy Smith may be a smart lawyer, but he's an idiot if he doesn't realize you're the best eligible female in Milton County."

TWENTY-SEVEN

GRACIE WOKE UP EARLY SATURDAY MORNING. AFTER getting dressed, she inspected herself in the mirror. Trying to look ten years younger might be a common goal for some women, but it had never been part of her mind-set. Her mother didn't look her age even after having four children, and Gracie relied on genetics, a healthy diet, and exercise to slow the advance of the years. After discussing options with Mayleah, she was wearing a contemporary pair of jeans, a casual top, and sandals. The trickiest part was her hair. Long hair was the sign of the times, and Gracie's short haircut was an exception. They decided to address it by using a ball cap. She struck a teenage pose in front of the mirror and immediately abandoned it as totally fake. The girls on her team wouldn't come across like that. Neither would she.

Gracie, Mayleah, and Buddy had agreed to meet for breakfast at the Crossroads and then take two cars to Atlanta. Buddy was already at the restaurant when Gracie arrived. He saw her and did a double take. Buddy was wearing jeans, a T-shirt, and running shoes. There was no sign of Mayleah. Gracie walked over to the table and removed her sunglasses.

"Our waitress is going to ask for your ID before serving you a glass of orange juice," Buddy said.

"I feel silly," Gracie said, glancing around to see if anyone else who knew her was in the restaurant.

A woman who worked for a local insurance company saw her and hesitantly raised her hand in greeting. Gracie responded.

"There's Nancy Monroe," Gracie said as she slouched down. "Whose idea was it to meet here?"

"Mine," Buddy replied. "I swear you don't look a day over twenty-one."

"Do you think I look old the rest of the time?"

"No, you don't look your age. It's just that—"

Buddy stopped and stared. Gracie turned in her chair as Mayleah approached. The detective had gone completely Western: boots, jeans, shirt, and hat, with her hair captured in a ponytail. Her makeup captured a youthful appearance.

"You two are amazing," Buddy said when Mayleah joined them. "I feel like a chaperone."

"That describes your role accurately as far as I'm concerned," Mayleah responded with a smile.

They ordered coffee.

"I talked with Patricia Nichols last night," Mayleah continued. "There's a change in plans. We're going to meet with the dog breeder at five o'clock this afternoon, then go to the apartment complex for a cookout with some of her friends."

Gracie felt anxious at the thought of having to be Pixie Carpenter for more than five minutes. "I'm not going to say anything," she said.

"Which is the way I've set it up with Nichols," Mayleah said. "She knows you're shy around new people and understands that's one reason I'm coming with you today. I suspect in her mind this is a time for her to check us out."

Gracie hated the prospect of being evaluated like a piece of meat. The waitress came and took their food orders.

"Before we do anything else, I want to pray," Buddy said.

Gracie knew she shouldn't be shocked, but it was still so new for Buddy to say something like that. He bowed his head and prayed a short prayer, asking God for help and safety.

"And success," Mayleah added after he said the amen.

While Mayleah and Buddy discussed other aspects of the day, Gracie nibbled her eggs and bacon in silence. She was so completely out of her comfort zone that she didn't have anything to contribute.

"You're being quiet," Buddy said to her. "What do you think?"

"That I'd rather be on my way to a softball tournament."

"Understood," Mayleah replied. "But don't underestimate the power of your innocence. When you feel weak, you'll come across as vulnerable. If there's a point at which Nichols wants to talk to you alone, go for it so long as you stay in the same room with me."

"I'm not leaving your sight," Gracie said.

"And I'll be close by," Buddy added. "Cue up a text message, and I'll be there in seconds."

Gracie left to go to the restroom. As soon as she was out of earshot, Buddy turned to Mayleah. "Are you sure Gracie should be going with us? She is really uptight."

"I'm concerned about her too," Mayleah said. "But at this point she's such a big part of the plan that I don't see how I could cut her out."

"You could tell Nichols that she asked you to pick out a puppy and bring it back," Buddy suggested.

"Maybe, but it was clear to me from our communications on social media and my phone calls that she really wants to meet Gracie, not me."

"Why?"

"For whatever reason, she probably sees Gracie as an easier or better target. I'm the one in boots and a hat. Gracie comes across as more innocent and vulnerable."

"Which is true."

"And has helped sell the story."

"I'm not sure Gracie can sell anything."

"I'll talk to her during the drive," Mayleah said. "She's not going to have to act. I want her to be herself, only fifteen years younger."

"Twenty-year-old Gracie Blaylock wouldn't have wanted to run away from home in search of adventure in Atlanta."

"I'm sure that's true, but after what you told me about the encounter at the pharmacy, I think Gracie may be the best person to talk to Reagan if we're able to make contact."

"That's true," Buddy agreed.

"Do you have the cash in case we need to show it to Nichols or the dog breeder?"

"Yes." Buddy tapped the front pocket of his jeans. "Do you want it now?"

"Keep it until we see how things unfold."

Gracie returned. Most of the food remained on her plate.

"Finish up," Mayleah said. "We need to leave soon."

"I'm done," Gracie replied. "No appetite."

Gracie and Mayleah rode in silence over the same stretch of road where Gracie prayed fervently when she and Buddy drove to Atlanta. Today she felt dry and empty, which made her wonder if she'd stepped out of the will of God at some point in the process.

They were barely outside the city limits of Clarksburg when the detective turned to Gracie and asked a question: "Do you remember the first time we ate dinner together at the Southside Grill, and I asked if you'd ever dated Buddy when you were in high school?"

"Yes, and I told you no. Why?"

"Because I could really see the two of you as a couple."

Gracie was so surprised she didn't know what to say.

Mayleah continued, "It crossed my mind when we first met, and that's why I asked you about him. But once my ex-husband and I started talking again, I told Buddy right away that's where I wanted to focus my attention. The only date Buddy and I had was to the softball game, and that didn't really count. Since then we've just been working together trying to find Reagan and Elise."

For the next twenty miles, Gracie listened to the story of Mayleah's marriage and the recent changes in Clay's life. Gracie told Mayleah about David and Missy Whitaker. Unlike Buddy, the detective wasn't skeptical.

"That's encouraging," she said.

"I hope it works out for you and Clay," she said. Then she quickly added, "But not because I'm interested in Buddy."

"Thanks. I know you'll be praying for us."

They slowed for a line of cars caused by a traffic accident farther up the road. Buddy was directly behind them.

"I've known for a while that you viewed Buddy as more than a friend," Mayleah said when they were able to pick up speed. "Whenever his name came up in conversation you gave it away."

"My mom says I'm an open book," Gracie sighed. "I guess I'd

rather have an honest face than a lying one. Do you think Buddy is interested in me?"

"He respects you, but I'm not sure if there's anything else there. You're friends with his mother, aren't you?"

"Yes, and she's dropped hints that she would like to see us together."

"If she's said that to you, I bet she's done the same thing with Buddy."

Thinking about Beatrice as her champion encouraged Gracie. "I already love his mother," she said.

Airing out the situation with Buddy caused Gracie to relax and realize how uptight she'd been at times around Mayleah. She told Mayleah about the shift.

"I wish we'd talked about this earlier," Mayleah said with a smile. "Even though we're trying to be young today, we're too old for that sort of stuff."

On Saturday morning it was slightly over a two-hour drive to the east side of Atlanta where the apartment complex was located. Shortly after 10:30 a.m. they exited the interstate onto a four-lane highway with a lot of residential and commercial development. It wasn't a part of the city familiar to Buddy. They then passed neighborhoods of smaller homes built in the 1950s, which now commanded prices that would have shocked the original owners. Mayleah slowed and turned into the apartment property. There were ten two-story buildings that didn't appear to be modernized. Buddy guessed there were at least twenty apartments in each building. It was the kind of development his father would have loved—buy it cheap, do minimal repairs, and collect rent. They passed the common area with park benches surrounding the green space. Buddy recognized it from the pictures Mayleah took. There were people with their dogs enjoying the morning but no sign of Patricia Nichols or her little white dog. Mayleah parked her car, and Buddy pulled in beside her. They got out to stretch.

"You can't see the building where Nichols lives or hangs out from here," Mayleah said.

The parking lot was filled with a wide range of cars and trucks, from old and worn-out to brand-new and expensive.

"Let's get in position so we can watch the apartment and see who comes and goes," Mayleah continued. "It would be great if we could intercept Reagan without having to go to the dog breeder."

"What if I've decided that I want a dog?" Buddy asked. "Gracie doesn't need one, but now that I have the money in my pocket, it feels like I've already paid for it."

"Everyone needs a dog," Gracie replied with a smile. "They make life richer in so many ways."

"Or a parrot," Buddy answered. "I haven't made up my mind."

"Listening to the two of you has made my first decision easier," Mayleah said. "You two sit in Buddy's car and talk about dogs and parrots. I'll be in mine."

They took up positions so they could observe the building linked to Nichols while Mayleah conducted surveillance. Buddy and Gracie were closer, with Mayleah in a spot where she could easily follow anyone who left. Gracie and Mayleah decided to make a quick trip to the apartment complex clubhouse to find a restroom.

"People on a stakeout never have to go to the restroom in the movies," Buddy said.

"You can pretend you're in a movie if you want to," Gracie said. "This is real life for me."

Buddy reclined his seat so he could relax. Gracie returned and slipped into the passenger seat. Buddy had brought several bottles of water and offered her one.

"Thanks," she said, unscrewing the top.

"What did you and Mayleah talk about during the drive?" he asked.

Before Gracie answered, someone came out of Nichols's apartment. It was a blond-haired young woman wearing shorts and a T-shirt. Buddy sat up. The woman leaned against a metal railing and looked up and down the parking lot.

"Look!" Buddy said.

Gracie leaned forward. "She's not the woman we saw at the pharmacy, but it looks like she's waiting for someone to arrive."

Buddy's cell phone vibrated. It was Mayleah. "Is that the woman from the pharmacy?" the detective asked.

Buddy put the phone on speaker. "Gracie says no," he said.

The woman turned sideways. She was clearly heavier than the blonde they'd encountered earlier in the week.

"And she's right," Buddy added. "It's not her."

Leaving the call open, they watched in silence for a few moments. A white van drove past and backed into a parking spot across from the apartment building. Seconds later four young women and a young man got out. The girl on the landing waved to them. The girls from the van moved together in a tight group, making it hard for Buddy to distinguish among them. They separated as they approached the stairway leading up to the landing.

"That's her!" Gracie said excitedly. "The girl from the pharmacy is the last in line!"

"Are you sure?" Mayleah asked.

"Yes," Buddy said. "It's her. No doubt."

They watched as the group climbed the stairs.

"Does it look to you like the girls in front are moving slowly and having to be pushed along?" he asked.

"Maybe," Gracie replied.

The group reached the top of the landing and, with the man leading them, entered the apartment. The door closed behind them.

"Did they go into the apartment?" Mayleah asked. "I can't tell from where I'm parked."

"Yes," Buddy replied.

"Then we're in the right spot at the correct time," Mayleah said.

When nothing happened for several minutes, Buddy decided it was his turn to go to the clubhouse for a bathroom break.

Gracie adjusted the rearview mirror so she could check her makeup. Her attempt at eternal youth would definitely require a significant touch-up before late in the afternoon. She turned the air-conditioning vent so that it didn't blow directly in her face. The outside temperature was in the eighties and would reach ninety by midafternoon. The arrival of the girls had given her an excuse not to answer Buddy's question about what she and Mayleah discussed during the drive to Atlanta. He returned to the car.

"Did I miss anything?" he asked, sliding in behind the wheel.

"No. Do you want to listen to a podcast? Mayleah told me about one on the way down that I think you'll like."

Several uneventful hours passed. Breakfast seemed as distant as the Milton County line, and Buddy was hungry. Gracie had stepped over to spend a few minutes with Mayleah, leaving him alone. Normally, Buddy didn't mind sitting in his car, but after several hours he was uncomfortable. He opened the glove box, hoping to find a spare energy bar tucked away in a corner. No luck. He closed the lid and glanced out the windshield. Two women and a man were descending the stairs. Buddy didn't know which apartment they came from. He quickly phoned Mayleah.

"Are you watching the people who just came down the steps?" he asked.

"Yes, one of them is Patricia Nichols."

The group got in a black car and backed out of the parking spot.

"Gracie needs to get over here," Buddy said.

"No time," Mayleah responded. "We're going to follow the car and see where she goes."

The black car passed. Buddy stepped on the gas and shot out of the parking space faster than he wanted. Concerned he might have attracted attention, he slammed on the brakes.

"What's wrong?" Mayleah asked through the still-open phone call.

"I've been sitting here so long I forgot how to drive. Do you want me to be in the lead or follow up?"

"You stay close to Nichols until we're on a major street, then I'll pass you."

They turned left out of the apartment complex in the direction of downtown Atlanta, which was about fifteen miles away. Within a half mile Buddy ran through two orange lights that then turned red as Mayleah passed beneath them. They turned onto a different four-lane road.

"I'm coming around you now," the detective said.

"Good. That was a bad sequence of lights."

Buddy slowed as Mayleah passed him. It was interesting to see how Mayleah tailed the vehicle. She didn't stay directly behind it but drove to the side, seemingly without trying to block any car from getting between them. However, when two vehicles tried to squeeze in, she smoothly prevented it. They entered an aging industrial zone interspersed with self-service laundries, fast-food restaurants, pawnshops, and other low-rent commercial businesses. The Nichols vehicle slowed and turned into the parking lot for a large commercial building with neon signs not currently lit up. At this time of day, the lot was empty. It was a strip club.

Mayleah continued past the building and turned into a convenience store lot. She parked in front of the gas pumps so that her car faced the roadway with a clear view of the club. The Nichols car was behind the building and out of sight. Buddy pulled in beside Mayleah. Turning off the engine, he got out and joined the two women. Gracie had a tissue in her right hand. Buddy slipped into the rear seat.

"It's a shock but not a shock," Mayleah said bluntly. "At least we know one place to look for Reagan."

Gracie sniffled and blew her nose. "If she's been here, maybe they had her working as a waitress or something," Gracie said. "She's not the type—"

Gracie stopped. Buddy looked across the street.

"We don't know anything for sure," Mayleah continued. "But a common practice is to get a girl involved with drugs, then use that dependency as leverage to control them."

"I understand about the oxycodone," Gracie said. "But why would she want a refill of Ambien? That's not very dangerous."

"People get so high and strung out they need something to help them come down and sleep," Mayleah replied.

"Oh," Gracie said, grabbing another tissue.

Buddy didn't know what to say. Perversion hit hard when staring a person in the face. They sat in silence for several minutes. A phone with a tinny sound rang, and Mayleah reached for her purse.

"That's my burner phone," she said. "Nichols is calling."

TWENTY-EIGHT

AT THE MOMENT, GRACIE COULDN'T STAND THE THOUGHT of being within a hundred feet of Patricia Nichols and doubted she'd be able to pull off any ruse if they met in person. Even though she hadn't looked in a mirror, Gracie knew her makeup was a total disaster. Mayleah answered the call and listened. Gracie couldn't hear anything that Nichols was saying.

"Pixie has the money," Mayleah said. "Two thousand, and we can get more if she loves the puppy."

Mayleah listened for a longer time. Nichols must be a chatty person.

"No problem if you're short of cash. It was sweet of you to offer. No, we don't want to waste a trip. And you don't have to be there."

Mayleah listened again. "Hey, thanks for all you're doing. Pixie wants to thank you in person, so we can wait until then. Just let me know. Bye."

Mayleah lowered the phone.

"What's going on?" Buddy asked.

"She lied and said she was calling from the dog breeder. There is one supercute male left. The breeder is going to put a hold on him, even though Nichols didn't have the money to lay down a deposit. If Pixie wants the dog, we're supposed to come tomorrow, not today. Nichols put a woman on the line who claimed to be the breeder and told me all about the dog. She says the male is the pick of the litter, a real champion. That's what took so long. Nichols is going to take a picture of him and send it to me."

"Why not meet with Nichols and the breeder today?" Buddy asked.

"That was a convoluted story. Nichols made two commitments at the same time and had to rush over to the breeder to grab the best puppy for Pixie."

"I'm glad I don't have to see her," Gracie said. "Not today, tomorrow, ever."

"Don't shut the door on it yet," Mayleah cautioned. "If nothing else happens today, we may need to use the dog connection."

The burner phone chirped.

"That's the photo," Mayleah said.

She handed the phone to Gracie. In the center of the frame was a fluffy golden retriever puppy.

"Wonder what internet site she pulled that from?" Gracie asked as she passed the phone to Buddy.

"Maybe one of us should go back to the apartment," Buddy suggested. "Our first priority is trying to find Reagan, not following Nichols around."

"That thought crossed my mind too," Mayleah replied. "Why don't you and Gracie go to the apartment while I stay here? Now that we're not going to try to meet with Nichols today, we can drop any effort to present ourselves as Ahyoka and Pixie."

Gracie and Buddy got out of Mayleah's car and into Buddy's vehicle.

"Call if anything happens," Mayleah said through an open window.

Buddy and Gracie left the convenience store parking lot and retraced the route to the apartment complex.

"Even though I'm upset, it takes a weight off my shoulders that I'm not going to have to pretend to be Pixie in a meeting with Nichols," Gracie said.

"It would have been hard to pull off, but I believe you could have done it."

They stopped for a red light at an intersection. Buddy pulled into a fast-food restaurant that featured chicken.

"Do you want anything?" he asked. "I'm starving."

The tension of the day had continued to numb Gracie's appetite. "Maybe something to drink and a few fries," she replied.

Buddy ordered an extra-large meal at the drive-through window. At the apartment complex he laid out the food like a picnic in the front seat of the car. The white van was in the same place. He offered Gracie a piece of chicken.

"Thanks," she said. "Even if I'm not hungry, I need something in my stomach."

Buddy wiped a crumb from his mouth with a thin paper napkin. A female figure appeared on the landing of the building's second floor.

"It's the blonde from the pharmacy," Gracie said.

The young woman scanned the parking lot. Even though the windows of Buddy's car were tinted, Gracie slouched down in her seat. The girl disappeared from view in the direction of the apartment and didn't come back out.

"Evidently someone else is on the way, but they're not here yet," Buddy said.

Buddy ate quickly, partly because he was hungry but also so he'd be ready to react. Nothing happened outside the apartment before they finished the meal. Gracie, who had been understandably upset when they followed Nichols to the strip club, seemed to have calmed down.

"I'm going to eat salads every day next week," Buddy said as he put the trash in a paper bag. "Have you tried that new place on Baxter Street? I went there last week with Chris Henley."

"No, I haven't. After today, though, I can understand why police officers who spend a lot of time watching suspects gain weight."

An SUV approached from their left. Buddy instantly recognized it. "It's the silver Cadillac from the pharmacy," he said.

Gracie leaned forward as the vehicle passed by. "It's the right color, but the license plate is different."

"They stole another plate."

The driver parked beside the white van. Three people, two men and one woman, exited. The two men stood on either side of the woman and helped her to walk. The woman was wearing a ball cap.

"Is that Reagan?" Gracie asked. "It's hard to tell because she's crowded in between those two men."

Buddy couldn't tell either. When they reached the bottom of the steps, the men almost carried the woman up the stairs.

"Something is wrong with her," Gracie continued. "Do you see how the men are helping her climb the steps?"

The group reached the landing at the top of the stairs. The blonde came out of the apartment and took over, helping escort the other woman into the apartment.

"The young woman they brought in is either sick or drugged," Buddy said.

They settled in to continue their watch. Over the next two hours, both of them got out of the car to visit the clubhouse and stretch their legs.

"After being cramped in this car all day, I'm ready for a run," Buddy said when he returned after one of his breaks.

Buddy's cell phone vibrated. It was Mayleah. He put the call on speakerphone so Gracie could listen.

"Nichols finally left the club," the detective said. "She's alone, and I'm following her now. Unless she makes a turn, it looks like she's returning to the apartment. There's more going on at the club, most likely employees getting ready to open later this afternoon."

"This afternoon?" Gracie asked. "I thought a place like that wouldn't open until it was dark."

"They probably want to catch the crowd going home from work on a Saturday."

Buddy told Mayleah what they'd seen.

"Okay. Let me know if you can confirm that it's Reagan. I'll probably be there in a few minutes myself."

Thirty more minutes passed. When Mayleah didn't appear, Buddy called her back.

"Detour," she said. "Nichols drove to a different apartment complex not far from where you are. It may be another hub. There were a lot of people coming and going. As soon as we're finished today, I'm going to let the Atlanta police know what I've seen in case they want to investigate."

"Are you going to stay there?" Buddy asked.

"Yes. I think there's just as much of a chance for Reagan to show up here as where you are."

"Unless there are even more places we don't know about," Gracie said morosely. "Atlanta is a big city."

"We're doing what we can," Mayleah replied. "This is better than working the dog breeder angle. Keep me posted."

"I get the idea Mayleah is enjoying this," Gracie said after the call ended.

"That's why she's a detective," Buddy replied.

"I don't want to give up," Gracie sighed. "But this is wearing me down."

"Don't be so hard on yourself. For me, I'm trying to break it down into thirty-minute segments."

They sat quietly, but Buddy's mind continued working. His simple attempt to encourage Gracie reminded him how much she'd helped him over the past weeks. And not just the evening when they sat on his mother's porch. No one except his mother cared as much about his search for his daughter. Mayleah had been a great help in Soddy-Daisy, but Buddy knew Gracie's heart had been invested for a longer period of time at a much deeper level.

"Gracie, I really appreciate you," he said.

"Why?" she asked.

"Because you truly care about other people, and even though you're kind, you can be tough when it's necessary."

"I don't consider myself tough."

"Ask anyone who's tried to hit your rising fastball. But I'm not talking about being athletic. If someone was threatened and you could do something to help, you'd step in without hesitating. That's why you're here now when you could be doing a thousand other things."

"You're here too."

"Yes. But this is my opportunity to tell you why I appreciate you."

Gracie smiled.

"And I like your smile," Buddy continued. "It's never connected to anything negative but comes from the joy and happiness that live deep inside you."

"Buddy, you're painting me in a much better light than I deserve."

"You've always liked my drawings, haven't you?"

"Yes."

"Then let me keep painting the picture I see of you. You do a great job at the courthouse. All the lawyers are glad you're the clerk because it makes their jobs easier. I've heard Judge Claremont praise you more than once."

"Really?" Gracie raised her eyebrows.

"He ought to tell you himself." Buddy paused. "And you always pay your rent on time."

Gracie laughed.

Buddy was silent for a moment before continuing, "You've been a true friend to me as long as we've known each other. We've been through a lot together recently, and I don't want to mess up our friendship, but it's made me wonder—" He stopped and pointed. "Look. A lot of people are coming out of the apartment."

Gracie quickly lost count of the number of people descending the stairs. Some had drinks in their hands. Others were vaping, sending up huge billowing puffs of smoke.

"There must be twelve or fifteen people," she said.

Buddy was silent for a moment. "Fourteen," he said. "Five men and nine women. Can you pick out the woman they had to almost carry up the stairs a little while ago?"

Gracie stared at the group that quickly made its way to the white van, the Cadillac, and another large silver car. "No, it looks like a party that's about to move to a new location."

Buddy phoned Mayleah.

"Follow them," the detective said. "It sounds like they cleared out of the apartment. Nothing like that has happened over here yet."

"What if the vehicles don't stick together?" Buddy asked.

"Stay with the Cadillac. We know it's been connected with Reagan."

Buddy started the engine. Fortunately, the silver SUV was the last in the line of cars.

"I'm going to wait," he said. "Otherwise, it will look obvious that I'm following."

"Don't wait too long," Gracie replied. "And based on what we just saw, I don't think they're worried about someone following them. They have other things on their minds."

Buddy delayed so long that they could barely see the Cadillac when they turned out of the apartment complex.

"They're going right," Gracie said excitedly.

"I see them."

Buddy reached the exit and turned right. The Cadillac was out of sight over a hill. Gracie bit her lower lip. Buddy accelerated, and when they topped the hill, the Cadillac came into view.

"Sorry for sounding so panicky," Gracie said.

"Hey, I'm nervous too. I just hope this doesn't turn out to be a dead end."

"All three cars are staying together. That should make it easy to follow them. Did Mayleah give you the address for the apartment where she's watching Nichols?"

"No. Text and ask her. Then put it in your phone to see if that may be where we're heading."

Gracie did so and watched as the route appeared.

"According to the GPS, they could be heading toward Mayleah," she said. "I'll let you know if they go in a different direction."

The group ahead slowed to a stop as a traffic light turned red. There was another vehicle between the Cadillac and Buddy. When the light turned green, the line of cars turned right.

"They're off course for Mayleah," Gracie said. "They should have stayed on this road for another three miles."

"Keep it on," Buddy said. "It may be a detour or they may stop to pick up someone else."

The three vehicles turned into a much larger and nicer apartment complex than the one they'd left. Buddy continued past the entrance before stopping to turn around. When he entered the apartment property, Gracie's heart fell. It was gated. There was no sign of the Cadillac or the other vehicles.

"Hopefully, there's only one exit," Buddy said as he backed into an empty parking spot in front of the leasing office. "We can either wait here or get out and see if we can locate them on foot."

"Let's get out and search," Gracie replied. "If this is their destination for the night, I'm ready to go home. I can't hang around here until 3:00 a.m."

"I agree, but if we spot them and then they go on the move, we're going to have to sprint back to the car."

"I can't keep up with you, but I'll be close behind."

They entered the complex through an unlocked pedestrian gate.

"Let's split up," Buddy said. "Call if you spot any of the vehicles."

Gracie headed left. The terrain was hilly, and she was able to find a vantage point that gave her a clear view of a long, sloping parking area that served multiple buildings. There was no sign of the Cadillac or the other cars. She went around another line of buildings to a much smaller lot and saw the Cadillac. A man came out and got in. The SUV moved away from the curb. Gracie started jogging back to Buddy's car while trying to text him at the same time. Her fingers slipped. She stopped and called him.

"I see it," Buddy said before she could speak. "Run!"

Gracie slipped off her sandals and took off barefooted. Buddy was already sitting in the car when she burst through the pedestrian gate and hopped in. He shot out of the parking space.

"The Cadillac left thirty seconds ago and turned the way we came," Buddy said. "The windows have a heavy tint, but there were several people inside."

There was no sign of the vehicle on the roadway, and Buddy had no choice but to stay in the line of traffic for the two-lane road.

"Do you still have the route to the apartment where Mayleah is waiting available on your phone?" he asked.

"Yes."

"Let's follow it."

They reached the main highway and continued for three miles without seeing the Cadillac. Two turns later they arrived at the address for Mayleah. Buddy called the detective.

"I see you," Mayleah said. "The Cadillac pulled in a couple of minutes ago."

Gracie spotted Mayleah's car. Buddy parked beside the detective, who rolled down her window.

"Are we making any progress?" Buddy asked.

"Welcome to police work," Mayleah answered. "I have a hunch about what's going on."

Gracie leaned forward so she could hear.

"They're taking people places as part of a prostitution operation," Mayleah continued. "It involves both men and women."

Gracie felt like she might throw up. This was even worse than what she had imagined when they followed Nichols to the strip club. She closed her eyes and leaned back against the seat.

"If that's true, I definitely think you should notify the Atlanta police," Buddy replied.

"I will, and I'll send them a report of what we've observed today."

Gracie opened her eyes as the Cadillac glided past. She didn't want to follow it. She wanted to go directly home to Milton County. Buddy's words that she wouldn't hesitate to step up and help someone in trouble had limits. If Reagan was ensnared in the situation Mayleah described, Gracie couldn't handle it. She turned toward Buddy to let him know. He was still looking at Mayleah.

"Follow the Cadillac," the detective said.

Buddy backed out of the parking space.

"I'm done," Gracie said before he put the car in drive. "This is so much worse than trying to have a talk with Reagan and convince her to come home."

"I know what you're saying," Buddy said grimly. "But we've spent the entire day here, and I want to do what Mayleah asks. Who knows? Whatever we uncover might help someone later."

Buddy continued to follow the Cadillac. Gracie took a deep breath and stared out the passenger-side window as she fought back tears of exhaustion and despair. The sun was setting. Night would soon fall.

TWENTY-NINE

BUDDY KNEW GRACIE WAS EMOTIONALLY LOSING CONtrol. Mayleah's words hit him hard too. But he couldn't cut and run. Not now. He hadn't been in a fistfight since middle school, and that wasn't his goal now, but a rush of prefight adrenaline coursed through him and banished the fatigue of the day.

The strip club came into view. Instead of parking across the street at the convenience store, Buddy slowly rolled into the rear of the parking lot for the club. At least twenty cars and trucks were already there. The Cadillac stopped beneath a streetlight close to the rear entrance. Several people, both men and women, started to get out. Helped by the light, Buddy immediately recognized one of them.

"There's Reagan!" he said, pointing to a figure who was slightly slumped over and standing between two other girls.

Buddy opened the car door.

"What are you going to do?" Gracie asked.

"Anything I can."

"I'm coming with you."

Buddy stopped and looked at her. "Are you sure?"

"Yes. We've come this far. I want to see this through."

Buddy's feet touched the cracked asphalt of the lot. Gracie opened the passenger door.

"Do you have your phone?" Buddy asked.

"Yes."

"Start recording, but stay behind me."

Buddy waited for Gracie to take her phone from her purse.

As he made his way through the cars, Buddy saw that another group of people were talking in loud voices with the people from the Cadillac. Coming closer, he began to pick out words.

"Don't go in there!" one man called out.

A man who'd been in the Cadillac turned to the blond-haired girl. "Get security out here now! These people are trespassing!"

"Come over here, honey!" an older woman yelled in the direction of Reagan and a couple of girls who were now huddled against the Cadillac. "We're here to help you!"

Buddy glanced over his shoulder at Gracie, who remained directly behind him.

"Don't come any closer," he said to her. "It's some sort of confrontation with demonstrators."

There were six or seven people in the protester group near the Cadillac. Buddy counted four women and two men. He slowed to a stop when he was about twenty feet away and stood next to a red pickup truck.

Still recording, Gracie joined him. "Reagan!" she called out in a loud voice. "It's Coach Blaylock!"

Everyone turned and looked at Buddy and Gracie. The man from the Cadillac pointed his finger at them with a menacing expression on his face. "Leave! Now!" he yelled.

Buddy could see Reagan take a couple of steps in their direction. The young blonde grabbed her arm, but Reagan jerked free and stumbled forward. The blonde followed. At that moment a young woman with the demonstrators rushed up to Reagan, put her arm around her shoulder, and said something to her.

"She wants to talk to you!" the young woman called out to Buddy and Gracie.

The man who'd yelled at them was facing the demonstrators. He turned to see what was going on. Buddy stepped forward with Gracie, who held her phone in a way that made it clear she was recording. If the man decided to lunge forward and grab Reagan, Buddy was determined to block him.

"Turn that off!" the man shouted at Gracie.

The blonde jumped in front of Reagan and pointed her finger at the woman who'd come alongside her. The young woman didn't back off but continued to steadily guide Reagan forward. The blonde screamed some profanity. Attempting to move faster, Reagan stumbled forward. As she got closer, Gracie handed the phone to Buddy, who kept recording as Reagan fell sobbing into Gracie's arms. The woman who'd guided Reagan stood beside Buddy as the man and the blonde came closer. The man was shorter than Buddy but stocky and muscular.

"I'm recording this too!" a woman called out from the crowd near the Cadillac. "If that girl wants to leave, you can't stop her!"

The stocky man glanced over his shoulder and spoke to the blonde: "Get everyone inside." He then turned to Reagan and said menacingly, "I'll be back for you."

The man and the blonde retreated. The demonstrators continued to call out to the other girls, but none of them responded. The women entered the rear door of the club.

"You need to get her out of here now," the young woman said to Buddy. "Are you her father?"

"No, I'm a lawyer hired by her parents to find her."

The young woman didn't look much older than Reagan. Something about her face caught Buddy's attention.

"Who are you?" he asked.

"Elise Fleming. I'm a volunteer with a group that helps these girls."

Gracie, who was guiding Reagan toward the car, overheard the girl tell Buddy her name.

"Mary Elise Fleming?" Buddy managed.

"Yes," the girl said. "Do I know you? Have you been here before?"

A woman from the group of protesters was walking quickly toward them. When she came closer, Gracie realized it was Amber. Her former classmate was wearing a white ball cap, gray shirt, and jeans. Her hair was light brown. Otherwise, she looked similar to the photos from the reunion in Soddy-Daisy, only with a resolute gaze in her eyes.

"Buddy?" Amber asked.

"Mom," Elise said in an anxious voice, pointing at Buddy, "he knew my first name."

Three burly men came out the rear door of the club. Two came toward them. The other one headed toward the protester group.

"Don't stay here," Amber said to Buddy. "Take the girl to Southeast Hospital. It's on this road a couple of miles south. Elise, come with me."

"No—" Buddy started. "I have to talk to you!"

"Not here and not now!" Amber said. "I'll come to the hospital."

Gracie started guiding Reagan toward the car. She glanced

over her shoulder as Amber and Elise hurriedly made their way toward the demonstrators, who surrounded them. The two guards continued in Buddy's direction.

"Buddy!" Gracie called out.

Buddy turned and jogged toward the car. Gracie pushed Reagan, who was still unsteady on her feet, into the rear seat and got in after her. Buddy jumped in behind the wheel and locked the doors. The security detail reached the car and banged their fists on the hood so hard that it made Gracie jump. Reagan whimpered. Buddy started the engine and backed rapidly away from the men, who didn't try to follow. Gracie could see Amber and Elise's group entering a gray van across the parking lot.

Reagan's eyes fluttered open. She slowly turned her head to look at Gracie. "Where?" she mumbled.

"We're taking you to the hospital to get you checked out and make sure you're okay," Gracie said.

Reagan closed her eyes again and slumped over against the door.

"Faster!" Gracie said to Buddy.

Buddy zipped beneath a yellow light as it turned red. Gracie reached over to prop Reagan up before exclaiming, "I think she's unconscious!"

Buddy turned sharply into the hospital parking lot. There was a large neon sign identifying the emergency room. He pulled up in front of the doors and stopped.

"I'll go inside," he said.

Walking rapidly, he approached the desk. Within a couple of minutes, Reagan was wheeled into the hospital. Gracie stayed with her to provide information while Buddy parked the car. Sitting in the parking lot, Buddy tried to call Mayleah. When she didn't answer, he left a voice mail that they'd found Reagan and taken her to Southeast Hospital due to a probable drug overdose.

Buddy crossed the parking lot to the hospital. Inside, a young black man at the intake desk directed him to the triage room where they'd taken Reagan. Buddy peeked past the curtain but pulled back when he saw they were removing part of Reagan's clothes. Gracie was with her. Buddy found a chair in the hallway and sat down to wait. His phone vibrated as he received a text from Mayleah:

YES!!! About to meet with a detective from the Atlanta Police Department. Will call later.

Buddy considered passing on the news regarding Amber and Elise but decided to wait until he could talk to her. He called Sammy Landry. Crystal answered.

"I'm in Atlanta," he said. "We have Reagan. She's getting checked out at the hospital for a possible drug overdose."

Crystal gasped and began to cry. Sammy joined the call, and Buddy told them that Reagan came with him and Gracie voluntarily.

"Where was she?" Sammy asked.

"The east side of Atlanta, only a few miles from the hospital," Buddy said vaguely.

"What was she doing?" Sammy continued.

"She was with the blond girl from the pharmacy and some other people. Gracie helped Reagan into the car and we brought her here. The doctor is examining her right now."

While Buddy was talking, Gracie appeared.

"Here's Gracie," he said. "She's been with her. I'll let her talk to you."

He handed the phone to Gracie. "It's Sammy and Crystal."

"Reagan is groggy but conscious," Gracie said. "She was able to tell the doctor that she'd taken some kind of speed or amphetamine and then crashed."

Gracie was silent. Buddy could imagine the emotions on the other end of the line. Gracie pressed her lips together tightly. "I believe they'll admit her."

Gracie listened again for a much longer time. She put her hand over the phone's microphone.

"How much did you tell them?" she whispered to Buddy.

"Very little," Buddy replied, holding his index finger close to his thumb.

Gracie continued to listen. "Of course," she said. "We'll keep you updated."

The call ended.

"They're just relieved that she's safe," Gracie said. "I'd better get back to her."

Buddy told her about his conversation with Mayleah. "I'll be here or in the area near the entrance waiting for Amber. Let me know how Reagan is doing."

Gracie looked into his eyes for a moment. "I hope she shows up."

Buddy swallowed. "Thanks, me too."

Buddy walked the hall for a while, then ventured outside. His mind was racing much faster than his feet as he thought about Elise and Amber. It had been only forty-five minutes since they'd left the strip club, but it seemed like hours. He found an empty chair in the waiting area near the ER entrance and sat down.

/ / /

Gracie stood at the foot of Reagan's bed. The doctor had just left after giving encouraging news: Reagan's vital signs were stable.

The young woman opened her eyes. "Coach Blaylock," she said in a subdued tone of voice. "You were at the drugstore the other day."

Gracie moved closer so she could hear. "Yes."

"I was so strung out I don't remember much about it. And today was worse, but when I heard you calling my name—" Reagan stopped and closed her eyes. "It sounded so loud and clear."

Gracie sat quietly. Her silent prayers were a mix of thanksgiving and intercession. In her mind's eye, she saw Reagan wearing her softball uniform and running onto the field to play first base. For the young woman to be restored to innocence again would be one of the greatest of miracles.

"Thanks," Reagan continued. "I wanted to get out of that mess. It wasn't what I thought it was going to be."

"You're not there now."

Reagan nodded slightly. "Where are my parents?"

"On the way from Clarksburg. They should be here in a couple of hours."

"I'm scared to see them."

"I spoke with them a few minutes ago. They just want to see you, and they're thankful that you're safe."

Reagan bit her lower lip. "I'm going to have to apologize, especially to my dad."

"And get help for what you're struggling with."

"Yeah, I know."

They sat in silence. Gracie thought Reagan may have gone back to sleep, but the young woman opened her eyes.

"I know it sounds crazy, but over the past few days I've remembered some of the things you used to say to us when we'd stand in a circle at the end of softball practice. And then when I saw you at the pharmacy, I freaked out."

Gracie reached out and took Reagan's hand. "I don't know what I said, but I'm glad you remembered."

"Just about knowing that God loves us and made us special. I've felt so unloved and dirty—" Reagan heaved as a sob escaped her chest. Gracie's own heart cracked in two, and tears rolled from her eyes.

A few moments later someone pulled back the curtain. It was a woman in her early forties.

"Are you Grace Blaylock?" the woman asked.

"Yes."

"I'm Reagan's aunt. Crystal asked me to come over until she and Sammy get here."

Reagan's eyes fluttered open and quickly filled again with tears. "Aunt Polly," she managed. "I'm so sorry. I should have called you for help."

The woman rushed over to the bed. She and Reagan hugged for a long time. When they parted, Polly also wiped away some tears.

"We're together now, and you're safe," she said and then turned to Gracie. "You can leave if you'd like. I talked to Crystal, and she knows I'll be with Reagan until they get here."

Reagan wiped her eyes with a tissue that her aunt had given her. She looked at Gracie. "If it's okay, I want to talk to you when I get back home."

"Anytime. And if you don't call me, I'll call you."

/ / /

Buddy looked up as Gracie joined him. She gave him an update about Reagan and told him about the arrival of Aunt Polly.

"I checked back in with Sammy and Crystal, so they know what the doctor said," Gracie told him. "They're fine with Reagan's aunt staying with her until they get here."

"We could head back to Clarksburg," Buddy said. "There's no sign of Amber. But now that I know they're here in Atlanta, I can probably find them again."

"No," Gracie responded. "I thought some more about it. If Amber said she was coming to the hospital, I believe she will. When she gets here, I'll find someplace else to wait while you talk."

"You really think she'll show up? She's been hiding from me for seventeen years."

"Yes. Anyone who's brave enough to do what Amber was doing at the strip club isn't going to be afraid to face the past."

"Maybe," Buddy said with a small shrug. "If she does show up, I want you with me."

"Are you sure?"

"Yes," Buddy responded emphatically.

They watched as a young man helped an elderly woman with a homemade bandage on her head enter the ER. Ten minutes passed. Buddy's doubts increased. Then Amber appeared. She'd changed clothes and was wearing a yellow top and black slacks. Her brown hair touched her shoulders.

Buddy and Gracie stood, and Amber came over to them. "How's the girl doing?" she asked.

Buddy watched and listened as Gracie provided a summary of

what they'd found out about Reagan's condition. Amber asked a few questions. The natural way the two women interacted helped Buddy relax. Amber was no longer a flirtatious seventeen-year-old. And Gracie wasn't a tomboy athlete anymore.

"I know you must be exhausted," Amber said, "but we could go someplace close and grab a cup of coffee if you'd like. There's a place around the corner from the hospital."

"Let's do it," Buddy replied.

The three left the hospital together.

"When I heard you call out to Reagan, I knew within a couple of seconds who you were," Amber said to Gracie. "Are you the coach of the girls' softball team?"

"I coach a summer league team but work at the courthouse. Reagan was one of my players until she disappeared."

They reached a red Volvo. "This is my car," Amber said.

Buddy pointed. "I'm over there."

"I'll be waiting at the parking lot exit."

He and Gracie got in his vehicle.

"Amber seems nice," Gracie said. "And don't feel like she was putting you off. She just didn't want to talk to you about something this important in an ER waiting room or a hospital parking lot. That's why she suggested the coffee shop."

They followed Amber onto a main roadway and through two intersections to a shopping area with a coffeehouse on one end. As they entered, Buddy saw a wedding band on Amber's finger. There was a table for three in the rear corner of the shop.

"That was scary back at the club," Amber said when they sat down with their coffees. "It's not usually like that. Most of the time we're dropping off gifts for the girls and trying to set up times to talk to them when they're not on the property. The situation tonight changed because the Cadillac showed up, and we saw how young the girls were. One of the men in our group is a retired police officer and stepped in. Elise was supposed to stay back, watch, and pray. When she jumped forward to help Reagan, I thought I was going to have a heart attack."

"I wondered about her being there," Gracie said.

"Yeah. Ever since she was a little girl, she's always tried to rescue the underdog."

"Buddy is like that too," Gracie said.

"Maybe," Buddy said, looking at Amber. "But from the safety of a courtroom. Not on the streets like you."

"I knew you became a lawyer," Amber said. "I wasn't surprised. You were always smart."

Amber took a sip of coffee. Buddy felt like a racehorse in the starting gate, but he was determined to be patient.

"A lot has changed over the past seventeen years," Amber said to him. "Where do you want me to begin?"

Buddy quickly replied, "Why did you leave Milton County without saying anything to me?"

"Because the situation with my father was so dangerous that I didn't believe I had a choice. Before Elise was born, I could run to a friend's house, but that wasn't an option with a baby. The last night I saw you, there was a terrible fight between my parents. I don't remember what you saw."

"We were in the kitchen," Buddy said. "I was holding Elise. Your father grabbed her, shoved her at you, and ordered me out of the house."

"Yeah," Amber said with a slight nod. "That's right. After you left, he started pushing my mother around. When I tried to get him to stop, he punched me. He'd done that before, but this was the worst. I called your house, and your father answered. I blurted out what had happened. He said you were asleep but that he would come get us. Elise and I left the house with nothing except what we were wearing. Your father took me to get something to eat. We talked everything over, and he promised to help me escape."

"You could have called the police."

Amber shook her head. "I can't tell you how many times the police came to our house from when I was just a little girl. Sometimes it was because my mom threw something and hit my father. Or it might be when he knocked her around. If the police came and didn't do anything, what would have happened to Elise and me when they left?"

"Is that when my father started giving you money?"

"Yes, although he always said you didn't know anything about it."

"I didn't. But not long ago I found the canceled checks in the basement at my mother's house."

"Your father was very faithful in supporting us. When I married Charlie, he insisted on continuing the payments as a college fund for Elise. She has enough in her account to attend any school she wants to."

Buddy was silent for a few moments. "We could have faced this together," he said.

"No." Amber shook her head emphatically. "This wasn't something a couple of teenagers could have handled. It was even worse than I'm telling you. I desperately needed to leave town and go where my father couldn't find me. Please don't try to make me feel guilty for the choice I believed I had to make."

"No, no . . . I'm just trying to understand."

Amber spoke rapidly. "Twice my father found out where I was living and showed up. The first time I'd just moved to Savannah. I recognized his truck in the parking lot and didn't go back into my apartment. A few years later he found out where I worked here in Atlanta and waited for me outside. He tried to run me over in a parking lot, but I jumped out of the way."

"Why did he want to hurt you after you were out of the house?"

"Because he was insane, and what I knew could have sent him to prison for a long time if he'd been prosecuted and convicted. But it would have been hard to prove, and, once again, if I failed, who was going to keep Elise and me safe? He died from a brain tumor five years ago. It was the first time in my life I was able to sleep without fear."

"And your mother?" Gracie asked.

"Living in Los Angeles not far from my brother. She has a lot of emotional and mental issues, but we stay in touch."

"After your father died, is that when you went to the family reunion in Soddy-Daisy?" Buddy asked.

"Yes," Amber answered, looking at him with surprise. "It was the first contact I'd had with my father's extended family in years. How do you know about that?"

Buddy told her about the visit with her great-uncle in Soddy-Daisy and the photos Vick gave him.

Amber seemed puzzled. "I had no idea you were looking for us," she said.

"My father never told you?"

"No, I thought you'd moved on with your life."

"Is that what he said?"

"Not in those words exactly, but that's the strong impression

I received. I knew you went to college with the intent to go to law school and have a career. Your father and I rarely talked, but he made a few comments that led me to believe things had worked out for the best for you after I left town. I let him know where to send the support for Elise, and he faithfully did so. I used a post office box in Atlanta for years, even when I wasn't living here."

"But you also came to Clarksburg."

"Yes. One time I met your father's bookkeeper. And then I drove to Clarksburg a few months before your father passed away." Amber paused. "I came to his funeral."

"What?" Buddy's eyes opened wider.

"Out of respect. I sat at the back of the church, which was packed, and I left early. I thought about saying something to you, but I didn't. That was a mistake, and I'm sorry."

"Why did you continue to hide after your father died?" he asked.

"Charlie is a computer analyst who works for the government. Even now I don't know exactly what he does. They have all these guidelines our family has to follow about avoiding social media. We don't even receive our mail at our house and other stuff like that. Charlie is out of the country now for at least a month. When we met and started dating, I eventually told him about my background. He told me marrying him would help keep us safe."

"Does the government know you're involved in trying to help the women at the clubs?" Gracie asked.

Amber shook her head. "No, and if his bosses found out, I'm sure we'd have to stop. But when a group at our church started the outreach and intervention, I wanted to help for as long as I could."

"What does Elise know about me?" Buddy asked.

"Nothing beyond the fact that I had a boyfriend in high school, got pregnant, and ran away from home because of the abusive situation with my father. The emphasis was always on avoiding my father, not anything negative about you. I cut off all ties with my family to make it hard for my father to track us down. I didn't see my mother or brother for over ten years. Even then, it was in Florida while I was living in Atlanta." Amber paused. "But all this was part of the pressure that brought me to faith."

"I'd like to hear more about that," Gracie said.

Amber took another sip of coffee. "When Elise was five, I started attending a church so she could go to Sunday school. I'd been a few times as a small child when a neighbor took me, and it was a glimmer of light in the darkness. Elise liked the church, but the big impact was on me. I encountered the Lord's love and healing, which I desperately needed, and that's where I met Charlie. After dating for a year, we married. He adopted Elise, and we have a son named Bo. He's eight."

Gracie drew out more details with gentle questions to Amber. As he listened, Buddy realized Amber's story made much more sense to him now than it would have even a few weeks earlier.

"Because of what I've suffered, I can help others in a way not everyone can," Amber said.

"That is beautiful," Gracie said.

The coffee in their cups was gone. Buddy had to ask the most important question in his heart. He turned to Amber. "Are you going to let me get to know Elise?"

"That will be up to her. She considers Charlie her father, but I've already told her I'd support her if she wants to spend time with you."

"Did you talk about it tonight?" Buddy asked.

"Yes," Amber answered. She smiled as she continued, "And if I'd answered all her questions, I wouldn't have been able to come to the hospital or here. But there are some things I think she should hear from you, not me."

They exchanged contact information. That simple act held enormous significance for Buddy. His search was over.

"I'll get in touch with you," Amber said as they stood outside on the sidewalk in front of the shop. "I want to let Charlie know what's happened first."

"Sure." Then he had to ask: "Do you think Elise is going to say yes to getting to know me?"

"After what I tell her about you, I think I know what her answer will be."

On their way out of the city, Buddy called Mayleah. The detective was going to spend the night in Atlanta after meeting with the APD.

"What we provided filled in some gaps for an ongoing investigation," Mayleah said.

Buddy told her about the encounter with Amber and Elise. He wished he could see the detective's face. When he finally paused, Mayleah didn't say anything.

"Hello?" he asked. "Are *you* there?"

"Yes," Mayleah managed. "But I'm having trouble talking or seeing through my tears."

"Thanks for your part in making this happen," Buddy said.

"You're welcome, and I want to hear more when we're together."

Even a late-night cup of coffee wasn't enough to keep Gracie's eyes open. By the time they reached the interstate, she was asleep. It was 1:35 a.m. when her eyes opened and she checked the time on her phone. They were in Clarksburg, about to turn into Gracie's driveway. She ran her fingers through her hair and stretched her arms out in front of her.

"You're home," Buddy said.

"Did I sleep the whole way?"

"Except for the time you talked in your sleep. We had an interesting conversation about softball."

"I don't talk in my sleep, but if I did, there's a good chance I would talk about softball."

Still groggy, Gracie opened the car door.

"What time do you want me to pick you up tomorrow?" Buddy asked.

"Pick me up?" Gracie replied.

"To take you to church."

"Are we really having this conversation?" Gracie asked. "Or am I talking in my sleep?"

"I'm serious. I thought about it during the lonely drive home."

"Sorry I wasn't good company. We just spent eighteen hours together. Are you sure you want to see me tomorrow?"

"If you need to sleep in, I'll understand."

"Let's go to the later service."

"What time should I come by?"

"Ten minutes before eleven."

THIRTY

BY THE TIME GRACIE WOKE UP, THE MIDMORNING SUN was casting bright streaks through the cracks in her bedroom curtains. Sitting in the kitchen with a cup of coffee on the table and Opie lying at her feet, Gracie turned on her tablet. If ever there was a day to record answered prayer, this was it. As she wrote, the thankfulness in her heart welled up so strongly that it overflowed. She grabbed some tissues, not to stop the tears, but to make room for more.

The clothes she'd worn the previous day were on top of the hamper in her closet. Glad she didn't have to pretend to be fifteen years younger, she put on a light green dress that was one of her favorite summertime outfits. The doorbell rang. It was Buddy. He was wearing a blue sport coat and khakis.

"You look nice," he said when she opened the door.

"Thanks. As soon as I put Opie in the backyard, I'll be ready to go."

Gracie slipped into the front seat of Buddy's car. "This looks familiar," she said.

"I had the same thought," he replied. "It made me want to trade it in for a new model."

"Maybe not for a while," Gracie said as she patted the leather seat. "You and this car share some important memories."

It was only a mile and a half to Gracie's church. Curious stares followed them as they walked down the aisle to her usual place a third of the way from the front. Shortly before the service started, Gracie received a text message from her mother inviting her to lunch. She entered a quick reply.

May I bring Buddy Smith?

While she waited for the answer, Gracie imagined what might be going on between her parents. Her mother would be telling her father about the text and discussing if they needed to modify the menu. As the choir filed in, her mother answered simply:

Yes

Gracie leaned over and conveyed the invitation to Buddy.

"I'd like that," he replied.

Gracie was amazed how comfortable she felt with Buddy beside her. She didn't fidget or worry about what he was thinking. After the service, he greeted several people he knew as they made their way to the vestibule.

"What did you think?" Gracie asked when they crossed the parking lot.

"It's different from my mother's church, but in a way, everything about faith is new to me."

"That makes sense," Gracie replied. "Would you want to come again?"

"Only if we can sit together in the same pew."

Buddy's statement was far from the most romantic thing a man could say to a woman, but for Gracie, in that moment, it sent shivers down her spine.

"Deal," she said.

They left the parking lot and headed out of town toward the Blaylock farm.

"When are you going to tell your mother about finding Elise?" Gracie asked.

"I haven't decided. Maybe drive her to Atlanta for a surprise meeting." Buddy paused. "But I don't want to get ahead of myself. Amber and Elise will decide what they want to do."

Buddy parked behind a green pickup truck in the driveway at the Blaylock homestead. Wearing a checked apron, Maxine greeted them in the foyer of the rambling house.

She hugged Gracie tightly before saying, "Frances Mulhaven was in church this morning. She told me that you and Buddy found Reagan."

"Yes. Sammy and Crystal are with her now."

"Is she okay?"

"I can say that she's safe," Gracie answered. "Beyond that, I'd better leave it up to her folks to share any news."

"That's fine. I'm just glad she's been found." Maxine turned to Buddy. "How's your mother doing?"

"Well," Buddy answered. "She likes it when Gracie stops by for a chat."

Gracie followed her mother and Buddy into the dining room where Lauren waited. When Buddy moved on to be with the men, Lauren pounced.

"Did he go to church with you?" she asked.

"Yes."

"It was bold of you to invite him."

"Actually, he invited himself. We spent all day and most of the night together in Atlanta yesterday, and he brought up going to church when he dropped me off at my house around one thirty this morning."

"One thirty in the morning! What were you doing?"

Gracie leaned in closer. "We went places you'd never guess in a million years and saw God work miracles. It was one of the most amazing days of my life. At one point we were sitting in Buddy's car, and he listed all the things he likes and admires about me. I wish I'd recorded it."

Lauren was shocked speechless. When they were all gathered around the table, Gracie asked Buddy to pray.

Without hesitation, he bowed his head. "God, bless this family and this food. Thank you for what you are doing in my life, and how you helped Gracie and me yesterday in Atlanta. Amen."

Buddy was relaxed and friendly around Gracie's family. After they finished eating, she helped her mother in the kitchen.

"I really like Buddy," Maxine said when they were alone.

"All he needed was Jesus."

It was after 3:00 p.m. when Gracie and Buddy drove back to town.

"I enjoyed being with your family," he said.

"We do this most Sundays."

Buddy was silent for a few moments. "We didn't finish our conversation yesterday in Atlanta," he said.

"Which conversation? There were a lot."

"The one when I was telling you all the things I admire and like about you," Buddy said with a smile. "I didn't get to the part about wanting to spend more time together if you're open to it."

"I am," Gracie replied and waited.

Buddy glanced over at her. "And I'm not just talking about going to church."

"Sounds good."

"You're being very efficient with your words," he said.

"Because my heart is about to pop with joy," Gracie answered.

"That's better," Buddy replied. "Today was a good start, and I'm looking forward to tomorrow. Breakfast or lunch at Crossroads? Which would you prefer?"

"Lunch," Gracie answered. "It will give me something to look forward to all morning."

/ / /

Buddy rarely took naps, but after dropping off Gracie, he stretched out on the sofa in his den. Still sleep-deprived from the previous day in Atlanta, he soon entered a familiar dream in which he was in the midst of a run and suddenly became disoriented. As he retraced a convoluted loop and ended up in the same spot, a figure stepped from the shadows and pointed down a road Buddy hadn't noticed. Moments later he burst into the sunlight near his car. Buddy lifted his arms in celebration. He woke up, replayed the sequence, then fell back to sleep. When he awakened the second time, his first thought was about Gracie and how natural it felt to be around her. He'd always had a sense of anxiety when entering into a relationship with a woman. This time he felt at peace. His phone that was on the coffee table beside the sofa vibrated. It was a text from Amber.

Could Elise and I come to Clarksburg on Tuesday around eleven in the morning—and stay until five?

Buddy sat up and immediately replied:

Yes. What would you like to do?

A few seconds later an answer came:

Elise wants to spend time with you.

Buddy stared at the seven words until they were permanently etched into his memory. His daughter wanted to spend time with him. And if she spent time with him, that meant he could spend time with her. He picked up his phone.

May I include my mother at some point in the day?

He was relieved at the response:

I'm sure Elise would like that.

Buddy sent Amber his home address and immediately called his mother. He hadn't told her about the trip to Atlanta yet.

"How are you doing?" Beatrice asked.

"Fine," Buddy replied. "Are you busy Tuesday? I'm going to take a day off work and want to spend some time with you."

"It's not a holiday."

"Right, but I'm in the mood for a break."

"That's a new kind of mood. Are you sick?"

"No. Please look at the calendar in the kitchen and tell me what's on it."

"I'm there now," his mother replied. "I have a brunch at eleven with Kitty Dawson and her sister who's visiting from Jacksonville. Other than that, I don't have any plans."

"So you'll be there in the afternoon?"

"Kitty likes to talk, so it will be around two o'clock before I'm home. Why does that matter?"

"I'll plan on stopping by around three o'clock. That way you don't have to rush."

Buddy ended the call before his mother could ask any more questions. His next call was to Gracie.

"Buddy, that's wonderful," she said after he'd given her the update. "What are you going to do with Elise?"

"Stare at her and listen to the sound of her voice."

"She's seventeen years old, not seventeen months."

"I'll feed her solid food. Maybe I'll take them to the Southside Grill for lunch. I've set up my mother for a surprise visit at three o'clock."

"Are you sure you should surprise her?"

"Yeah, it would be more stressful for her thinking about the visit than if we just showed up."

"She's going to cry."

"I might cry too."

"Anyone would cry. Have you talked to Mayleah yet?"

"No."

"She called me after you dropped me off. She's on her way back from Atlanta. The police have already brought Katrina Caldwell, alias Patricia Nichols, in for questioning and have a search warrant for the apartments."

Buddy checked the time on his watch. "Mayleah should be back by now, but I bet she's exhausted. I'll wait to talk to her."

"Yeah, she didn't sleep any last night."

/ / /

The following morning Buddy arrived early at the office.

"What brings you in at the crack of dawn?" Millie asked.

"I need to clear my schedule tomorrow. I'm going to be out of the office most of the day."

Millie pulled up his calendar. "You don't have anything until Pete Molitor comes in around lunchtime."

"I'm going to reschedule with Pete, and also push the conference call with Merriwether Wells to another day," Buddy said casually. "I met my daughter in Atlanta on Saturday, and she's coming for a visit."

Millie's mouth dropped open. "Elise is coming here?" she said as her hands went to her heart. "This is unbelievable," she said. "After all these years. How? Where?"

"There's a lot to tell."

Millie settled into her chair. "Jennifer won't be here for another hour. I'll log out so you don't have to pay me."

Buddy smiled and said, "That's okay—you deserve to know."

In telling Millie, Buddy focused on the encounter with Amber and Elise, not the dark saga with Reagan.

"And Amber is okay with you being in Elise's life?"

"So far."

"Why not earlier?"

"She wasn't hiding from me; she was hiding from her father. After he died a few years ago, she thought about reaching out to me but didn't."

"Because Rascal told her you'd moved on with your life?"

Buddy nodded. "Pretty much, yes. That part stung. You were probably right about his motive in thinking he was protecting me from an obligation I didn't want or a responsibility I couldn't carry."

"I'm sorry," Millie said and slowly shook her head. "But that's in the past, and I'm excited about tomorrow."

/ / /

The following day Buddy nervously paced through the house as it got closer to the time for Amber and Elise to arrive. Eleven o'clock came and went without anyone turning into his driveway. Fifteen minutes later he heard the sound of a car outside, but it was someone turning around to head down the street in another direction. He picked up his phone and sent Amber a text asking if she was having trouble finding the house. She immediately replied:

No. We're here.

Throwing open the front door, Buddy saw the red Volvo pull into the driveway. Amber was in the passenger seat. Elise was behind the wheel and wearing sunglasses. They got out. Elise had on jeans and a turquoise top. Her wavy brown hair looked much like the style Maddie adopted when she was in college. His daughter removed her sunglasses and walked up to him with the same firm footsteps that had compelled her across the parking lot to help rescue Reagan Landry.

Buddy started to hold out his hand, but Elise stepped forward and gave him a quick hug. Even the brief touch was indelibly imprinted on Buddy's mind.

"What do you want me to call you?" she asked in a voice that held hints of the same tones as her mother's.

"I don't know," Buddy managed. "I guess you could call me Buddy. You already have a dad, and I'm not here to take his place."

A broad smile creased Elise's face. "Okay, Buddy it is. Until we agree on something else."

"Come inside," he said. "We can sit on the back porch. I thought we might grab lunch later at the Southside Grill."

Sitting on the porch, Buddy felt awkward. As he'd mentioned to Gracie, he simply wanted to stare at Elise and listen to her talk without caring what she said, but she seemed to be holding back. He didn't know what to say to a seventeen-year-old woman to jump-start a conversation. He wished Gracie were present.

"I talk all the time in my job," he finally said. "And I've

rehearsed a thousand times what I'd say if this moment came, but right now I'm tongue-tied."

Elise smiled. "Why don't you tell me about the first time you saw me?" she suggested.

Buddy's paralysis lifted. "You were a beautiful baby," he said. "Way cuter than any of the other infants in the hospital nursery."

For the next few hours they talked back and forth. Instead of going to the Southside Grill, they fixed deli sandwiches at Buddy's house. Having Elise in his kitchen made the house seem more like a home than it ever had.

"Have you thought about where you want to go to college after you graduate from high school?" Buddy asked after they finished eating.

"My dad went to Georgia Tech, so that's on my list. But I'm also thinking about liberal arts schools like Vanderbilt and Wake Forest."

Buddy remembered what Amber said about Elise having the funds to go anywhere she wanted because of the money paid by Rascal. As he listened to his daughter, Buddy picked up on other traits that existed in his family line. Elise liked to paint and be outside in nature.

"Tell him about running," Amber said.

"I'm on the cross-country team. I was second-team all-conference last year, and I hope to do better this year. My goal is to run a marathon this winter."

"That's good," Buddy said. "I've completed several marathons."

"Would you like to do another one?"

Despite his having advised Dr. Simpson that he'd given up marathons, Buddy made a split-second decision: "Yes. Could we do it together?"

"I wouldn't want to hold you back—"

"Don't worry about that. My goal would be to keep up with you and finish. Did you ever play fast-pitch softball during high school?"

"I made the junior varsity team when I was in the ninth grade, but when they started throwing curveballs, I struck out all the time."

"I know that pain."

It grew closer to three o'clock. Buddy told them what he had in mind regarding his mother.

"That's fine with us," Amber said. "I was hoping it would work out for today. But I think you should let her know we're coming."

Buddy didn't argue. He placed the call.

Beatrice answered. "I left Kitty's house fifteen minutes ago," she said. "Are you on your way?"

"In just a few minutes. Is it okay if I bring a couple of guests?"

"Who is it?"

"Amber and Elise. They're with me now at my house."

There was silence. Buddy hoped his mother hadn't fainted.

"I think that would be a wonderful surprise," Beatrice said.

"We're on our way."

Buddy drove them the short distance and pointed out a few landmarks. They pulled into the driveway.

Beatrice opened the door as they walked across the porch. "Good to see you, Amber," she said, and then she fixed her eyes on Elise.

"And I'm Elise, your granddaughter."

"Oh my goodness," Beatrice said and the tears began to flow.

As Buddy watched, Elise wrapped her arms around her grandmother. This wasn't a quick hug. It was a total embrace.

Buddy turned to Amber and mouthed the words, "Thank you, thank you."

Later, Buddy called Gracie, who left the courthouse early and came over to Beatrice's house so she could spend a few minutes with Amber and Elise before they returned to Atlanta. The five of them sat on the front porch together. Gracie's eyes seemed to stay constantly moist.

"If this was spring, I could blame it on the pollen," she said as she pulled another tissue from her purse. "But it's just so beautiful to be sitting here with all of you."

"I told Elise you can't have enough loving family members in your life," Amber said to Beatrice.

Gracie's admiration for Amber skyrocketed. To say those words after what Amber had experienced in her own family was as amazing a testament to healing as Gracie had ever heard. And Elise was a bright, articulate young woman. When it was time for them to leave, Beatrice asked Gracie to stay behind while Buddy drove Amber and Elise back to his house.

"I had no idea why Buddy was taking off work on a Tuesday," Beatrice said when they were alone. "Thank goodness he gave me a few minutes' notice."

"It was still a good surprise."

"The best," Beatrice said, then sighed. "And having you and Buddy here together with Elise. I'm not sure how to describe how that makes me feel, except that it's like family."

"He invited himself to church this past Sunday, and I took him to dinner at my parents' house."

Beatrice beamed. "I didn't think this day could get better, but it just did."

Gracie drove directly from Franklin Street to softball practice.

News about Reagan had reached a couple of girls on the team. All they knew was that their former teammate was in the hospital in Atlanta. No one was aware of Gracie's involvement.

"Is she going to be okay?" Laura asked when they gathered to pray at the end of practice.

"That's why we do this," Gracie answered.

As the girls scattered, a familiar truck pulled into the parking lot. It was Mayleah, wearing her trademark cowboy hat and boots. She got out and came over to Gracie.

"Have you recovered?" Gracie asked. "I couldn't have done what you did."

"Mostly," Mayleah replied, taking off her hat. "I talked to Buddy, and he told me that Amber and Elise came to town for a visit."

Gracie told her about the time at Beatrice's house.

Mayleah nodded. "And the circle is closed."

"Yes, and I hope it gets stronger."

"It will." Mayleah glanced down at the red clay dirt for a moment before looking up. "And as long as I'm in Milton County, I'm going to enjoy watching that happen."

THIRTY-ONE

SATURDAY MORNING BUDDY PUT HIS GOLF CLUBS IN the trunk of his car. A couple of minutes later he pulled up to Gracie's house. He could hear Opie barking when he approached the side door. Gracie was wearing golf shorts and a white top. A light blue visor was already on her head.

"I'm here for my golf lesson," Buddy said.

"You must have the wrong address," Gracie replied with a grin. "I haven't played in almost a year."

Driving to the club, Buddy told her about his last golf outing with Sammy Landry: "We went to the range a few days later, and I was spraying the ball all over the place, more like a baseball player trying to get on base than a golfer trying to hit the green."

"I'm very rusty," Gracie replied. "I brought some cut balls to use on the holes with a water hazard."

"I hope you brought extras for me."

The country club was just outside the city limits. The entrance was framed by pecan trees.

"I talked to Crystal last night," Gracie said as they drove toward the clubhouse parking lot. "Reagan spent the night with Frances and has an appointment with Dr. Simpson next week."

"That's good. I hope she agrees to meet with you too."

"I'm going to invite her to a game so the girls can show her some love."

Gracie turned down the offer of an electric cart, which pleased Buddy. He enjoyed walking a course, especially earlier in the day. Throughout the round, he couldn't stop smiling. Not at his shots, but in watching Gracie. She was intense and focused. And he enjoyed every nuance of what she said and did. The cut golf balls came in handy. Buddy complimented Gracie on the symmetry of one of her splashes. He then dropped two straight balls into the same pond. As the sun rose higher in the sky, they stood side by side on the tee box for the eighteenth hole.

"It's time to get serious," Buddy announced.

"I've been doing the best I can all morning," Gracie replied. "But my putter isn't cooperating."

"I mean put something on this hole."

"A bet?" Gracie raised her eyebrows.

"Yes."

"I've never done that. I don't need an incentive to play my best."

"You haven't heard my wager."

"Okay," Gracie said slowly.

"If you win this hole, I have to do something you want to do," Buddy said, then stopped.

"And if you win?" Gracie asked.

"You have to do something I want to do."

"That's it?"

"Yep."

Buddy waited as Gracie studied him. He knew it was a moment for her to decide if she trusted him.

"You're on," she said. "You hit first."

The eighteenth hole was a 355-yard par four with a dogleg to the right, two fairway bunkers, and a tiny creek past the bunkers. Three sand traps protected the green. Everyone who played the course considered it the toughest hole.

"Watch out for the bunkers," Gracie said as Buddy placed his ball on the tee. "The large one is right where you've been landing your drives all morning."

Buddy, who was bending over, looked up at her. "That won't work with me," he said. "Pressure is my middle name."

"I thought the 'C' stood for Christopher."

Buddy took a practice swing and then struck the ball solidly with a loud *thwack*. It sliced over the bunker and landed just on the other side of the trap at the edge of the fairway.

"Don't try to match that," he said, turning to Gracie. "I suggest you lay up short of the bunkers."

"That's my intention," she answered.

Gracie had a smooth swing that made Buddy jealous. It showed off her excellent hand-eye coordination. As she brought down the driver, it didn't look like she was going to have much power, but over the last couple of feet the head speed accelerated. For a woman her size, she crushed the ball. It flew out and up and landed in the middle of the fairway about forty yards short of Buddy's ball.

"So far, so good," she said.

They walked side by side across the green grass until they reached her ball.

"I recommend a 3-iron," Buddy said. "You still have a long way to the green and need to bounce it up."

"Thanks," Gracie said as she took a 5-iron from her bag.

She lined up the shot but then stepped back. Buddy expected her to change clubs, but she returned to her ball and hit it sharply. It sailed higher than Buddy expected, took four bounces, and rolled onto the left front edge of the green. It was a fabulous shot.

"I'd like to bottle that," Buddy said.

"That's the thing about golf," Gracie replied. "Once you hit a nice shot, you're always chasing it, hoping to do it again."

"I guess that's common to all good golfers. Sammy Landry says the same thing."

They walked over to Buddy's ball. He could barely set his feet without having to stand on the edge of the bunker. He took out a 7-iron. Without taking a practice swing, he hit a ball that arced nicely and landed in the sand trap on the right front of the green.

"Perfect," he said.

Gracie laughed. "Explain, please."

Buddy picked up his bag. "My sand game is my strongest component because I've had so much practice. I think my golf balls have something like a magnetic attraction to sand."

They made their way to the green.

"Even though I'm in the trap, I'm actually closer to the pin," Buddy said. "You hit first."

"Seriously?" Gracie asked.

"Yes."

"Okay."

Gracie lined up and hit a putt that crossed over a rise and rolled down to within four feet of the hole. She had par in her sights. While Gracie was marking her ball, Buddy stepped into the sand trap with his wedge. His ball rested nicely on top of the sand, which was harder than normal due to a rain shower the previous evening. He took a couple of practice swings. Taking a deep breath, he exhaled and hit the ball. It shot up out of the trap along with a splatter of sand, then rolled down toward the hole and in for a birdie. He dropped his club in shock.

Gracie's eyes were like saucers. "Did that just happen?" she asked.

"You are my witness, because none of my friends will believe it."

Buddy retrieved his ball and raised it to his lips. Gracie stroked in her ball for a par. They walked off the green and toward the clubhouse. Buddy didn't say anything.

"Don't leave me wondering," Gracie said. "What do you want me to do? Cook you a peach cobbler?"

"That would be nice, but it's not what I had in mind."

They reached Buddy's car, and he opened the trunk. "That was fun," he said. "You only beat me by five strokes."

"But you won the hole that mattered. Please tell me?"

Buddy closed the trunk lid and faced her. "You have to come over to my mother's house this evening so we can sit on the porch together."

Gracie's jaw dropped. "That's it? I would have done that anyway."

"I know, but winning the bet makes it feel more special."

They got in the car.

"What was I going to have to do if you'd won the hole?" Buddy asked as he backed out of the parking spot.

"Oh, I'm saving that for another day," Gracie advised him with a smile. "But don't worry. You'll like it."

/ / /

Gracie changed outfits twice before leaving her house. She didn't know whether to dress up or be more casual. As she and Lauren had discussed, the porch was such an old-fashioned spot for a rendezvous that Gracie decided to put on a nice dress, fix her hair, and add a touch more makeup. Buddy's car wasn't there when she arrived. Beatrice opened the door for Gracie.

"You look lovely," the older woman said. "I hope Buddy doesn't show up in a T-shirt and running shorts."

They went into the kitchen.

"Have you eaten supper?" Beatrice asked.

"I had a snack before I left the house. Buddy was vague about what he had in mind, so I didn't know what to do about food."

The side door opened and Buddy entered carrying a brown bag. He was wearing a collared shirt, navy blue pants, and loafers. Gracie was glad she'd dressed up.

"Hors d'oeuvres," he said, holding up the bag.

"I'll go upstairs and leave you two alone," Beatrice said.

"No, let's eat together in here," Buddy said, then turned to Gracie. "Is that okay with you?"

"Sure, you won the bet," she replied.

"Bet?" Beatrice asked.

Buddy told the story while he emptied the bag. He'd picked up a fancy combination of seafood, fruit, and cheese.

"Where did you find this?" Gracie asked.

"Holcomb's Catering. I know Richard pretty well, and he put it together."

Beatrice brought out the fine china, and they sat at the round table in the kitchen as they ate. It was very different from a Sunday meal with Gracie's family, but it felt just as friendly and natural.

"I talked to Elise on the phone after we played golf," Buddy said. "She's serious about running a marathon in November, so I'm going to begin a regular running schedule. Would you be interested in joining us?"

"No, thanks." Gracie shook her head. "My specialty is a sprint from home plate to first. Long distances have never been fun for me, but I'd love to come and cheer you on."

"Where will the race be held?" Beatrice asked.

"In the countryside south of Atlanta," Buddy replied. "That means it won't be too hilly. I also talked for a few minutes to Amber. She's been good about continuing to answer my questions."

"What did you ask her?" Gracie asked.

"I wanted to know why Elise's birth certificate lists the father as 'Unknown.' Amber had a simple explanation. When they brought the form to her at the hospital, she was mad at me and left my name off."

"Both of you have come a long way since then," Beatrice said.

Gracie nibbled a piece of Camembert. "Anything else you wanted to know?" she asked.

Buddy paused before answering. "I needed to better understand why she never reached out to me, even without telling me where she was living. I didn't want her to feel guilty, so I had to be careful how I asked the question."

"Were you able to do that?" Gracie asked.

"I think so. I phrased it differently but got an answer. It turns out I was more attracted to her in high school than she was to me. Based on how bad things were in her family, she wasn't interested in a long-term relationship with me or anyone else, so it wasn't that hard for her to leave Milton County and not look back. All she cared about at that point was Elise. Contacting me would have required bringing up a period of her life she didn't want to remember. It stung, but I was glad to know the truth."

"I'm not looking back either," Beatrice said in her kind voice. "My heart is happy because we're getting to know Elise."

Buddy nodded. "You're right. And Amber invited all three of us to come to Atlanta toward the end of the month. She's not trying to keep us out of Elise's life now."

When they finished eating, Beatrice began to clear the table.

"No," she said to Gracie when she started to help. "I have a surprise for you on the front porch."

"I didn't see anything when I drove up," Gracie said.

"I did it when I excused myself from the table a few minutes ago. But it was Buddy's idea."

Curious, Gracie followed Buddy through the living room and out the front door. Beatrice had put a small white linen cloth on the table between the rockers and placed a spectacular arrangement of flowers in a large vase in the center.

"She wants you to take them home, along with the vase," Buddy said.

"They're gorgeous. So far I'm glad you won the bet instead of me."

They sat in the same chairs as the night Buddy encountered the Lord. The heat of the day had retreated as the sun dipped below the trees, but it was still light outside.

As she gently rocked, Gracie felt enveloped in peace. "This is amazing," she said. "Do you feel the peace?"

"Yes," Buddy answered. "And that's not all."

Gracie glanced over, and their eyes met. She became still as unspoken communication flowed between them.

"What else do you feel?" she asked in a soft voice.

Buddy smiled. And brightness shone from his face. He reached out and took her hand in his. "I think you know," he said.

They sat beside each other. And received the gift of unconditional love into their hearts.

ACKNOWLEDGMENTS

THANKS TO ALL WHO ASSISTED AND INSPIRED THE writing of this novel, especially my wife, Kathy, and editors Becky Monds, Jacob Whitlow, and Deborah Wiseman. Each of you played a unique and important part.

And to those who read what I write: It is a privilege to invite you into the world of my stories.

DISCUSSION QUESTIONS

1. Amber saw running away as her only option to protect herself and her baby. Imagine yourself or your child in a similar situation. What would you do? How might things have been different if Amber had told Buddy of her plans or asked for his help?
2. Millie made a promise to her late husband that she would never tell Buddy about the checks. Would you have done the same in her shoes? Was she right to tell Buddy or should she have honored that promise?
3. Have you ever been in a situation where the more you learned, the more you wanted to stop searching for answers? Do you think knowing the truth is worth the search, even if it means learning something difficult?
4. Social media has changed the way we interact with people. The ability to keep in touch with friends and family is a wonderful benefit, but there are also some very real dangers, as shown in this novel. What are some ways that parents/guardians can protect teens from the risks of social media (without banning them from it entirely)?

5. How did Gracie's community involvement work in the story? In what ways did her coaching the softball team help Buddy?
6. In regard to raising Reagan, Sammy told Buddy it was "better to keep the peace than start a war." Are there times when keeping the peace is best? Why might it be necessary to "start a war" with your child? Is it possible to find a balance?
7. What did you think of Judge Williams? And, of course, Bailiff?
8. Gracie and Buddy start off the novel at different places in their faith. Talk about those different starting points and how their faiths worked together. When did Buddy first start to change and deepen in his faith? What factors led to this? How might he have reacted differently in the end if he hadn't changed in that way?